THOSE EYES

They burned him and would leave an afterimage branded into his mind. Never had Nathan seen such eyes, the hue of clouds just before a storm. It wasn't their color so much as the depth of feeling he saw within them that seared him. Haunted, hunted. A feral creature, trapped within the body of a striking woman. That creature called to him, even more than the wilderness outside. A kinship there. Something dark inside of him stirred and awakened as he gazed into her eyes.

An animal within himself. He'd always felt it, fought it down every day. White men thought Indians were animals. He would prove them wrong, even if it meant brutally tethering a part of himself. But that hidden beast recognized her, saw its like within her. And demanded.

The Blades of the Rose

Warrior

Scoundrel

Rebel

Coming Soon

Stranger

Published by Kensington Publishing Corporation

REBEL
The Blades of the Rose

Zoë Archer

ZEBRA BOOKS
KENSINGTON PUBLISHING CORP.
http://www.kensingtonbooks.com

ZEBRA BOOKS are published by

Kensington Publishing Corp.
119 West 40th Street
New York, NY 10018

All Kensington titles, imprints and distributed lines are available at special quantity discounts for bulk purchases for sales promotion, premiums, fund-raising, educational or institutional use.

Special book excerpts or customized printings can also be created to fit specific needs. For details, write or phone the office of the Kensington Special Sales Manager: Attn. Special Sales Department. Kensington Publishing Corp., 119 West 40th Street, New York, NY 10018. Phone: 1-800-221-2647.

ISBN-13: 978-1-4201-0681-7
ISBN-10: 1-4201-0681-3

First Printing: November 2010
10 9 8 7 6 5 4 3 2 1

Printed in the United States of America

For Zack:
giving me strength
when I need to rebel

Chapter 1

Encounters at the Trading Post

The Northwest Territory, 1875

The two men tumbled over the muddy ground, trading punches and kicks. A sloppy fight, made all the more clumsy by a surfeit of cheap whiskey and punctuated by grunts and curses. Nobody knew what the men were fighting about, least of all the men themselves. It didn't matter. They just wanted to punch each other.

They rolled across the soggy earth, gathering a few interested onlookers. Bets of money, beaver pelts, and tobacco were placed. Odds were six to one that Three-Tooth Jim would make pemmican of Gravy Dan.

No one counted on the lawyer.

Jim and Dan, throwing elbows and snarling, careened right into the path of Nathan Lesperance, actually rolling across his boots as the attorney crossed the yard surrounding the trading post. Lesperance calmly reached down, picked up Three-Tooth Jim, and, with a composed, disinterested expression, slammed his own fist into the big trapper's jaw. By the time Jim hit the ground, Lesperance had already performed the same service for Gravy Dan. In seconds, both trappers lay together in the mud, completely unconscious.

Lesperance sent a quick, flinty look toward the onlookers. The men—hardened mountain dwellers, miners, trappers, and Indians who had seen and survived the worst man and nature could dole out—all scurried away to other buildings surrounding the trading post.

Sergeant Williamson of the Northwest Mounted Police looked down at the insensate bodies of the trappers. "That wasn't necessary, Mr. Lesperance," he said with a shake of his head. Two young Mounties, Corporals Hastings and Mackenzie, hurried forward to drag the trappers away to the makeshift jail. "My men could have seen to the disturbance. *Without* resorting to fisticuffs."

"My way's faster," said Lesperance.

"But you're an *attorney*," Williamson pointed out.

"I'm not your typical lawyer," said Lesperance, dry.

On that, the sergeant had to agree. For one thing, most lawyers resembled prosperous bankers, their soft stomachs gently filling out their waistcoats, hands soft and manicured, a look of self-satisfaction in their fleshy, middle-aged faces. Nathan Lesperance looked hard as granite, hale, barely thirty, and more suited for a tough life in the wilderness than arguing the finer points of law in court or from behind a desk.

Williamson said, "I've never met a Native attorney before."

Lesperance's gaze was black as chipped obsidian, his words just as sharp. "I was taken from my tribe when I was a child and raised in a government school."

"And you studied law there? And learned how to throw a mean left hook?"

"Yes, to both."

"You must have a few stories to tell."

A brief smile tilted the corner of Lesperance's mouth, momentarily softening the precise planes of his face. "More than a few. I'll tell you about the time I took on three miners making trouble in town—the only gold they found came out of their own fillings. But later, over a drink." His smile faded. "I came here all the way from Victoria, so first let's get this business taken care of."

No Native had ever talked to Williamson this way. For one thing, Lesperance spoke flawless English, better, even, than most of the Mounties at the post. And there was no deference or hesitancy in Lesperance. In his words and eyes was a tacit challenge. Williamson had no desire to take up that challenge, lest he wind up lying in the mud, unconscious. And that seemed the least of what Lesperance seemed capable of. He wasn't an especially big man, but no one could doubt his strength, judging by the way he filled out the shoulders of his heavy tweed jacket and by the facers he'd landed on both Jim and Dan.

"Of course, Mr. Lesperance," the sergeant said quickly. He tugged on the red wool tunic of his uniform. "Please follow me. The Mounties keep a small garrison here. We have our own office, which serves as our mess, too, and a dormitory." He gestured toward two of the low structures clustered around the main building of the trading post. Both the Mountie and the attorney began to walk. They passed fur trappers, clusters of Indian men and women, some white men in well-cut coats who could only be representatives for the Hudson's Bay Company, here to buy furs, and horses and dogs. The Indians stared at Lesperance as he walked, no doubt just as amazed as Williamson to see a Native with his hair cut short, like a white man, and wearing entirely European-style clothing. Lesperance didn't even walk as a Native might, with soft, careful steps. Instead, Williamson had to lengthen his stride to match Lesperance's. "We do appreciate you traveling so far."

"You could have just sent Douglas Prescott's belongings to Victoria," Lesperance said. "His next of kin agreed to it."

"The Northwest Mounted Police take their responsibilities very seriously," Williamson replied gravely. "We were created only last year to cnforce law and order out here in the wilderness."

"I thought it was to fight the whiskey trade."

Williamson flushed at Lesperance's blunt words. "That, too." He cleared his throat. "I think you'll find that Mrs. Bramfield also wants to conclude this Prescott business as soon as possible."

"Bramfield. The woman who found Prescott."

"The same."

"And then her husband brought Prescott's belongings to the fort."

"Oh, no. Only she came to report Prescott's death. She lives over a day's ride from this trading post in a cabin by herself."

This stopped Lesperance. He frowned at Williamson as the sergeant stumbled to a halt. "Alone?"

"Entirely alone."

"Sounds dangerous."

"It is," agreed the sergeant. Lesperance resumed walking, so Williamson followed, saying, "But the locals say Astrid Bramfield has been on her own ever since she came to the Northwest Territory four years ago. She must know how to take care of herself. She even buried Prescott on her own, then brought his belongings to the Bow River Fort."

"Maybe Mrs. Bramfield killed Prescott," Lesperance suggested.

Williamson shook his head. "She's a tough woman, but no killer. If murder was her aim, she didn't need to bring Prescott's possessions to the fort."

"She may have kept some for herself." Lesperance's direct, forthright way of speaking reminded Williamson of his superiors at nearby Fort Macleod. He wasn't certain whether the Mounted Police took Natives into their ranks, but Lesperance would have made an excellent Mountie—straightforward and determined.

"No, her honesty is impossible to deny, yet she refused

to go back to the fort when it came time to meet you. This trading post was as far as she would come, and only then with quite a bit of reluctance."

"A recluse."

"Indeed. Even the Indians call her Hunter Shadow Woman. But you'll find that these parts are full of peculiar characters. Here we are, our office-cum-mess. Right now it's an office."

They had reached one of the small log buildings that huddled near the trading post. It was barely more than a shack, a testament to the trading post's rough surroundings. Out in the Northwest Territory, people made do with what they had. Over two thousand miles of prairie, mountains, and lakes stood between the Territory and the civilization of Toronto or Quebec. Sergeant Williamson stopped in the doorway and looked apologetic. "She's inside. Please give me a moment to speak with her alone. Then we'll have you and Mrs. Bramfield sign some papers and Prescott's belongings will be released to you."

Nathan gave a clipped nod and turned away when the sergeant went into the building. He heard voices within, the sergeant's and a woman's, and something, some rich quality in the timbre of her voice, sent immediate awareness tightening the surface of his skin. Something inside of him sharpened, like a knife being turned to the light. With a frown, he stepped farther away from the building and breathed in deep, looking around, assessing.

The trading post and the buildings that surrounded it were situated at the base of wooded foothills, and just beyond rose the jagged, snowcapped peaks of the Rocky Mountains. Even from a distance, such impassive, raw mountains awed, becoming godlike as they stretched toward the heavens. No shelter, only rock and sky. A cold wind blew down from the mountains, swirling in dusty clouds around the trading post yard. A man's life would be a fragile thing out in those mountains, even more tenuous than within the isolated woods surrounding the post. Hard not to feel small and temporary when faced with beautiful, pitiless wilderness.

Home. Of a sort. His mother's grandmother had come from these mountains, journeying all the way to Vancouver Island and taking a husband from one of the local fishing tribes. The few times Nathan had seen his mother, she would tell him stories of the mountains, legends of magical creatures and elemental spirits that lived within each spruce and aspen, but the teachers at his school always said such tales were at best only ridiculous and at worst idolatrous. He paid neither his mother nor the teachers any mind. He had his own path to follow.

He'd lived almost entirely in Fort Victoria, a bastion of Britishness on the west coast of a fledgling territory. Not once had he traveled the hundreds of arduous miles to see his great-grandmother's ancestral home. He had never wanted to. The mountains were the past, and he moved forward. His business, his needs, kept him elsewhere. Until now.

No one at the firm where Nathan worked wanted to make the journey to some hardscrabble trading post out in the middle of rough country. Someone had to go. Douglas Prescott had been a valuable client, and remained so even after he abandoned his family to find adventure as a trapper. Poor sod had found more than adventure. He'd found death. And somebody from Steedman and Beall must go out and claim his belongings. A trip to the Northwest Territory meant weeks of grueling travel through unmapped terrain. And then turn around and do it all over again to get home.

In the silence that greeted Mr. Steedman's announcement, Nathan had stepped forward to claim the task. Somebody muttered, "Of course, Lesperance. He's just the contrary bastard to do it."

So he'd gone, and thought of nothing in his long journey but returning and throwing down the packet of Prescott's belongings on Steedman's desk as everyone gaped. Yes, he was a savage, as they said he was behind his back, but it had taken a savage to get the job done. He liked nothing better than defying expectations.

But as he stared out at the pearl gray sky, stretching above the harsh, magnificent mountains and deep green forests, Nathan couldn't shake the oddest sensation of being drawn toward the mountains and wilderness, invisible hands reaching out to him. *Come to us*, the woods seem to call. *We are waiting*.

"Mr. Lesperance?"

Nathan almost snarled in surprise as Sergeant Williamson appeared at his shoulder.

"Sorry," the sergeant gulped. "I called your name several times, but you didn't hear me. Mrs. Bramfield is waiting."

Shaking his head at his imagination, Nathan followed Williamson into the low building. It took a moment for his eyes to adjust to the changing light. Small windows cut into the west-facing wall allowed watery sunlight to wash into the single room. A heavy, crude table and several chairs composed the room's sole furnishings. Primitive as it was, there were homes in Victoria equally simple, especially belonging to the Indians and Chinese laborers. Once his vision cleared, Nathan barely noticed any of this. His attention was claimed entirely by the woman standing on the other side of the table.

From Sergeant Williamson's description of Astrid Bramfield, Nathan had expected a much older woman, someone well on the other side of middle age, with the rough features and sturdy build of a female living alone in the wilderness. Beauty, youth, and femininity could not survive out here. He'd met fresh-faced girls going out to live pioneering lives with their husbands, only to return a few years later, haggard, weathered women with girlhood left long behind. Mrs. Bramfield would likely be much the same.

Yet Astrid Bramfield took his few preconceptions and obliterated them. She was much younger than he'd believed, closer to his own age of twenty-eight. She wore men's clothing—a heavy coat, jacket, shirt, and slim trousers tucked into worn boots. The hilt of a stag-handled knife peered above the top of her boot. Despite the coat's bulk, her figure revealed itself to be an elegant collection of curves, her waist narrow, the flare of her hips tapering down into long legs. A gun belt hugged her hips, a revolver holstered and ready for use. Her hair, the color of wheat in high summer, had been pulled back into a long braid, revealing a face of pristine, solemn loveliness. The golden freckles playfully dotting the bridge of her nose contrasted sharply with her gray eyes.

Those eyes. They burned him and would leave an afterimage branded into his mind. Never had Nathan seen such eyes, the hue of clouds just before a storm. It wasn't their color so much as the depth of feeling he saw within them that seared him. Haunted, hunted. A feral creature, trapped within the body of a striking woman. That creature called to him, even more than the wilderness outside. A kinship there. Something dark inside of him stirred and awakened as he gazed into her eyes.

An animal within himself. He'd always felt it, fought it down every day. White men thought Indians were animals. He would prove them wrong, even if it meant brutally tethering a part of himself. But that hidden beast recognized her, saw its like within her. And demanded.

He felt his senses sharpen almost painfully, becoming aware of everything in the room—the fly buzzing in one corner, the sap smell of the wooden table. Most of all, her.

She stared at him with equal fascination, her hands spread upon the table as though leaning toward him without thought. Her breath came faster, her ripe pink lips slightly parted. He heard each intake and exhalation, saw the widening of her pupils within those storm eyes of hers.

A deep, barely audible growl rose in the back of Nathan's throat as he started toward her.

The sound seemed to rouse them both from a trance.

Nathan forced himself to take a step back, cursing himself. Hell. He wasn't truly a damn animal.

Astrid Bramfield curled her hands into themselves and glanced away. The next time Nathan saw her eyes, they had become as remote and cold as a glacier.

"Mrs. Bramfield," Sergeant Williamson said, entirely unaware of what had just transpired, "this is Nathan Lesperance. He is an attorney from the firm that represents Douglas Prescott."

She gave Nathan a clipped nod but said nothing. He returned the nod, wary of her silence. Some white women found his presence to be an affront, the savage aping the dress and manners of a superior race; others thought him dangerously intriguing, like a pet wolf. How did Astrid Bramfield see him? And why did he care?

Despite her reserve, something charged and alive paced between them in the small room. They continued to regard each other across the table.

"Why don't we sit?" the sergeant offered.

"I'll stand," Mrs. Bramfield said. Her voice was sensuous and low, unexpectedly cultured. She was English. That wasn't entirely surprising. Canada was full of Britons, both English and Scottish. Why Astrid Bramfield's Englishness, out of everything, should surprise Nathan, he had no idea, but the thought of a well-bred Englishwoman living the life of a solitary mountain man caught him off guard. He wondered what had driven her to seek isolation in this untamed corner of the world. At some point, there had to be a *Mr.* Bramfield.

The sergeant shifted uncomfortably on his feet. "Very well." He gestured toward a small wooden box on the table. "Would you be so kind as to confirm that the items in that box are the same you found on Mr. Prescott's body?"

Mrs. Bramfield opened the box and, as she did so, Nathan noticed her hands. At one time, they might have been a lady's hands, slim and white. Now they were still slim, but they looked far more capable and used to hard work than any other lady's hands. His vision, still sharper than he could ever remember, noted the calluses that thickened the skin of her fingers and lined her palms. For some reason, he found the sight arousing. A plain wedding band gleamed on her left hand.

One by one, she took items out of the box and laid them onto the table. A pocket watch. A battered book. Packets of letters. Nothing of real value. Nathan ground his teeth together. For *this* he had traveled hundreds of miles? Damn overzealous Mounties, taking their new responsibilities as peacekeepers too seriously. But then he watched Astrid Bramfield as she removed the dead man's belongings from their container, and couldn't feel that this journey had been entirely worthless.

"Yes," she said after examining everything in the box. "These are the same items. Nothing is missing."

"Very good." The sergeant handed her several pieces of paper, as well as a pen and bottle of ink. "If you'll just sign these affidavits, we can release the items into Mr. Lesperance's custody."

Wordlessly, she bent over the papers and signed them. The only sound in the small building was the pen's nib scratching over the paper. As she wrote, Nathan saw that, in the pale sunlight, a few glints of silver threaded through her golden hair. But her skin was unlined and smooth. Something had marked her, changed her, and he wanted to know what.

"Please countersign the documents, Mr. Lesperance," Williamson said when Mrs. Bramfield was done.

Nathan reached for the pen to take it from her. Doing so, his fingers grazed hers. A brush fire spread from his fingertips through his whole body at the brief contact. She drew in a shaking, startled breath. The pen fell to the table, scattering droplets of ink like dark blood across the papers.

Sergeant Williamson darted forward, quickly blotting the ink with a handkerchief. "Not to worry, not to worry," he said with a nervous laugh. "If you like, I can have Corporal Mackenzie, our clerk, draw up some new affidavits."

"No need," Nathan said. At the sound of his voice, Astrid Bramfield pressed her lips together until they formed a tight line. She suddenly paced over to where a Hudson Bay blanket was tacked to the wall as a gesture toward décor, and became deeply engrossed in studying the woven pattern.

Nathan could practically see her vibrating with tension. She wore it all around her like armor. He knew she didn't want to be at the trading post, but there seemed to be more to her sense of unease. *He* was unsettling her. Well, now they were even.

Intrigued, Nathan signed the documents, noting that Mrs. Bramfield's handwriting was both feminine and bold. *Astrid Anderson Bramfield.* He found himself touching her name, little caring that the ink smudged on the paper and stained his fingertips. Nathan had the urge to inhale deeply over the affidavits, as if he could draw her scent up from the paper. He shook himself. What the hell had gotten into him? He must be tired. He'd been riding hard for weeks, and it had been nearly two months since he'd been with a woman. That was the only explanation that made any sense.

Once the papers were all signed, Sergeant Williamson examined them. "Everything looks to be in order. The Northwest Mounted Police will be happy to release Mr. Prescott's belongings into your care, Mr. Lesperance."

"Am I finished here?" Mrs. Bramfield said before Nathan could answer the sergeant.

Williamson blinked. "I believe so."

"Good." She picked up a broad-brimmed, low-crowned hat and set it on her head. Without another word, she strode from the building, but not before stepping around Nathan as one might edge past a chained beast. Then she was gone.

For a moment, Nathan and Williamson stared at each other. A second later, Nathan was out the door and in pursuit.

He caught up with her near the corral. She was already

shouldering a pack and a rifle with practiced ease, taking the muddy ground in long, quick strides. Nathan didn't miss the way most of the men's eyes followed her. Women were rare sights out in the wild, and trouser-clad, handsome women even more rare. Yet he had the feeling that even if the trading post yard was full of pretty women in pants, Astrid Bramfield would stand out like a star at dawn.

"Douglas Prescott's family appreciates you giving him a decent burial," Nathan said, easily keeping pace. "They want to give you a reward."

She shot him a hard look but didn't slow. "I don't want anything."

"I'm sure you don't," he murmured.

They reached the corral, and she walked briskly toward a bay mare. She threw the Indian boy watching her horse a coin. The boy said something to her in his language, glancing at Nathan, and she answered sharply. The boy scampered off.

"What did he say?" Nathan asked.

"He wanted to know what tribe you come from," she said. "I said I didn't know." Without asking for any assistance, she hooked her boot into the stirrup and mounted her horse in a single, fluid movement. She tugged on some heavy rawhide gloves before taking up the reins.

"Cowichan," he said. "Government people took me when I was small. Raised me in a school. I never knew the people of my tribe."

Something in his tone had her looking down at him. Their eyes caught and held, and he felt it again, drawing tight between them, a heat and awareness that had a profound resonance. "I'm sorry," she said. Her simple words held more real sympathy than anything anyone else had ever said to him.

"You could have kept Prescott's things for yourself," he said, gazing up at her. "People die out here all the time, and no one ever knows."

"Those who love him would know," she said, her words

like soft fire on his flesh. "And it was for them I took Prescott's belongings to the Mounties. They would want something of his to help them remember."

She spoke plainly, almost without affect, but he heard it just the same, the raw hurt that throbbed just beneath the surface. She'd shown him a small piece of her heart, and he recognized it as a gift.

Looking into her eyes, into the stern beauty of her face, he dove through the surfaces of words and gestures to the woman beneath. Wounded within, a fierce need to protect herself. And beneath even that, a heart that burned white-hot, blazing its way through the world.

He understood just then that Astrid Bramfield spoke to him like a man, not a barely tamed savage or object of curiosity. The only woman to have ever truly done so. Even the Native women he knew could never place him, since he was neither entirely absorbed into the white world nor fully Indian. But this guarded woman saw him as he was, without judgment.

He placed a hand on the reins of her horse. "Don't leave." He truly didn't want her to go. Nathan had a feeling that once Astrid Bramfield left this dingy little trading post, she would disappear into the wilderness and he would never see her again. The thought pained him, even though he'd met her just minutes before.

"I can't stay."

"Have a meal with me," he pressed. He struggled not to seize her, pull her down from the saddle, and drag her to some shadowed corner. He clenched his jaw, fighting the urge. He was *civilized,* damn it, not the savage everyone thought him to be. But the compulsion was strong, growing stronger the more he thought about her leaving. He switched tactics. "It's already growing dark. Could be dangerous."

She said with no pride, "The dark doesn't frighten me."

"Not much does."

Her jaw tightened and a flash of something—pain, regret—

sparked in her eyes before she tugged the reins from his grasp. She wheeled her horse around, forcing him to step back.

"Good-bye, Mr. Lesperance," she said. Then she set her heels to her horse, and the animal surged forward, out of the corral. It cantered across the rough trail leading away from the trading post, taking her with it. Nathan battled the urge to grab a horse and follow. Instead, he turned and walked toward where Sergeant Williamson stood holding the box of Prescott's things, deliberately not glancing back to try to get a final glimpse of Astrid Bramfield before she vanished. His inner beast snarled at him.

His senses were still unusually keen. Scents, sights, and sounds inundated him until he felt almost dizzy from them. The minerals in the mud. The horses' snorting and pawing, rattling their tack. A man's laugh, harsh and quick. And, more than ever, the persistent pull winding down from the mountains like a green surge, drawing him toward their rocky heights and shadowed gullies.

"What do you know about her?" Nathan demanded of the sergeant without preamble.

Williamson seemed more accustomed to the way Nathan spoke. He hardly blinked as he said, "Very little. She comes to the post a few times a year. Never stays overnight."

"Tell me about her husband."

"All anyone knows is that she's a widow." The sergeant shrugged. "Honestly, Mr. Lesperance, she spoke as much to you in the past fifteen minutes as she has to anyone in four years. Interested in paying court?" Williamson sounded both amused and appalled by the idea that a Native, even one as civilized as Nathan, would consider wooing a white woman. White men took Native wives, especially out in the wilderness, though few genuinely married them in the eyes of God and the law. It almost never happened the other way around, with an Indian man taking a white wife. If he'd been inclined toward marriage, which he wasn't, Nathan's choices would have been slim. Still, he didn't like to be reminded of yet another way he lived on the fringes of society. The idea that a woman like Astrid Bramfield could never be his particularly stuck in his craw.

"I'm leaving tomorrow," Nathan growled.

"Your guide won't be willing to leave again so soon," Williamson said in surprise.

"I'll find another." Everything about this place set Nathan on edge, unbalanced him. Victoria wasn't anything more than a decent-sized town, its ranks swelling periodically when gold was discovered nearby, so it wasn't wilderness itself that troubled Nathan. What unsettled him, roused the animal within, was *this* wilderness. And Astrid Bramfield.

"There's no shortage of men who'd oblige," the sergeant said, "if the price is good."

Nathan had money in abundance, not only provided by the firm, but his own pocket. "They'll be satisfied with my terms."

"You can find good trail guides at the saloon." Williamson grimaced. "It isn't so much a saloon as it is a cramped room where they serve whiskey. Legal whiskey, of course," he added quickly.

"Of course," Nathan replied, dry. "Keep hold of Prescott's belongings for a little while longer. I don't want some drunk trapper getting curious."

"You can handle yourself in a fight," Williamson said.

"Getting another man's blood on my clothes is a damned nuisance."

After Williamson nodded, Nathan set off for the so-called saloon. He wanted to secure his return journey as soon as possible. He needed to get back to the cold, moist air of Vancouver Island. This mountain atmosphere played havoc with his senses, luring the beast inside of him with siren songs of wild freedom. He didn't care what that damned animal wanted—he would leave here and leave *her*.

An hour later, Nathan had drunk some of the most

throat-shredding whiskey he'd ever tasted and found himself a guide who went by the name Uncle Ned. Nathan doubted anybody would willingly claim Ned as a relative, given the guide's preference for wolverine pelts as outerwear, complete with heads, but Ned's skill as a guide weren't in doubt. Even Williamson said that Nathan had made a good choice in Uncle Ned.

When Nathan emerged from the saloon, dusk had crept further over the trading post and its outbuildings. The men had grown more raucous with the approach of darkness. And there was considerable commotion surrounding a group of riders who had entered the yard around the post while Nathan had been securing a guide. One of the men had a hooded peregrine falcon perched on his glove. Not only were the riders all equipped with prime horseflesh, but also their gear was top of the line. Saddles, guns, packs. All of it excellent quality. As Nathan walked past the riders, he noted their equipment was English, likely purchased from one of London's most esteemed outfitters. He'd seen a few examples pass through Victoria and could recognize the manufacturers.

"You," snapped one of the men to Nathan. Like Astrid Bramfield, this man had a genteel English accent, but none of her melodiousness. He glanced around the trading post with undisguised disgust. "You guide us? Big money. Buy lots of firewater." The man, tall and fair, jingled a pouch of coins at his waist.

"I'm not from these parts," Nathan answered, his voice flat. "But I'd be happy to lead you straight to hell."

The man gaped at Nathan. As he stood there in astonishment, his companion with the falcon approached.

"This Indian giving you trouble, Staunton?"

Before either Nathan or the man called Staunton spoke, the falcon let out a sudden, piercing shriek. Nathan's sensitive hearing turned the sound to an excruciating screech, and he fought the urge to wince. Both Englishmen stared at the bird, amazed, as it continued to cry and flap its wings, struggling against its jesses as if it meant to swoop at Nathan. The men traded looks with each other, and their other two companions also took keen notice.

As did the rest of the inhabitants of the trading post. The falcon persisted in its noise, drawing the attention of everyone, including Mounties and Natives, who gawked as though Nathan and the bird were part of the same traveling carnival.

Nathan wanted to grab the bird and tear it apart. Instead, he made himself stride away. He didn't know what had disturbed the falcon, but he wasn't much interested in finding out. If he stayed near the Englishmen any longer, he'd wind up punching them as he had the two drunk trappers earlier, only with less delicacy. He heard the Englishmen murmuring to each other as the bird's cries died down. With his hearing so sharp, he could have learned what the men were saying, but he didn't care. They reminded him of some of the elite families on Victoria, touring the schools for Natives and praising the little red children for being so eager to adopt white ways. But when the red children grew up and presumed to take a place in society beside them, then they were less full of praise and more condemning. Let the Natives become carpenters or cannery workers. Respected, affluent citizens? Government officials or attorneys? No.

Nathan had spent his life challenging people like that, but his vehicle was the law. From the inside out, he'd smash apart the edifices of their prejudice, and the victory would be all the sweeter because they'd put the hammer into his hands.

Not now. All he cared about now was rinsing off some of the day's grime, getting a hot meal, and having a decent night's sleep. It had been a long day, an even longer journey, and tomorrow it would begin all over again. He'd forget about Astrid Bramfield. She seemed eager to forget him.

As Nathan headed toward the Mounties' dormitory, a flash in the corner of his eye caught his attention. He turned, thinking he saw a woman, a redheaded woman, skulking close to the wooden wall enclosing the trading post. He saw nothing, and debated whether to investigate. Normally he would have dismissed such a suspicion. After all, anything could exist in the margins of one's vision, even monsters and magic. But ever since he'd met Astrid Bramfield, there was no denying his senses were sharper. He started in the direction where he thought he'd seen the red-haired woman.

"Mr. Lesperance," called Corporal Mackenzie, waving to him, "please, come and have supper with us."

Nathan cast a look over his shoulder, where the woman had possibly been, but then cleared his head of fancies. It didn't matter if there were passels of redheads haunting the trading post. He was leaving there soon, as soon as possible.

Mounties worked well with Natives. Without Native guides, they all would have been dead on the slow, far march from Winnipeg to the Northwest Territory. Tribes respected the Mounties for curbing the devastating border whiskey trade. So Nathan was welcomed at the Mounties' table that night, the company consisting of him, Sergeant Williamson, and Corporals Mackenzie and Hastings. They ate a spread of roast elk, potatoes, and biscuits while telling stories of their adventures bringing order to the wild.

"Sounds damned wonderful," Nathan admitted over his beer. "Getting results through brains *and* action." More satisfying, in the short run, than what he tried to accomplish in Victoria.

"It is," agreed Corporal Mackenzie. "It's what we all signed on for. Being out in the field, tracking criminals, keeping the peace." He grinned.

"Everyone saw how you put down Three-Tooth Jim and Gravy Dan," said Corporal Hastings, a man hardly old enough to shave. "Maybe you should consider joining up. You'd be grand as a Mountie."

Williamson and Nathan shared a look. The boy was too young and naive to realize that what he spoke of would likely never be accepted by headquarters at Fort Dufferin.

"Thanks, all the same," Nathan said. "But I've got a life waiting for me in Victoria." A life that seemed, at that moment, too tame. He already chafed against the restraints of society there, and no one, not a soul, knew about Nathan's late-night restlessness, his compulsion to run. He was always careful.

"Just think about it," pressed the young corporal. He yelped. "You kicked me, Mackenzie!"

Corporal Mackenzie rolled his eyes, and Sergeant Williamson hurriedly changed the subject. "What do you know about those Englishmen who arrived today, Hastings? The ones with the falcon."

"The falcon that took an instant dislike to Mr. Lesperance," Corporal Mackenzie added with a wry smile. Nathan scowled down at his battered enameled tin plate.

Hastings, eager to shine in the eyes of his superior, pulled out a notepad from his pocket. "A scientific expedition, all the way from London," he read.

"Scientific," repeated Williamson. "Botany? Zoology?"

Hastings flushed. "He wasn't specific, sir. I tried to get more details but he gave me a lot of bluster, saying he was a very important man in England and he didn't have time to waste on"—he cleared his throat and turned redder, matching his jacket—"'boys in pretend uniforms.'"

All the Mounties grumbled at this.

"But they did hire three mountain men as guides," Hastings added. "And I heard they're heading west at first light."

"Good work, Corporal," Williamson said, and Hastings beamed. He turned to Nathan. "Are you sure you want to leave tomorrow, Lesperance? It's jolly exciting around here. Always something going on."

"I'm sure," said Nathan, thinking once more of Astrid Bramfield's silver eyes. A welcome distraction came when something brushed against his leg. He glanced down to see an enormous orange tabby cat twining between his boots. The cat placed its paws on his knee and chirped.

Nathan stroked the cat's head and was rewarded with a series of purrs.

"That's Calgary," said Mackenzie. "I named him after the place in Scotland where my pa is from. He isn't usually this friendly. Just eats and sleeps all day. Terrible mouser."

"You've got a way with animals," Williamson noted as Calgary tried to climb into Nathan's lap.

"Except those Brits' falcon," Nathan said.

The men continued to share stories until darkness fell completely, and the only light came from their pipes and the lantern on their table. At last, aching with fatigue, Nathan stood, dumping the irate Calgary from his lap, and bid the Mounties good night. Tomorrow would be another long day.

Once outside, Nathan took a deep breath of night air. Most everyone at the trading post was either asleep, passed out, or had since left, so the evening was cold and silent. Hardly any light penetrated the darkness, save for the glinting stars and waning moon. Yet Nathan felt them, just the same, the huge, dark forms of the mountains, pulling on him like a lodestone. He'd struggled against it all evening, and now that he was out of doors, their draw became sharp, insistent. He gritted his teeth against it. *Come to us. We await you.*

So strong was their pull, Nathan didn't notice the shadowed forms creeping up behind him. By the time he became aware of them, it was too late. He felt several men leap upon him, binding him, forcing a gag into his mouth. He struggled fiercely, almost dislodging them, but there were too many. A falcon cried. Something exploded behind his eyes and then he was swallowed by nothingness.

Chapter 2

Solitude Shattered

Morning frost turned her lungs brittle, each inhalation a reinforcement that she continued to breathe and live.

There was a time when even that reminder would have been too much. Astrid had hated the fact that, despite everything, her body persevered, pressing on, a machine with no consideration for her heart or soul. Each dawn had proven again and again that she must go on without Michael, regardless of what she wanted. So she did. She awoke and moved and, eventually, fed herself, dressed herself, and went about the business of being alive. In time, living no longer was an effort of titanic proportions. Birthdays passed. She turned thirty-three last May. She went forward.

Now she rode through the low mountain pass leading to her homestead, glancing about her. Gold-glimmering mountains rose out of the morning mist that seeped up from the evergreen woods. In the scrub, animals returned to their burrows after their nighttime forays for food. Thrushes sang to each other. And nowhere could be heard the sounds of human habitation.

Being out in the expanse helped. In this wild place, every day she fought to survive. No room or time to huddle into herself. Self-pity opened the door to disaster. She pushed herself ahead and had done so for four years. She would continue to do so until she stopped appearing at the trading post, and some curious trapper or dutiful Mountie made the trip out to her cabin to find what remained of her. But her loss wouldn't matter, because she had been careful, very careful, to form no attachments.

Something shifted in her peripheral vision. Astrid swiftly took up the rifle slung over her shoulder, then lowered the gun when she saw it was only a fox trotting home from a nocturnal hunt. A beautiful creature, sleek and red, all economy and motion. The animal barely sent her a glance—it had too little exposure to man to see her as a threat—before darting into the brush to seek its den.

"A wise choice." Astrid chuckled to herself. Thoughts of her own secluded homestead, as comfortable as a place could be well away from civilization, had her urging her horse on. She'd spent the night sleeping on pine needles with her rifle cradled in her arms. Her bed at home offered better rest.

Her solitary bed.

Against her will, her thoughts turned back to the man she'd met at the trading post yesterday. Nathan Lesperance. Just thinking his name sent a shiver of heat and awareness through her. There were men in these mountains who were bigger and brawnier, but the raw masculinity of Lesperance's lean and muscular body, even underneath his heavy traveling clothes, hit her at once with the strength of a hot avalanche. A striking man, with high cheekbones, aquiline nose, and full mouth, his skin the color of cinnamon, sculptural in his virile beauty. Hair and eyes as black as mystery. Her own body, so long used to its seclusion, thrummed into wakefulness, stirred by the male splendor of him. Even the sound of his deep, smoky voice enthralled.

An attorney from genteel Victoria. She never would have believed it. Not because he was Native, but because she sensed it at once, the elemental wildness in him, barely contained, glittering in the jet of his eyes.

There had been something else, too, a kinship. She felt instantly that he knew her, knew her innermost self—the hurt, the anger, and, yes, even the fire that burned in her deepest recesses, the fire for life itself. That fire had brought her to the Blades, made her love her work with them. To seize the world with both hands and never let go. She'd tamped it down after Michael's death. But it never truly extinguished. Lesperance, somehow, had seen it. He'd done the impossible, piercing the fortifications she had raised. No one, not even her closest friends or her family, had been able to do that in all this time. She could not fully understand how Lesperance managed it, only that he had.

He had looked into her. Not merely seen her hunger for living, but felt it, too. She saw that at once. He recognized it in her. Two creatures, meeting by chance, staring at each other warily. And with reluctant longing.

Yet it wasn't only that immediate connection she had felt when meeting Lesperance. There was magic surrounding him.

Astrid wondered whether Lesperance even knew how magic hovered over him, how it surrounded him like a lover, leaving patterns of nearly visible energy in his wake. She didn't think he was conscious of it. Nothing in his manner suggested anything of the sort. Nathan Lesperance, incredibly, was utterly unaware that he was a magical being. Not metaphorical magic, but *true* magic.

She knew, however. Astrid had spent more than ten years surrounded by magic of almost every form. Some of it benevolent, such as the Healing Mists of Ho Hsien-Ku, some of it dark, such as the Javanese serpent king Naga Pahoda, though most magic was neither good nor evil. It simply *was*. And Astrid recognized it, particularly when sharing a very small space, as the Mounties' office had been.

If Nathan Lesperance's fierce attractiveness and unwanted understanding did not drive Astrid from the trading post, back to the shelter of her solitary homestead, then the magic enveloping him certainly would. She wanted nothing more to do with magic. It had cost her love once before, and she would not allow it to hurt her again.

But something had changed. She'd felt it, not so long ago. Magic existed like a shining web over the world, binding it together with filaments of energy. Being near magic for many years had made her especially sensitive to it. When she returned from Africa, that sensitivity had grown even more acute. She had tried to block it out, especially when she left England, but it never truly went away.

Only a few weeks earlier, Astrid had been out tending to her horse when a deep, rending sensation tore through her, sending her to her knees. She'd knelt in the dirt, choking, shaking, until she'd gained her strength again and tottered inside. Eventually the pain subsided, but not the sense of looming catastrophe. Something had shaken and split the magical web. A force greater than anyone had ever known. And to release it meant doom.

What was it? The Blades had to know how to avert the disaster. They would fight against it, as they always did. But without her.

A memory flitted through her mind. Months earlier, she'd had a dream and it had stayed with her vividly. She dreamt of her Compass, of the Blades, and heard someone calling her, calling her home. Astrid had dismissed the dream as a vestige of homesickness, which reared up now and again, especially after she'd been alone for so long.

The jingle of her horse's bridle snapped her attention back to the present. She cursed herself for drifting. A moment's distraction could easily lead to death out here. Stumbling between a bear sow and her cub. Crossing paths with vicious whiskey runners. A thousand ways to die. So when her awareness suddenly prickled once again, Astrid did not dismiss it.

A rustle, and movement behind her. Astrid swung her

horse around, taking up her rifle, to confront whoever or whatever was there.

She blinked, hardly believing what she saw. A man walked through tall grasses lining the pass trail. He walked with steady but dazed steps, hardly aware of his surroundings. He was completely naked.

"Lesperance?"

Astrid turned her horse on the trail and urged it closer. Dear God, it *was* Lesperance. She decocked her rifle and slung it back over her shoulder.

He didn't seem to hear her, so she said again, coming nearer, "Mr. Lesperance?" She could see now, only ten feet away, that cuts, scrapes, and bruises covered his body. His very nude, extremely well-formed body. She snapped her eyes to his face before they could trail lower than his navel. "What happened to you?"

His gaze, dark and blank, regarded her with a removed curiosity, as if she was a little bird perched on a windowsill. He stopped walking and stared at her.

Astrid dismounted at once, pulling a blanket from her pack. Within moments, she wrapped it around his waist, took his large hand in hers, and coaxed his fingers to hold the blanket closed. Then she pulled off her coat and draped it over his shoulders. Despite the fact that the coat was quite large on Astrid, it barely covered his shoulders, and the sleeves stuck out like wings. In other circumstances, he would have looked comical. But there was nothing faintly amusing about this situation.

Magic still buzzed around him, though somewhat dimmer than before.

"Where are your clothes? How did you get here? Are you badly hurt?"

None of her questions penetrated the fog enveloping him. She bent closer to examine his wounds. Some of the cuts were deep, as though made by knives, and rope abrasions circled his wrists. Bruises shadowed his knees and knuckles.

Blood had dried in the corners of his mouth. Nothing looked serious, but out in the wilderness, even the most minor injury held the potential for disaster. And, without clothing, not even a Native inured to the changeable weather could survive. He was in shock, just beginning to shake.

"Lesperance," she said, taking hold of his wide shoulders and staring into his eyes intently, "listen to me. I need to see to your wounds. We're going to have to ride back to my cabin."

"Astrid . . ." he murmured with a slow blink, then his nostrils flared like a beast scenting its mate. A hungry look crossed his face. "Astrid."

It was unexpected, given the circumstances, yet seeing that look of need, hearing him say her name, filled her with a responding desire. "Mrs. Bramfield," she reminded him. And herself. They were polite strangers.

"Astrid," he said, more insistent. He reached up to touch her face.

She grabbed his hand, pulling it away from her face. At least she wore gloves, so she didn't have to touch his bare skin. "Come on." Astrid gently tugged him toward her horse. Once beside the animal, she swung up into the saddle, put her rifle across her lap, and held a hand out to him. He stared at it with a frown, as though unfamiliar with the phenomenon of hands.

"We have to go *now,* Lesperance," Astrid said firmly. "Those wounds of yours need attention, and whatever or whoever did this to you is probably still out there."

He cast a look around, seeming to find a shred of clarity in the hazy morass of his addled brain. Something dark and angry crossed his face. He took a step away, as if he meant to go after whoever had hurt him. His hands curled into fists. Insanity. He was unarmed, naked, wounded.

"*Now,*" Astrid repeated.

Somehow she got through to him. He took her hand and,

with a dexterity that surprised her, given his condition, mounted up behind her.

God, she didn't want to do this. But there was no other choice. "Put your arms around my waist," she said through gritted teeth. When he did so, she added, "Hold tightly to me. Not that tight," she gasped as his grip turned to bands of steel. He loosened his hold slightly. "Good. Do not let go. Do you understand?"

He nodded, then winced as if the movement gave him pain. "Can't stay up."

"Lean against me if you have to." She mentally groaned when he did just that, and she felt him, even through her bulky knitted vest, shirt, and sturdy trousers. Heavy and hard and solid with muscle. Everywhere. His arms, his chest, his thighs, pressed against hers. Astrid closed her eyes for a moment as she felt his warm breath along the nape of her neck.

"All set?" she asked, barely able to form the words around her clenched jaw.

He tried to nod again but the effort made him moan. The plaintive sound, coming from such a strong, potent man, pulled tight on feelings Astrid didn't want to have.

"Thank . . . you," he said faintly.

She didn't answer him. Instead, she kicked her horse into a gallop, knowing deep in her heart that she was making a terrible mistake.

Her cabin sat in an isolated meadow, a flat expanse of grass that rested in the shelter of the mountains. A small creek ran through the meadow, cold with melting snow, and spruce trees dotted its banks. In spring, the meadow was dotted with snow lilies and cow parsnip, but now, in the first weeks of September, the blossoms were already gone. Feed for her horse was abundant, though, and it made for a good place to situate herself. She had the creek for water, the mountains shielded her from cold winds, and she was utterly alone.

Until now.

"Lesperance, wake up," she said over her shoulder. She slowed her horse to a trot, and it snorted with relief. The poor beast wasn't used to carrying two people. It couldn't be more uncomfortable than she was, though. She'd endured hours with Nathan Lesperance pressed close, his weight and muscle tight to her, his cheek resting on her shoulder. "We're here."

He stirred behind her, muttering something in a language she didn't recognize.

Astrid brought the horse up to the step leading to the low porch at the front of the cabin. She dismounted, slinging her rifle onto her back, and was relieved to see that Lesperance had enough strength now to sit up on his own. The blanket had loosened from his grip, however, giving her far too good a view of his flat, ridged abdomen.

"Can you get down?" she asked, forcing her eyes up to his face.

He nodded and awkwardly lowered himself from the saddle, with Astrid providing support. As the blanket at his waist slipped farther, she lunged, grabbing it and hauling it up. She closed his grip around the blanket.

When he swayed on his feet, Astrid stepped to his side and draped his arm over her shoulder. "There's a step here. Lift your foot. That's right." She guided him up the step and across the porch. "Wait here." She leaned him next to the door frame. Satisfied that he wouldn't topple over, Astrid pulled her revolver and carefully opened the door, using the wood to shield herself.

She peered into the cabin, just as she always did when returning. A quick scan revealed everything exactly as she had left it: a single room, sparsely furnished with a table, one chair, her bed, a cupboard, and three shelves holding her books. At the foot of her bed stood a small chest, where she stored shells for her rifle and bullets for her revolver. A quill- and bead-decorated elk hide on the wall was the cabin's only adornment. The wood stove that served to heat the cabin and cook her food was cold—no trapper or squatter or anyone else had moved in while she had been at the trading post. And no opportunistic raccoons or hungry bears had plundered her larder. Muslin covered the small windows cut into the log walls. She had never put glass into the window frames. Too expensive, an unnecessary luxury. In the depths of winter, she simply wore several layers of clothes and huddled close to the stove.

It was so far removed from what she had been raised in, Astrid almost smiled.

There was no time or room for remembrance. Satisfied that her home was undisturbed, she fetched Lesperance from where he was propped against the door frame. With him leaning on her, they stumbled into the cabin. She glanced around, looking for a place to set him down. There was only one option, an option she hated.

They staggered toward her bed, and she tried to lay him down carefully across the quilt covering the mattress. Gravity worked against her. Lesperance went down heavily onto his back, and the momentum took her with him. She sprawled on top of him, their legs tangling together, bodies pressed close. She braced her hands on his broad, smooth chest and glared down at him as his arms came up to wrap around her waist. Even through her coat and the blanket, she felt his hips against hers.

"Let go," she growled.

Yet he didn't. He actually pulled her closer. "Astrid," he murmured. "Your voice." His head came up from the bed as he nuzzled the juncture of her neck and jaw. "Your smell. Mmm."

She fought to keep her eyes open. Resentment propelled her forward, away from longing. "Let go *now*." With a surge of anger-fueled strength, she reared back, unclasping his arms from around her.

Astrid pushed up to her feet, backing away from the bed. He grumbled a little but made no further protest. Her chest rose and fell with each strained breath. How long had it been since she'd been so close to a man? Five years and she felt her isolation with every part of her. And now, here was this man, this wounded stranger, invading her home, lying upon her bed.

Astrid strode from the cabin. She took her horse to the corral next to the cabin, then stripped off its tack and rubbed it down as quickly as she could. She didn't want to leave Lesperance alone in the cabin, even though every instinct she had screamed at her to just run, run and abandon him. Protect herself.

Instead, after attending to the horse, Astrid made herself go back inside. She removed her hat and put it on the peg by the door. Lesperance had managed to get himself fully onto the bed. She pulled her one extra blanket from the cupboard and covered him with it. When she tugged off her gloves, she reluctantly touched her palm to his chest to test the temperature of his skin.

At the flesh-to-flesh contact, they both gasped, as though a current passed through them. His closed eyes flew open and an animalistic growl curled in the back of his throat. Astrid skittered back, stunned by both the immediate response and the feral sounds he emitted.

To get away, she lit the fire in the stove. Even though the feel of his skin had rocked through her, she possessed enough sense to recognize that he was very, very cold and needed warmth and rest in order to heal. The process of lighting the fire—cleaning out the old ashes, putting kindling into the stove, adding dry twigs and wood as the flame caught, adjusting the damper—helped calm her, remove her, and she took shelter in the routine, as she had for the past four years. She hurried out, pumped some water into a bucket, then came back in and filled her kettle. She set the kettle on the stove.

For longer than she needed to, she stared at the fire. It

had such purity, fire, clean and merciless. If only life was as simple and spare as flame.

Satisfied that the cabin was receiving sufficient heat, Astrid turned back to Lesperance. He was her patient now. The sooner she healed him, the sooner he could disappear from her life forever.

Astrid poured some water into a basin and knelt beside the bed, grateful to see that Lesperance had calmed. Carefully, she peeled back the blanket to look at his injuries. Even before she'd come out to the Northwest Territory, she knew about field dressing. Many times had she tended to Michael's wounds received on missions, just as he had seen to hers. What she saw now on Lesperance turned her blood to sleet.

These were no accidental injuries inflicted by the landscape or animal. His wounds were man-made, save for the scrapes on his feet, clearly indicating he'd walked a goodly ways without shoes. Thank God, not too serious, but a grievous sign nevertheless. Someone had deliberately done this to him. But who? And why?

She dampened a clean rag and dabbed it at the cuts marring his arms, shoulders, and chest. He hissed a little at the cold before subsiding back into semiconsciousness. Soon, the water in the basin was pink, but the blood on his body was mostly gone. No need to use ashes to stanch the bleeding. The blood in the corners of his mouth washed away, and she could find no wounds on his lips or, after carefully prying it open, inside his mouth. Strange. She examined the rope abrasions at his wrists. Bound. Tied like an animal. Yet the bruises on his knuckles showed he had fought his captors. Somehow he'd freed himself. Examining his hands further, she found dried blood under his nails, but again, there were no actual cuts anywhere near them.

It wasn't his blood.

Her mind whirled with the possibilities, yet she made herself focus on tending him. A poultice of dried arnica for the bruising. Honey and chamomile on the rope burns. As for the cuts . . .

Must not have been as severe as they first appeared. Astrid bent closer, forcing herself to ignore the proximity of his satiny copper skin to her mouth. The cuts had stopped bleeding and, in truth, seemed to be more scratches than cuts.

She sat back with a frown. She'd seen his lacerations earlier and they *had* been deeper. Damn. Damn and hell.

She closed her eyes to feel the magic around him. Still there, and growing in strength. It lit the air around him with energy, invisible but alive, the touches of the other world that existed just beneath this one.

The kettle whistled, piercing her apprehension. She busied herself with making tea—an English pleasure she simply couldn't forsake—for herself and Lesperance. Only when she readied to pour the water did she realize she had only one mug. Which would be worse? Drinking from the mug and then placing it to his mouth, or giving him the mug first and then having to place her mouth where his had been?

He was her patient, so his needs came before her own. She dribbled a bit of tea into his mouth. She felt a surge of gratification when he swallowed easily. He would be better soon. And that meant his departure.

Astrid desperately wanted some tea, but, as she considered the mug in her hands, she found she couldn't do it. She couldn't share the same cup as him. Altogether too much intimacy. So she left it on the table, to wash later.

After eating a small meal of bread and cheese, taken from her cool cupboard, and performing meaningless, mindless tidying around her already clean cabin, Astrid found herself with nothing to do. Ordinarily, she would spend her days hunting or cultivating the small garden behind the cabin, but she was loathe to leave this stranger in her home unattended. As much as she hated sharing the small space with him, her conscience wouldn't allow her to stray far from his bedside. He might need something, might get worse, his injuries might demand attention. Right now he slept, seemingly at peace.

Wait, then, until he awoke.

She went to her bookcase and selected Scott's *Ivanhoe.* She'd lost count how many times she'd read it, but she wanted to immerse herself in the familiar comforts of knights and ladies. She always identified more with the knights than the ladies, though, riding around, performing feats of heroism, rather than embroidering in the solar. Michael used to tease her because of this, calling her Sir Astrid. He didn't laugh as much when she called him Lady Michael.

Yes, she told herself, think of him, and not the man in her bed now. She would get Lesperance well again and then send him packing. Whatever trouble he'd gotten himself into, magical or no, he must deal with it on his own. She was through with magic.

His groan, several hours later, brought her to his bedside. He was awake, struggling to sit up.

"Don't aggravate your wounds," she cautioned.

He glanced down at his bare torso, drawing her attention to the chiseled muscles there, the dark brown of his nipples. Like other Natives, he hadn't any hair on his chest, only the faintest dark trail that began just below his navel and led downward, covered, thank heavens, by the blanket.

"What wounds?" he rasped.

Her gaze flew back up to where the worst of his injuries had been. She swore. The cuts were gone now, barely red lines crossing his skin. Same with the rope abrasions. And the bruises were a healing yellow.

Astrid swore under her breath.

He lifted up the blanket just enough to ascertain that he was completely naked. "You took my clothes."

"You were naked when I found you. Do you remember what happened?"

Anger and confusion darkened his face. He sat up fully. "There were men," he said, struggling to recall. "A group of men. Spoke with English accents."

A flare of alarm, but she tamped down her fear. Englishmen filled Canada. "And these Englishmen, what did they want?"

"Hell if I know." He scowled. "Tied me up like a damned dog. They took me from the trading post. Don't know where."

"How did you get free?"

His look turned even blacker as he grew more frustrated, his hands forming fists. "I can't fucking remember." He shot her a glance. "Sorry. Taught not to curse in front of ladies."

Astrid eyed her clothes wryly. A man's shirt, vest, trousers. Heavy boots. She wasn't wearing her gun belt at the moment, but she was seldom far from it. "No such things as ladies out here."

"You've got a lady's accent."

She ignored this comment. "Is there anything else you can remember? Anything those men said?"

He shook his head. "Little bits float in and out of my head, but nothing to grab onto. Damn frustrating. But . . . I kept hearing a falcon, screeching."

Her fear sharpened. "Falcon," she repeated.

Memories began to collect in his mind; she could see the growing clarity in his coal black eyes. "There was a falcon . . . at the trading post. I think it was the same one."

"I didn't see it," she said quickly. "Flying above the post?"

"Showed up after you left. Not flying. It was with some men, some Englishmen." His dark brows drew down as he fitted pieces of remembrance together. "They were looking for guides, said something insulting to me. Then the bird, the falcon. It got agitated. Started shrieking and flapping for no reason."

"Were you standing near the falcon when it did this?"

The words felt like ice in her mouth. She already knew his answer.

He frowned up at her. "Yes. How would you know?" A cold rage sparked in his eyes. "You working with them?" He swung his legs around so his feet were on the ground. Before he could rise and let the blankets fall away entirely, she held out her hands as if to hold him back.

"I'm not working with anyone," she clipped.

"But you knew about the bird. How?" This was a demand, not a request. He grabbed her wrists.

There was no diminishment of sensation. If anything, it had intensified, so that they both jolted the moment he touched her. Around him, the aura of magical energy grew, so much so that it was a wonder it wasn't visible. His skin was warm now, almost sultry to the touch. Not in the way of a fever. Something else heated him.

He drew in a hard breath, then grimaced. "Everything's become so sharp. Clear. Sounds. Scents." He locked eyes with her. "Touch."

Molten awareness gathered. "Since when?"

The tropic intensity of his gaze could have incinerated the cabin around her. Even in this heightened state, she felt it again, the connection between them. If anything, it had grown stronger. A wounded wildness they shared. "Since yesterday, when I met you." He drew her toward him, until she stood between his legs. His calves were leanly muscled, his feet long. "You've done something to me." An accusation, rough, searching. "Some kind of drug. I'd say you put a spell on me, but there's no such thing as magic."

"Then you really don't know," she said softly, more to herself than him.

His glower was ferocious. "Don't know what?"

Before she could think up an appropriate answer, he stiffened, tilting his head slightly to one side. "I hear someone coming. On horseback. They've got a pack mule, too."

At first, Astrid heard nothing, but then, very faintly, came the sounds of hoofbeats. She stared at Lesperance. They shared surprise at his extraordinary hearing.

She pulled away and grabbed her rifle. "Stay inside. Don't go near the windows."

"If there's trouble, I'll handle it." He rose to his feet but at least had enough presence of mind to keep the blanket at his waist.

"This is *my* cabin, *my* homestead," she gritted. "It's mine to protect. And if we can stave off trouble by keeping you hidden, then we'll do it. Understand?"

He wanted to argue with her, but the attorney part of him recognized her logic. Scowling, he nodded, and crouched down so that he could not be seen from the outside. She could have sworn she saw his hackles rising. Satisfied that he was in place, Astrid headed for the door.

"Be careful," Lesperance said. "I'll watch your back."

She stopped at the door but didn't turn. It had been so long since anyone had said that to her, when she had been so used to it before. She didn't want someone watching her back. No words came from her mouth. Instead, she stiffly left the cabin, securing the door behind her.

Afternoon sunlight filled the lea, briefly dazzling her. She stood on the porch and watched a rider approach through the one pass that led to her meadow. That was one of the primary reasons Astrid had chosen this spot for her homestead. Only one way in and one path out, both passes she could easily monitor. There was a second way out of the valley, but she alone knew about it. No one could enter or leave without her knowing.

She slightly relaxed when she recognized the horse and rider. The man waved his fur cap and smiled as he neared. "Mrs. Bramfield!"

Lowering the rifle, she called back, "Hello, Edwin."

The trapper stopped his horse several yards from where she stood on the porch. Hanging from his saddle and on the back of his mule were the accoutrements of his trade—

beaver traps and pelts, black fox skins, snowshoes, and grappettes for navigating ice. She was relieved to see his rifle was in its scabbard on his saddle.

"How are you, Mrs. Bramfield?"

"Very well, thank you." As she exchanged pleasantries with Edwin, Astrid never forgot that a nude, somewhat wounded, and extremely angry man was crouched beside her bed inside. A man who was hunted.

"Summer's just about over."

"Looks like it."

Astrid first met Edwin Mayne shortly after she came to the Northwest Territory. He had been one of the men she'd had to hire to help her build the cabin. Surprisingly, men out in the Territory were among the most respectful of women she had ever met. Even though she lived alone, and Edwin knew it, not once did he or any of his fellow trappers attempt liberties with her person. He might stop by for a moment on his way to set and check traps, but he never stayed long, knowing that she wanted solitude rather than company.

"Mind if I come in?" Edwin asked.

"Oh," she said, "I don't think so. I just did some washing and I have some . . . feminine things hanging up."

Edwin blushed underneath his bushy beard. "A' course! Can't stay long, anyway. I just came to warn you."

"Warn me?" she repeated. "About what?"

The trapper looked grim. "Wolf."

"I haven't any livestock in pasture," she noted. "And wolves don't attack people." The fairy-tale legends and popular lore often painted wolves as cruel man-killers, but Astrid's time out in the wilderness had taught her that wolves wanted nothing to do with people and stayed well away from them.

"This one did. Gave one of 'em a good bite, got a few more with his paws. Maybe it was sick or wounded. You ought to keep a sharp eye out. I'm trying to track it now. Might be able to get a good price for the pelt."

"Who did the wolf attack? One of the settlers by the lake?"

"No, ma'am. Some English fellers. Between here and the post."

Astrid did her best to keep her voice steady, her face betraying nothing, but growing horror crept through her, numbing her at the same time she felt acutely aware of herself and her surroundings. All the instincts she had spent years honing came blazing back to life. She felt again that rift in magic, that encroaching sense of doom.

"I'll be vigilant," she said. "Thank you for letting me know. I should get back to my washing."

Edwin looked reluctant to leave, but he didn't press the point. Instead, he touched his hand to his cap in a gesture of farewell. The trapper set his heels to his horse, clicking his tongue, and man and animals started away from the cabin.

Astrid let out a breath and turned to go back inside. The sound of a rifle going off had her whirling around, her own rifle cocked and ready. She heard Lesperance inside, leaping for the door. She only just managed to hold it shut as his body connected with the wood, and was actually grateful for his slightly weakened condition. If he'd had his full strength, there would have been no way she could have kept him back.

"Wait," she hissed through the door. "It wasn't aimed for me or the cabin." Lesperance cursed but did as she said.

Edwin, a few dozen yards off, held his rifle across his lap and smiled sheepishly. "Sorry, Mrs. Bramfield. Thought I saw that wolf and took a shot at it. But it was only a shadow."

Her only response was a nod. This time, she waited until Edwin had ridden far off before she went into the cabin.

Lesperance stood just on the other side of the door. His breath came shallowly, in angry surges, as she closed the door behind her and leaned against it. Less than two feet separated them, and she felt the heat of him, the size and masculinity of him, to the point where she was nearly overwhelmed.

"You could've been killed." Fury shadowed his arrow-sh features. "I should have been out there, protecting you."

"I don't need or want protection," she answered. "Not by you or anyone. If anybody needs looking out for right now, it's you."

He scowled at her reminder of his current vulnerability.

"You said at the trading post you were Cowichan." She edged around him, needing to put distance between them, and set her rifle on the table. "Do you have any other tribal background?"

Her abrupt change of topic puzzled him, but he said, "Another Siwash tribe from around Vancouver Island."

"Anything from these parts?"

"My great-grandmother, on my mother's side. Stoney tribe. Somewhere in these mountains. Why?"

Astrid swallowed hard as her heart slammed in her chest and a net of old memories ensnared her. Lesperance had no idea. He would never believe her. But he had to. Because it was the truth, and the truth wouldn't allow itself to be hidden away for the sake of convenience or peace.

"There are Stoney legends," she said at last, "of people who can change their form, change into animals. Perhaps you've heard them."

He nodded guardedly, unsure where she was headed. "When I was allowed to see her, my mother told me stories she had heard from her grandmother. The people who ran the school didn't like her filling my head with 'heathen' tales. After a while, she wasn't permitted to visit anymore. But I remembered what she said. A legendary race of changers lived in the sacred mountains."

Astrid shouldered past the pain she felt for him to be separated from his family at so young an age. All that mattered at this moment was now.

"The race of changers are called Earth Spirits," she said. "I have heard the legends, too. But I learned long ago that there is much more truth to legends than society would have us believe. Often, the truth surpasses the legend."

He stalked toward her. She had no desire to be chased like a rabbit around her cabin, so she held her ground as he loomed over her. "Tell me what the hell you're suggesting," he demanded.

She looked up at him, careful to keep her own gaze steady and serious. "I'm *suggesting* nothing. I am *telling* you."

"Telling me what?"

She stared at him for a moment, understanding full well the implications of what she was about to say. Not only would his life change completely, but hers would as well. Damn.

"*You* are an Earth Spirit."

Chapter 3

Transformation

Laugher. Anger. Astonishment. Astrid expected any one of these reactions from Nathan Lesperance after revealing to him that he was not a mere man, as he had long believed, but a shape-changing Earth Spirit.

Instead, he stalked around her cabin, throwing open her cupboard, hauling up the ticking-covered mattress so that the bedding tumbled everywhere, shoving books out of her bookcase.

"What the hell are you doing?" she demanded.

"Looking for whiskey," he growled over his shoulder. "Either you're drunk, or I need to be." He threw more books onto the floor, heedless.

Astrid stomped over to him, determined to keep him from wrecking her once-orderly home. She grabbed his arm. "Stop it."

He whirled to face her, and only a few inches separated them. "Thank you," he said, low and fierce. "I didn't say that before. Thank you for finding me out in the wilderness and bringing me here to your cabin. I probably would've died if you hadn't taken me in. I know you don't want me here. So, don't think I'm not grateful, because I am. But *like hell* will

I be lied to or mocked. You think I'm a stupid Indian—the way they all do."

"That's not what I think," she shot back. "I'm not lying. I'm not making fun of you."

He glanced down to where she still held his arm, his eyes narrowing at the sight. His arm was tight and hewn with muscle. Warmth flooded her, and she pulled her hand back.

"Explain yourself," he rumbled, "before I smash this cabin into matchsticks."

She cast a quick look around, as if actually assessing whether he could reduce her sturdy cabin to kindling. At the moment, he was so ferocious, she almost believed it was possible.

"When I found you," she said, "you were covered in cuts. Not little scratches, but actual wounds that might need stitches. And now look"—she gestured to his chest, forcing herself to consider the sleek contours of his skin—"they are practically vanished. Healed within hours."

"Always been a fast healer."

"No one mends that quickly. Not without some assistance."

He shook his head. "So my wounds are almost gone. That's not enough to convince me I'm some kind of man-beast."

"I did not say you were a man-beast. A man who can change into an animal. That is different."

His bark of laughter held no humor. "Stupid of me not to see the difference."

Astrid held up her hands. "I know this is difficult to comprehend—"

"Difficult?" His mouth twisted. "Try ridiculous."

"But it is true," she persisted, clenching her teeth. "Edwin, the trapper who was outside, said a wolf attacked a group of Englishmen. The wolf bit someone and clawed them. You had blood in the corners of your mouth and under your fingernails. Blood that wasn't yours."

This made him pause, but for a bare moment. "Still a

damned far leap to make. Maybe an animal attacked *me* when I was wandering around."

Astrid wanted to pummel him. She had not spoken this much at one time in years, and the effort cost her patience. "Somewhere, buried in your stubborn head is the memory of your abduction and escape. In that memory is the truth."

He swung away from her, gripping the blanket to his waist. "The laughable truth that I—me, a man—can shift forms into a wolf—an animal."

"Exactly," she said.

"Not 'exactly,'" he fired back. "You may consider me some ignorant heathen savage—"

"I never said that!"

"But the stories my mother told me are just that, stories. I knew it as a child and I know it now. This is a world of steam engines and gunpowder. Magic isn't real."

"Trust me," Astrid said darkly, "it is." And she had the loss to prove it.

He glowered at her. "Trust. You're asking me to trust you. Based on what?"

She should have expected resistance from him. After all, a person wasn't told he was a supernatural being every day. Even so, his stubbornness was a stone wall she battered herself against. How unlike gentle, soft-spoken Michael this man was. But then, she realized belatedly, Lesperance was much like her. She always demanded proof, would never give her trust readily, even before her husband's death. Michael had been the one to believe, to befriend everyone, while she guarded herself and him like a tigress. Lesperance had the same wariness.

"You said it yourself," she countered. "I could have left you to die, but I did not. Even if your wounds did heal quickly, you were in the wilderness alone and dazed." *And naked,* she silently added.

"If I *could* turn into a wolf," he said as though humoring a fanciful child, "I think I'd know. I've never done it before."

"Things change," she said, grim. "People change."

"But not into animals," he countered. "Just find me some damned clothes and I'll get the hell out of here. I don't care how beautiful you are, I'm not going to listen to you—" He stopped, tensing, then inhaled deeply.

Her heart, already racing, began to knock forcefully in the cage of her chest. "What is it?"

His eyes met hers, ebony to steel. "Trouble."

"Can you hear something?"

"I smell it." He drew in another breath through his nose. "The men who captured me. It's their scent." A moment's rare bewilderment crossed his face. "I don't know how I know, I just do."

Astrid did not doubt him. She took a spyglass from her pack, still resting on the floor, and darted to the window. As Lesperance watched in puzzlement, she drew back the curtain, then pulled herself through the window.

"There's a new invention called a door," he said drily as she stood on the windowsill.

She ignored him, instead climbing up onto the roof. The pitch of the roof was not very steep, so she easily held her footing. Her hands, however, shook slightly as she trained her spyglass on the lone pass leading into the meadow. She would not be visible to whoever tried to breach the lea, and had a good enough vantage to see whoever dared disturb her isolation.

What she saw caused her heart to seize. Curses or swears refused to come to her lips. Instead, a cold sense of inevitability threaded through her. She could not see the faces of the men riding in the pass, but she was able to count their number, and knew them at once from their posture. A sense of entitlement radiated from them like noxious vapor. The world belonged to them, and whatever was not already in their possession soon would be.

She knew these men, knew them almost as well as she once knew herself. They were a blight upon the earth, an engine of destruction and enslavement that she had once foolishly thought she could stop. Until the day when Michael was taken from her. Then she no longer believed whatever she or any of her friends did made any difference. Their enemy was and would always be stronger, more ruthless. She had tried to leave them, and her friends, her work, behind. Yet even here, in this wild place, the enemy had found her and even now was less than a half an hour from her home.

The Heirs of Albion.

Balanced on the roof, balanced on the cusp of her own conscience. What to do? A few, far too few, options. She could get her rifle, wait for the Heirs to come within range, and then pick off as many of them as possible. But there were too many. At best, she could hit two or three before their own shooters took her down. No, she refused to throw her life away for a petty victory.

It isn't me they want. The Heirs wanted Lesperance. He was their objective, not her. Years she had spent nursing her seclusion, far from everything and everyone who meant anything to her. The deprivations she had suffered just to carve out a corner of the world where she could be alone. *Do nothing, let the Heirs take him. Reclaim your peace.*

Impossible. She cursed at her integrity. No matter how much she wished, her honor rejected the idea of allowing the Heirs to capture Lesperance. Even if he possessed the ability to shift into wolf form, he could never face the Heirs by himself. They were far too powerful, too brutal. And his survival in the wilderness, alone, was next to impossible. He didn't know the terrain. Without a guide, without protection, he would be vulnerable to the wild and, most of all, to the Heirs. She had to get him to safety.

She was down from the roof, inside her cabin, within seconds. She did not spare a glance toward Lesperance. "We have to leave immediately," she said. She dashed around the single room, throwing gear together for a longer trek into the wild. Her mind and body switched far too easily into a mode of being once thought forgotten. Everything became clear and precise. Uncertainty led to hesitation, which led to death. So, no uncertainty.

A revolver's hammer clicked behind her. She spun around.

Edwin stood near the open door, his gun pointed at her. To one side lay Lesperance, dazed, struggling to sit up amid the splintered remains of the chair. Astrid immediately deduced what had happened. The trapper was a big man, incredibly strong. It was a wonder Lesperance wasn't completely unconscious.

"What are you doing?" Astrid asked, even though she knew perfectly well what Edwin was doing.

To his credit, the trapper looked contrite, though he didn't lower his weapon. "I'm sorry, Astrid. They offered me too much money to say no."

She didn't have to ask who "they" were. The Heirs. Her mind raced. It wasn't the first time she'd been on the dangerous end of a gun, especially that of one of the Heirs' hired mercenaries. Her own revolver was still in her gun belt on the table, her rifle by the door. She could go for the knife in her boot.

Astrid was still calculating odds when a gray, snarling blur leapt onto Edwin. She barely saw the movement. One moment, the trapper had his gun aimed at her, and in the next, he rolled on the floor, screaming, as an animal attacked.

Not any animal. A wolf. Huge, much bigger than any wolf she had seen in these parts. And merciless as it tore into Edwin.

Astrid ducked as the trapper's revolver fired, the shot going wild and slamming into the wall. When she looked up, it was all she could do not to turn away in horror. The wolf had Edwin by the throat. The trapper gave another scream, then the sound collapsed into a wet gurgle. Blood splashed across the wooden floor and stained the wolf's maw, crimson on the silver fur. Edwin's limbs twitched, and he went still.

Wolf and woman stared at each other.

The wolf snarled from his crouched position over the trapper's body as Astrid took a careful step forward. Dear God, it was enormous. At least thirty inches at the shoulder. Silver and black fur bristled with aggression. A mouth full of white, tearing teeth. Eyes of glinting topaz.

It was those eyes into which she stared, searching for the man within. "I am your friend," she said slowly, hands upraised. "I am no threat to you."

The wolf relaxed slightly from its crouch, its snarl easing. It tilted its head a fraction, as if considering her.

"Please," Astrid whispered, drawing nearer even as her mouth dried and her hands grew slick. What if he was too far gone to recognize her? She would die beside traitorous Edwin Mayne, her blood mingling with the trapper's, as the Heirs neared. "You and I are in danger. We must leave at once. I am your friend," she repeated, holding out one trembling hand. The wolf leaned closer, cautiously sniffing her palm.

She expected, at any moment, to have her hand torn from her body. Instead, the air shimmered. A vapor gathered around the wolf, silvery light gleaming through the mists, like clouds covering the moon. The vapor swirled, then dissolved, revealing Nathan Lesperance on hands and knees where the wolf had been. Blood smeared his mouth. He glanced down at the trapper's corpse, then lurched upright and back until he connected with the wall.

Lesperance stared at her, utterly, profoundly shocked by what had just happened. He brought shaking fingertips to his mouth and started when they came away wet and red. He did not seem to care that he was completely nude. What was modesty compared to the incredible, awful truth?

Before he could speak, Astrid crossed the cabin to him. She stepped over the splayed, still form of Edwin, unconcerned that she tracked his blood over her formerly clean floor. From her back pocket, she produced a kerchief.

Lesperance reared back when she reached for him, knocking his head into the wall behind him.

"Easy," she murmured, bringing the square of fabric up to his mouth.

"Don't want to hurt you," he said hoarsely.

"You won't." She carefully wiped the blood from his lips until it was completely gone. The kerchief was ruined, though, and she tossed it to the ground.

"I've never . . ." He swallowed hard, then shut his eyes when he tasted blood. But he was strong, because he opened his eyes a second later. "I've never killed anyone before."

Astrid turned away. "It doesn't get easier."

Considering that Astrid Bramfield had just watched him change into a wolf and rip a man's throat out, she was damned calm. Nathan, buried in layers of shock, watched her bustle around the cabin with a levelheaded precision that would have shamed the most seasoned soldier.

"Help me strip the body," she said, tugging on the dead trapper's buckskin coat.

Nathan normally bridled at being told what to do, but in this instance, he couldn't bring himself to be angry. At least *someone* was thinking clearly. He moved to follow her command, helping her to pull off the trapper's coat, deerskin leggings, wool shirt, and boots. Blood stained the coat and shirt, blood that was still wet because Nathan had taken his teeth to the man's throat and torn at the flesh until the man died. Holy hell.

"Lesperance." Astrid Bramfield's voice cut into the downward spiral of his thoughts. "Don't travel that road. Put the clothes on."

Numb, Nathan did so. The garments were ill-fitting, cut for a heavier, taller man, and they still held the warmth of the trapper's body. Soon, the body would be cold.

As he dressed, he kept his eyes trained on Astrid Bramfield, knowing instinctually that if anything could keep him from losing his mind entirely, it would be her. He felt her strength, her presence. Normally, he relied on his own. But he'd lost his mooring and found steadiness in her. It shouldn't be a surprise. He knew the moment he met her yesterday that this was a woman of uncommon will, a will that matched his own.

She pulled on her heavy coat and her broad-brimmed hat, then culled items from the cabin, things needed for a journey. She knelt in front of a box at the foot of the bed. From this, she loaded a cartridge belt with rifle shells. Women who lived in the wilderness had to be familiar with using firearms, but this woman possessed a long familiarity with weapons. That much was evident in her economic, efficient movements.

Nathan, tugging on the trapper's oversized boots, saw her hesitate over an item in the box. Eventually, she seemed to make a decision, and put what looked like a field compass into her coat pocket. Odd that she'd hesitate over something so ordinary. She took a few more small objects from their hidden places around the cabin, also stuffing them into her pockets. She wavered over the pile of books—books he'd thrown to the ground when refusing to believe her claim that he was a shape changer—then decided against them.

"I made a mess of your place," he muttered.

She dismissed this brusquely. "Doesn't matter. I'm not coming back here."

The implications hit him. Her cabin had been her refuge, though from what, he still didn't know. And now she had to abandon it. Because of him.

"No time for apologies," she said, seeing he was about to offer exactly that. "We must leave now."

Easier for him to find shelter in movement and action than dwell upon what he had just done, what he had now become. She headed for the door, a revolver in her belt, rifle slung across her back, and he followed, but not before taking the trapper's fallen revolver and tucking it into his belt. She gave an approving nod. He found a gleam of satisfaction in getting her approval.

Once outside, sensations battered him. The sound of the wind in the pines. Trails of scent telling thousands of stories. He tasted the deepening afternoon. Everything had become too sharp, too present. Somehow, he must find a way to navigate this new world, or else risk being drowned by his senses.

She watched him struggle, her own expression remote. This was a battle for her, he realized, as much as it was for him.

It shook him that he could read her so intimately, and that she, too, could see into him. No one, especially no woman, had ever done the same. He'd never let them and never wanted anyone prowling around the inside of his mind. But he and Astrid Bramfield shared a connection. Whether either of them wanted to.

"Take Edwin's horse," she directed. "And we'll keep the mule, too." She didn't look behind her to see if he did as she bid him. Instead, she trotted toward the corral and readied her own horse. The trapper's animals seemed indifferent to their change of owner. He smelled the horse's and mule's momentary confusion and then acceptance.

In moments, she saddled and mounted her horse, then joined a mounted Nathan in front of her cabin.

"Their scent's growing stronger," Nathan said. "The men who took me." A coil of fury unwound within him, strong and fierce. He wanted to hurt those men as they had hurt him.

"You and I can't fight them," she said, somehow reading his thoughts. "I know those men, and we could not defeat them on our own."

He wanted to press her on how she knew those bastards, but she had already set her heels to her horse. Nathan followed her lead, spurring his horse into motion.

They plunged their horses into the woods bordering the

west end of the valley, and then up steep, forested hill slopes. Nathan was no stranger to riding, but he would never have found the route on which she led them, narrow passes between rocky ridges all but invisible to any but the most experienced mountain dweller. She never stopped to look back, not at him, and not at her now-abandoned home. He didn't ask where they were headed. All that mattered was moving forward.

The mountain's secrets she knew well. They slid up between the hills, barely a notch, and then they rode downward, putting the valley behind them. Dense stands of spruce trees kept them in lengthening shadow. Nathan watched her watching, her eyes constant in their movement, assessing, thorough. What manner of woman was she, to carry herself like a veteran?

She sat tall in the saddle, moving easily with the horse. He followed the golden rope of her braid hanging down her back and thought of what it might look like unbound. Those trousers showed her legs to be long and sleek.

Hot, swift hunger clawed through him. He saw himself leap toward her, drag her off her horse, and, wrapping her legs around him, thrust into her as she moaned her pleasure. A claiming. Pure visceral demand. He saw it clearly but fought the urge to act. He stayed on his own horse and beat his thoughts and needs down, stunned by their savagery and strength. It had to be the animal within him.

He didn't know who the hell he was anymore. He was a stranger to himself, a stranger who was not another man but, incredibly, a wolf, capable of killing with nothing more than tooth and nail. Wanting a woman in the most basic and elemental way. Demanding to make her his. His study of the law meant nothing compared to the unleashed truth of his body and mind.

She turned in her saddle at his rueful laugh. "You find this amusing?"

"No. Yes." He shook his head. "The world's changed."

"It often does."

He nudged his horse so that he rode beside her, and considered the clean lines of her profile beneath the brim of her hat. "Tell me what you know."

Her shoulders rose and fell in a shrug. "I know as much as you."

"Don't lie to me. You saw me *turn into a wolf,* and it didn't shock you at all, like you'd seen something like that before. You know the men who abducted me, who paid the trapper to capture me. For someone who claims to be ignorant," he said, his voice hardening, "you sure know a hell of a lot."

A slight tension in her jaw drew his gaze. So subtle, the shifts of her emotions, yet he could read them. She wanted to bury those emotions, but there was too much fire in her to be dampened. She debated with herself, what to say, what not to say. She was a keeper of many secrets. He wanted to know them, to know her. The glimpses of herself that he caught tantalized and made him need more.

"Tell me, damn it," he growled.

Her nod of acquiescence was so small as to be almost invisible. "There is," she said after a pause, "real magic in the world. The magic of legends and tales. You said you did not believe in it, but, after what happened at my cabin, it is safe to assume you believe now."

"I've got proof," he said, grim.

"Your mind is open now." She gave him a quick glance of approbation. "That's good. You will need to keep it open." She guided them down a series of switchbacks through the trees, using a trail only she could see. "This magic can be found everywhere, all over the world. When humanity created civilization, it created magic, and placed it into objects both for protection and to coalesce the magic's power."

"What kind of objects?"

She gestured with a gloved hand. "Anything, everything. A coin, a knife, even something as mundane as a rock. Such objects are known as Sources."

Just the word alone sent a cataract of wakefulness swirling through him. He felt it, the animal inside himself, respond, pacing and alert, as though responding to a long-awaited call.

"The Sources are prized beyond all reckoning," she continued. "They must be kept hidden from those who would exploit them. And there are many who do just that."

"The men who abducted me," he deduced.

Again, she looked approvingly at him, though it was only a slight thaw in the gray ice of her eyes. "They are called the Heirs of Albion, an organization of British men who plunder Sources in order to make Britain master of the globe. If the Heirs had their desire, Britain's empire would see no limits."

"They didn't come all the way from England just for me," he objected. "I'm just one man." He stumbled over that word, knowing he was something more than a man. He felt it now when she spoke, how her voice lured the beast within him. He pushed it down when it coiled to spring. "Not enough to make a difference where building an empire is concerned."

"They probably did not come for you. I've heard legends of magic in these mountains. Monsters living in the lakes. A giant serpent." She said these fantastical things as though they were as familiar as house pets. Maybe to her, and those Heirs, they were. "The Heirs must have come for one of those, and to scout for other Sources. That's why they brought a falcon with them. Birds are extremely sensitive to magic, so when their falcon came near you, it sensed the magic within you and reacted. That was enough for them to decide they needed to capture you."

She held his gaze. "It's a fortunate thing you escaped their clutches. They would have made your life a hell, had they taken you back to England. Dissect you with magic, see how you work, perhaps to reproduce your changing ability in one of their own."

The flatness of her tone, more than her words, chilled him. "Were you one of these Heirs?"

A tiny, mirthless smile notched in the corner of her mouth. "Heirs have no women in their ranks. They believe we are too weak and fragile for such dangerous work."

"They've never met you, then." He meant it as a compliment. The courage of this woman made most men look like green saplings. The animal inside of him rumbled its approval, knowing she could meet his strength with her own.

Her smile, small as it was, disappeared. "They've met me. Watch out." They had reached the bottom of the hill, and now the horses had to pick their way through a quickly moving stream.

He was careful to lead his horse exactly where hers had walked. Soon they reached the opposite bank of the stream, coming up on shingled gravel flats.

"Sources," she continued, "are not entirely undefended from organizations like the Heirs. They have their own shielding magic, and the wisdom of the ancients, but there are people who make it their life's work to protect Sources."

"People like you."

She spoke stiffly, refusing to look in his direction. "Not anymore."

"Why did you leave them, these . . . whoever they are?"

"They're called the Blades of the Rose, but that doesn't matter," she said quickly. "What matters now is to keep running."

"I can't run from the Heirs forever. I won't." The idea of fleeing like a wounded deer infuriated him and his inner beast. He never turned from a fight, no matter what form it took.

"We cannot fight the Heirs," she protested. "We don't even know what's happening inside of you."

The animal was a betrayal and a blessing. All these years, never knowing what he truly was, what he could be capable of doing. It was terrifying and liberating. The impossible now possible. Men turning into animals and back again. Magic throughout the globe, and secret societies battling for it. What had become of the world?

He'd make a place for himself. That meant knowing more, battling toward a goal.

"I don't run," he said.

She flushed, because that was exactly what she was proposing.

"And if I can't fight the Heirs alone," he said, "I'll find people like me—the other Earth Spirits—and we can face the Heirs together."

"You'll never find them," she pointed out. "Local tribes say the Earth Spirits are secretive and elusive, living far from others, somewhere deep in the wilderness. Only a few bands in this area know of them or where they might be."

"Then I find one of those bands," Nathan said, decisive. "Even if they don't stand with me against the Heirs, I'll learn more about who, and what, I am. Why the change happened now, after all this time. Make them tell me what they know."

"You cannot 'make' the Native bands do anything." She pursed her mouth wryly. "Out here, one doesn't storm onward, heedless of everything but one's own objectives."

He quirked a brow. "You think I have no finesse."

"As much finesse as a wildfire."

His sudden crack of laughter startled her, almost as much as it did himself. "Back in Victoria, they called me a 'hard-headed son of a bitch.'"

He watched, fascinated, as she fought down a smile. He wanted to see the progress of her smile, how it might change her, lighten her. But her will was strong, and she wouldn't allow such lightness.

Instead, she glanced up at the sky and the deepening shadows cast by the trees.

"Finding a band of Natives will have to wait until tomorrow," she said. "Right now, my concern is putting enough distance between us and the Heirs so we can make camp."

He noticed she included herself in his plans. Not unwanted—she intrigued the hell out of him and the animal within. But, even though he knew she was as capable, if not more so, than any man he'd ever met, the idea of needing her help, of needing *anyone,* riled him. He'd spent too long alone, fighting for himself.

"I've drawn you back into something you want to avoid," he growled.

She didn't try to deny this.

"Point me in the right direction," he said. "I can do this on my own." He didn't want to part with her, not when too many of her mysteries tantalized him as a man, not when that primal inner beast wanted to claim her for its own. But this was bitter medicine, dragging her into the dangerous—and baffling—morass his own life had become.

She brushed away his proposal as a horse might twitch away a fly. "You cannot do this alone," she said. "Whether either of us like it, you need an ally. God help us both, but that ally is me."

Thoughts of Heirs, Blades, Earth Spirits, and his own complex, changeable nature spiked in and out of his mind in the preparation of camp. His fascination with Astrid Bramfield grew each moment he spent with her.

The journey from Victoria to the trading post had taken Nathan through some of the wildest and roughest terrain he'd ever encountered. He knew a fair amount about life out of doors—no matter how much the school administrators had tried to coax or beat the Native out of him, he'd been determined to learn something of his tribal self. And the *voyageur* who'd served as his guide between his home and the trading post seemed to have tree sap running in his veins, his knowledge was so deep, and had taught Nathan a few things about surviving in the wild.

Though the *voyageur* had many years on Astrid Bramfield,

he didn't possess her instinct or expertise. She chose the site of their camp with a keen eye, close to a river, but not so close that the site might flood should the waters rise. Ample feed for the now-hobbled horses and mule. His heightened sense of smell told him she'd steered clear of game trails. No unwanted guests during the night.

"The Heirs might come," he said as they spread dried bracken on the ground for bedding.

She shook her head. "They will, but not today. Even their guides cannot find the hidden pass out of the valley. They'll lose time doubling back and skirting it. Besides, we are far enough from the river so I can hear them coming."

"I can help with that, too," he pointed out, touching a fingertip to his ear. "Unexpected gift." He could also hear the sounds of her body in motion, so that he was aware of every shift, every sigh.

Kneeling, she began to dig a fire pit. He noted that she made one hole in the ground, and then a smaller connecting hole beside it. He saw the rationale when, after she lit a fire, the smoke dispersed.

"Clever," he murmured. He lowered down to sitting, cross-legged. "Our position won't be given away by the smoke."

"A war-camp fire," she said. The flames were low in the pit, barely giving off any light. In the growing dusk, her cool remove kept her distant, even as she sat opposite him.

"Did you learn to do that out here," he asked, "or when you were a Blade?"

She scowled. "I thought Indians were supposed to be stoic and silent."

"I'm not your typical Indian," he noted, a fair amount of pride tingeing his voice. He'd worked like a fiend to ensure no one mistook him for ordinary. And now he was far beyond ordinary, in ways even he couldn't have envisioned.

She regarded him steadily, the fire pit between them. In her eyes was a tentative reaching out, a marked contrast to her tart words. Her voice softened, became pliant with curiosity. "I cannot figure it. You seem remarkably . . . adjusted to your new magic."

"I won't let myself go mad, even if a man doesn't often learn he can change into a wolf."

"Usually someone doesn't have a say in the matter of madness. It takes them, whether they want it to or not."

"Like grief," he said.

Vulnerability flared in her gaze. He wanted to take that vulnerability into himself, shelter her.

"Like grief," she answered, then looked away, breaking the connection.

The truth was, and he could hardly voice it to himself, let alone Astrid Bramfield, he felt . . . relieved. Late at night, he had lain in bed, at war with himself, struggling to contain something he couldn't name, something animal inside of him that scrabbled to be let out. When he dreamt, his dreams were of moonlit forests, of nocturnal hunts and flight. Those who ran the school that raised him, they insisted Natives were wild, savage creatures that wanted taming. He had to prove them wrong. So he rebelled against not only them, but himself.

"Why—" she began, then stopped herself.

"Yes?"

She made a dismissive gesture, but he wouldn't let her retreat so easily. "Ask your question."

She tried again to wave it away.

"Short of being bludgeoned with a heavy log," he said, "I refuse capitulation."

"How aggravating," she muttered.

"Effective," he countered. "No one was going to hand a Native a law degree. I had to seize it for myself."

She seemed to respect that. "Are there any other Indian attorneys in Victoria?"

"No, and probably not in all of British Columbia, either. And I wasn't called to the bar by falling for such simple attempts at distraction. Ask your question," he repeated.

Knowing that she couldn't shake him, she finally asked, "Why did you turn into a wolf at the cabin? How did you know how to do it? You didn't believe it was possible."

He turned his gaze to the fire she had built with such skill. Only the tips of the flames showed at the rim of the pit. One would hardly know a goodly blaze burned beneath the surface. "The first time—I'm not sure. Can't even remember. But the second time . . ." He frowned. "I saw that trapper's gun pointed at you. He wanted to hurt you. And I couldn't let that happen."

His answer caught her off guard. "You were protecting me?"

"Yes."

Her jaw tightened as it did, he began to learn, when she was angry. "I don't need protection."

Nathan's own temper flared. "Tell that to the wolf. We both saw you threatened. And he came out. You look tough, but you're also a woman."

"*Tough?* Like an old, stringy hen?"

He almost laughed at her look of outrage. She might have been one of the most unusual women he'd ever met, but she had her feminine vanities, just the same. Made him wonder what other parts of her were as purely female.

His animal rumbled in his chest. Man and beast were both intrigued with Astrid Bramfield. He had felt it earlier and he felt it now. The man was drawn by her mind, her tenacity and will. The beast's interest was much more primitive but just as powerful. He was both, animal and man. Each moment from now on would be a fight between the two parts of himself. Unless he found balance.

"So, to answer you," he said, "instinct guided me."

"And, when you were the wolf, was it *you*? Did you have the same thoughts, the same feelings?"

"I was there," he said, after considering her question. "But I was also the wolf. His mind and mine . . . blended together. Hard to explain. I want you to feel it with me."

The idea seemed far too intimate for her. Without another

word, she got to her feet and went to the packs taken from the horses. Nathan almost believed she, too, had some animal within her, she moved with such lithe grace, like a sleek mountain cat. But this cat would sooner claw him than accept a caress. He grappled with the urge to stalk her now like prey. Or a mate.

She rummaged in the packs until she produced what Nathan recognized as dried meat and pemmican, and a canteen.

"Dinner," she said, coming back beside the fire. "Courtesy of Edwin. We've enough provisions to last us awhile without hunting." She handed him the food, careful to keep their hands from touching. It was the same with the canteen.

Nathan was ravenous. He hadn't eaten anything since the night before at the trading post. Hell—had it been only a day since the world as he knew it had changed completely? Yesterday, he'd been an ordinary man. If not ordinary, then certainly less unusual. He had believed himself on a certain path. Retrieve Douglas Prescott's belongings, take them back to Victoria, and then continue his pursuit of justice and equality for Natives.

Now he'd discovered something about himself, something that tested the strength of his will. A man who could transform into a wolf. Yet even this was a small piece within a larger wonder. He stood in the middle of an ongoing war. A war for the world's magic. Heirs of Albion. Blades of the Rose. Even the names were fanciful. He'd wandered into an adventure story and found that it was not fiction, but truth, and he was part of this fantastical, yet real, world. It was a world that Astrid Bramfield knew well. He wondered what she had seen. Enough to have her accept his shape-changing ability immediately.

As Nathan watched her, the beast tried to push its way out, but he held it down. A dark smile curved his mouth. *She* might be able to accept him as a shape changer, but she didn't have to wrestle with the damned thing every time he looked at her.

They ate without talking, but he heard everything: the pop of the fire, the horses and mule cropping grass, the nearby river flowing over rocks, and the profound loneliness surrounding Astrid Bramfield, revealing itself through her silence. He knew that loneliness. It marked him from the moment he awoke to when he lay down to sleep, and in his dreams, too. They both belonged to no one, and no one was theirs.

Night descended, enveloping them in darkness.

After trading sips of water from the canteen, she struggled yet again to keep herself from speaking. Maybe this was why she had become a Blade, her relentless curiosity that even she couldn't contain. He thought about what she must have been like all those years ago, bursting with a need to know, a need that propelled her toward defending the world's magic. It was the same demand for knowledge he'd felt as soon as he was aware of his own consciousness.

He wanted to see that part of her, unguarded, eager. He would find a way to bring it back.

So now he waited. Like a wolf stalking prey.

Finally, she asked, lowly, "Can you do it now? Change into the wolf?" In the darkness, he couldn't tell whether she blushed, but he felt it, the subtle warming of her skin. His own flesh heated in response.

Nathan hadn't tried to deliberately change, not yet. "I feel it. Just beneath the surface. It wants to come out." *Wants you,* he added silently. He knew she'd flee at the first open mention of the pull between them.

"Then it shouldn't be difficult," she said.

He couldn't resist. "I'd have to strip."

He didn't miss the way she swallowed hard. He wasn't alone in this desire. Not much comfort, when the woman in question was more closed-off than a vault. Buried beneath ten feet of solid stone. Defended by man-eating dragons and poisonous, carnivorous vines.

"And if you did . . . undress," she rasped, "could you then?"

Could he? Reach into himself and channel the beast inside of him? The thought both unnerved and thrilled him. Without telling her so, he let slip a little the bonds he'd lashed around the animal, but then, seeing her watching him carefully, he forced the beast back under control. It growled in frustration.

He toyed with an evasion. Or an outright lie. But the only way past her armor was to show her that he wasn't without his own vulnerability. "Not now," he said, "even though I'd be a ferocious animal, something about it, about changing, that's exposed. Unguarded. Maybe that doesn't make sense."

"No," she said slowly. She seemed to recognize what he had done, how he had opened himself to her as a show of faith. Her gaze fastened to his and he saw the shadows fall away, just a little. "It makes perfect sense."

Man and beast were one at that moment. They both saw in Astrid Bramfield courage and need, strength and softness. And they both wanted her.

Her eyes widened slightly as she held his gaze. She read in his eyes his intent. Before she could push it away, a responding desire gleamed in her silver smoke eyes. Not just desire of the body, but of the mind and heart as well.

Then she stood and grabbed her bedroll. "Get some sleep," she said gruffly as she unrolled the blanket. "All the days now will be long." She didn't take off her boots or coat, only her hat, which, after she laid down, she used to cover her face.

The drawbridge is up, Nathan thought. A siege it would be, then. But not one of outright force. No matter what the beast demanded. He was still a man and had his own needs. This woman would be his, but she would give him herself by her own desire.

He took the blanket that once belonged to the trapper, then lay on the grass bedding and looked up at the stars. There were legends and stories about the stars, tales he once thought were nothing more than fancies dreamed up to while away long nights. Now he knew differently.

And all around him, the mountains whispered. *You are very close. Come, we await you.*

Chapter 4

The First of Many

Renewal here, in the mountains and alpine meadows. She had felt it when first arriving in the Rocky Mountains, and she still felt it to this day.

As she and Lesperance rode along the base of one mountain spur, the sky gleamed in a chalcedony of blue and white, and the ground still wore its carpet of green velvet. Autumn would soon arrive, but its season was short, and winter beckoned in traces of frost upon the grass.

Home. This was home to her.

After Michael's death, Astrid had lost her mooring, herself, swept into a tide of grief that saw no cessation. She'd taken the voyage from Africa back to England, alone, dressed in the widow's weeds she purchased from an English tailor in Cairo. A black shade of herself, she stood upon the ship's deck and felt nothing. Not the punishing sun, or the sway of the ship upon the waves. She spoke to no one and could not sleep because Michael was not there. They had been married for five years, and she needed his large, solid presence beside her to guide her into dreams.

In Southampton, her parents met her at the dock. Catullus Graves had been there, too, with Bennett Day, Jane

Fleetwood, and nearly a half dozen other Blades. All full of condolences, their sorrow at Michael's loss sincere. Tears marked Catullus's and Jane's faces. And yet Astrid remained numb, even when her mother, her dear, middle-aged, lilac-scented mother, embraced her, whispering, "My poor little Star," Astrid remained entombed in ice.

She couldn't go home with them, to their little Staffordshire house. It was in that ivy-covered house that she had met Michael. The walls were saturated with him, her father's study where he'd gone for education, all the bridle paths and garden gates imbued with his gentle presence. So she remained in Southampton for a year, at the Blades' headquarters, wandering back and forth along the docks late at night as if anticipating a ship carrying Michael—though she'd had to bury him quickly in Africa. Catullus scolded her for inviting peril. The docks were dangerous, full of rough sailors and unsavory types. She could protect herself, though. Hadn't *she* been the one to survive, and not her husband?

One night, she could stand it no longer, and left with one of the ships in the harbor with a satchel bearing few belongings. She had no idea where the ship might be headed, only that it took her away. She wrote letters back, to Catullus and her parents, telling them of her latest whereabouts. New York. Chicago. Farther west. Where might she lose herself? To the mountains and wilderness of western Canada, still an embryonic land, where she had land and silence, and the towering, snowcapped mountains stripped her of everything but bare existence with their magnitude.

She never lost her healthy awe of the wild. Complacency killed. Though her heart she kept shuttered, she left herself open to the mountains and found, in their impassivity and beauty, sustenance.

Lesperance, riding beside her, wore an expression of sharp-eyed fascination as he took in the land unfolding around him. He'd been mercifully silent since breakfast. She had been afraid he would pepper her with more questions about her life with the Blades, questions she had no desire to answer. That chapter was done. She would not go back, not even in remembrance.

Yet in his silence, Astrid still sensed him. She told herself it was because she was unused to traveling with another person, but something smaller, wicked and insidious, whispered other reasons why she watched him from the corner of her eye. She kept revisiting their conversation from the night before—the words, the gazes. He saw into her, no matter how much she tried to shield herself from him. But his interest did not feel exploitative, a means to take her apart to suit his own needs. He understood her grief, having experienced his own, but he had a will and strength that she had to admire. Few possessed enough spirit to gain her respect. Even Michael, much as she had loved him, wavered at times. Not Lesperance. He was her equal. In many ways. A frightening prospect.

She told her inner voice to be quiet and leave her in peace. But Astrid had always been a headstrong, rebellious woman. Now was no exception.

They reached the top of a rock ledge and stopped, looking down. Below them shone a small aquamarine lake, its golden sandy banks frilled by aspens. From the farthest bank rose steep-sided mountains, still crowned with snow despite the lateness of the summer season. No artist could do it justice, and to think of capturing the scene on canvas or paper seemed the height of hubris.

"This feels right," he said. The corners of his eyes creased in pleasure, warming the striking planes of his face, and it was more arresting than the view.

"Don't forget," she said, forcing her gaze to the glinting surface of the lake, "this is a hard place. With respect, however, it gives back even more than it takes." Why had she said so much? She hadn't intended to.

Holding his horse's reins, he dismounted smoothly and

bent to grip a handful of earth and plants. She watched, curious, as he inhaled deeply, the soil cupped in his long-fingered hand.

"So much here," he said. He gazed at the humble clump of earth intently.

"It's the wolf in you. It can smell things a mere human cannot."

He shook his head. "I can scent more—a rabbit passed this way early this morning, it was a damp summer, those Englishmen are still following us, they're far, but out there—yet, even so, it isn't just animal senses. There's blood, living blood, in these mountains." He looked up at her, holding her gaze with the intensity of his own. Her pulse quickened. "You can feel it, too."

She could only nod, entranced by the onyx fire of his eyes. The sense of magic clung to him stronger now, its energy turning the air around him alive. Yet she knew, deep within, that her response came not just from his connection to magic, but his own inner brightness, his active power. She saw it in the way he took in the world, open and ready, but also consumed it. A conflagration of a man. Who was more than just a man. She'd said he had the finesse of a wildfire, and realized now the truth of her words. In his heat and passion, the dryness of her heart and body would catch like tinder and be reduced to ashes in moments. A danger she must avoid.

"This," he said, pointing to a jagged-leaved plant. "What is it?"

"Field mint. Its blossoms are little purple flowers. But they are gone until next year. I love to see the wildflowers in spring, so hopeful after the long, cold winter." Something about Lesperance's presence, his energy and stillness, pulled words and thoughts from her.

"Edible?" At her nod, he plucked a leaf with surprising dexterity. Astrid flushed to see the small green leaf cling to his tongue, then disappear into his mouth. When he plucked another leaf and held it up to her, she felt herself lean down and take the mint into her own mouth, inadvertently brushing the sensitive skin of her lips against his rough, blunt-tipped fingers. She tasted the clean brightness of mint and the spice of his flesh.

Astrid almost fell off of her horse, she pulled back so quickly.

She nudged her horse forward, and Lesperance was on his own horse and at her side within moments. They wended down the slope to the lake. She wondered whether he could hear her heart sprinting in her chest.

"What has it given you?"

She blinked. "Excuse me?"

"You said that this place gives back more than it takes. Must have given you something."

Astrid considered. "Purpose," she said, then, casting a quick glance at him, "and solitude."

"I always had purpose. Solitude is overvalued."

This surprised her. "Have you never been alone, Lesperance?"

"All the time." He said this without a trace of self-pity, only a straightforward relating of the truth. "More now than ever."

"I don't count?" she asked, gruff, and was shocked by her own hurt.

"I scratched your pride." He raised a brow, the picture of arrogant masculinity.

"I've no desire to be your bosom companion," she clipped, then grew heated at her use of the word "bosom." Especially as her own had been growing increasingly more sensitive since meeting him. She craved his touch with a need that embarrassed and angered her.

Perhaps he took pity on her, because he said, "Alone, meaning I'd always been a rarity. Not white, not Native. Now I'm also a man who can change into an animal. There might be no one else like me."

An outsider, like her. Without wanting to, she placed

herself in his life. A Native, taken from his family and tribe, raised by strangers and taught that those familial, tribal ways held no value. But if he aspired to integrate himself into white society, he would never be accepted, not fully. From an early age, he must have been torn, a creature of uncertainty, neither of one world nor another. And that divide had only grown larger within the past few days.

Threads of empathy and connection threatened to bind her to him. No. She wouldn't allow it. Not after so much time, not after the wounds she had suffered.

"But I'll find the other shape changers," he said, resolve strong in his voice. He wouldn't mire himself in defeatism. Wouldn't run from the obstacles in his path. She couldn't stop her admiration for him. She'd never respected those who surrendered easily.

A cold, biting emotion stirred inside her, something she did not want to face. She immersed herself in the land rather than look inward.

At the lake, they both dismounted and let their horses and the mule drink, while they themselves knelt to gulp handfuls of cold water. The day was clear, but dry, and her thirst was strong. She took greedy swallows. In her work for the Blades, Astrid had experienced the privilege of the finest, rarest beverages—teas for maharajas, devastating liquors from the Italian hills, even the variety of whiskey said to be Admiral Nelson's favorite. Yet, to her, nothing compared to cold, fresh water that had been, not long ago, snow atop a nearby mountain. Astrid felt droplets fall from her mouth and slide down the front of her throat, dampening the collar of her shirt.

She heard an animal's rumble and was suffused with heat when she realized it was Lesperance making the sound as he stared at her. Stark desire chiseled his face into something altogether feral.

To her rage—and mortification—her body responded

immediately. Liquid need turned her blood both sluggish and fast. Something clenched low in her belly.

She hauled to her feet and stalked to her horse. "Enough. The more time we waste, the closer the Heirs get. They could make a move at any moment, and we still don't truly know where we are headed." She checked the cinch on her saddle, even though she knew it was perfectly fine. Yet, when Lesperance rose up and strode over to stand next to her, she pretended deep involvement with the latigo connecting the cinch to the saddle's rigging. His masculine presence threatened to overwhelm her.

"Astrid," he said, putting his hand over hers. Damn, why hadn't she put her gloves back on? It galled her that the feel of his large hand covering hers sent a jolt of raw hunger to her core.

She still would not look at him. "You have no permission to use my given name."

"Those rules don't matter out here."

She pulled her hand out from under his and quickly tugged on her gloves. "If we continue on north," she persisted, "by tomorrow we should reach the late summer encampment of a band of Stoney Indians. They might know—"

"Backing down?" he challenged.

She turned so she faced him, knowing that anything less would be a capitulation. "I'm keeping us on track." Her voice held more heat than she realized. "You must see me as your guide and ally, but nothing more."

He narrowed his eyes. "That can't happen."

"It will," she insisted. "Anything else is not possible."

"Sounds like a dare." He crossed his arms over his broad chest, confident as an undefeated pugilist. Under other circumstances, she would have admired his self-assurance and tenacity. But when the obstacle in his path was her own preservation, admiration turned to anger. Yet even anger was too hot. It masked another passion.

She retreated behind icy detachment. "I will only guide

you and help you. That is all. If you seek anything further from me, you will find such a pursuit to be impossible."

He smiled, predatory. "My favorite word."

Dark was coming. Camp would have to be made. She was bone-tired, worn thin not so much from the day's hard riding as blocking Lesperance from her mind. Not once over the hours or miles did she forget him, riding beside her. She tried to retreat into herself, but, even silent, he threaded into her awareness. His presence, the force of his will, glowed like a brand. The way he took in the world around him, with a ferocious intensity, stirred her.

He was like what she had been, before Michael's death. A woman hell-bent on seeing and experiencing everything. She had loved the Blades, loved Michael, because they both accepted that hungry, determined part of her. To her parents, she was a beloved anomaly, the adventure-seeking daughter of a quiet scholar. She had never had a place in rural English life. She could not be part of higher society, could not be meek and fragile. A terrible candidate for domesticity. Yet she had found rare understanding with the man who would become her husband, and more in the circle of the Blades.

And now she had found it again. In Nathan Lesperance. Even without the wolf inside, he was an unstoppable force. The shared intimacy of camp would be difficult to withstand, even with the campfire between them.

They rode through a patch of swampy muskeg, the horses and mule slogging across the peat. A bad place to spend the night, too wet, no possibility of fire. Lesperance also took note of the growing shadows heralding the end of day. He knew they needed a place for the night but didn't question her when she had them press onward.

He trusted her decisions. That itself showed respect. Many men would not rely on a woman's judgment, even if the woman's experience was greater than their own. Lesperance was different, for more reasons than the obvious. She scowled to herself. This would be much easier if he wasn't so damned captivating.

A rustling in the scrub. Astrid held up her hand, signaling silence, as she and Lesperance drew up on their reins. He kept mute as she reached slowly toward her boot. Her hand curled around the handle of her knife. Then, with a single move, she drew the blade and threw it into the scrub. There was a small squeak, then nothing.

Astrid dismounted and gingerly stepped into the undergrowth. Moving through the brush, she felt it, the difference.

"You're frowning," he said. "Did you miss?"

She ignored his comment. "Magic is strong here. I feel it in the ground, the plants."

"Magic's everywhere, so you said."

"See this?" She plucked, then held up, a purple-tipped gold flower. "Isis's Eyes. This isn't their flowering season."

"A seasonal anomaly?"

"More than that. Strong magic makes them bloom out of season. Blades use them to track Sources." She frowned down at the little flower, a portent of something much bigger than its size would indicate. "Changes are happening. But I don't know what's stirring to life."

The flower was edible, so Astrid chewed on it meditatively and resumed her initial search through the scrub. She found what she was looking for. With tall grass, she wiped the blood off the hunting knife's blade after pulling it up.

When she held the rabbit up by its ears, showing Lesperance her prize, frank appreciation lit his face. She had to admit, it had been a good kill.

"Looks like we're having meat for supper," she said, and liked it too much when he grinned in anticipation.

Instead of watching her dig the fire pit, he wanted to try his hand at it. She was obliged to give him direction—but not much, for he learned quickly, and soon had their fire beautifully built and flickering. She skinned and cleaned the rabbit. Before long, it sizzled as it cooked on a spit, and the dusk filled with the sounds of roasting meat and nocturnal insects striking up their song.

"See that?" she said, nodding toward the sky. Lesperance followed her gaze to some low-hanging clouds in the east. "That faint glow at the bottom of the clouds. It's light from the Heirs' campfire."

He scowled. "A taunt."

"Exactly. They want us to know they're coming for you, and there's nothing we can do to stop them."

He looked murderous, but it was one small drop of the Heirs' arrogance. "We know where they are. We can stop them—use magic against them."

"I've none to use," she answered. "The code of the Blades demands that Blades may only use magic that is theirs by birth or gift."

"Damned inconvenient," he muttered.

"It can be."

"You're not a Blade anymore," he pointed out.

Hell. The prohibition of magic use was deeply ingrained into all Blades. She'd forgotten that their code no longer applied to her. Astrid knew it was inscribed in her very blood, no matter how much she wished otherwise.

"Just be cautious," she said instead. He gave a clipped nod. Even though the Heirs were nipping at their heels, she needed to think of something else. "Take care with rabbit," she advised him. "They are too lean to live on. You can gorge yourself on them and still starve to death. Be sure to eat enough fat. Even pure suet, if you must."

He looked at her without hiding his interest. "You know a hell of a lot about living out in the wilderness."

"If I did not, I would be dead."

"And did you know as much, before you came to the Territory?"

She gave a noncommittal shrug. "I knew some things."

"What brought you out here?"

Astrid glowered. "This is the edge of nowhere, and you're cross-examining me."

He refused to look abashed. In truth, he appeared downright arrogant. "I studied law for three years and took up at the firm right after that. Nobody argued a case better than me. Even ones that others thought unwinnable. I helped a Chinese laborer with settlement against a white banker who cheated the laborer of his savings. Everyone was sure the banker would win. The Chinese have hardly any rights in Victoria. But the banker lost, because I got the truth out of him. I always do."

She believed all of that. She felt her own truths laid bare before him. And as for arguing, she and Lesperance did that very well.

It would be better if she kept quiet, if she knew as little about him as possible, yet she could not stop herself. "Will you go back to Victoria, go back to the law, after all this?"

Arrogance fell away as he considered his options. "I'd be the only wolf in the courtroom."

"I've heard that lawyers are jackals."

A corner of his mouth turned up, wry. "Then it could be my advantage. Wolf beats jackal." He shook his head at the fancy. "Maybe I can't return. Maybe I won't be able to find other Earth Spirits. All I know for certain is that I want to rip out the Heirs' throats." He gave a small self-mocking snort. "Finding out I can turn into a wolf, and that there's a gang of murderous Englishmen after me, threw off all my pretty plans."

What those plans were, he didn't say, but she was surprised at the loss coloring his deep voice. He didn't show his vulnerability if he could help it. A twinge of shame pierced her, having, up to that point, mostly considered her own unhappiness at being drawn into this mission. It wasn't a mission to Lesperance. It was his life.

"I'm sorry," she said, for that was all she could offer. She knew what it was to have dreams for the future, and those dreams to blow away like ashes.

"I'll find my way. Could use guidance, though. A firm hand." He raised his eyes to hers, and a heated interest glowed there.

"You don't need *that* kind of guidance," she answered tartly.

His scarce smile flashed. "A man who believes he's nothing more to learn about women is a damn fool."

Her sudden laughter caught them both off guard, but he chuckled with her.

"That's a nice sound," he said.

"Rusty," she replied, grimacing. How long had it been since she'd laughed with another person?

He fed twigs to the fire, but she could not help but notice the masculine grace of his hands. A traitorous thought teased her: How might he touch a woman? With a firm hand, no doubt.

Astrid took her knife and carved the roast rabbit into pieces. Rather than bother with dirtying plates, she shoved a cooked leg into Lesperance's hand and took one for herself.

She muttered something in Swedish about her disloyal mind, but, before she could take a bite, he asked, "What language is that?"

Astrid sighed. "I'm not used to all this conversation."

"You intrigue me," he said simply.

Her body gave a sudden pulse of answering interest. "I shouldn't."

"But you do."

She had been so far withdrawn into herself for all these years, the idea that she could draw any man's interest—particularly one as devastating as Nathan Lesperance—stunned her. "Why?" she asked, genuinely baffled.

"You're not like any woman I've met before." When Astrid gave an indecorous snort, he said, "Don't scoff. We're alike, but not the same. Tied together somehow, you and I. I knew it the moment I met you. You felt it, too."

She wanted to deny it but couldn't. She tried to shield herself behind flippancy. "Who knew a shape-changing attorney could be so sensitive? You should write poetry."

"Throw your barbs," he said with a shake of his head. "You can't scare me off. I want to know you from the outside in."

Oh, Lord. She could well imagine.

"And," he added, nostrils flared, "there's a hell of a lot more heat than poetry in what I feel for you. The animal in me feels the same way."

She, who had faced enemy gunfire, water demons, sandstorms, and cannibal trolls, trembled at his words. Images flickered through her mind of her and Lesperance, slick and tangled, mouths and hands and flesh. His growls. Her moans. And not only bodies entwined, but minds and hearts as well. Exactly what she wanted. Exactly what she feared.

She had to change the subject before she gave in to her body's darkest desires. "If I tell you what language I was speaking, do you promise not to say another word all night?"

"I'll be quiet for ten minutes."

"Ten! Thirty."

"Fifteen."

"Twenty."

He held out his hand to shake. "Done."

Her fingers slid into his grasp, and the sensation of fingers pressed against each other echoed in humid pulses through her body. "How did you talk me into this?" she asked, breathless.

He smiled, wry but also confident. "I'm a very good negotiator."

That, she did not doubt. She wondered how many women he had "negotiated" into bed. A goodly amount, she wagered. Perhaps all his talk of being intrigued by her, their connection, was merely that—talk.

She wished that was true. Yet knew, somehow, it wasn't.

He was no polished city attorney, beguiling women into his bed with glossy words of seduction. What he wanted, he achieved through strength of will. And he wanted her.

It took longer to retrieve her hand than it had taken to give it. The drag of skin contacting skin. Her starved body wanted more. She refused to acquiesce. Yet he knew, too, the effect he had on her, blast him.

She finally pulled back and kept her hand cradled protectively in her lap. "It's Swedish," she said, trying to herd her thoughts and the conversation toward more secure ground. "I learned from my father. Bjorn Anderson, born in Uppsala. He was a great naturalist." Her father's fame as a naturalist had brought Michael as a pupil, and it was over Latinate texts of botanical disquisitions that her and Michael's love had taken root and blossomed. In particular, they were both fascinated by the works of one of England's only female botanists, the Viscountess of Briarleigh. Astrid dreamed of exploring the world as Lady Briarleigh had, with her beloved husband by her side, and soon Michael came to share that dream. Shortly after she and Michael were married, Catullus Graves approached them, offering places within the Blades, the opportunity to travel and study while protecting the world's magic. It had seemed perfect.

"Was?" Lesperance asked. "Your father is no longer living?"

"Is," she corrected, relieved that he was willing to talk about something other than the attraction between them. "Alive. In England."

"You must send him hundreds of specimens for his studies. Plenty to investigate out here."

She shook her head. "I cannot remember the last time I wrote him," she admitted. Her father's correspondence, however, arrived as regularly as post could out in the Northwest Territory. The last letter had related that Michael's youngest sister had been married and was presently on a bridal journey in the south of France. Astrid had realized that everyone else had picked up their lives, yet she continued her self-imposed exile. The idea had left her moody and restless for weeks.

Lesperance's brows drew down. "Are you feuding with your father?"

"No. We've always been close." Except for the past four years.

"Why the hell don't you write him?"

Astrid drew back from the anger in Lesperance's voice. How could she answer him? She could not even answer herself. When she had first arrived in the Territory, she sent her parents and Catullus a letter each, assuring them she was still alive but had no wish to return home. Their letters, however, did not stop. At first, they pleaded with her to come back, said they were worried, that it wasn't right or healthy for a young woman to consign herself to a living afterlife. She need not contemplate another marriage. If she was done with the Blades, everyone would respect her decision. But please return, however she wanted.

Her replies, when she had written them, were terse. No, she was staying. If her parents and Catullus wished to keep writing, they were free to do so, only know that she would no longer open their letters if they insisted on pressing her to come back.

"I just . . . ran out of things to say," she said to Lesperance after a moment. To write to them of her life in the mountains, her observations of the flora and fauna, her interactions with Natives and trappers—it was too much like returning to life, to admit that her grief was loosening its hold, and what held her immobile in the wilderness was something else. Something she dared not name. "I fail to see why that should upset *you.*"

Lesperance's handsome face was stark with fury. He jabbed a finger at her. "Unlike you, who chose to abandon your family, mine was torn from me. They wouldn't let me see my parents after I turned eight. Didn't want me to be tainted by their heathenish ways. I saw them alive only once more after that."

He didn't explain the circumstances of this final visit, but she did not ask for further details, knowing instinctively that his pain would become her own if she knew more.

"And when I was old enough to leave the school," he continued, "I went to find my parents."

"Did you locate them?"

"By the time I reached their village, I learned they'd died the week before from smallpox."

Astrid swallowed, an ache in her throat.

"I made the medicine man show me the bodies," he said, bitterness hardening his words. "I didn't recognize them."

She struggled not to look away. "I didn't know—"

He was on his feet, a shadow hovering large and dark, with the glow of the fire turning him gilded, sinister. "My parents were illiterate, but I would've killed for something from them, even a damned rock. Didn't matter. I just wanted them, a family to belong to. And you're throwing that away." To punctuate, he threw the cooked rabbit leg into the dirt, then turned to stalk off into the night.

"The Heirs are out there," Astrid said to his retreating back.

He pulled at his clothes, so she was forced to look away. "The wolf will take care of me." Moonlit mists began to gather around him, as if he prepared to change, but then he saw her watching him, and the clouds dissipated. He pushed farther into the shadows.

"What about supper?" Astrid asked.

The vicious smile he sent over his shoulder chilled her. "The wolf can take care of that, too."

Then he was gone, disappearing into darkness. She thought she heard the sounds of paws upon the ground, racing into the night, but the night's noise soon hid this.

He would come back. He had no choice but to stay with her, since, even with the wolf in him as protection, he would die in this wilderness without her. Yet she did not doubt that, under different circumstances, he would have left her then, to forge his own path.

Though she was hungry, it was a struggle to force herself to eat. She told herself that she didn't give a damn, that Lesperance could do whatever he pleased, and if he starved out there or got himself killed by a bear, it mattered not a whit. If the Heirs captured him, she might have to come to his rescue, but the location of the Heirs' fire showed they were at least a day behind, likely more. He was in no danger on that front. And the man had turned into a bloody wolf. He was well situated.

Astrid lay down to rest, uneasy but insisting in her mind that there was nothing to be troubled about. She had spent weeks on her own in the wilderness away from her cabin. She wasn't afraid.

Had she been selfish, shortsighted? Callously tossing aside love. When she knew that there was all too little of it in the world. The idea disturbed her.

She looked at the empty space across the fire. For the first time in years, she felt very alone.

A warm muzzle nudged her from her light doze.

Astrid's eyes opened to see a large silver-and-black wolf hunkered over her. She bolted upright, hand flying to her gun.

The wolf made a sound, halfway between a growl and a whine. An alert. It paced closer, brushing against her, moving in a circle around her. A primal fear snaked through her to be so close to the massive animal. Yet she fought against the fear. Even in the darkness, she saw its topaz eyes, the man within.

Her hand dropped from her revolver. "Lesperance?"

He made a small yip of acknowledgment, followed by another warning growl as he looked off into the woods, his ears swiveling toward an unheard sound.

"What is it?" Astrid whispered, rolling up into a crouch.

An odd conversation. She'd never met a shape changer. But the novelty of this had no place now as her senses struggled to full wakefulness. There was a threat out there.

Lesperance moved as though to head toward it, but stopped a few feet away. He swung back to her, pacing around her, as if forming some kind of barrier between her and whatever lurked in the darkness. A low growl rumbled in his throat, deep and continuous.

Suddenly, Astrid heard it. Rhythmic beats upon the ground. Steady and fast. A horse. Big, by the sound of it, and riderless. Even a bareback Indian would change the sound of a horse's hoofbeats. Wild horses weren't unknown in these parts, but they roamed in small herds, never alone, as this one was. She could only hear it as it headed directly toward her and Lesperance.

Astrid drew her revolver, cocked it, and waited. The wolf's growls grew louder as the hoofbeats drew closer.

The trees at the edge of the campsite exploded. The air filled with awful screams as a beast plunged out of the night, straight toward Astrid. Lesperance darted forward with a snarl, shoving her aside, and snapped his wicked teeth at the creature.

It was a horse, but no ordinary horse. Bigger than even the sturdiest draft horse, black as tar, with eyes blazing like an inferno and hooves the size of trenchers. Its mane was a black tangle, and about its neck swung heavy iron chains. The fetid smell of the underworld clung to its flecked hide.

She heard, distantly, the sounds of their horses and mule neighing and braying in fright. At least they were hobbled so they couldn't run off, but they surely wanted to. Astrid could not blame them.

"Hell," she muttered. "A *púca.*" A particularly nasty creature from Ireland. And she knew precisely who had summoned it. She leapt backward to shield herself from its flying hooves and hot breath. Its mouth was full of cutting fangs that tore at the air.

Lesperance shot toward the monster, snarling, lunging for its legs. The *púca* clumsily dodged the wolf's advances and let out a screeching whinny when Lesperance tore a chunk from its front leg. Sticky black blood spurted onto the ground and Lesperance's fur.

So the beast *could* be harmed. Good. Some magical creatures couldn't be affected by such things as knives, teeth, or bullets. But this one could. Steadying herself, Astrid took aim with her revolver.

The *púca* bolted toward her as she readied her shot. Abruptly, the chains about its neck unwound themselves and flew at her. Astrid cursed and flung up an arm for protection. A heavy chain wrapped itself around her forearm. Astrid clawed at it, but the chain would not release her.

Then it was pulling at her, dragging her toward the *púca*. She dug her heels into the ground, scattering their gear lying there, but could not stop the chain's relentless tugs. Her arm blazed with pain as she fought to liberate herself. She had to get free before she was forced onto the beast's back. Anyone who mounted a *púca* would be carried off, never to be seen again—alive.

The Heirs must want her out of the way to get to Lesperance, but like hell would she let that happen. She pulled harder against the chain. Yet it made it damned difficult to aim her revolver.

A wild growl tore the night, something silver and black flew through the air, and the *púca* shrieked. Astrid was tugged off her feet as the monstrous horse reared up, the wolf gripping the *púca*'s back with sharp nails. Astrid fell to the ground and rolled, dodging hooves as the beast tried to shake Lesperance from its back. But he held firm, digging into the creature's flesh. He plunged his teeth into the *púca*'s neck. The monster screamed.

Drops of thick blood spattered onto Astrid as she struggled to avoid the careening, wounded creature's enormous hooves. She might have her head smashed in by the panicked beast.

She pulled again on the chain around her arm and let out a gust of relief when she found she could tug free. The wolf's attack distracted the *púca* and its dark magic. Without the chain's restraint, she rolled away, out of the path of the bucking monster. Astrid leapt to her feet and steadied herself, legs braced wide, as she aimed her gun.

"*Jävlar,*" she cursed. Lesperance still clung to the creature's back, biting whatever he could sink his teeth into. No matter how hard the *púca* bucked, it couldn't dislodge him. But it was too dark and the monster too frenzied for Astrid to take a proper shot, not without possibly hitting Lespérance.

"Let go," she shouted.

The wolf's ears swiveled to catch her words, but the animal didn't release its hold on the *púca.* In fact, the damned wolf snarled at *her.*

"Let go," she yelled again, "so I can put a bullet in its damned head!"

That seemed to convince him. With a final growl, Lesperance released his death grip and sprang away. The moment he was clear, Astrid fired. Her bullet slammed into the *púca*'s eye.

An ordinary horse would have fallen to the ground, dead, in an instant. Even, perhaps, in other circumstances the *púca* would have been killed. But the world's magic was stronger now. The *púca* shrieked once more and wheeled away. It dove for the shelter of the trees, and Astrid shot again. If she hit the creature, she couldn't tell, because it evaporated into a noxious mist. In a few seconds, the only thing remaining of the beast was the smell of putrid, stagnant water.

She let out a slow breath, holstering her gun. The wolf trotted up to her.

They stared at each other in the sudden silence of night. It licked at the blood on its muzzle as it gazed levelly at her—almost a challenge, both to itself and to her. *This is what I am.*

And this is what I am, she thought in answer.

Lesperance let out a small *woof* of understanding. She almost smiled. Both of them, barely civilized.

Astrid reached out as if to scratch between the wolf's ears, then stopped herself. He was not a pet. This was a man within a wolf. As for the man . . . she and he were allies, but not friends.

He must have seen this in her face. Lesperance backed up, then cast a glance over to the pile of clothing he'd left behind earlier. He made a soft whine of distress, looking back at her. She understood.

Astrid turned away and heard the sounds of shifting, movement. Clothing being gathered and donned. When she turned back, Lesperance in his human form stood by the remains of the camp, dressed. A curious and uncharacteristic vulnerability hung about him, even though he still had blood on his mouth, blood he'd drawn with his wolf's teeth and wolf's nails.

"Still hard to believe I can do that," he said, low. He wiped at his mouth and smiled grimly at the dark smears left on his sleeve. Yet another bloodstain on his clothing.

"You did, and did it well." She also dabbed at the gore on her clothes. She began to move through the camp, gathering up the things that had been scattered during the fight.

He snarled, "The Heirs sent that . . . thing." He glared toward where the *púca* had dispersed. "I'll rip their fucking guts out. You could've been killed."

"I have faced worse," she noted, but did not miss how his outrage was on *her* behalf.

"That's not a consolation," he growled, dragging his hands through his hair.

She had to disabuse him of the notion that he was her sole means of protection and safety. She'd done perfectly well before he slammed into her life. "Truly, Lesperance, far more dangerous magic exists. Not only does it exist, but I've faced it and survived."

"You've seen that creature before?" he demanded.

"The *púca*? No. But many other magical creatures."

"Demon horses," he said with a shake of his head. At least he'd calmed down and wasn't threatening to single-handedly take on the Heirs. "I shouldn't be amazed, considering." He glanced down at the blood on his garments and on the ground. "But I am amazed. Amazed and furious."

"The *púca* is merely the first of what will be many," she cautioned, "so save your fight for another day. They are determined to have you."

His mouth flattened. "And I'm determined to be rid of the Heirs. I can find their camp, go after them."

"Even though you are a powerful wolf, you could never defeat them." She rubbed at her arm where the chain had dug into her flesh. "Magic such as the *púca* is nothing to what they are capable of."

"Why don't the Heirs send more?"

She sunk down onto her heels, suddenly exhausted. She knew she should thank Lesperance for coming to her aid, but all she could feel now was weariness in the aftermath of the fight. If she needed convincing that the Heirs were truly in pursuit, she had her proof now. "They will."

Chapter 5

Astrid Awakened

A strange mood the following morning. She awoke in the gray of dawn to find Lesperance sitting across from her, cross-legged, feeding kindling to the fire. His face looked carved from jasper, hard and immobile.

Their morning meal was wordless. Too much had happened the night before—their argument, the fight with the *púca,* the fact that the Heirs snapped at their heels—and the weight of everything pressed down upon them. She cooked bannock over the fire and they ate it without speaking or even truly looking at each other. Astrid distracted herself with other thoughts. Soon, she would have to forage to supplement their stores. Autumn frosts hadn't come yet, so there would be enough to sustain them.

After tending to their personal needs, they readied their horses and struck camp. The process went much faster now. Lesperance's skills in the wild grew hourly. No wonder he had been able to break past societal boundaries to become a learned professional. His mind was as forceful as his determination. Yet she knew the other side of him, the side that had charged and attacked the *púca,* spilled the monster's blood.

He was both, beast and man. But it was the man that disturbed her most. He cut to the very heart of her, through force of will as well as softer, subtler means. One of the few men who accepted her as she was, yet challenged her. And, reluctantly, she admired him. Courageous, almost to the point of being reckless. A deep generosity despite having so many barriers set before him. Perceptive—too much so, for her comfort.

She said none of this. They went on in labored silence. She could not feel the same restorative joy in the glinting snow atop the mountains, nor the lush green depths of the woods, not while she and Lesperance both clung to their stubborn silence. She had been so used to going without words. No longer. Damn and damn again. He'd taken her perfectly good isolation and punctured it, making her aware of the hollowness at its center.

They sought his true people, the tribe to which he belonged. And where did *she* belong? She knew, but did not want to know.

At midday, as they followed a creek, he drew up short on the reins, narrowing his eyes and drawing in a breath.

"Smoke," he said. "Dogs and horses. And people."

Sure enough, as they pushed around the bend of the creek, there it was. A collection of elk-hide tepees rising close to the creek's bend like conical mushrooms. Strips of meat dried in the sun as women in beaded deerskin dresses scraped at more elk hides, preparing them for tanning. Horses roamed at the edges of the camp, guarded by boys in fringed leggings. As Astrid and Lesperance slowly rode closer, their appearance was noted by a small girl, who ran, shouting their arrival, with a dog barking excitedly at the girl's heels.

Astrid could see the encampment was already in the process of being broken down for a move to the winter grounds. Several women were packing travois to be hitched to the backs of horses.

"This is the tribe we're looking for?" he asked.

She nodded. "They might know where to find the Earth Spirits."

"You've dealt with them before?" he pressed.

"Not this band," Astrid answered. She could well imagine what a good attorney he might be, demanding answers, exacting information through strength of will.

Two men on horseback, wearing the feathers of warriors in their braided hair, trotted toward them.

"Friendly?" Lesperance asked, low. She followed his eyes to the rifles the men carried, and the heavy, blunt war clubs hanging from their saddles.

"The Stoneys here are peaceful," she answered, equally low. "They want to be left alone." But she did not want to push them. Even a peaceful creature grew fierce when it perceived an attack.

The warriors stopped their horses in front of Astrid and Lesperance. They gave a quick look at Astrid, noting her men's garb with barely revealed curiosity, before turning to Lesperance and speaking.

Lesperance could only frown when the men spoke Nakota to him. He glanced, frustrated, at Astrid.

"Forgive me, warriors," Astrid said in Nakota. "This man is not of your tribe. He comes from the Western Sea and cannot speak Nakota."

If the Native warriors were surprised, they did not show it. "We know some English," one said, "from the trappers and the men who tell us of their God and His dead son." He took note of the furs still hanging on the pack mule. "You are a trapper, though," he glanced back at Lesperance, "you have the look of a warrior."

Astrid wondered how to properly phrase who, or what, she and Lesperance were. Something much more complicated than she knew how to describe.

"We are travelers," Lesperance answered, while she debated with herself. A fitting description.

The second warrior spoke. "You are far from your tribal lands, friend."

Again, Lesperance took command of the exchange. "I seek answers about myself."

Both warriors nodded with understanding. The pursuit of one's truth was well regarded.

"And you mourn as well?" the first warrior asked.

Lesperance looked puzzled.

"This man was taken and raised by the white man," Astrid interjected. "He wears his hair short as they do." She whispered to Lesperance, "When a Native grieves, they cut their hair."

She saw him struggle not to touch the back of his neck self-consciously. It was such a boyish gesture of uncertainty, so unlike him, especially given the way he took charge of their dialogue with the warriors, she almost smiled.

"You speak much for a woman," the second warrior noted.

At that, Lesperance chuckled, then composed himself when the Natives stared at him in perplexity. Most Natives retained a good deal of reserve, especially in the presence of strangers, and warriors were famed for their stoicism.

"She is Hunter Shadow Woman," Lesperance said.

Astrid turned to him, surprised. "How do you know that?"

"Sergeant Williamson at the trading post."

She had no idea she had developed a reputation. And, judging by the slight shifting in the Native warrior's expression, the barest hint of esteem glinting beneath the smooth surface of their impassivity, her reputation was a good one. How odd, but somehow gratifying.

The first warrior called something over his shoulder. Another man near a tepee answered, then went into the tent. Within a few moments, he emerged and shouted back to the mounted warriors.

"Hunter Shadow Woman and He Who Is Far are welcome," the second warrior said. "Our chief will smoke a pipe with you."

Both murmuring their thanks, Astrid and Lesperance followed at a slight distance. As they rode into the encampment, they drew the unconcealed stares of everyone. But it wasn't Astrid, with her white skin, blond hair, and men's clothing, that attracted attention. It was Lesperance, a Native man dressed like a European, hair shorn, who, it was already known, could not speak Nakota and was taken by white men and raised as one of them. He was more alien to the Indians than she.

He bore their staring with restraint, though she could detect, in the slight tightening of his jaw, his discomfort. This troubled her for many reasons—including the fact that she was coming to know him well enough to read his emotions, and that his unease should bother her at all.

They were led toward one of the larger tepees. Several boys came forward to take their horses and mule. As the animals were led away, the chief emerged from the tepee, wearing the beads and eagle feathers of his office. Through the opening to the tent, faces of women and children peered out with interest. One of the women was only just on the side of marriageable age, no doubt the chief's eldest daughter, and she looked at Lesperance with sizable attention.

"It is a shame about his hair," she whispered in Nakota to her mother. "He would be most handsome with warrior's braids."

Her mother hushed her, and the daughter disappeared into the recesses of the tepee.

The chief gestured that they were to sit. Some nearby women giggled when they watched Astrid sit cross-legged, like a man, and not with her legs tucked under like a modest woman, but she paid them no heed. But, again, Astrid held much less fascination than Lesperance. Judging by their discreet but admiring glances, it wasn't only Lesperance's curious amalgamation of Native and white man that held their interest. Astrid wondered if it was the beast inside him that made his presence so arresting, so fascinating. No, it was not that, but his inner strength that glowed with an unseen heat. This was a man who fought for his beliefs, with the face and body of temptation. Lord knew she was tempted.

"You frown, Hunter Shadow Woman," said the chief in Nakota. "Does something displease you?"

"No," she answered quickly. "Your band is prosperous, and the smoke of many fires may sting my weak eyes."

That answer pleased him. As the pipe was being prepared by one of the warriors who met them, the chief introduced himself. "I am Thunder Eagle, and I have heard tales of you, Hunter Shadow Woman. Your companion—my warriors say he searches for answers about himself."

Astrid glanced quickly at Lesperance, who was attempting to follow the conversation despite the language barrier. How strange it must be to not speak the language of one's people, even if the divide of generations separated them. She would not exclude him, as others had done. "Wise Thunder Eagle, if you have the knowledge of English, I humbly ask you to use it," she said, with a meaningful look toward Lesperance.

The chief nodded, taking up the prepared pipe. It was decorated with feathers but was not as elaborate as some war or peace pipes Astrid had seen. Thunder Eagle took several draws upon the pipe before handing it to Lesperance, who mirrored the chief's actions. Astrid gave a tiny shake of her head when Lesperance started to hand the pipe to her. She might be an anomaly to the Natives, but male rituals were still forbidden to her.

"I have made such searches, He Who Is Far," Thunder Eagle said to Lesperance in careful English. "When I was only allowed to hunt with a bow, still a boy, I had dreams that I was meant for more than being a hunter or warrior. So I went away for seven nights to seek my answer in fasting and prayer. My brother Eagle showed me I was to be chief."

"And were you made a chief when you returned?" Lesperance asked.

Thunder Eagle's eyes glittered with a smile. "When I

returned, I ate half an elk and slept three full days. Being chief could wait."

Astrid and Lesperance laughed softly.

"Many years later, I became chief," Thunder Eagle continued. "But my search led me to the right path. What answers do you seek, He Who Is Far?" Thunder Eagle asked Lesperance.

"I must find the Earth Spirits, great chief," Lesperance answered without preamble.

Those Natives nearby who understood English gasped audibly. Soon, the encampment burbled with the news that the white Indian sought the shape changers.

"This, you cannot do," Thunder Eagle said, clearly taken aback. "They do not wish to be found."

"What do you mean?" Astrid asked, fighting a shiver.

"Since the coming of the white man," the chief explained, "their tribe does not leave their territory. They come out only when something is needed, such as horse trading or finding husbands and wives outside of the tribe. Then they disappear again, like smoke in the rain."

"No one seeks them out?" Lesperance pressed.

Thunder Eagle looked grave. "There are tales. Five summers ago, a foolish warrior from another band claimed he would storm the Earth Spirits' lands and count coups. A great feat, to touch or strike such powerful spirits."

"What became of him?" asked Astrid.

"His war club was found near a river. But that was all." The chief frowned. "Stoney leave the Earth Spirits in peace. You must do the same."

Astrid pushed her disappointment aside. More than once as a Blade had she faced obstacles in her quest to protect Sources. She urged, trying to keep her voice respectful, "If you know where we may find them, please, tell us." When Thunder Eagle looked reluctant, she continued, "It is most important that we find the Earth Spirits. Men are coming who will harm not only their tribe, but all tribes in the mountains. Not just Nakota or other Natives are in danger. But *all* people are threatened, white, red, black. These men bring a dark medicine from across the water. We have seen it. I . . . *we* know its destruction."

Something of her past wounds must have resounded in her voice and revealed itself in her eyes, for the chief seemed to relent slightly. "There are old stories that tell us where the Earth Spirits might be found, but even these tales are shrouded in mist." He paused.

"There's more," Lesperance said, honing in on Thunder Eagle's slight silence. "Please, whatever you know, tell us."

"How do I know you are not like the foolish warrior, who went to find death? Or perhaps you are part of those men who you claim are coming to harm the tribes."

"The white man took me when I was small," Lesperance said. "I've never known this." He gestured around, indicating the bustling village of tepees, children with their mothers, hunters and warriors repairing weapons and saddles. "I've never known myself. I can't even speak the language of my ancestors." He scowled at his history, at himself.

Astrid ached for him, understanding how much he needed that connection. And she had thrown away what he wanted most.

"White men are worse than dogs to do that," the chief said, anger chipping into his words.

Thunder Eagle seemed to have forgotten that Astrid was white, but she bore his insult. Many white people hadn't been good to Natives, either from outright bigotry or well-intended meddling. She kept silent, watching Lesperance make his case, the raw need in his eyes that left her feeling equally defenseless.

"The blood of the Earth Spirits is in me," Lesperance continued, impassioned. "They are all I have left. They hold the answers to the riddle of myself, and that is why I seek them now."

"*You* are an Earth Spirit?" Thunder Eagle asked.

Lesperance's nod was brief. His confession cost him. This was a powerful secret to share, one he hadn't fully adjusted to, either to reveal or to himself. "It's only been a few days since I learned of it, but I am."

"This is difficult to believe," said the chief.

"It's true," Lesperance growled. He seemed to force the words out. "I can take the form of a wolf, if I have to."

The chief's impassivity fell away for a brief moment as his eyes widened. "I never thought to speak to, or even see, an Earth Spirit."

"You see now why we must find their tribe," Astrid said, "what it means. We have questions that can only be answered by the Earth Spirits."

"Whatever you know, I need you to tell us." Lesperance stared hard at Thunder Eagle, burning intensity in his dark eyes.

The chief drew on his pipe, deeply contemplative. After a moment, he said, "Swift Cloud Woman could find the Earth Spirits. She was once part of their tribe. But," he added darkly, "she is bad medicine."

"I have heard of her," Astrid said.

Lesperance shot her a glance. "You never said anything."

"I had no idea," she fired back. "I only heard her name, and that she is avoided by all Natives. But I never knew she was part of the Earth Spirit tribe."

"There is a shadow over Swift Cloud Woman," Thunder Eagle said. "She has lured men into destruction. Makes promises she cannot keep. Strips warriors of their honor to serve her purposes. Two young warriors from my own band have fallen to her. If you *must* find the Earth Spirits, you must never seek her help to do so. It is better we tell you what we can than you search for her."

"Anything you know," Lesperance urged.

"The way will be dangerous," warned Thunder Eagle. "The Earth Spirits guard their secrets well."

Astrid shared a glance with Lesperance. Tension still

hummed between them, unsaid words, stung feelings, anger, vulnerability, and, yes, strengthening tendrils of attraction and connection. Yet, despite all this, neither could quite contain their mutual excitement. Or adventure. Astrid had once loved it, and she knew, deep within herself, that Lesperance not only shared her love, but was glad to have hers reawakened.

The line of men moved silently through the alpine pass. They seldom wasted time with idle chatter, especially when in pursuit. Their guides, three hard-bitten mountain men, dreamed of wealth. To ensure their loyalty and services, each had already been given a purse full of British pound sterling, but there would be more, much more, with the successful completion of the mission. So they kept their positions, at the head and the rear of the column, eyes and ears alert and sharpened with greed.

Four others made up the rest of the party. As they navigated the narrow, rocky pass, they, too, dreamt of wealth, but even more, they craved power. Such hunger drove them to the farthest, most inaccessible and perilous corners of the globe. Power was theirs, by right, by birth. They were Englishmen. The world's magic belonged to them alone, the Heirs of Albion.

Albert Staunton glanced behind him with a scowl, making sure his compatriots kept pace. Halling was nodding in his saddle again. Idiot. Staunton had come halfway across the earth for this mission and sure as hell wasn't going to let some doughy laggard like Richard Halling slow him down. Succeeding in a mission meant greater rank and prestige within the Heirs. Each mission was a building block upon which he planned to construct the fortress of his power. And this one was most important of all.

"Look lively, Halling," Staunton barked.

Halling snapped awake and looked annoyed, wiping his sleeve across his mouth.

As Staunton muttered a string of curses, a marked contrast to his aristocratic breeding, Lesley Bracebridge drew up alongside him, smirking. The falcon on Bracebridge's arm seemed just as smug.

"Whose palm did Halling's father grease to get him here?"

Staunton grunted. "Had to have been Fawler. He's got the final say on field teams."

"At least Milbourne's worth something."

Both men regarded the fourth member of their team with approval. John Milbourne sat tall and alert in the saddle, revolver and rifle both at the ready. One of the Heirs' best marksmen, and a prime addition on this most critical mission.

"That *púca* didn't do the trick," Staunton noted. "Our hands are still empty."

The mage glowered. "A first attempt."

"And what about the spell you've been tinkering with?" Staunton pressed.

"Needs more work." Bracebridge rubbed at his dark beard. "The transformation isn't lasting long enough. And it isn't 'tinkering.' One doesn't 'tinker' with dark magic."

"Whatever you call it, keep working. We need that spell to go up against the shape changer."

Even though Bracebridge had seen, and done, some wonderfully brutal deeds in his time, he still could not suppress a shudder, making the falcon shift on its perch on his arm. "What that Indian did to the *púca* . . . and the way he tore out Mayne's throat . . . vicious."

"But useful," Staunton reminded him.

"Very true." Bracebridge's horror was lost in a smile as he contemplated not only possessing Lesperance's shifting abilities, but having his own magical transformation. He thought of his future exploits, his conquests, and stroked his beard gleefully.

Staunton smiled as well. Despite the failure of the *púca,*

Bracebridge's magic could be relied upon. The mage coveted power, and that pushed him always forward, to wherever and whatever the mission demanded. Excellent. This mission was Staunton's to command, and he was determined to succeed.

The Primal Source—the world's first and most potent magic—belonged to the Heirs now. It had been awakened, and Staunton vowed to see its power, and his own, fully realized. His successful completion of the mission here in the wilds of Canada would ensure the Heirs' command. And if, in his pursuit, he got to inflict some bodily harm on Astrid Bramfield, so much the better.

Nathan stood at the bank of the river, waiting. Packs and gear were piled by his feet. A cluster of children, crouched in the dust, watched him. Behind him, Astrid spoke with Thunder Eagle in Nakota, so he had no way to know what they discussed. Judging by the glances they both sent in his direction, he was the subject. Still, both the chief and Astrid were too damned good at hiding their feelings, so whatever it was they said about him, he would never know. He could only stand nearby and watch.

"Not a hell of a lot new there," he muttered to himself, then shook his head at his own moodiness.

Nathan existed on the margins. Even with the other Native children at school—he hadn't fit in with them. Those boys and girls read and learned their catechisms, learned to play the piano, sang hymns, took up carpentry or spinning, and played football on the pitch on Saturday afternoons. Nathan got into fistfights. He brooded his way through his lessons and wouldn't attend innocent Thursday night dances held in the refectory. The last time he had been permitted to see his mother was when he was eight, and four years later, he ran away to his parents' village, but both his mother and father urged him to return, to make something of himself in the white man's world. The Indians' world was dying, they said, despite the white man's promises. He must learn to live as the ghost-colored men did.

He did return, digging knuckles into his eyes to keep them from leaking. But instead of joining the other Indian children in their play or schoolwork, he kept to himself and applied all his energy toward his studies. He wouldn't take up carpentry or blacksmithing or cannery work or any of the other manual skills the teachers pressed upon the students. No—he would learn the white man's own system, law, master it, and use it like a hammer to demolish the world that was killing his own.

There is no such thing as a Native attorney, they told him.

There will be, he answered, and became just that.

He didn't expect his social standing to improve by becoming a professional. And it didn't. He was invited to a few parties and dinners, but he knew they saw him as a novelty, not a man.

Unlike Astrid. The barriers between them were not founded on the color of skin. That ordinary prejudice would almost be easier to face than what kept her fortified like a citadel. Even now, talking with Thunder Eagle, her arms were crossed over her chest, her posture protective.

Some of the anger he'd felt at her self-imposed estrangement from her parents dissipated, especially after they had fought side-by-side. He was honest enough to realize he wasn't angry with her, but at the sense of his displacement that never truly went away. Hard to reconcile himself to his life when every step he took, every word or gesture directed toward him, only reinforced the fact that he was, and would always be, an outsider, even among those who supposedly were his people.

Yet they weren't his people. The deeper he got into the mountains, the closer to the Earth Spirits' lands, he felt it. Drawing him. Pulling him. Toward what, he didn't know. All he knew was that his whole life, he'd felt a profound difference, never at home, never himself. He hoped finding the other shape changers could give him the belonging he'd never felt.

Two men carried down to the river a birch bark canoe. They watched Nathan from the corners of their eyes, as if he might spring at them like a cornered wolf.

He gave the men a grin that was more flash of teeth than welcoming smile. They set the canoe down upon the sandy riverbank and hurried away.

"Stop scaring them," Astrid said, approaching.

Nathan didn't try to refute this.

She planted her hands on her hips. It continued to floor him that a woman in trousers and a gun belt could look so damned alluring. Maybe he was more rebellious than even *he* gave himself credit for, to find Astrid Bramfield with her blunt speech and heavy boots seductive. He wanted her, wearing her boots, or barefoot—her toes curling into the soft earth of the forest floor. The beast in him rumbled with approval.

Only he knew the direction of his and the beast's thoughts. Astrid was brusque efficiency. "Thunder Eagle said we were to follow this river for a day and a half to reach the border of the Earth Spirits' lands." She squinted up at the sun. "There's still plenty of daylight left, so we can make good progress."

"A canoe, food, and direction, in exchange for the horses and a few pelts. You made a good bargain."

She seemed relieved that they had reached détente. She actually blushed a little at his praise. He kept discovering how sensitive she truly was, despite her plain speaking and skill with knife and gun. Astrid was much more responsive than she realized.

"Do you know your way around a canoe?" she asked.

"There are lakes and rivers on Vancouver Island." He began to load their gear into the small boat, careful to keep everything balanced in the middle.

She noted and approved of his technique, then helped to pile their packs into the canoe. "Not like the rivers in these mountains. Many are fast-moving and full of rapids. And I am sure that the Earth Spirits keep their territory well protected. This river is certain to be dangerous. Deadly, even."

"You can't discourage me."

"As if such a thing was possible." She smiled. Not a big smile, only the slightest upturn in the corners of her mouth, yet to Nathan, the sight hit him like sunrise over the mountaintops. "I think the wolf in you has made you arrogant."

He hefted another pack. "Always been that way."

"How fortunate," she said drily. Her braid dangled down her front, hanging in front of her breast, and she flipped it back with a practiced motion.

Nathan was ready to cut off a limb just to take her hair out of that damned braid. If he could remove her coat and shirt, touch her bare skin . . . His beast paced in the cage of himself, wanting.

Thunder Eagle approached them, trailed by the two warriors who had escorted them into the encampment. The chief looked grim. "You must be careful. If the river does not claim your lives, the tribe may."

"We will take that chance," Astrid said, without a flicker of fear.

Nathan wondered whether all women in the Blades of the Rose were as courageous. Even if the female Blades had the bravery of armies, he doubted they resembled Astrid in any but the most superficial way.

"Now *I* must warn *you,* Chief," Astrid continued. "The men who are following us, they are cruel, more cruel than any white man you have ever met. And they are not far behind. They will be here in a day or two. They will ask questions about us, questions you should not answer, for everyone's safety."

"My band is honest," said the chief, but added with a wry gleam in his eye, "but not always. We can tell good stories."

She was not amused. "These men know falsehood when they hear it. And if they *do* catch you in a lie, they will make war upon you, a terrible war."

"My band's warriors can fight," Thunder Eagle said,

slightly stung at the implications that he and his men could not defend themselves against the Heirs.

Astrid placed her hands on her hips. "Not against these men. They use dark medicine, the darkest there is."

The chief frowned. "If we cannot fight them, how can I protect my people?"

"I see you are moving camp." She nodded toward where women were disassembling the wooden racks used for drying meat.

"To our winter grounds," Thunder Eagle confirmed.

"The sooner you move, the better. Leave by tomorrow, and no later."

The chief looked surprised at Astrid's commanding tone. No doubt no woman ever spoke to him as she did. Nathan knew exactly how Thunder Eagle felt. There wasn't a single woman like Astrid Bramfield.

Thunder Eagle recognized her rarity, too. "I see why you are called Hunter Shadow Woman," he said, reluctant admiration in his spare words. "The women will grumble to have to move so quickly."

"Then the men must help."

"Oh, they must?" Thunder Eagle asked with a raised brow.

"If they value the lives of their women and children," Astrid said, her voice so stark that the chief paled slightly, and Nathan, too, felt his blood chill. Even though Nathan had seen some of the Heirs' magic, he still did not know what they were fully capable of doing—but Astrid did, and he wondered at the horrors she'd seen. And survived.

"It will be done." The chief turned to Nathan. "He Who Is Far, your journey is not over."

Nathan looked at the river, moving fast and cold over rocks, and then at Astrid, just as swift and cool, but warmth was in her, like the light shining upon the water.

"It's just starting," Nathan answered.

* * *

Astrid took the front position in the canoe, and Nathan's seat was close enough that he could catch her subtle, verdant scent above the freshwater. He clenched his teeth as he fought the beast. Damn his sharpened animal senses. The next few days on the river promised to be hell.

As they pushed off from the riverbank, Thunder Eagle and most of his band gathered to watch. Some of the children shouted what Nathan had to assume were farewells, and ran alongside the river as he and Astrid began paddling. When the river turned a bend, the children stopped and waved. Another bend, and the children disappeared.

"We should practice our strokes," Astrid said.

He didn't think she meant the kind of strokes that he'd been imagining with more and more frequency. Images of him buried deep inside of her. Her sleek legs wrapped around him. And the even darker demands of the beast. Him covering her from behind. Seizing her neck with his teeth as he claimed her.

"I'm ready," he said, a little more huskily than he'd intended.

He had his share of female company in Victoria—mostly married women with neglectful or unfaithful husbands, no one with whom he could ever have or want a future—and he thought he had a normal man's sexual appetite. But ever since meeting Astrid, he battled constantly the demands of his beast.

It wasn't just the animal desire to mate that drew him to her. They shared a bond beyond their immediate goals, the parallels of their lives, something that pushed into the realm of the unspoken. Her intriguing combination of toughness and vulnerability. Her acceptance of him, as a shifter, as a man. And those long legs, her rosy, full mouth, the storm gray of her eyes. Either way, he was balanced on a knife's edge of need, getting sharper by the day, the hour and minute.

Making love in a canoe wouldn't work. He could never

move cautiously enough to keep them from tipping over. Get to the shore, then—

"Follow my lead," she said briskly, breaking into the haze of his erotic thoughts.

As the river wound gently past tree-fringed, rocky banks, they practiced their strokes. It had been awhile since Nathan had been in a canoe, but as he and Astrid worked out their pivots, draws, and braces, they fell into an easy, instinctual rhythm. Without speaking, they understood just how to maneuver the boat, how to lean and balance their weight when needed, avoiding large rocks and eddies with hardly a word exchanged, only an innate awareness of what needed to be done and how to work together.

He drew in a deep breath, taking in the clear, bright air, the evergreen needles in the afternoon sunlight. Even though the perfume of her skin aroused, having her so close, the forest and river around them as they journeyed toward the lands of his true people—everything felt right. For the first time in . . . maybe ever.

"I need to learn that language you spoke," he said, interrupting the sounds of flowing water and dipping paddles.

"Swedish? Why?"

"What you spoke with Thunder Eagle."

"Ah. A dialect of Nakota. It's Siouan."

"Can't get answers if I can't speak the same language as my ancestors."

"Mine is not a perfect understanding," she cautioned.

"Doesn't matter. Whatever you can teach me."

She turned slightly so he could see the curve of her cheek as she smiled. "Are you sure it isn't because you do not like relying on me to translate?"

Perhaps because she faced away from him, he found it easier to speak, and what he said next surprised him with its candor. "I'm not used to relying on anybody."

She was silent for a moment, and he thought he'd said too much, but then she said, "It leaves you open, exposed." Her voice was meditative. "You think if you depend on someone, then, when they leave, you are weak and likely to be hurt."

"Yes," he answered, hoarse. She cut straight to the heart of him. With knowledge she gleaned from herself.

She made a soft exhalation, part humor, part regret. "A fine pair, we are."

"Better we are who we are, than who the world expects us to be."

"So young," she murmured, "but almost wise." She was definitely laughing now. He couldn't make himself mind, to hear the sound, even more liquid and bright than the river. He only wished he could see what she looked like at that moment. "How old *are* you, Lesperance?"

"Twenty-eight," he said.

"Oh, God." She shook her head. "A child. I am going up against the Heirs with a child."

He snorted. If she was older than him, it couldn't have been by more than a year or two. "Damned ill-bred of you to ask my age."

"It's the mountains," she answered. "They took all my polish. I was a jewel, but now I'm a rock."

"Rocks are much more useful than jewels."

Her words grew quiet. "The most powerful Source is merely a rock. But it has the strength to destroy everything."

She'd gone back to that dark place within herself, and he had to draw her back out. "So, you're scared."

"What?" she demanded sharply.

"Scared to teach me Nakota. Afraid I might surpass you."

She made a noise of exasperation at his goading, but he didn't care, because the darkness around her fell away. "Do not blame me if you say the wrong thing and wind up getting scalped."

He again resisted the urge to touch his short hair, another clear marker that he was not truly part of the Native world. The teachers always insisted boys kept their hair cut short, to indicate they were civilized, and he'd continued to do so out of habit. Now he wondered whether he might let it grow but then, he had no idea what came next for him in his life. All he could focus on at the moment was finding the Earth Spirits and learning more about his ability to change into a wolf. There were those son-of-a-bitch Heirs of Albion to contend with, too.

And Astrid.

As they navigated the river, wending through narrow stone gorges, over widening and then tapering stretches, passing fields of late summer flowers, she did teach him. Despite what she claimed, her knowledge of Stoney Nakota was extensive, and she was a hell of a teacher. Patient, but also demanding, correcting his pronunciation, making him repeat words and phrases until he got them exactly right, yet she was complimentary. She didn't praise him often, but when she did, it was simple and heartfelt, and that meant a great deal more than effusive lauding.

"How do you say 'rain'?" she prompted.

"*Marazhud.*"

"And to say, 'It is raining hard'?"

"*Nihna marazhud.*"

"You learn quickly," she said. "It would take most people weeks or more to reach this point."

"I keep telling you that I'm not most people," he chided, "but you don't listen."

"I only pay attention to the things that matter."

He didn't mind her teasing—it meant his persistence with her paid off. He could not imagine the ice fortress of a woman he'd met only a few days ago at the trading post would have even spoken more than a few words, let alone teach him Nakota or make fun of him. But there was a wide gulf between teasing and trust.

That gulf was more treacherous than the river. Until now.

Astrid was teaching him the difference between *Daca canuca?*—What are you doing?—and *Dudiki naca*—Where are you going?—when the river began to move faster. The canoe heaved as white, churning froth crested the water's surface. Large boulders along the bed turned the once-placid river seething. Directly ahead, two rocky outcroppings jutted into the water just as the river narrowed.

"This concludes today's lesson," Astrid said, readying herself for the rapids.

"Or it's just about to begin," said Nathan. He felt a spike of mixed fear and excitement. None of the rivers he'd navigated on Vancouver Island were like this.

The canoe shot forward as the water picked up speed. They bounced along, dipping low and rising high with the swells.

"We need power," Astrid called over her shoulder. "Put your weight into it."

They both began digging hard into the water with their oars as they neared the narrowing. She guided them straight down the middle, shouting directions above the now thunderous river, and dodging obstacles. The outcroppings suddenly loomed above them as they plunged forward.

"Keep your shoulders in," she yelled.

Nathan hunched down but still felt one of the outcroppings scrape his shoulder. He hissed in pain as the rock bit into him.

"Are you all right?" she shouted.

"Fine," he gritted. "We're not done."

The canoe burst out from between the outcroppings into a steep dive. They careened onward in a chute, the boat angling so far down both Nathan and Astrid had to brace their feet and knees against the hull of the canoe to keep from tumbling out. A sharp curve ahead threatened to smash them into the rocks. Nathan threw himself to the side, using his weight to counterbalance the canoe, as Astrid steered them through the turn. Spray washed over them both as they banked, went backward, then turned in an eddy.

They followed the river as it terraced in broad pools, down, farther down. He saw the water break ahead of them.

"Falls!" Astrid yelled, but he saw.

"Holy hell," he muttered.

Chapter 6

Rapids

They launched over the top. For a moment they flew, roiling water below. A brief, wonderful weightlessness. Then, descent. With a splash, they landed, jolting, her hat falling back, dangling from its cord, and she was ready, guiding the canoe onward.

Suddenly, they were through. The water calmed, as placid as if the rapids had been a brief display of bad manners. He glanced back to see the way they had come. Damn—without Astrid's guidance, the canoe would be slivers of birch floating on the river's surface. But she'd gotten them through, and it had been a hell of a ride.

Nathan shook the water from his hair, laughing, torn between relief and wanting to do it all over again. Astrid's shoulders shuddered. Only when she turned to him, he saw it was from silent laughter. She'd enjoyed those rapids, the thrill of them, every bit as much as, if not more so than, he had.

His laughter stopped as he stared at her. The beast within growled its praise. Gems of water clung to the gold of her hair, which had partially come loose from its braid. A few damp tendrils clung to her neck and cheeks. The storm gray of her eyes changed to sparkling silver, alight with joy, and she smiled now. Not the usual small, reluctant curve of her mouth, but a true smile, and, though she was handsome before, with this rekindled fire in her, she glowed, became luminously beautiful.

Beast and man had to touch her. Nathan reached out with one hand to stroke his fingers down the curve of her cheek and over the column of her throat. The softness of her. Every part of him roared to life, the beast lunging and straining on its chain, the effort to keep it back pushing him almost to breaking. He was already roused from taking the rapids. Now, to touch her like this, feel her skin—he wanted to launch himself at her.

She gazed at him, her laughter lost as she caught her breath. Longing suffused her face. Her eyes fluttered closed as she leaned into his caress, her lips parting. He knew it. It had been a long time for her, so long since she'd permitted a man to touch her.

Not content with merely the brush of his fingers on her flesh, Nathan's hand cupped the back of her head, threading his fingers into her hair. He pulled her closer. She did not resist.

He brought their mouths together. With that small contact, Nathan erupted into flames. Some rational part of him—a *very* small part, getting smaller by the heartbeat—knew he should go slow, be gentle, coax her into the softest of kisses. But he lost all rationality as soon as their lips contacted. The animal inside broke from its restraints.

Hard to say who was more greedy. The kiss turned wild in an instant. Her mouth opened to his as their tongues met and stroked, wet and searching. She tasted of honey and milk.

This was not a girl's shy kiss. Astrid kissed like a woman, full and unashamed. She knew her hunger and claimed it. The same way he claimed her lips. He growled into her damp mouth and was rewarded a hundred times over when she growled in response. His beast recognized the rightness of this.

The paddle slid from his other hand to the floor of the canoe as he released it to stroke over her shoulder, down her arm, then move to her waist. But she was wearing that damned heavy coat, so he shoved back the fabric impatiently, delving beneath to feel her curves. Her shirt was warm, having taken on the heat of her body, and beneath that, he felt the whisper of a camisole. God, to touch her there, with nothing between them. Demanding more, he tugged at her clothes, pulling her shirt up, and her breath hitched when he caressed his palm over the bare skin of her waist and higher.

He thought she might feel good, because women did feel good, so different, so yielding. Yet the feel of Astrid devastated him. The finest silk, liquid and hot, and, though supple, lean and tight with muscle. Life in the wilderness shaped her, strengthened her. Most men loved the softness of women, their need for protection. He saw now that a woman of strength, *this* woman, overwhelmed him and his beast with wanting, knowing she could meet his strength with her own. He stroked upward and met the delicious swell of the underside of her breast.

They both jolted, and he nearly toppled on top of her.

With a snarl, he lifted his head to see that the canoe had bumped against the shore, lodging itself between trees that had fallen into the water. She saw this, too, her eyes drifting open. A flush spread over her cheeks, across the bridge of her nose, as she gazed at him.

They had to get to dry land, now. He needed more. More of her.

He began to stand, tugging on her hands to follow. She made a strangled sound, looking downward, and he followed her glance. His cock, hard and demanding, pressed against the front of his trousers, its need and intent obvious. Not a surprise. Though he couldn't remember wanting a woman more than he did at that moment. He started to pull her to her feet.

"Not here," she gasped.

"Fine," he rumbled. "In the canoe. On a mountaintop."

She pulled away, tucking her shirt in. She looked rumpled and fogged, far removed from a flint-eyed recluse. "We have to . . . keep moving." She shook her head as though to clear it. "The river. We need to get farther. Before dark. We—"

"Astrid." His voice barely sounded like him, octaves deeper, more animal than human.

"No!" She was fierce, turning away. "Not now. Not yet."

"Soon."

She shoved at the riverbank with her paddle. To keep from tumbling into the water, Nathan lowered back down to sitting, though he grimaced in pain from his aching cock. He breathed in hard, forcing himself and the beast back under control but having a hell of a time. The beast demanded more. He never took an unwilling woman—even if the woman's body was so damned willing she could start a firestorm with her heat.

"I don't know," she said, and it ripped at him, to hear the gravel of emotion in her words. "Damn it, I don't know a bloody thing. I just want to be left alone."

He clenched his jaw so tightly it throbbed, felt the animal in him growl, demanding to be set free. But he was more than animal. He had to prove that to her, and to himself.

In silence, they pushed back into the river. As they did this, they took up their paddles to ride the currents, and Nathan vowed that he'd untie the tangles knotted around her, or shred them apart, before he, too, was torn to pieces by the beast of his own desire.

They ran out of river. It didn't disappear, but it pushed between narrow, steep cliffs, impenetrable by canoe. Nothing left to do but portage.

Which suited Nathan fine. He'd tried to wear himself and the beast out paddling, throwing as much energy as he could into tackling the river, and his arms burned with the punishment he meted out. But it still wasn't enough. He felt ready to kick mountains into rubble, tear fir trees into splinters—anything to exhaust the fury of frustration and ravenous beast inside of him.

Carrying a canoe over several miles might serve. Astrid was a physically capable woman, but she didn't have his strength, so she took the burden of a few of their packs and the paddles. The rest of the gear was draped over him. He picked up the canoe, rolled it overhead, and then balanced it carefully, supporting its weight with a leather tump strap across his forehead. Astrid had tied a rope to the bow of the boat, and, with him holding the rope, he used it to steer as he walked.

It took a few minutes for him to adjust to moving with the burden of the canoe. Once or twice, he came close to flipping over like a turtle. He grit his teeth to master the movement. He was as ill-tempered as a bear, and watching Astrid striding ahead of him on her slim, long legs while he fought for footing didn't improve his mood. Soon, though, he found a pace and stride that worked best.

"Let me spell you," Astrid said after an hour.

"I've got it," he growled back. Like hell would he let her carry the load. Besides, it felt too good to push himself until his legs and arms ached. He wanted the beast beaten down with exhaustion, but the damned thing seemed tireless.

She shrugged and moved ahead.

They tramped through a mile of boggy muskeg, making his mood even more foul. Thank the devil it was late enough in the season that the mosquitoes were in short supply. Fortunately, they cleared the muskeg and moved into denser forest—though that made his job a little less easy. Then, just as the sun began to dip behind the western mountains, clouds descended. Afternoon turned to dusk.

"Smells like rain," he said.

With a crack of thunder, the sky opened. They were

drenched in seconds. Nathan decided it was as good a time as any to recite the foulest curses and swears he knew.

Astrid watched him, unimpressed. Her eyes didn't even widen.

"Finished?" she asked.

He repeated some of his favorites. "Now I'm finished."

"Good. Because we've work to do. Put the canoe upside down, and help me build a shelter."

They gathered branches and pine boughs, Astrid hewing smaller branches with her knife, and he kicking into proper size more stout tree limbs, until she pressed a small hatchet into his hands.

"This might serve you better."

"Not as satisfying." But he took the hatchet just the same, and soon they had a goodly pile of wood.

They worked quickly, taking the sturdiest branches and leaning them against each other to form the shelter's frame. The limbs that still held foliage were woven between the poles, and she stuffed the driest moss she could find into any small openings, providing insulation. Soon, they had fashioned a space that, while small, held them both as well as their gear.

The only light came from the opening, leaving them to sit in hazy shadow. For a while, they both watched the rain fall in sheets. The noise outside only made the space within feel all the more secluded and close. The air hung heavy, scented with rain, pine, damp wool, but mostly he was aware of her skin. Short of going outside to be soaked by the storm, there was nothing for him to do but sit close to her, and burn, throwing his will on top of the beast to keep it down.

This was going to be a long night.

"No fire," she said. She pulled off her gloves and rubbed her hands together, then breathed onto them for warmth.

Without speaking, he took hold of her hands and rubbed them with his own. As he did this, he felt the thin metal band of her wedding ring against his hand. He hadn't realized how small and slender her hands were until they were cupped between his palms. They were still chilled, so he bent forward and exhaled over them with deep gusts of warm air. He wanted to lick her wrists, but ran his thumbs over where her pulse beat instead.

She went very still.

"My husband was also a Blade of the Rose," she said, soft.

He glanced up, still bent over her hands, his own unmoving. Her gaze had turned far away, toward memory, a place inside of her he could never go, not without permission. And he couldn't, wouldn't, force his way in.

Nathan held himself motionless, as if any sudden movement might break the spell.

"We became Blades together," she continued, "within months of being married. And I loved our work, but not as much as I loved him. So kind, so careful." Her mouth curved in a bittersweet smile. "So different from me. We were always together. I couldn't imagine life without him."

He watched her and wondered whether he was a bastard for being jealous of a dead man.

Astrid whispered, "Five years we were married. Almost as long now as he's been dead." Her gaze sought and found his. "That's strange, isn't it?"

"Not so strange. Not if you loved him." He kept his voice low, like one might when coaxing a mountain cat to eat from one's hand.

"Perhaps not." She still had not removed her hands from his, which he took as some sort of progress.

"How did he die?"

She swallowed and was silent for so long, he thought either she had not heard him, or else she had and refused to answer. But then she said, "We were in Africa, in Abyssinia. Studying the Primal Source—the most powerful, most ancient Source, the Source from which all others originate. We were there just to learn from it, find out what we could, and allow the Primal Source to remain hidden and safe in its home."

"But it wasn't safe," Nathan deduced.

"The Heirs of Albion found it, found us. There was a battle." She sounded remote, the events she recounted separated by years and immeasurable grief, as she looked down at the band of gold on her finger. "Michael and I against two Heirs, Albert Staunton and Neville Gibbs. But the Heirs had a dozen mercenaries and dark magic. We had . . . only us." Her lips pressed tight. "Staunton killed him in the battle. Shot Michael straight through the heart, which was a kind of mercy. He died quickly."

Nathan asked, hoarse, "And where were you?"

"Beside him. I held him as his blood seeped out, onto the ground, onto my clothing. I tried to stop the flow, but it went everywhere. He was dead long before the bleeding stopped."

Nathan swore quietly. Her husband had died in her arms, saturating her with his blood.

"I had to leave him to escape," she continued. "Leave his body. I came back later, when it was safe, to bury what remained."

He tightened his grip on her hands, yet kept silent.

She met his gaze and was there, drawing toward the shore. "I've never spoken of this to anyone. Not even my parents, or the other Blades."

The impact of this truth wasn't lost on him. The strangest gift, to be given that much trust. Or perhaps, because he was a stranger, there was safety in her confession. Didn't matter.

"Thank you," he said, and meant it.

"You needed to know," she replied. "Because there's nothing left in me. This woman you see sitting here," she nodded down at herself, "she is an empty husk, and that's all she will ever be."

Astrid moved to withdraw her hands, and he let her go. Even the beast knew enough to give her freedom. Eventually, they murmured idle conversation about the rain, and the continuing course of the river. They shared a meal of pemmican, roots, and berries, then curled into themselves to sleep, listening to the rain.

He heard her breathing deepen. He reached across and put his hand lightly on top of hers, and she sighed in sleep, turning her own hand over so that their fingers interlaced.

She thought herself an empty husk. Nathan knew otherwise.

Sergeant Williamson sat at his makeshift desk—a table with a desiccated biscuit shoved under one leg for stability—writing up his latest report to headquarters. He had planned to be back at the Bow River Fort by this time, but recent events demanded his attention.

> *An extensive search for Mr. Lesperance was undertaken when he failed to appear for breakfast on the morning of 3 September. Speculation cast suspicion upon a scientific expedition who arrived the same day, but leads pursued in this direction proved fruitless as the expedition in question has similarly disappeared with no signs as to their whereabouts. I have not had the resources to send either Corporals Mackenzie or Hastings to inquire with Mrs. Bramfield, a local widow last seen in conversation with Mr. Lesperance, though—*

"Excuse me, Sergeant," Mackenzie said, standing in the doorway. "I think you may want to come out here."

Williamson set down his pen, aligning it carefully with the ink pot. It would not stand to have any kind of disorder out here in the Northwest Territories. "What is it, Corporal?"

"Two men have just arrived, Sergeant."

"Men arrive here all the time," Williamson pointed out. The trading post saw a usual amount of activity for a tiny bastion on the edge of the civilized world—trappers, traders, men from the Hudson's Bay Company come to buy furs, prospectors, whiskey runners, government surveyors, Mounties, Natives, fortune hunters, criminals, and men of every nationality and stripe, both respectable and suspect. Women were less frequently seen, usually as the wives of homesteaders or representatives of the HBC. Astrid Bramfield had been entirely unique. "You or Hastings can speak with them and ask them their business."

"I think it would be best if *you* did so, Sergeant."

Frowning at Mackenzie's insistence, the sergeant rose and, after tugging on his scarlet jacket and donning his hat, strode outside to see what sort of visitor to the wilds of Canada demanded his particular attention. "What's this all about, Mackenzie?" he demanded. "I'm still writing this report, and it's deuced difficult to explain the utter disappearance of someone as noteworthy as Lesperance."

"There, Sergeant." Mackenzie pointed to the two men who were currently the object of attention. Everyone at the post, including the most jaded *voyageurs,* stared. And no wonder.

One of the men was an exceptionally tall fellow, with a lean, lanky build and sandy hair and moustache. He was handing over to an Indian boy two saddled horses, as well as two packhorses loaded down with as much equipment as three scientific expeditions. When the lanky man spoke, it was with the flat vowels of Boston.

Americans, even tall Americans, were not so unusual out here in the Territory. It was the American's companion, however, who drew most of the interest.

Williamson doubted he'd ever seen a finer-dressed man, and that included his visits to Toronto and Montreal, where, it was alleged, tailoring came straight from the finest fashion houses in Paris. From the shoulders of his pristine hunter green jacket to his slim gray trousers and all the way to his gleaming black tall boots, the man dazzled. And that was not taking into account his blue-and-silver embroidered silk waistcoat, so beautifully cut that even a man who cared little for fashion, as Williamson did, could but weep in envy. Everything was fitted to perfection on the man's lean but well-built frame. He didn't look like a dandy. He looked exactly as he should, even out here in the middle of the wilderness.

The fact that this model of sartorial excellence was Negro almost, but not quite, obscured his elegance. Before and after the war between the states, Negro men came up to Canada to seek their fortunes away from the blight of slavery. These men had little except what they wore on their backs, and that was threadbare. There was absolutely nothing threadbare about this gentleman. He had a neatly trimmed goatee, close-cropped hair. He gazed through gleaming wire-frame spectacles around the trading post with a pair of intelligent, inquisitive eyes that missed absolutely nothing.

Williamson did not miss the revolver holstered at the man's waist, nor the stag-handled knife also on his belt. Both looked well used.

As Williamson approached both men, he heard them speak to each other.

"You sure this is where she's supposed to be, Graves?" the tall man asked his comrade. "Seems more populated than she'd want."

"She didn't live here," came the answer, in an English accent so refined, Williamson would have thought him a member of the royal family, if such a thing were possible. "From what I understand, Quinn, she lived a substantial way out."

"Good afternoon, gentlemen," Williamson said, nearing. He introduced himself and the men politely nodded their greeting. "Can I help you with something?" It was the duty of the Mounties to keep a vigilant eye on all comings and goings in their jurisdiction. Williamson fervently believed in his responsibilities.

The elegantly dressed man, identified by his companion as

Graves, nodded. "We will need to hire a guide, someone who can be relied upon for his knowledge and discretion."

This piqued the sergeant's interest. "Is there something you need to be discreet about?"

"We are investigating certain natural phenomena," Graves answered, "that is highly sensitive."

"Sensitive in what way?" Williamson eyed the shotgun slung over Graves's shoulder. The man might be a scientist, but he knew his firearms as well as his fashions. It was a hunting gun, sawed down for quick use. The metal was blued dark, making the ornate gold carvings stand out.

Quinn, the tall man, said, "Other men of sciences are in pursuit of the same phenomena. You could say we're rivals."

"If that's so, then your rivals have already been here," Williamson said. "A group of four Englishmen came to the post several days ago and hired several guides. They, too, said they were on a scientific expedition."

Graves tensed. "Did they have a bird with them?" he demanded.

An odd thing to ask. "Come to think of it, they did. A variety of falcon. Something got the bird riled up—it made a substantial racket."

Both men exchanged alarmed glances. The American cursed.

"You fellows must take this scientific discovery business quite seriously," Williamson said, noting the men's expressions of mixed apprehension and anger.

"Sergeant," Graves said, grim, "that is an exceptional understatement."

Williamson looked back and forth between the two men, a feeling of unease prickling along his neck.

"You may be familiar with our colleague," Graves continued. "A woman, about this tall," he held his hand up to the height of his shoulder, "with blond hair, gray eyes. She generally keeps to herself."

"Mrs. Bramfield," Williamson said. "I didn't know she was also involved in the field of natural phenomena."

"She used to be," Quinn answered.

Williamson shrugged. "I have only met her on a few occasions. The last time was a few days ago."

Now Graves looked truly alarmed. "Around the same time that the other expedition was here?"

"Yes—she left only hours before they arrived. They found guides and headed in her direction. West. Perhaps they wanted her to join their team."

Graves stepped closer, and suddenly Williamson realized that the elegant man could be quite intimidating. "A guide," he said, low and demanding. "We need one *now.*"

The sergeant pointed him toward the saloon. "You'll find one there."

"Thank you, Sergeant." With those clipped words, Graves strode toward the saloon, Quinn fast on his heels. Williamson stood and watched them go, wondering how he might explain this in a letter to his superiors.

Catullus Graves spared little thought to the mud spattering his boots, or the stares directed at him—he was used to both. He had also already dismissed the inquisitive Mountie Williamson from his thoughts. The only thing on his mind was getting to Astrid in time.

"How much lead do they have on us?" Max Quinn asked him. Catullus had only just met Quinn a month ago when he docked at Boston, but Quinn's service as a Blade was well regarded back at Southampton headquarters.

"Too much," Catullus answered. "We'll have to push ourselves to catch up."

Quinn nodded. Good man—he knew how important this mission was, not only to the Blades, but to Catullus personally.

They entered what the sergeant had optimistically called a saloon, and went up to the chipped, barely standing bar. A handful of men gathered at tables openly stared at Catullus and Quinn. The man behind the counter eyed the Blades warily, particularly Catullus, until a neat stack of Canadian coins appeared on the scarred wooden bar. Then the bartender was much more affable.

"Two whiskeys," Catullus said. "And the whereabouts of a good guide."

Before the barkeep could answer, a shadow fell across the bar. Catullus turned to see the unmistakable form of a woman standing in the open doorway. He knew at once she was not Astrid. For one thing, Astrid did not have fiery copper hair that formed a blazing corona when lit by sunlight. And also, to put it delicately, Astrid's curves were far more subdued than this woman's lush figure. As she stepped into the saloon, Catullus felt himself immediately regress into stammering, libidinous boyhood. She was shaped like a temple goddess, the kind of woman who filled young men's thoughts with aching, impossible lust—full breasts, a waist hardly more than a hand span across, and sumptuous hips.

He dragged his gaze up to her face to see her watching him with ironic amusement in her clear blue eyes. She seemed to know the effect her body had on men, and was not entirely pleased about it. It was then that he realized what he saw in her appealing face piqued his interest as much as, if not more than, her figure. Perception, a shrewd intelligence, determination. And freckles.

Catullus had a weakness for freckles. Even more so than his weakness for waistcoats.

When she moved farther into the saloon, Catullus saw she was dressed in a serviceable riding skirt and plain jacket and blouse, all perfectly ordinary for this wild place, and though the garments were somewhat boxy, they could not disguise the splendor of her shape. Belatedly, Catullus noticed she also carried a notebook and pencil.

Every one of the seated men leapt to their feet, stumbling over themselves like eager bear cubs. Their voices clamored against each other. "Please, Miss Murphy, take my seat."

"Would you do me the honor, Miss Murphy—?" "What can I get you to drink, Miss Murphy?" Such chivalry in a saloon that would make a Whitechapel gin house look opulent by comparison.

"I'll take a whiskey, thank you," she said in a husky, American-accented contralto, as she lowered herself into a now-available seat.

Four men launched themselves at the bar. Catullus and Quinn were forced to jump backward, lest they be crushed to death by a stampede of trappers. The woman, Miss Murphy, barely noticed. She was busy writing in her notebook and absently nodded her thanks when the requested whiskey appeared in front of her.

The commotion slowly died down, and the trappers, seeing that Miss Murphy was not there for conversation, went back to their own dialogues. Periodically, she would glance up, gaze about her with that same cutting perception, and then return to her writing, with an occasional sip of whiskey.

Once the bar was no longer a potential scene of asphyxiation, Catullus and Quinn took up their places.

"We still need our drinks," Catullus reminded the bartender, "and information about a guide. A *trustworthy* guide."

Two whiskeys were poured into glasses much more chipped and grimy than the one Miss Murphy had received. Then the bartender muttered something to one of the men at the bar, and this man promptly left the saloon.

"Slately will bring your man," the bartender said. He went back to his preoccupation with wiping down a streaked mirror mounted on the wall behind him.

Catullus took a drink and felt his throat catch on fire. Someone must have distilled the whiskey through a sock. How the hell had that Murphy woman taken such dainty sips? She had to have a constitution stronger than an ironclad battleship.

"I think you have an admirer," Quinn murmured, low.

When Catullus frowned in perplexity, Quinn darted a look toward Miss Murphy. Catullus, using the mirror, surreptitiously studied the woman. Sure enough, she would pause in her work, stare at him for a little while, then return to her notepad, writing more furiously than before. For a moment, it looked as though she were sketching him as well. He didn't know whether to be suspicious or flattered. The part of him that was entirely male preened under her scrutiny, but the part of him that was a Blade wondered what kind of agenda this woman had out here in the midst of the Northwest Territory.

The Heirs of Albion did not have women in their ranks, but recent activities in Greece proved that, when the situation was crucial, even this steadfast rule could change. Fortunately, in Greece, the woman who had been unknowingly employed by the Heirs had turned out to be an ally. More than an ally, actually, since she had gone on to marry reprobate Bennett Day, who was now thoroughly devoted to his wife. But one could never be certain of such a felicitous outcome. As much as Miss Murphy intrigued him, he would have to remain on his guard.

Slately returned with a man of mixed Indian and white blood following.

"I hear you're looking for a guide," the Métis said. "I'm Jourdain."

"You know this area well?" Catullus asked.

"As well as you know waistcoats," answered Jourdain, glancing down at Catullus's chest.

Quinn chuckled. "I think we've found our man."

"How soon can you leave?" Catullus pressed.

"Today, if you want. Within the hour, if time's important."

"It is." Catullus handed both Slately and the barkeep more coins, then headed for the door, Jourdain and Quinn at his heels. He had to reach Astrid before the Heirs did. Everything else fell away from his thoughts, including the enigmatic Miss Murphy.

* * *

Astrid stood on the bank, studying the river. Unlike the incessantly shifting sea, a river's currents did not change from moment to moment. It had its terrain, just like a landscape, and so if one wanted to plot a course of navigation, to plan strategies and tactics, it could be done. There was a kind of stability in a river.

Behind her, she heard Lesperance unburdening himself of the canoe. They had portaged for several hours this morning, until finding a traversable leg of the river. Paddling was much easier than portage, so it was back into the water for them. The Heirs were behind them—she knew without doubt, but just *how* far back those bastards were, she didn't know. And that infuriated her. She hated being powerless against them, but she was and would always be at a disadvantage where Heirs were concerned.

The river might mask her and Lesperance's trail. That was a small solace.

She did not watch Lesperance setting down the canoe, though she knew if she did, what she would see: supple muscularity in the art of motion, pale sunlight glinting in his night-dark hair. His serious, handsomely severe face too alive to be a sculpture yet too striking to be ordinary flesh.

She would not think of his flesh. She would not consider him in that way.

Oh, she was a fine one, telling herself something that was impossible. Ever since she first met him at the trading post, she'd been aware of Lesperance as a man. And each moment she spent with him made her all the more aware. The tie between them strengthened the more she knew of him. He was strong, but not rough. He'd warmed her hands and truly listened to her, revealing a tenderness that was all the more incredible because of his potency. Yesterday's shattering kiss had proven to her that the desire she felt for him was mutual, and that didn't make her life one bit easier. Everything became a thousand times more complex.

"Let's take the canoe to the water," she said over her shoulder, "and then we can load our gear into it."

He made a wordless sound of agreement. Their silence had changed over the past days. It held much more than before, thick with unspoken words and waiting. In the silence, he crouched, a beast hunting.

Soon, they were both carefully packing their kits into the slender boat, readying it and themselves for what was sure to be a treacherous crossing.

But not as treacherous as the feelings she battled. She remembered vividly a morning, a year after Michael's death, when she had awakened from heated dreams to discover herself slick and needy. She refused to give in. Her body's demand for release infuriated and shamed her. It, clearly, had moved out of mourning, but her mind and heart had not. She resented her body's hunger for pleasure, its will to cling to life.

Eventually, she had to acquiesce or else face madness. But she took little gratification from her self-induced release. It was simply a necessity, like eating or bathing, that had to be taken care of. She missed the nights and sometimes days of lovemaking she and Michael had shared, but all she wanted now was to sate herself and proceed with the business of existence.

Being so close to Lesperance, his touch, his scent, his devastating kisses, his force of will and unexpected compassion, reawakened her, making her confront the truth that Michael was long dead, and she . . . she was not. She lived. She *felt,* and it scared the hell out of her.

Once the canoe was loaded, Lesperance pulled off his coat, then his shirt. Her eyes were filled with sleek copper muscle, the ridges and planes of his torso, his taut, banded arms.

"What are you doing?" Her voice sounded shrill in her ears.

"Don't need them." He stuffed the garments into his pack.

Her breath misted in front of her mouth in the frigid morning air. "It's cold!"

"Not for me. Not since I started changing into the wolf." He gazed at her with desire and challenge. "Now I'm always hot."

Her mouth dry, Astrid tore her gaze away. She and Lesperance took up their places in the narrow boat. At least he was sitting behind her, so she wouldn't have to stare at the bunch and play of muscles in his back, shoulders, and arms. But still, knowing he was shirtless did not help her already strained strength.

They pushed away from the bank and settled quickly into the rhythm of paddling. It was a good partnership, she realized. He read the river well and took her guidance without a moment's hesitation. Their strengths and pace were evenly balanced.

As the river curved through forest and meadow, she felt herself staked upon pleasure and pain. The silence was broken as Lesperance asked her questions periodically about the surrounding wilderness. She liked the direction his mind took, his need to absorb more and more, his open-mindedness. Yet beneath his questions and her answers stretched an undercurrent of tense awareness, waiting. This was a pause in his pursuit, but it was far from over.

Whenever she glanced back at him, she saw how moved he was by the land. She discovered, through his eyes, her own renewed delight in these mountains. The freedom and purpose of a river. And, after so long without, the bittersweet demands of attraction and connection.

Yet she didn't want to feel any of these things, did not want any of it. And she never forgot that the Heirs were hard behind them. Her fear of them had never dulled. Nor had her hatred. Both were sharp and exacting.

And she could not lose that ever-present sense that something was deeply wrong in the fabric of the world's magic, as though a tear had appeared, far away, but was slowly, inevitably rending everything apart.

The river gave her enough to think about, for now. She put aside thoughts of Michael and Heirs and magic and fear and desire—especially when the river picked up speed.

"You've a good memory, is that right?" she asked Lesperance.

"For most things," he answered. "I can recite a page of text after reading it once." The canoe rode a swell of water and slapped back down.

She fought against the strengthening current. "No text here, except what's written on the river. I hope you remember how to tackle rapids."

The river steepened, rocketing the canoe forward as if released from a slingshot. Trees and rocks passed in a smear of green and gray. They couldn't speak, except to shout directions to each other over the growing roar of the water.

Eddies boiled around them. Lesperance battled to keep the canoe from slamming into boulders that menaced up from the river's bed. They careened like a twig, caroming from bank to bank, rising up, then plummeting down with greater and greater speed.

Astrid's alarm swelled with the river. Yesterday's rapids seemed a gentle trickling stream compared to this. Her grip on her paddle grew damp as the rapids stretched on, no signs of abating.

Life was measured out in paddle strokes. Everything around her became white water and bleak stone. The violence of these rapids astonished her—she'd never experienced their equal—as the canoe hurtled on, borne upon the back of a vengeful serpent.

The water ahead formed a razor line, foaming at its edge. Above the snarling rapids, she heard an even larger boom, the sounds of water hitting water. Falls. *Enormous* falls. From the sound of it, over twenty feet high. Straight in front. She couldn't even see where the river took up again below.

"We're going over," she yelled just before they reached the lip. "Paddle faster—we need more speed!"

It seemed a ridiculous thing to ask for, speed, but it was what they needed to survive. They had to stay upright, had to move forward quickly, or else they wouldn't make it. Lesperance, thank God, did not question her. They threw themselves into matched, powerful strokes.

"As soon as we clear the edge," she shouted, "shove with your hips. We have to clear the canoe's stern before the bow drops." He made a growl of agreement.

They launched over the lip of the falls.

A free fall. It went on forever, as though the world shifted on its axis. She felt cold air whip around her, pushing upward, and struggled to keep her eyes open.

"Lean back!" she yelled. "If we're too tilted, we'll flip over when we land!"

His knees were against her spine as she leaned back as far as she could, and they both groaned, fighting gravity. She could only pray that there was enough space for them at the bottom of the falls. They could be smashed against boulders and be torn to shreds.

The canoe hit the base of the falls. Her jaw slammed together. It felt as though they'd hurled themselves against twenty brick walls. But they landed flat, without flipping, and that was a consolation.

There wasn't time to revel in their landing, or even to breathe. Enormous rocks thrust up from the bed, having tumbled down into the river from some great height millennia ago, leaving her and Lesperance the narrowest path to navigate at topmost speed.

They threaded through, their paddles scouring against the close-lying rocks. The canoe's hull shrieked. Hell, if they took on any water from a cracked or splintered hull, they'd either sink or be pulled even faster in the current.

She allowed herself a moment of relief when they cleared

the boulders. Her respite had barely begun when he warned, "Another eddy."

Not so much an eddy as it was a cataract. It caught them, the swirling whirlpool, spinning them in hard, tight circles. She and Lesperance thrust their paddles into the churning water, struggling to right themselves.

Lesperance snarled as he fought to keep them under control. Yet there was nothing he could do when the stern swung around and crashed against a large rocky outcropping. Astrid jolted with the collision, but he took the brunt of it. The impact roughly tilted the stern and she hadn't even time or means to lunge for him before he was thrown from the canoe.

He disappeared into the seething water.

Chapter 7

Crossing the Boundary

Astrid's arms ached with exhaustion, but she did not notice or care as she dug her paddle into the water with all the force she could marshal. She had to get to Lesperance, had to reach him. *Oh, God, where was he?* She couldn't see him anywhere in the swirling, foaming water. He'd drown, or be pummeled against a boulder, break an arm, a leg, it was all fatal, and—

A dark head bobbed up a dozen yards ahead of her. Was he . . . ? No, his arms moved as he wrestled with the river. She let herself be joyful for only a moment before plowing forward. He shot onward, faster than the canoe.

Lesperance tried to swim against the current, fighting it as he sought the shore. The river had too much force, buffeting him.

"Don't try and swim," she shouted over the clamor. "Angle yourself feet first!" He'd only exhaust himself by swimming, and there was a much higher chance that, going headlong, he'd be thrown against a rock and crack his skull, if not snap his spine.

He must have heard her, because he did as she directed, leaning back so that his feet led the way. And he maneuvered himself with his arms, steering his course. Thank heavens he was strong, or else the river would have claimed his life in moments.

Her attention was torn away from him when the canoe, battered by the angry river, knocked against a cluster of smaller rocks and tilted. Icy water poured into the boat, soaking her boots and coming halfway up the sides of their packs. Now weighted with water, the canoe sped forward, more rapidly than before. With only her paddling in a canoe meant for two people.

Astrid watched as Lesperance hurtled toward a boulder near the riverbank, then disappeared behind it. She looked farther down the river and could not see him. He never surfaced or appeared.

"Lesperance!" Her throat burned with the force of her shout. "Lesperance!"

No answer.

No. No.

The water in the canoe was getting worse. The boat sunk even lower. She didn't have a choice. It was time to abandon ship. She didn't want to—her chances of reaching Lesperance were better in the canoe—but if she didn't give up the boat, she'd be taken by the river, too.

She piloted the canoe toward the same boulder around which Lesperance had disappeared. As soon as the bow of the boat slammed into the rock, Astrid leapt out. The canoe shot around the boulder, stern first. She clung to the boulder for only a second before scrambling up its side. Everything she needed to survive in the wilderness was in their gear, still in the canoe, though she had her rifle on her back and her gun on her hip. But if she could save the boat, she could use it to search for Lesperance. She would not let herself believe he was dead. Her mind simply shut out the possibility.

Astrid clambered up the boulder to reach its top. She saw farther down the river. Not a sign of Lesperance. Crouching there, she cupped her hands around her mouth.

"Nathan!"

"Here."

She let out a gasp of relief. Looking down, she saw him gripping the other side of the boulder, thoroughly soaked but mercifully alive. His eyes met hers for a moment. Something loosened around her chest, the smallest easing of constriction.

He broke the contact when the canoe came racing around the boulder. With one hand grasping the rock, he swung himself out to seize hold of the boat just before it darted past him.

"Don't bother with the boat," she yelled. She worried that he wouldn't be able to hang on to the safety of the boulder with just one hand while the canoe tried to drag him with it farther down the river.

"Get our packs." He gritted his teeth against the force of the water.

She didn't waste time arguing. Clinging to the rock, she eased her way down, closer to him. He groaned with exertion as he pulled the canoe nearer, swinging it around so she could reach their gear.

The packs were heavy, yet she found surges of power in herself to haul each one up and throw them to the nearby riverbank. As soon as the last of their gear was out, he released the canoe.

They both watched as the boat plunged down the river, then careened into a massive pile of rocks covering the entire width of the river. Above the din came the sounds of wood splintering as the canoe, within seconds, broke apart. Nothing was left but small chunks of birch. Even the paddles were torn to slivers.

She and Lesperance stared at each other as the implications hit them. They would not have survived, either of them.

Astrid leaned down to help pull him to safety.

"Get to shore, damn it," he growled at her. "I might pull you in."

"Give me your hand!"

"No."

Swearing in English, Swedish, and every other language

she knew, Astrid dashed to the riverbank. The moment her feet touched dry land, she searched for, and found, a stout, long tree branch. She grabbed it, set down her rifle, then ran toward the bank. Digging her heels into the ground, she held the branch out. It just reached him.

"Take it, you stubborn son of a bitch," she snarled.

At least he wasn't too stubborn to listen. He snared the branch, letting go of the rock. Immediately, she was forced to lie almost flat on her back to combat the force of the river tugging on him. She pulled and pulled, grunting with effort, as he hauled himself toward the shore.

And then he was safe, reaching the safety of the riverbank. He crawled up on hands and knees, panting, dripping, torso and arms covered with scratches and cuts, smeared with mud, and the most welcome sight Astrid had seen in a long time. She still lay on her back, and he collapsed onto his stomach next to her. For some time, neither of them spoke as they both fought for breath and understanding that they had survived, but only barely.

Finally, he said, "Nathan."

She turned her head to stare at him. "What?"

"You called me Nathan, not Lesperance."

Astrid covered her eyes with one shaking hand. "After we just faced rapids so fierce they would make a deity cry, *that's* what concerns you?"

"My needs are simple."

She hadn't a moment to respond when she felt his lips on hers, chilled, but alive. Her response was instantaneous as she kissed him back, wrapping her exhausted arms around his solid shoulders. She didn't have the strength to fight herself anymore, and threw herself into her desire as one might leap into a volcano for sacrifice.

It was worth almost drowning if it meant kissing Astrid. And having her kiss him in return with a blazing need that had the power to reduce them to ashes. He was bone weary, stretched thin with the fight to stay alive, to keep her safe. Yet everything receded to nothingness as soon as their lips met.

His tongue delved into the warm wetness of her mouth and she stroked it with her own. He rolled, coming to rest on top of her, her legs twining around him as he braced himself over her. She rose to meet his hips with her own. He growled into her mouth at the contact, that welcoming place, even separated by too much fabric. When he pressed his length against her, she surged up, moaning. He'd never been harder in his life. His cock was a branding iron that wanted her flesh. As she wanted his burn.

Faintly, he realized he shouldn't be doing this, that he was getting her clothes wet with his damp skin and she would be cold. He couldn't make himself stop, not when she laced her fingers into his hair and pulled him fierce and close to her.

It wasn't gentle or sweet or tender. It was rough and urgent, primal. The beast in him snarled its demands. When he dragged his mouth from hers to bite at her neck, she arched. The effort it took to keep from actually piercing her skin with his teeth made him shake. Instead, he shoved off her coat and almost tore her shirt right down the middle, but that small rational part of his brain reminded him that she needed clothing and might not have anything to replace it. So he clawed at the buttons with hands that felt more like paws. Her own trembling hands came up to help, their fingers tangling.

Then her shirt was gone, and all she wore beneath was a camisole. Beneath the thin fabric, her breasts were perfect, high and full, her nipples tight, stretching the cotton. When he took them in his hands, they both moaned, and he stroked her, drinking in the feel of her skin with a visceral savagery.

Through lust-hazed eyes he gazed down and what he saw made him growl. The dampness of his skin soaked through her chemise, turning it transparent. Her nipples were the color of rosy dawn against the cream of her skin, hardened into beads. His beast broke free of its leash. She gasped when he tore the chemise, and gasped again when he took the tip of her breast into his mouth. She pulled him even closer as she ground her hips into his.

With each of his licks and each of her moans, arousal grew, his beast becoming wild, until he became mindless, wanting only her, needing to be inside her. He fumbled with the buttons of her trousers.

Then she shoved him away. The beast bayed in frustration and loss, the sound echoing inside him. God, no. He was too close. He wanted her too badly.

It took him a moment to understand what she was doing before fierce exultation hit him. She tugged off her boots and threw them carelessly aside, unbuckled and set aside her gun belt, then began to wriggle out of her trousers.

The sight was too much, her hips undulating, the skin of her belly and lower being exposed. As soon as he saw the faintest trace of golden down between her legs, he leapt upon her. Nathan yanked off her trousers in one motion, then cupped her sex with his hand. His fingers were drenched immediately. The scent of her, damp and musky with passion, urged his beast to frenzy.

His fingertips brushed against the bud of her clit. She stiffened with a cry. Holy hell, had she climaxed already? Even as shudders racked her body, she growled into his mouth, "More."

"More," he rumbled in response. He caressed the liquid core of her, his fingers dipping into her, while the demand and weight of his cock grew monstrous. She tumbled through another and then another orgasm, her eyes squeezed shut, the expression on her face bordering on torment if not for the pleasured sounds she made.

"Inside me," she panted. "Now."

Nathan lifted himself up enough to undo the fastening of his breeches. His cock sprang free, the relief from pressure enough to make him groan. When her fingers stroked along his shaft, over the aching head and across the weight of his balls, he drew upon wellsprings of control he barely knew had not to explode in a second. And when she guided him toward her slick opening, as impatient as he, Nathan went to the brink of madness. He thrust into her with one hard, sure stroke.

She was hot and sleek and gripped him like the beginnings of time. They moved together, possessed, and there was no way to know who was more wild because they were both fierce, racing toward pleasure, throwing themselves into it mindlessly. She clawed at him, and when he bit her again, harder, at the juncture of her neck and shoulder, she came with a cry.

He let himself go then. A few more deep, thick thrusts and his own climax tore through him. It was fire, liquid fire, and he realized only later that the feral, animal rumblings of satisfaction and release came from him, from somewhere deep inside.

There was a word for what happened to living matter when it returned to the earth, breaking down to its elemental, liquid state and soaking into the ground to feed another generation of trees and plants. Deliquescence. Nathan, draped over Astrid as they both lay panting and shaking, felt he would deliquesce, dissolve into the soil and leaves, nothing remaining. Spent. He was spent in every sense of the word and could hardly move, weighted down with exhaustion and contentment. Even his beast could barely stir. It curled up inside of him, rumbling as it slept. Now there was nothing for him to do but melt.

She shoved at him.

"I'm crushing you." He immediately rolled aside.

When she sat up and began picking at the leaves in her hair, he also sat up—though his body protested at any angle other than horizontal—and brushed at the twigs and leaves clinging to her back. She waved him off.

"I can do it," she said.

"You can't reach your back."

Instead of letting him assist her, she stood and shook out her shirt. She did not seem to care that all she wore at the moment was a shredded chemise. He took a moment to admire her, especially her legs: They were, as he had suspected, long and slim, and sculpted from years of mountain living. He'd felt their strength wrapped around him, pulling him deeper. Gorgeous legs that he wanted to lick.

Which seemed to be the furthest thing from her mind. With quick, methodical movements, she pulled off the remains of her chemise and stuffed it into one of their packs. She dressed herself just as mechanically, as one might dress before setting off to conduct important business elsewhere. There was nothing in her manner suggesting she had just survived dangerous rapids and then made fevered love on the forest floor.

Nathan, sluggish, could only watch her as she bustled about and set herself to rights. Shirt, drawers and trousers, boots, belt. And not once did she look at him.

"I got your clothes wet," he said. More complex sentences and thoughts eluded him.

She glanced at her damp shirtfront, and the wetness on the front of her trousers, concentrated especially at her hips and between her legs. Where he had lain, and moved.

"It's fine," she said through stiff lips, looking away. "It will dry."

His mind slowly began collecting itself. Something was very wrong. Maybe he had been too rough. He'd never taken a woman with such force. But then he felt the lingering heat of her nails on his back, sharp lines scraped into his skin. If he had been rough, she had been equally so.

"You should cover yourself," she said.

Nathan got to his feet, tucking himself back into his trousers. The action was all the more difficult because his trousers were still wet from his trip in the river.

She went to the packs and rifled through them.

He followed, reaching out to stroke her hair, but she ducked from his hand and sidled away.

"We should go," she said. "I don't know how far it might be to reach the Earth Spirits, and we need to cover more—"

He'd had enough. "What the hell are you doing?"

She stared at him, unblinking, removed. "I'm putting us back on track for our objective."

Anger flared at her retreat. "Astrid. We just—"

"I know what we just did," she said, her voice glacial. "I was there."

"Me, too," he growled. Her determined indifference dug at him. He wanted some kind of reaction from her, anything. Even anger. So he goaded. "Or maybe you were too busy throwing yourself onto my cock to notice."

She winced slightly, his crudeness shaming him, but it was some kind of reaction rather than icy impassivity. "Don't confuse yourself," she said. "What happened was only an expression of lust."

He crossed his arms over his chest. "More than that."

"It wasn't." She hardened her chin, almost surly. "I've not had sex in five years. It's only natural that, after being in such close contact with a man as we have been, and then surviving the rapids, I needed some release. You were convenient."

The word was like a slap. He glowered as he stalked to her. "I've spent my life being dismissed, pushed aside because I'm an Indian, but I pushed back. And I'm damned well not going to allow it now."

She looked offended. "This isn't because you are Native."

"No," he answered. "You're afraid."

"Afraid?" she shot back, disbelieving. "I've faced fire demons while trapped inside a collapsed pyramid. Crossed the icy wastes of Siberia with nothing but a knife. I'm not afraid."

"But you *are* frightened."

She stiffened. "Getting bloody presumptuous just because I let you roger me."

"It was better than a rogering."

"Now you're being arrogant." She tried to brush past him, but he gripped her arm. She glared up at him. "Lesperance—"

"No going back," he said. "It's Nathan now."

"What sodding difference does it make?" she snapped.

"It makes a hell of a difference," he fired back. "It means we're more than strangers fucking each other."

Hurt stained her cheeks. "We have just crossed the boundary of the Earth Spirits' territory. A tribe that is feared by all the Natives in these mountains, and likely with good cause. The Heirs of Albion are close behind us, ready to use the darkest magic they possess to capture you and kill me. Now is *not* a good time to have this discussion." She tried to pull away, but he held tighter.

"No running," he growled.

She turned mulish. "You can't browbeat me into submission."

He scrubbed one hand over his face, frustrated with her and himself. "Astrid. You loved your husband. I can't pretend to understand what it must be like to love someone and lose them, to have them die in my arms—"

She tried again to wrench away. He still would not release her.

"But I know I would be afraid, too," he continued. "Afraid to feel anything again. And I'd fight like the devil to keep everyone away. It was like that after I lost my family. But I didn't live the rest of my life that way. I didn't bury myself in the wilderness, hiding."

"I'm not hiding, damn you!" Her eyes shimmered. "I built a new life for myself. A life apart."

"Never answering letters? Abandoning friends, family? Living in an isolated cabin with only books for company? That's not a life apart. That's hiding."

Anguish and anger suffused her face, and he hated

causing her any pain, but feeling something, anything, was better than numb detachment. She was too bright, too alive, to waste herself as she did.

"What do you want from me?" she demanded.

"I won't let you run like a deer. Everyone else let you scamper into the bushes and stay there. It's not going to work with me. I'll hunt you out."

For some moments, she was silent, staring at him with silver smoke eyes filled with guarded trepidation and the smallest, barely perceptible beginnings of hope, before glancing away. "You are a stubborn son of a bitch."

"Always have been."

"An *arrogant,* stubborn son of a bitch," she amended.

"And you're a recluse, a mountain cat who's just as stubborn." He unclasped his fingers from around her arm. A softer woman would bruise, but she wouldn't. "We need to get back on the trail," he said, yet added when she let out a small sigh of relief, "but don't think this is over between us. I never back down from a challenge."

She tilted up her chin. "Is that what I am to you, a challenge?"

"Oh, no, love," he said softly. He stroked the skin just beneath her bottom lip with the pad of his thumb and was rewarded with a blaze of returning desire in her eyes. "You're much more than that."

Even to an experienced mountain woman such as Astrid, these lands were unknown. She took in the landscape—snow-crowned peaks, open and shaded valleys, evergreen woods—with a careful, assessing eye, but underneath that caution, a gleam of excitement. The same as when she and Nathan had conquered the river rapids.

Yet none of this resonated as deeply as what had just happened.

She'd never been so wild. She had wanted him—still

wanted—with a hunger and need that alarmed her. Not only his body within hers, but that greater, subtler connection she had not felt in so very long. And this frightened her as much, if not more so, than the Heirs. They could only hurt her body. But her desire for Nathan could tear her completely apart and leave her in ruins. She knew it the moment they touched. She'd had to protect herself after the searing intimacy of their sex—but Nathan was too strong to back down, to let her retreat. He would not accept her flight.

Infuriating, but liberating, as well. His extraordinary strength shattered her defenses, freeing her, and that freedom was a joy and a terror.

Face this moment, she told herself. The land and people within it were treacherous. She would face those threats and wonders rather than the ones within herself.

He, too, felt the excitement of discovering a new land, she saw, but there was more than that simple emotion.

"Hear that?" he asked as they wended through a sloping pine forest.

She stilled. "An animal? People?"

"A heartbeat."

Her brows went up. "Perhaps your own."

"No." He gazed around, upward, trying to isolate the noise. "Not my own. It's coming from"—he gestured, taking in the land surrounding them—"everything."

She felt her gaze softening. "Even if I had your sharp hearing, I think that sound is yours alone."

He nodded slowly, half dazed, as though suspended in a dream. Not a sleepy, languorous dream, but the kind that revealed hidden truths previously unknown to the dreamer. "This place wants something from me. I can feel it. . . ."

She stepped closer to him, compassionate, cautious. After their sex had shattered the walls between them, something had shifted, a tentative intimacy growing in their now exposed and tender core. "These lands, they are in you, just as the wolf is in you. Buried for years. Until now. A homecoming."

The word was so foreign to him he started. "Homecoming," he murmured. "Home. Never had one, not truly. Are these ancient mountains and primeval woods my home?"

"Nathan," she said softly, drawing his attention, "I think you should change into the wolf."

He looked at her with surprise but said nothing.

"Whatever it is in this territory," she explained, but gently, "it's calling to you. It *wants* you to find the other Earth Spirits."

"And the best way to do that is to take on my other form," he concluded.

"At the least, you could scent the Earth Spirits out. Your senses are better when you become the wolf, aren't they?"

"Yes, but I wouldn't recognize their scent."

"I think you will." Quiet confidence in her words, both in herself and him.

Woven into his flesh and soul were the means by which he could transform himself. The world he had known no longer existed. The man he'd been seemed to fade into something else, but what that "else" might be remained to be discovered.

"You would have to carry both packs," he cautioned.

"I'm strong."

"That I know," he said, admiration plain in his voice. He glanced around. They stood amid bracken and pine. It would not be difficult to step behind a tree, take off his clothes, and there, unseen, shift into the wolf. She could sense that it was easier for him to summon the animal now. He didn't have to wait for a threat. He could do it. Privately, as he'd done before.

Astrid saw the hesitation on his face. "I can look away or," she pointed several yards distant, "wait for you there." She understood the exposure he felt to have anyone, even someone who knew his secret, watch the transformation. She understood vulnerability, going to great lengths to hide her own.

He seemed to come to a decision.

"Stay," he said. He slipped the pack from his back. "Will you put my clothes in the pack?"

She nodded, mute, eyes wide. "I'll—" She swallowed and tried to turn away but seemed unable to move at all. "I will look away."

"Don't. We shared something before," he nodded toward the direction from which they'd come, the riverbank on which they'd made love. "We'll share this now." He pulled off his boots with hands that shook slightly with the intimacy of what he was about to do. A greater intimacy than the joining of their bodies in sex. They both knew that no one had ever seen him so unguarded, so truly exposed as he would be in a moment.

Nathan tried to calm his thundering heart. She knew he could shift into a wolf and wasn't afraid or disgusted. But that might change to see him actually transform in front of her.

He had to take that risk. Had to show her what it meant. To him and to her.

He unfastened his breeches and slid them down his legs. A momentary gratification to see the purely female appreciation in her face. He couldn't think of that now. The breeches were folded and put beside his boots, then he rose to his full height. Naked. Poised on the edge.

Hard to tell who was more apprehensive. Her breathing, like his, came in short, shallow gasps, measuring life in tiny increments.

Then, holding her silver gaze with his own, he let it happen. He reached into himself, where the animal dwelt, pacing inside of him, alert and keen. The part of himself he'd always fought against. Indians were animals. That was all they could ever be. That's what he was taught. He'd pushed it away, fighting himself, but that time was past. Now he summoned it.

The wolf stirred and began to push out. It climbed through him with the heat of its being. Hunt. Run. Chase the moon. Mate.

He stared at her, still a little afraid.

Astrid gave him the smallest nod of encouragement. In her face, he saw acceptance, trust. Not only of him as one who could change into an animal, but acceptance of the gift he was about to bestow upon her.

Warm, moonlit mists enveloped him as the wolf sprang forth. It shaped his body. Fur, paws, teeth, ears, tail. Not pain, but the hard, swift change of his bones, his muscles. As the mists dispersed, he threw himself forward. His paws hit the ground.

He and the wolf became one.

He looked around. This was the same world, and entirely different. Filled with scent and sound and life. He could smell it now, the scent of the Earth Spirits, dark and rich, beckoning.

He started toward it, then stopped and turned to Astrid. She stared at him. There was no disgust or fear in her face. Only wonderment. Humility. And ambivalence. She was not certain she wanted his trust, the intimacy, but he had given both to her.

She took a step closer. He crossed the distance. Her scent enveloped him, her woman scent, her flesh, and even the smell of himself on, and in, her. In this form, the combination of him and her together lured, made him demanding, far more possessive than he ever knew himself to be. He rumbled.

"Nathan?" She held out her hand to him.

He pushed his head into it, and growled to feel her fingers in his fur. Experimentally, he licked her hand and growled again to taste her this way.

"Can you find them?" she asked, voice slightly breathless.

He gave a small chuff of confirmation. He had no voice—and felt its loss. He wanted to tell her what it felt like, what new explorations there were behind the senses of a wolf.

"We must go," she said. "Before it grows too dark for me to see."

He softly barked an assent. Even enfolded within the beast of the wolf, it pained him to watch Astrid hoist up the other pack with obvious effort and not be able to help. Some rules of society were too deeply enmeshed to be lost. When at last she gained her balance, she said, "Lead. I will follow."

Her words set him free. He bounded forward, drawn by the scent of the Earth Spirits, feeling the ground beneath him, the joy in running and tracking. The man receded. The wolf came forth. Around him were the mountains and forests and millions of other animals and insects all living and breathing together in the oldest rhythm, of which he was but one small pulsation. It felt right, impossibly right, to run with Astrid. To have her close, sharing the true core of himself with her. Only she understood, only shc could run with him in both his form as a man as well as him as a beast.

He felt her. He took in the stories around him. A doe and her fawn had passed this way. A young wolverine, on the cusp of maturity, had hunted nearby. Squirrels chattered to each other in alarm to see a wolf out during the day. He had no way to tell them it was not prey he sought, but his own history.

He leapt over grasses and rocks, splashed lightly through a creek, drawn forward by scent. *This* was what he wanted, for all those years in Victoria, lying awake at night and curling his hands into fists to keep from throwing open his window and leaping out to run through the darkened streets and on into the wild.

"Nathan!"

He whirled around. Astrid struggled to keep up, not only

on her less swift human legs, but also carrying two heavy packs and her rifle. He trotted back to her.

"Be mindful of your speed," she gasped. She wiped one sleeve across her damp forehead.

His quiet whine was apologetic, but she smiled her cautious smile.

"Keep going," she said.

He did, but reined himself in enough that she could keep pace. The scent was stronger now, its demands insistent, so that to keep himself in an easy lope rather than breaking into a flat run was a struggle. They took a steeply pitched rocky slope, him moving straight down, her with more careful switchbacks. The slope led into more forest of spruce, ancient trees taller than he had ever seen, whose branches interwove to form thick canopies. Their dried needles under his paws released sharp scents of longing and remembrance. He could taste it as he panted.

Close. He was so close. The path was before him. He had but to follow it.

He didn't know how it happened. He was pushing onward, deeper into the forest, acutely aware of everything surrounding him. But he didn't hear, see, or smell the animal ahead until it blocked his path.

A massive bear, standing on all four legs, easily four feet at the shoulder. A female. He'd never seen a larger animal. Nor one so powerful. The size of her jaws alone ensured crushed bones. Her shaggy russet fur was tipped golden along her shoulders and back, but her straight, sharp claws held his attention. One swipe could gut a human.

Even though he could hear Astrid behind him, he had to glance back to ensure she was safe. Her eyes were fastened on the bear, her posture straight. She held her arms out, as if to make herself appear larger, as she began to move slowly backward.

"A grizzly," she murmured to him. "It may think we're

coming between it and some food. Or cubs. Just back away. As slow as you can."

He didn't know how a wolf might fare in an attack on a bear, but if the sow charged Astrid, he'd find out. Like hell would the bear reach her.

Something of the man prevailed, because he forced himself back. The bear stared at them, snorting, squinting, not entirely aggressive, but staking her claim on the path. There was a rustling sound behind the sow.

"Oh, my God," Astrid whispered.

Two more bears appeared, males, even larger than the sow. They lumbered up beside her, making guttural growls, heads hanging low in challenge.

He growled back. He wouldn't survive taking on all three, but he could give Astrid some lead. She could drop the packs and run. She had to know that a bullet could not stop these bears, not unless her aim was perfect, and he wouldn't let her take that chance.

"Nathan," she breathed, "adult grizzlies are *solitary.*"

That made no difference to him now. His only thought was how to inflict as much damage as he could before the bears killed him. He took a step forward. Then stopped.

A wolf trotted out of the forest, followed by five more wolves. They ranged in size, but they were all full grown, all focused on him and Astrid, all making low rumbles of warning. The wolves arrayed themselves in front of the bears in a semicircle.

Several screeches overhead brought his attention skyward. Red-tailed hawks circled, easily half a dozen in number, perhaps more. They flew lower and lower, gliding through the tree branches, eyes sharp, talons ready.

He crouched low, growling, baring his teeth, readying himself to spring.

When something brushed his neck, he snarled, then caught her scent. Astrid placed her hand on his neck as she stood beside him.

He wanted the power of speech, to shout at her. *Get back,* he thought savagely. *Run.*

"Wait, Nathan," she whispered. Then, louder, she said in Nakota, "We are friends."

He realized she was addressing the gathered animals.

Every one of them, bears and wolves, approached. The hawks made a final circle, then landed on the ground nearby.

It swept over him suddenly. A surge of power, of energy, beginning with the bears and then rippling outward to the wolves and hawks and then beyond. Even Astrid felt it, her fingers tightening in his fur. He lost his snarl and could merely stare, amazed.

He had only felt the change in himself, never seen it in others. The forest filled with power as bears, wolves, and hawks lost their animal forms, silver mists swirling around them, as they reshaped themselves. One after the other.

The female bear transformed herself into a tall woman with long, dark hair that swept over her bare shoulders. Beside her, the male bears took on the forms of large, powerfully built men. The wolves and hawks shifted and shimmered until they, too, reshaped into men and women, all of them lean and strong, their dark copper skin marked with scars from wounds new and old. No one wore clothing, but that did not lessen the fury sparking in their dark eyes, the threat in their postures.

The woman who had been a bear stepped forward. Her eyes were obsidian wrath.

She spoke a dialect of Nakota, yet he understood her words without trying. And wished he did not.

"Traitor," she said to him. "You have brought a human, a *white* human into our sacred lands. For this, you both must die."

Chapter 8

The Earth Spirits' Judgment

Astrid looked from face to face, searching for one who might be, if not an ally, then perhaps less hostile. She found none.

Under her hand, she felt Nathan change. A warm mist swirled, the fur at her fingertips shifted to smooth skin, and then he stood in front of her as though to shield her from the Earth Spirits. *She* was the one who was armed, but still, he guarded her, sending a challenging glare to the assembled shape changers, fists ready, posture poised to spring into a fight.

"I am one of you," he said in the Nakota dialect the woman had spoken. How he knew to speak it, she could not fathom, but, then, she had just witnessed nearly two dozen animals change into human form, so this mystery was less urgent. "We mean no harm."

The woman scoffed. "How can you say that? You have brought *her,*" she gestured toward Astrid, "to our territory, violating our secrecy. No white man or woman has ever seen our kind before."

"*I* have not seen our kind before," Nathan replied angrily. "I have come here to seek answers, and she—"

"Is your mate," said one of the men who had been a wolf. He said the word "mate" as if it were a curse.

Astrid fought her flush, realizing they could likely smell Nathan all over her, the scent of their sex.

"She is my friend," Nathan shot back. "And she knows more of magic and medicine than any of us. She helped me to find you."

"All the worse," the woman sneered. She nodded toward the men who had been bears. "Hold them, and we will take them to the village."

The men approached, faces stern, hands ready to grab them. Nathan snarled, priming to attack.

"Wait," Astrid whispered urgently to him in English. "If we are taken to the village, we'll speak with the chief."

"And run the risk that he'll kill us? I'd rather fight."

"*Nathan*. There are too many of them. We've no chance here."

The men came forward and seized their arms in unbreakable grips. Nathan growled at the man holding her, but Astrid sent him a quick, warning look. His growls subsided into low rumbling, and he looked as though he wanted to tear out someone's throat.

One man took her knife, rifle, and revolver. However isolated this tribe was, they knew about firearms.

Without any further words, the group of Earth Spirits turned and began walking farther into the woods, Nathan and Astrid their captives. Some of the wolves carried their baggage. As they walked, her mind raced. What could she say to convince them she and Nathan were not threats? That the bigger threat might be only a day or two behind? She would not allow herself to contemplate Nathan's death at the hands—or claws or talons—of his own people.

It was a little odd, being the only dressed person in a group of two dozen. Yet the Earth Spirits were unconcerned with their nudity, and Nathan was not self-conscious. She felt, in fact, out of place and awkward in her clothing, as though the construct of clothes was foreign and unnatural.

They wove deeper into the forest, down snaking trails, no one speaking. Her sense of direction had always been good, but she could not reckon where they were or how she might navigate out again. Perhaps a glamour further shielded their village. She remembered, suddenly.

In her coat was her Compass.

What had possessed her to take it from her cabin? No Blade was ever without their Compass. It was their prized possession. Even though it held no magic, all Blades cherished and protected their Compass, the signifier of their important role as guardians of the world's magic. She could make her way without its mechanical assistance, but she had taken it when abandoning her cabin. Why? Did she still consider herself a Blade?

The smells and sounds of village life reached her before they entered a wide clearing. And the strong reverberations of magic. She smelled smoke and heard voices, the nicker of horses. When the group came around a sheltering bend, she gave a small start. She was not certain what to expect from the Earth Spirits' village, but what she saw now had been far from her mind.

Despite the powerful, invisible emanations of its magic, the normalcy and ordinariness of the village surprised her. Hide tepees grouped in clusters. A rough guess numbered them around two hundred. And surrounding them were the perfectly normal routines of Native life. Women cooked and dressed hides, some with babies strapped to their backs. Men sat or stood in clusters, talking. Children played with dolls or tiny bows and arrows. Everyone was dressed, though some of the men were shirtless and wore only breechcloths, and a few women wore simple tunics rather than longer, more elaborately decorated dresses.

Only one thing truly distinguished this village from any other. Grizzly bears and wolves wandered freely, while red-tailed hawks circled and roosted. Astrid observed a woman talking to a huge bear. Two wolf cubs wrestled with a few children. A hawk landed on a man's outstretched arm and handed him a small fish.

As the group of shape changers and their captives neared, everyone abandoned whatever task they had been performing to stand and stare. Both Astrid *and* Nathan garnered the same amount of attention. While they were being pulled through the village, voices murmured together, some shocked, some angry, many curious. Even the bears, wolves, and hawks stared, several changing into their human forms to whisper to people nearby.

If she hadn't been concerned for her life and Nathan's, Astrid would have been fascinated. She longed to study these unique people, live among them and experience their world. But they were determined to keep themselves veiled, and while she could not fault their reasoning, she feared it would mean her and Nathan's deaths.

They were dragged before the assembled crowd and shoved forward. Both she and Nathan stumbled but remained standing. The crowd parted to allow a man to step forward. The chief, as evident by his eagle-feathered headdress. Yet this muscular man wore only a breechcloth and no moccasins.

"What is this, Yellow Bear Woman?" he demanded of the bear woman. "These strangers should be dead by your claws."

"He is an Earth Spirit," Yellow Bear Woman answered. "Yet he brought a white woman to our lands. The honor of killing traitors belongs to our chief."

The chief seemed mollified by this response. He pulled off the headdress and handed it to a warrior. Then, with a flick of his wrist, he loosened his breechcloth and almost instantly transformed into a massive charcoal-colored wolf. No one, not even the other Earth Spirits, had changed so quickly.

The wolf approached them, golden eyes narrowed but tail straight, ears forward. His hackles bristled. A dominant. No one would usurp him. A growl started in the back of the wolf chief's throat. Astrid could not help staring at his enormous, gleaming teeth. A single bite would tear her or Nathan open from throat to belly.

Nathan answered the chief's growl with his own.

The crowd gasped. None had ever challenged their chief. Yet here was an interloper, a rebel, doing just that.

Nathan bent low, readying himself to transform into his wolf.

"Don't," Astrid warned, low.

He sent her a rage-dark glance. "I'm not going to let this bastard just rip us apart."

"But you cannot speak as a wolf."

"Neither can he."

"You're also an attorney," she pointed out. "Argue our case, and maybe no one will be disemboweled."

He looked as if he was about to fight.

"There are only two of us, and dozens of them," she hissed. "Even if you kill the chief, we'll be dead." Still, he hesitated, preferring action to words. "These are *your* people, Nathan," she added. "Prove it to them."

Nathan scowled, but gave her a small nod. He stepped forward, rising to his full height. He was not especially tall, but he imbued himself with presence, so that none could look away from him. "Hold, Chief." His voice held so much authority, such confidence and strength, even the chief fell silent.

"Look around you," Nathan said. "At the faces of everyone here."

Amazingly, the chief did so. He gazed about, at the gathered crowd.

"These are your people," Nathan continued. "Your tribe. Since you were born, you have known them. You have seen many of them birthed and many die. And they will continue to come into the world and leave it, with you as their chief, secure in the knowledge of who they are and what it means to be both human and Earth Spirit. Though the outside world may not understand you, you understand yourself, your history, your birthright."

He slowly moved toward the chief. "Imagine, if you can, what it might mean to be taken by strangers. I remember the day I had to say good-bye to my mother, when the white men came to my village and said I had to go with them. She didn't want me to see her cry. She wanted me to be brave. She gave me a little wooden dog and said it would watch over me when I was far away. But when I got to the school, the teachers said the dog was heathen, and they made me throw it into the fire.

"Imagine," he continued, "if you were raised by people who were not your own, taught that the ways of you and your ancestors were savage and unworthy. Never knowing your parents, your home. And, all the while, you know that it is more than the color of your skin that divides you from everyone else, but something deeper, something held far within yourself that you cannot understand. It would destroy you, if you let it.

"So you fight," he went on, and Astrid, too, was held captive by his words. "You battle so as not to despise yourself. And you grieve for something that has never been yours.

"And when given the chance, the slimmest chance, to learn more about yourself, what can you do, but seize that chance. Yet, the path is treacherous and unfamiliar. On your own, you have no possibility or hope. There is only one person who can walk at your side. One person to guide you. The only person who sees you," he said, turning to Astrid, expression warming, turning thoughtful, "without judgment, only what is in your heart. And even seeing the darkness inside your heart, she accepts you and makes you feel, for the first time, truly whole. The emptiness is gone, because of her. No one has ever given you that gift before."

Astrid felt her eyes begin to burn, so she blinked them quickly.

He swung back to the chief, who was now sitting back on his

haunches, ears turning to follow each of Nathan's words. "Until one week ago, I lived as a man. In one night, in a few moments of fury and life and death, I learned that I was an Earth Spirit. The change, when it came, shocked me and made me the chosen prey of terrible, ruthless men. This woman"—he gestured toward Astrid—"gave me shelter when there was nowhere to turn. She knew I must find my people. She gave up everything—her home, her peace, almost her life—to help me. She knew the risks, and she took them. She has fought for me. She has given me myself. I will not repay her goodness through blood. I will battle any of you, all of you, to keep her safe.

"But that will not be necessary." He stopped in front of the chief, a yard between them. At any moment, the wolf could lunge for him, disembowel him, yet he showed no fear. His shoulders were straight, his chin high, and Astrid understood how he had become the sole Native attorney in perhaps all of British Columbia, if not Canada.

"It isn't necessary," Nathan said, "because the Earth Spirits know what it means to be different, they know what it means to be fearful and feared, and so they know what it means to be merciful. If I have broken any sacred commandments to find my people, it was not done so out of disrespect, but out of a need to know, at last, who I am. That is not a crime that warrants death. It means life. Finally, life."

For some time, no one spoke. No one moved. Nathan and the wolf stared at each other, unblinking. Astrid felt her heart attempt to slam its way out of her chest. She did not know whether what Nathan had said was mere oratory, but it shook her, touched her profoundly. She had not felt so much in many, many years.

But would this be the last emotion she felt? She watched the chief, willing herself to be utterly still.

With a shimmer, the chief changed into human form. He stood upright and studied Nathan for many long moments. Then he reached out a hand and clasped Nathan by his shoulder.

"You are welcome here, Lost Brother. You and your mate."

Nathan gripped the chief's shoulder in greeting with his own strong hand. He glanced back at Astrid with a smile that pierced her like fire while the words he had spoken filled her. She thought she might drown, then, drown in the flood of her undammed heart.

The chief was called Iron Wolf, and he waved both Astrid and Nathan into his tepee. A woman, Iron Wolf's wife, handed Nathan a breechcloth, which he donned, and for that, Astrid felt gratitude. She was no prude, but she could not look at Nathan's supple, sleek body without recalling that, earlier that same day, they had tangled together in ferocious sex. He had been inside of her. And she had wanted him there. Just to think of it brought heat to her face, her body.

And what he had said to the tribe . . . He demolished her defenses at every turn. Trust and acceptance. That she could be all that to him, had given him so profound a gift and returned it in kind, reduced her battlements to tottering walls, liable to fall with the slightest breeze.

As Astrid sat down opposite him inside Iron Wolf's tepee, she watched the firelight sculpt Nathan into planes of bronze and gold, and saw, as the light gleamed in his dark eyes, the fierce intelligence and passion within him. She noticed, too, in signs so subtle as to be almost undetectable, the searching in his gaze as he looked at Iron Wolf and some other shape-changing members of the tribe.

He's looking for himself in them. The first time he'd been among his own kind.

In the quiet, as a pipe was prepared, Astrid turned to him. She asked softly in English, "Did you mean what you said?"

He knew she meant his speech to the tribe. She was transfixed by the black depths of his eyes as he looked at her, nothing hidden. "Yes."

Silken ties wound between them, invisible but strong,

threading through every part of her. She wanted to cling to them, pulling him to her. She wanted to run.

She could do neither. Nathan, Iron Wolf, and three other warriors shared a pipe, and she must stay. The chief asked Nathan to recount his tale—his birth, his parents' tribe, his life among the white men in Victoria.

"And you live as they do?" Iron Wolf asked, incredulous. "In their wooden lodges? You speak their tongue and never follow the hunt, never release your wolf? How do you keep from ripping everyone to pieces?"

"It's a struggle," Nathan admitted. "But what do you know of my mother's grandmother? I was told she was once one of your tribe, and went west to marry. Her name was, I think . . . Little Creek Woman."

Iron Wolf frowned in thought, yet, as he did this, a thready voice came from the darker recesses of the tepee. A tiny, withered man ambled out of the shadows, draped in many blankets and robes, and as wrinkled as a knuckle.

"I remember her," the old man said. "I was a cub, barely weaned, when she left. Said she wanted to see the big water to the west."

Nathan sat up straighter, alert and intent. "Was she a wolf, too? Or a bear or hawk?"

The old man settled in front of the fire, his bones creaking like wood. "None. She could not change her form."

"Many of the tribe cannot," Iron Wolf said.

"How is it that I can change?" Nathan asked.

The chief made a small shrug. "No one knows where the Gift will show. Some women have only human babies, and others have only litters. A woman may also have a human child *and* an Earth Spirit child."

"Like Swift Cloud Woman and her brother," the old man said. The other warriors shifted uncomfortably.

"Quiet, He Watches Stars," the chief snapped. "Her name is not spoken."

Astrid and Nathan glanced at each other. What Astrid

knew of the woman was vague, but she seemed to be perceived as a threat by other Natives. Thank God she and Nathan had not tried to find her.

"Do some of the Earth Spirits show their powers later in life?" Astrid asked.

"No," said Iron Wolf. "All are born in their animal forms. Even hawks begin as eggs. Were you truly human at your birth?" he asked Nathan.

Nathan frowned. "My mother didn't say otherwise. I never knew I could change, not on purpose and not accidentally."

"Strange," murmured the chief. "I've never heard of one who is an Earth Spirit changing so late in their seasons. I cannot say why you are different from us."

Astrid's gaze flicked to He Watches Stars. The old man looked as if he wanted to speak, then held himself back. But she glanced at Nathan and forgot the old man.

Raw disappointment flickered across Nathan's face. He had wanted more answers, a stronger sense of belonging, but it evaded him. Astrid struggled to keep from reaching out and taking his hand to offer him comfort and support, knowing that most Native warriors would look poorly on the gesture. They would not tolerate anything that seemed to indicate softness or weakness. In that, they weren't dissimilar from the majority of British men.

Watching Nathan sit among his fellow Earth Spirits, Astrid's mind turned toward her former comrades, the Blades of the Rose. Though their members came from around the globe, most were British, yet they were far different from most Britons. True, male Blades did not sit around over pots of tea and iced petits fours discussing their feelings, but they held and prized an innate compassion that made them excellent protectors of the world's magic. Michael had been an outstanding addition to their ranks. And, in truth, so had she.

How were they now, her old friends? Names and faces flashed through her memory, especially that charming scoundrel Bennett Day, and her closest friend, Catullus

Graves. Urbane, clever Catullus, with his cunning inventions and dry humor. She missed him. Missed him terribly. And he had been more than patient with her, continuing to send her letters long after she had stopped answering his.

She loved her mother and father, but the Blades, with their purpose and determination in the face of incredible odds, they had been her family. With them, she had been her most authentic self.

In the years since she left the Blades, what dangers had they faced? How many of their numbers had fallen in the course of their never-ending battle? Perhaps the Heirs of Albion had finally eradicated the Blades. It had been some time since she'd heard from Catullus. He, and all the other Blades, might be dead. The thought was so painful, she could not bear to approach it.

But she could fight the Heirs now. She realized with a small, internal start that, ever since Nathan came into her life, since learning of his need, she'd been behaving as though she still was a Blade. And now she sat, surrounded by another culture, learning pieces of their mysteries. Just as she had done as a Blade.

Being a Blade was part of her. Like her muscles and nerves and breath. Inseparable.

"There are cruel, greedy men coming," she said to Iron Wolf, urgent. "They learned Nathan is an Earth Spirit, and tried to capture him. They pursue him even now. They will come here and enslave all the Earth Spirits."

But the chief chuckled, and the gathered warriors shared in his laughter. "Let them come. If they can make the crossing, they will face us. We have no fear of men or their guns."

"These men wield dark medicine, not just guns," Nathan said grimly.

Yet this amused Iron Wolf even more. "Even when I was a cub, another tribe tried to make war against us using medicine. They sought to make us their animal slaves, too. But they failed, just as all who try to bind us will fail."

"What makes you so certain?" Nathan asked.

"Three totems," cried He Watches Stars. "Each within the land. Each for each. Each to protect."

"I don't understand," Astrid said, frowning.

"Long ago," Iron Wolf said, "totems were created to ensure no Earth Spirit had too much power. One totem for each animal. Hawk, Bear, and Wolf. Whoever is in possession of the totem has command over the Earth Spirits."

"A safeguard," Nathan said.

Iron Wolf nodded. "These totems are hidden. No one can find them. Not even an Earth Spirit. It is enough to know they exist. This way, no Earth Spirit gains too much power and no one can truly hold dominion over an Earth Spirit. Everything keeps its balance. We are safe."

In English, Astrid muttered, "Sources." Nathan raised a questioning brow, and she said, low, "The totems are Sources. Surely *they* are what the Heirs seek."

Nathan, grim, nodded in understanding. "Then this tribe is in danger."

"More than anyone can understand." Astrid turned to the chief and said in Nakota, insistent, "I know the men who are coming. I have faced them many times. Five years ago, they killed my husband." Though it pained her to speak of Michael's death, it no longer devastated her as it once had. A bittersweet understanding. But she could not think on it now. Her mission was taking shape in front of her. "They are ruthless and unwavering. *Nothing* is safe from these men. Not even the Earth Spirits and their totems. They will not stop until they have the Earth Spirits under their control."

"And why would they want us?"

A terrible idea, so terrible as to be true, came to Astrid. "Captive breeding."

Iron Wolf, and all the men in the tepee, even Nathan, stared at her.

It all made sense to Astrid now. "When these men have the totems, they will control the Earth Spirits. They will force you into captive breeding and create their own army of shape changers." The notion was so disgusting, Astrid almost gagged, but she forced herself to keep talking. "They will turn the Earth Spirits into farm animals whose sole purpose is to churn out young. Young that could be molded into unstoppable warriors. It's the totems that they want. And then the Earth Spirits, and their power, will be theirs."

Nathan cursed in English, looking as though he, too, wanted to be sick.

"Do they have so many enemies, these men?" asked one of the warriors.

"Everyone who is not of their country is their enemy. They want the world to belong to them."

"Have you a name, Little Sister?" Iron Wolf asked.

She blinked, uncertain. "The Stoney call me Hunter Shadow Woman."

The chief seemed pleased by this name. He gave her an indulgent look. "Hunter Shadow Woman, your concern is appreciated by our tribe. But it is unnecessary. Whoever these men are, whatever dark medicine they bring, my people can defeat them. We always do."

"There is a first time for everything," Nathan pointed out.

Iron Wolf frowned. He did not like being contradicted in front of his warriors. "Enough. If these foolish men do come, we will vanquish them."

Astrid fought to tame her frustration. The chief wasn't listening to her or Nathan at all. Iron Wolf underestimated the Heirs, which always proved fatal. But there seemed to be no way of warning him. The Heirs wanted the totems. But Iron Wolf would not recognize the threat.

"Now," Iron Wolf said, "we will welcome our Lost Brother into our tribe. He is restored to his rightful place. A fine blessing."

The warriors and He Watches Stars all seconded the chief's words, and Iron Wolf's wife, who had been silently sitting nearby, quickly left the tepee. Astrid heard the woman shout to the assembled group outside the tent that there would be a celebration that night. The tribe, eager for amusement, readily agreed and hurried off to make preparations.

Astrid stared at Nathan, and he stared back. They had been drawing closer together, but now she felt the gulf between them widen. He was to be enfolded into the tribe, made one of them. The tribe's place was his place.

But the Heirs were coming for the totems, the Sources, and the Earth Spirits refused to acknowledge their threat.

A fearful ache wrapped around her chest, only partly due to the approaching danger.

Drumbeats and voices filled the night. Men circled bonfires, carrying small drums, rattles, and bells. Women sat at the edges, singing. Even in celebration, a plaintive tone permeated the song, as though sorrow drifted just beneath the surface of joy, ready to emerge from one breath to the next.

Astrid, seated alone, took those melancholy songs into herself. She watched the shadows cast by the dancers flicker across the nearby trees, the boundary between light and darkness, society and wilderness. One on the outside. The other within.

Nathan moved through the crowd. He still wore the breechcloth, but had also been given a loose, open hide shirt, handsomely decorated with beads. He looked more like the Earth Spirits now, save for his short hair, and, after the initial suspicion, was now happily welcomed into the tribe. People kept stopping him, talking to him, smiling. Several young women, at least ten years younger than Astrid, followed Nathan with their eyes, pleased by what they saw.

As was she. Pleased, but wary. He was a striking man, even amid many handsome men. Something burned within him to give Nathan a dark radiance, an energy, a strength. He would be a fine addition to the tribe.

Astrid forced her gaze away. Instead, she watched the

dancers, their sinuous forms as they circled the fire. Some had changed into their animal forms so that, interspersed throughout the crowd, bears nodded with the music, wolves yipped and leapt into the air, and a few daring hawks flew back and forth over the fire.

From her coat, she took out her Compass and opened its lid. Firelight gleamed over its glass face, so it was a thing of brass and flame in her hands. It had guided her once before. It would do so again.

She remembered the dream, calling her home. Back to the Blades. So strange that she should recall the dream so vividly, even much later, when most of her dreams evaporated like mist upon waking. Now it resonated as she prepared to take up the work she had cast away.

Her attention went back to Nathan as one of the warriors attempted to draw him into the dance. Nathan shook his head, holding up his hands, but smiling good-naturedly. The warrior laughed, then resumed his dance. Then more people surrounded Nathan, full of talk and big gestures. They called him Lost Brother Wolf, all aware that he was no longer lost, but found.

She got to her feet and started walking toward Iron Wolf's tepee. No one noticed her. Their attentions were all focused on Nathan and their own need for revelry. Life in the mountains was hard; they wanted release.

The celebration would likely go late. She would have enough time to catch a few hours of sleep. Deep weariness assailed her. Such a day. It was a wonder she hadn't collapsed into boneless exhaustion.

She moved into the darkness, alien and apart. These were not her people. This was not her home. That dream. It resounded again.

Someone took her arm and she spun about, pulling away. Nathan stood close. The firelight behind him outlined him in gold but left his face shadowed.

"I didn't hear you coming," she said.

"Drums," he answered. "Where are you going?"

She raised her brows at his abrupt change of topic. He never wasted time with niceties.

"It has been a most taxing day," she replied. "I'm going to bed." She turned to head toward the tent, but Nathan, silent and quick, blocked her path.

"I'll join you." Now the firelight was on his face, and she saw the heated promise in his words. Her heart hitched, and warmth gathered between her legs. Her body and heart now knew what they could feel with him, demanding more. She could not allow that.

"You will be missed," she pointed out instead. "This celebration is for you, to welcome you back."

He looked over to the revelers. Sensual need drifted from his face, replaced by a glimpse of uncertainty, which was not like him, always so confident and bold.

"Can't understand it," he murmured.

"Understand what?"

He turned shadowed eyes to her. "I *felt* it, I truly did, running through these woods, these mountains. Home."

"I'm glad for you," she said, and meant it, but could not stop the fractures spreading out from her heart.

"It isn't home," he said.

"Not yet."

He slowly shook his head. "I wonder, if ever."

"These are your people, Nathan," she said, taking hold of his wrist. "Whom you have been yearning for all this time, without knowing it. The missing part of yourself." Though he had said that day he did not feel anything missing when he was with her.

He glanced down at her hand on him, then covered it with his own. His hand was warm and strong, but his flesh revealed him to be human and, in his own tough way, vulnerable.

"I *want* it to be like that, Astrid," he said, frustration threading through his voice. "I want it to be, badly. But it isn't. I've been waiting all night to feel it, the peace, the belonging. But it hasn't come."

"It will," she said, trying to sound convincing, which was a challenge, as her heart broke for him. "You must give it time. You've only been with the Earth Spirits a few hours. It will take more than that to undo a lifetime of being an outsider."

He looked up, catching her gaze with his own. "You think so?"

"I do."

His expression shifted, turned hungry. "Wise Astrid," he murmured, drawing her closer. His eyes moved to her lips, growing even more feral. "Beautiful Astrid. I want to taste you again."

She wanted that as well, far too much. Lightning sped through her body, making her sensitive and needy. So she made herself pull away. "I'm exhausted. And you need to get back to the celebration."

He planted his hands on his hips. "It won't work."

"What?"

"I don't back down, Astrid. I don't give up."

Damn him and his tenacity. "Have you considered that I might not want you anymore?"

His smile was slow, arrogant, and wicked, and it tormented her. "You do," he said confidently. "As much as I want you."

"*Good night,* Nathan," she said and hurried back to the tepee as fast as she could. She did and she did not want him to go after her, and it was with a disheartening amount of regret that she reached her destination entirely alone.

Chill night air turned her lungs crystalline. She breathed in, taking in the frigid air, waking herself with each inhalation. After the close warmth of the tepee luring her back to sleep, she needed any form of impetus to move.

Overhead, the sky gleamed, each star a cut stone. And it

was hers alone. Everyone was asleep. The celebration had carried on late into the night, but now, fatigued and happy, the revelers were all snug in their tepees.

Including Nathan.

He'd been sleeping when she had crept out of Iron Wolf's tepee, laden with one pack, her rifle, and her pistol. In the dim glow of the fire's embers, she studied Nathan's face, the planes of his cheekbones, the fullness of his mouth. It had taken far too much strength to keep from going to him, pressing her lips to his in a farewell. But, despite what he had said to her earlier that evening, his place was here.

It was for him she did this. She had to remind herself of that. She alone truly knew what the Heirs were capable of, and so the task of protecting the Earth Spirits fell to her. Would she see Nathan again? If she survived this mission.

As she edged toward the limits of the village, through the clusters of tents, she passed the humped forms of bears curled in slumber, and wolves nestling together. Some twitched slightly as she passed, but she had learned long ago how to walk silently, and she kept herself downwind so that her scent would not travel and alert anyone to her disappearance.

Iron Wolf would try and stop her. Nathan might as well.

Yet she'd had a revelation back in Iron Wolf's tent. Nathan sought a sense of belonging. He would find it here, with the Earth Spirits. She, too, had something to which she belonged.

She had been, and would always be, a Blade of the Rose. Astrid knew this now. Fleeing from this part of herself was as impossible as fleeing from her own pulse. It was not duty. It was her. She had her Compass. Even alone, she was a Blade. That's what her dream signified, weeks before this journey had begun.

Which meant she had to act.

She passed the outer reaches of the village, where the horses were kept. Two human warriors as well as a wolf and a hawk guarded the enclosure. Yet they were asleep, too. Strange. She briefly contemplated taking a horse. It would make her own journey faster, but she did not dare risk waking the guards. And her actions might be misconstrued as theft rather than borrowing. Horse thievery was a grave crime. On foot, then. She had done it before.

Astrid crossed a dry, narrow creek bed. Then a large silver-and-black shape darted in front of her and blocked her path. In its maw, the wolf carried several pieces of hide clothing and a pair of moccasins. It stared at her, anger in its topaz eyes.

"Nathan," she whispered, torn between frustration and pleasure.

He changed forms, much more quickly than he had done before. That gave her some gratification, knowing that he was coming into the fullness of his ability, making it part of him.

He donned the breechcloth and shirt. "I didn't figure you for the sneaking-off sort," he said, tugging on the moccasins. His words were hard, like chipped flint.

"Iron Wolf would not have allowed me to leave had I gone during the day."

Arms folded across his chest, he stared at her, but it was too dark to see his expression. She felt rather than saw his anger, and had no way to answer it. So she let the silence draw out between them.

"You're going for the totems," he said.

Strange how well he knew her, this man who had been unknown to her a week before. "The Sources must be found and protected. Even if Iron Wolf thinks the tribe is safe, I know the Heirs are coming. They will find the totems and use them."

Quietly, but with steel in his voice, he said, "You're certain of this."

She stepped closer to him, feeling the heat of his body. Her own voice had its strength, its confidence. "I've never been more certain. The tribe must be defended from the enslavement that will definitely come. This *has* to be done."

Again, he fell silent. She could only wonder what he was thinking. Perhaps that she was a headstrong fool, meddling in affairs that did not concern her. But he could not think that. He, more than anyone, seemed to understand what drove her onward. Perhaps he would allow her to go. Though, she thought wryly, she never permitted a man to *allow* her to do anything.

"Wait here," he finally said. He started to move past her, back toward the village.

Anger shot through her. "I won't let you wake Iron Wolf."

"Wake him? He'll only try and stop us."

"'Us'?" she repeated with a spike of something that felt like elation.

He leaned closer, and his words were gruff. "If you think I'd let you face those son-of-a-bitch Heirs on your own, then I've made a damned poor impression on you."

Astrid struggled to keep the exhilaration from her voice, just as she struggled to keep from feeling that emotion. But the battle was lost all too quickly. "So, where are you going?"

"To the tepee for my pack."

"No need to go so far," said a reedy voice close by.

Both Astrid and Nathan spun to find He Watches Stars standing just behind them. The tiny old man had Nathan's pack at his feet.

Astrid gaped. She had not heard the wizened man, and could not believe such an aged person could even lift, let alone carry, the heavy rucksack.

"Don't try to stop us, old sage," Nathan cautioned. He shouldered the pack easily.

He Watches Stars chuckled, the sound like dry, rustling leaves. "Why would I do that? A grave threat to the Earth Spirits clouds the horizon."

Though she was profoundly relieved, she felt compelled to note, "Iron Wolf does not think so."

The old man waved a tiny, wrinkled hand. "Iron Wolf is a good chief, but he is too used to being pack leader. He cannot think anyone will challenge him. No one has. Except you," he added, looking back and forth between Nathan and Astrid with a smile.

"You believe me, then, about the threat?" she asked.

"It is not you I believe, Hunter Shadow Woman," said the old man. "I believe my dreams. And they have shown me what shall be, if the totems are not found and protected." His voice chilled with visions. "Betrayal. Death. Slavery. At the hands of those you call the Heirs."

Both Astrid and Nathan stiffened. Neither of them had mentioned the Heirs of Albion by name.

"Yes, children," He Watches Stars said, grim, "the Heirs come. My visions have foretold it. And if you do not act to secure the totems, our tribe's future is nothing but misery."

Chapter 9

In Pursuit

Hearing He Watches Stars' pronouncement, a sick dread plunged through Nathan, followed immediately by the need to fight. What the medicine man saw was a vision of what *might* be. Nothing was unchangeable.

"If there's anything you know about these totems," he said to the old man, "tell us now."

"There are legends of the three totems," answered He Watches Stars. "So that in times of threat, or when one Earth Spirit grew too powerful, they could be found. Only a handful know these legends."

"Including you, I hope," said Astrid.

Nathan shot her a quick grin. She was as ready as he to set off on their hunt. Later, he'd give her holy hell for trying to sneak away without him. For now, he was eager to take up the quest with her at his side.

"Yes, me," the old man said. He closed his eyes and spread his hands, and his voice chanted in a low and steady rhythm:

Brothers Wolf, Bear, and Hawk,
Guardians and warriors of these sacred mountains.

To the white lake where the pack hunts,
You must lend your voices to song.

Travel the path of the solitary hunter
To the gray forest.

From the sky, you see the way
Of the green river.

Incantation finished, He Watches Stars folded his hands and looked at Astrid and Nathan with eyes gleaming like his namesake stars. Nathan felt the chant resonating through his body, his heart and mind, as though he were a drum struck during a ritual.

"And that is all?" Astrid asked. "There is no more?"

"None, Hunter Shadow Woman," the old man said. He turned a shrewd gaze to her. "Is it not enough?"

"I've found more with less," she answered, a flat statement of fact that sent a jolt of pure desire shooting through Nathan. Her strength aroused him, and his beast, to madness.

He Watches Stars beckoned both Nathan and Astrid closer. When they approached, the medicine man placed a palm on each of their foreheads. A warm glow spread from the old man's hand and into Nathan. "Blessings of the Great Spirit on you. May you succeed in your quest—for the sake of your tribe. And the earth."

The glow receded, and He Watches Stars stepped back. "Go now, children. My medicine can only subdue the tribe until sunrise."

"What do you mean?" asked Astrid.

He Watches Stars chuckled. "Do you truly believe you could steal your way through a tribe of Earth Spirits and none would wake? Sister, you are a skilled hunter, but no one is *that* skilled."

"You cast a spell," Nathan said, startled. He still struggled for sea legs when it came to this world of magic.

"A small sleeping charm," the old man said with a modest shrug. "Iron Wolf would not have permitted you to go, had he been awake. Though, I must own, my medicine has been strangely strong lately. I feel something has changed."

Nathan noticed Astrid's small shiver of acknowledgment. She had felt the change, too.

"Will the Earth Spirits follow?" she asked.

He Watches Stars shook his head. "I will make Iron Wolf see reason. At the least, I will tell him that if you want to cast your lives away, it would be foolish to try and stop you."

"Thank you," Nathan said. "I think."

"Must I say it again? Go now."

Wordless, Nathan and Astrid set off, putting the medicine man and slumbering village behind them. They moved forward, into the darkness, and Nathan's heightened nocturnal senses guided them, so that their path was clear, even as the night and forest and mountains took them into shadow.

Catullus and Quinn stood in the doorway of Astrid Bramfield's cabin, their guide Jourdain outside with the horses. What they saw there made Catullus's heart sink.

"I don't know Mrs. Bramfield," Quinn noted drily. "But I'm going to guess she doesn't usually keep a dead body in her home."

"Not usually, no," said Catullus.

There wasn't much of a body left. Scavenging animals had gotten to it, but enough remained so that Catullus could identify it was a man—at least knowing its gender was a relief—whose clothes had been stripped off. Catullus carefully stepped forward over the piles of books and overturned furniture. The body smelled awful. Everything that had been edible was gone, but enough remained to fill the small cabin with the stink of decay.

Reaching into his pocket, Catullus pulled out a pair of very thin leather gloves. He had them specially made in Italy, and they were remarkably useful for handling things without leaving smudges from his fingers. He pulled on the gloves, crouched down, and methodically examined the body.

"He was killed by an animal," he said as Quinn came up to stand behind him.

"There's hardly anything there!"

"It's not so much the body, but what it left behind." He looked at now-dry rust brown splatters on the floor and even on the walls. "Blood here. And the markings on what had been the throat. The killing blow." Catullus pointed to deep scrapes across the remains. "Some kind of large cat or wolf tore the man's esophagus clean out."

"Explains the blood everywhere."

Catullus rose from his crouch, frowning at the stained floor and walls. God, he hoped the blood belonged only to the dead man, and none of it was Astrid's.

"Is he an Heir?" Quinn asked. "Sure hope so."

"No way to tell. Whoever he is, *was,* Astrid didn't kill him. But," he added, seeing smaller boot prints tracking blood back and forth over the floorboards, "she has been here, and she was alive after he died." A staggering relief. But there were other tracks. The bare feet of a man. Other men's footprints marked the floor, but the blood hadn't been as wet when they came through the cabin, judging by the marks. *Hell.*

"And then packed and left," Quinn said, gesturing toward an open chest at the foot of the bed.

A new hope surged through Catullus. He went to the chest and gingerly picked through it, feeling as though he was violating Astrid's privacy. He found empty boxes that once held rifle shells and bullets for a revolver. A quick search of her cupboard produced only a few garments, including some chemises and drawers, which made Catullus particularly uncomfortable. But the thing he was searching for wasn't there. And for that, he was grateful.

"She took her Compass," he said to Quinn.

The tall man straightened from his own examination of the cabin. "Thank God for that." He took from his jacket pocket his Compass, just as Catullus did. Both men flipped the lids open to stare at the devices' faces.

Every Blade of the Rose had in their possession the same Compass, its original created generations ago by Catullus's own great-great-grandmother Portia. No Blade was ever without their Compass, and would not part with it upon pain of death. It was used to recognize each other, as Catullus and Quinn had identified each other in Boston. But its use was not only decorative or symbolic. Aside from being valuable as a directional tool, Great-Great-Grandmother Portia had built into it another means of guidance.

"Disable yours," Catullus said.

"What do you mean?" Quinn frowned in puzzlement.

"A little family secret," said Catullus, "so you don't track the wrong Compass. Here." Catullus took Quinn's Compass and turned its outer rim. There was the sound of small metal disks sliding into place. He handed the Compass back to Quinn. "Shields the mechanism."

The Bostonian whistled softly in admiration. "You Graves folks are dangerous."

With a wry smile, Catullus twisted the dial on the face of his Compass, removing the front piece. He pulled out a miniscule pin located on the inner rim, releasing an internal device. The Compass needle spun for a moment, freed from true north, before finding and fixing on a spot to the west. Astrid. Or at least her Compass.

Great-Great-Grandmother Portia knew Blades would have to find each other. And so, in each Compass, she had provided the means by which they could do just that, a combination of metals that drew the needles of other Compasses. Every Compass could be used to track other Compasses within a range of fifty miles, the usefulness of which Catullus knew firsthand. It had saved his life, and the lives of others, countless times. He was damned glad that the family intellect ran through him.

"That's her, then?" asked Quinn.

Catullus replaced the front on his Compass. "She has her Compass with her."

"Unless it's another Blade," Quinn pointed out.

"I'd know."

"Then we'd better go after her." Quinn turned and left the cabin at once.

Catullus began to leave, but stood in the doorway for a moment, looking back at what had been Astrid's home for the past four years. It was difficult to picture her here. Obviously, she didn't usually have a body in her home, nor would she leave her books in chaotic tumbles, with her furniture upended and crockery everywhere.

But Astrid had forever been full of life. She was, as Michael once confided, life itself. An irrepressible energy, a force that no one could ever stop, and no one tried. Michael had been content to bask in her reflected glow, though he had his own quiet strength. Catullus always knew when she was at headquarters, even when he was in the quiet of his basement workshop. The whole building filled with her vibrancy. Blades, sequestered in their rooms, were drawn from their solitude by her energy. The parlor was never so full of people as when she was there, telling stories, acting out with a sheepish Michael their latest adventure. Laughter and exuberance. It felt much duller when she was away on a mission, as though all the lamps had been dimmed.

Yet here, in this homely little cabin, she had lived quietly, shut away not only from her family, the Blades, but also, Catullus realized, shut away from herself. The thought saddened and angered him.

"Hey, Graves," shouted Quinn behind him. "You better come out here."

Shutting away thoughts of Astrid's self-imposed exile, Catullus turned and went down the front steps. He found the guide Jourdain bent low to the ground, with Quinn standing concernedly nearby.

"These tracks," Jourdain said. "They say that your friend set out with a companion. A little while later, a group of men came, and now they follow her, but take a different track. She must know a secret way out of this meadow." The Métis stood and dusted his hands together.

"How far apart are they?" Catullus asked.

"Can't say. These tracks are far from fresh. But there are seven mounted men with pack animals following her."

Catullus swore and his hand tightened on the leather sling of his shotgun. The Heirs were most definitely pursuing her.

"Those men, the ones Sergeant Williamson told you about," Jourdain said. "I remember when they came through the post. They wanted me for a guide, but I didn't like them. Four Englishmen hired and left with three guides."

"You didn't say anything before," Quinn grumbled.

Jourdain shrugged. "Wasn't sure they were the same people. But it makes sense now."

"Did any of them give their names?" Catullus demanded.

The Métis frowned in thought. "Halling was one."

Catullus felt marginally better. Richard Halling, a baronet's son, was hardly a threat, though he could land a mean punch when finally cornered.

"Milbourne," Jourdain added, and that made Catullus a bit nervous, considering that Sir John Milbourne could shoot the kernel out of an apricot with surgical precision. "There was also . . . Buckbridge . . . Bracebank?"

"Bracebridge?" Catullus filled in.

"That's the one."

Catullus's lips thinned with concern. Lesley Bracebridge had been the protégé of the Heirs' most powerful mage. And now that Chernock was dead, killed in Greece, Bracebridge would be more than eager to prove himself as the

Heirs' most formidable dark-magic user. Who knew what kind of magic Bracebridge would use against Astrid, what untapped Sources he sought, not only for the Heirs' demands, but his own.

"And the fourth?" Catullus asked.

Jourdain stared at his boots for a long while, sifting through his memory. There were any number of names that Catullus did not want to hear, but two in particular stood out. He prayed that Jourdain did not say—

"Staunton." The guide smiled, proud to have recalled everyone's names, but his smile faded as soon as he saw Catullus's face.

Catullus immediately went to his horse and mounted. Without speaking, Quinn and Jourdain did the same. There wasn't time to waste on something as unimportant as words.

Astrid and Nathan didn't speak for hours. On foot, they needed to put distance between themselves and the Earth Spirits, and, even with He Watches Stars's medicine, did not want to risk any sharp-eared shape changer hearing them. So they moved onward by unspoken agreement, through forested slopes and past mountain-ringed lakes, as dawn blazed to life overhead.

The old medicine man must have kept his word to keep the Earth Spirits from pursuing. Astrid could not sense their magic nearby and, with each step she took away from their village, their presence dimmed.

They crossed a creek, and then another. He strode beside her and the rising sun glinted in the onyx of his eyes, revealing the hard sheen of anger within.

She knew he would be angry, should have counted on it, and every moment of silence thickened and strengthened his anger.

"You ran," he said, breaking the silence. He didn't hide his fury.

Her shoulders stiffened. "It had to be done. Sources are at risk."

"You weren't running toward the totems," he countered. "You ran from me. Scared." He clenched his jaw. "What I said about you to the tribe—it's true. True and you know it. You accept me as I am. When I am with you, I'm whole."

Astrid whirled to face him. Her cheeks burned as her heart sped at his words. They reverberated within her like a deep bell, a sound and a feeling. Yet she clung to the few tatters of her self-defense. "You've been looking for a place to belong, for people like you. And you found them. You're meant to be with the Earth Spirits, not risking your life with me to find Sources."

"I know this mission is important," he growled, "to me, to you, to the Earth Spirits, even to the damned Heirs of Albion. But you're hiding behind it."

A stab. "Rushing into danger is *not* hiding." She pressed her lips together until they whitened. "Just as your true home is with the Earth Spirits, my true home is this path, this mission. The Blades of the Rose are my people, their work is where I am meant to be, who I am. I must carry on their objectives."

"Not alone. From the beginning, it's been you and me. Together."

That silenced her. She had no rejoinder, because there was nothing she might say to shield her from such brutal, beautiful honesty.

"You came after me," she whispered. "Left behind what you did not need to abandon."

He did not answer, because the answer was in his eyes. She stared at him for a long while, her gaze moving over his face. They saw each other—perhaps more fully than ever before, perhaps more than anyone else had ever done. Who was this fierce man she had met by chance in the middle of the wilderness? He had a planetary force, a gravity, that drew her to him. Within herself she found a mixture of fear and desire and something even stronger, deeper than desire. He was drawn to her just as powerfully. But without fear.

Some daylight bird sang above them in the tree branches. Its mate answered.

"Thank you," she said, simply, quietly. "For . . . coming after me." She glanced up at the birds. "No one did. Before."

She saw that he understood. She'd held everyone back, even those who loved her most, yet none of them had faced her, challenged her. Except him.

Nathan stepped closer until only a few inches separated them. He took in the details of her face, and she imagined how she must look at that moment. A little weary, soft purple crescents underneath her eyes. The smallest lines at the corners of her eyes, traced by whispers, that showed a life lived fully. She was not a fresh girl. She was a woman, with the years written upon her face.

To him, she saw, she was beautiful. Yet when his hand came up to cup the back of her head, she stood, motionless, wary, and wanting.

He held her like that for a moment. Then they came together, brushing lips in a kiss. Only their mouths contacted, but everything gathered in that small connection.

This is right. This is as it should be.

She pulled away. "You . . . overwhelm me."

He whispered, his breath warm and feathering across her face, "I only give what I know you can handle."

Her rueful laugh. "Such conviction."

"When it comes to you and me, both alone and together, there is no doubt."

The smallest smile tilted the corners of her mouth, until it faded with the hard reality they now faced. "But we cannot take for granted the success of this mission. One of the first things we learn when initiated into the Blades: Complacency leads to failure."

"Complacent? Me? Never." He dropped his hand from where he touched her, reluctance in the gesture, and her own disappointment flared at the absence of his touch. "We need to find the totems. The answers are in the legend."

The fire of purpose flared to life within her. "I've been thinking about that since we left the village. *To the white lake where the pack hunts.* Wolves hunt in packs."

"The legend specified a lake," Nathan mused. "Wolves can't hunt on water. They would want a solid surface, I'd think."

"Solid . . . perhaps frozen?" Astrid suggested.

They looked at each other as understanding emerged. "And if water is frozen," he said, "it would be white."

"Numerous lakes freeze in winter." She chewed on her lip in contemplation. "The one we seek could be any of hundreds or thousands in these mountains. And we're at least a month away from that kind of cold. Unless . . ." Her words trailed away as she thought.

"Unless . . . ?" he prompted.

"There are ice fields that remain frozen," she said. "Year round. They never melt."

"Which would make sense—if they're in the legend, then they wouldn't change from season to season, and always remain white."

Excitement grew as they pieced together the meaning of the legend. They both began to grin like children opening the door to a secret room.

"How many ice fields are there?" Nathan asked.

"Several, but I don't know how many are within the Earth Spirits' territory. Nor how we would know if wolves hunt there."

Nathan would not be deterred. "A hunt of our own."

She found herself just as eager for the challenge. "It gets colder the farther north we go. The right environment for ice fields."

"North it is," he said with a smile. And something gleamed inside her as she answered it, the smile of shared expectation and eagerness.

From her coat pocket, she pulled out and then consulted her Compass. She thought about taking it from the chest in her cabin, the choice she had made. That day seemed a long time ago. Enough time for her to be reawakened. And discover the man she needed beside her. Within her, the rusty gates to her heart groaned as they slowly, slowly began to open.

"You're truly not cold?" Astrid's breath formed soft, warm clouds in front of her face. She pulled her heavy coat closer, then glanced down at his bare legs before focusing on the boulders she clambered over. A blush stained her cheeks.

That blush. Far too carnal to be girlish. He loved that he could do that to her, seasoned warrior that she was.

They climbed a rocky slope, nearing the top of a peak, but if Nathan did not see her breath hanging in the air, he wouldn't have known that the temperature was dropping. He felt insulated within the warmth of the Earth Spirits' magic, its elemental fire.

"It's refreshing," he said. "Cool against my skin." He didn't need the shirt he wore, either, but kept it on to prevent the pack from chafing his back. The moccasins, too, were almost unnecessary, but he kept them on. He pulled himself up another rock. The ascent was arduous, but it felt good to lose himself in movement, the simple demands of climbing when he became flesh and motion.

"I suppose making the transformation into an animal is easier," she said, "with such . . . scanty garments." Despite her heavy pack, Astrid moved fluidly over the rocks, taking the mountain as though born to it. "Less to remove."

"Liberating," he said. "Try it."

She chuckled, rueful, as she reached up to grasp the rock above her. "I can just picture me tramping up and down these mountains with icicles on my nose and my bum hanging out."

"So can I," he growled, assailed by images of her bare, supple legs, the creamy peach of her ass. As for the icicles on her nose, he'd have all of her warmed up within moments.

Then she cursed, softly, as she glanced up. He followed her gaze and joined her in a little bout of swearing.

A falcon circled high above them. Nathan's sharp eyesight revealed it to be the same falcon that belonged to the Heirs.

"They're tracking us," she muttered.

"Then we keep going forward."

Nathan and Astrid pushed themselves harder, climbing quickly, until they stood at the crest of the mountain. They gazed down into the valley below.

A plane of thick ice stretched along the bottom of the valley, its surface lined with crevasses. It looked to be about a mile across, bereft of life.

"Looks more gray than white," he said, surveying the ice's grimy surface.

"But it doesn't feel right, either." She planted her hands on her hips, frowning. "There's no magic here."

"How can you tell? A trick learned from the Blades of the Rose?"

"There is no trick to recognizing magic," she said. "Yet, when you are exposed to magic enough, as Blades are, you begin to get an innate sense of it."

"The totem could be buried," he noted. "There's a great deal of ice here."

"Do you remember when He Watches Stars said his medicine had been stronger lately? That something had changed?"

"I remember."

"I've felt it, too," she said, her expression grave. "This strange . . . rupture. As if all the magic in the world suddenly became amplified. I do not know how or why or even where this feeling comes from, but I know it is real."

He nodded in acceptance. "And you sense no such magic here," he said.

She gazed back out at the ice field huddled at the bottom

of the valley. "I cannot. I'm not an Earth Spirit, however. The totem's Source magic is within *you.* You can find it in yourself."

Recognition hit him. "So *that's* what that was."

She raised a questioning brow.

"Ever since I arrived at the trading post, I've been hearing this voice. A voice that wasn't a voice. Urging me toward the mountains, saying that it was waiting for me. It grew stronger the closer I came to the Earth Spirits' territory."

"Yes," she said softly. "That is the magic of the Earth Spirits, of the totems. It's within you. The moment I met you I . . . felt it. I feel it now."

They stared at each other for a long moment, golden awareness stretching between them like spiderwebs—finely wrought but incredibly strong. He stepped closer.

Her hands came up to press against his chest. "The question," she said, "is not whether I can feel magic in you. It's whether you can sense magic *here.*"

He took a reluctant step back, but there was a peace within him. She understood who, what, he was, and his connection to magic. He could free himself with her, and that was a gift he never thought to possess.

Nathan turned and contemplated the ice field, trying to open himself and his beast up to whatever energy or power lay within the land. He was a creature of magic, had seen magic with his own eyes, felt the call of the mountains.

He drew in a breath and the beast caught the scent and presence of the ice, the rocks, even the caribou miles away, heading toward a fresh place to graze. Astrid's warm presence beside him. Magic had its scent as well. The Earth Spirits' village had been alive with it. A sharp spice. It was more than a fragrance, it was a feeling, bright and shadowed, that drew along his every fiber, every nerve, and deeper.

Opening himself further, he sensed magic pulling him toward it. But not here. Here was its absence. A void as lifeless as ice.

"The totem's not in this ice field," he said at last. "We are close, but this is not the place. Farther north."

She smiled at him. And just kept getting more and more lovely. "There, you see? You did it." She turned and began to pick her way down the rocky slope, nimble and sure as a tawny cat.

Did she know? Following her down the mountain, Nathan felt it, its gleaming tendrils tugging on him. Within Astrid glowed magic—not the kind of Sources and totems and Earth Spirits, but a magic that was entirely and uniquely hers.

Albert Staunton paced the edge of the Heirs' encampment. He hated that the farther north they went, the less daylight they had for travel. Just ahead of them was Astrid Bramfield and the shape changer. Almost within his grasp. So the falcon had revealed to Bracebridge, who had translated the bird's shrieks. If the Heirs traveled all night, the Blade and Indian would be his by tomorrow.

"We shouldn't be stopping," he snapped to one of the guides.

The mountain man didn't look up from cleaning his rifle. "Can't travel at night," he said, then spit out some tobacco juice dangerously close to Staunton's boots. "Too dangerous."

"But you know this country!"

"And that's why I know only a damn fool goes stomping around at night. Sure way to get a man killed."

Staunton, irritated, looked toward the two other men he'd hired as guides. Maybe one of them could be persuaded to lead the Heirs after sundown. But all of them shook their heads and muttered about Englishmen who hadn't got a lick of sense when it came to mountain life.

Aggravated, Staunton paced over to Bracebridge. The mage had built his own, smaller fire a small distance from the larger campfire, where Halling and Milbourne now sat. The mage tossed handfuls of herbs and vials of powders into the flames, mumbling incantations. Duchess, Bracebridge's nasty-tempered falcon, perched nearby on a fallen tree, and her master's spellcasting made her shake out her wings and dance from foot to foot. Staunton made sure to stay clear of the falcon. She enjoyed biting.

Bracebridge threw what looked like toenails pulled from a dog's paw into the fire. Thicker smoke poured forth, black and acrid, swirling into the shape of a wolf. The mage smiled as his falcon gave a shriek. But when the smoke broke apart, Bracebridge cursed. He scowled when he saw Staunton watching him.

"I've almost got it," the mage said.

"We don't need 'almost,'" Staunton answered, causing Bracebridge to frown. "This mission is critical. You know that."

"Who do you think helped activate the Primal Source?" Bracebridge shot back.

"Me and Gibbs," replied Staunton.

"I had a hand in it, too."

"Hardly." Staunton kicked a piece of wood into Bracebridge's fire, sending up a small flurry of sparks. "Doesn't matter," he continued, when he saw the mage begin to argue the point. "There is still so much more to learn about the Primal Source. That's why we must succeed here. If Edgeworth's plan is to come off, we have to have the Primal Source completely in our power."

Bracebridge sorted through the satchel he was never without, full of potions and powders. "Never thought that black-tempered puppy would be at the head of our organization."

Staunton made a grunt of agreement. Jonas Edgeworth had taken over the high-ranking position within the Heirs after the death of his father, Joseph, in Greece. He'd never been a particularly promising prospect—impulsive and moody—and when he had returned from the failed Heirs expedition in Mongolia, terribly scarred, unwilling to leave his home, no one believed he would ever involve himself in the work of the Heirs again. But all that had changed when Bennett Day had killed Jonas's father. The worst betrayal came from Jonas's sister, London. She had not only taken Day as her husband, she'd become a Blade. Some even whispered that she'd been involved with her father's death.

Now Edgeworth had emerged from his seclusion, burning with a newfound hatred for the Blades. He vowed to punish and destroy them. He swore to complete his father's ambition: to make Britain master of the globe. And the Primal Source was key. Once the Heirs unlocked all of the Primal Source's secrets, they would be unstoppable. And the Blades would be annihilated.

Which suited Staunton's needs. But before that could happen, he had to reach one Blade in particular.

"Hey, boss," one of the guides said, coming to stand at Staunton's shoulder.

"Not 'boss,'" Staunton clipped. "It's 'sir,' to you." He hated the informality of North Americans, their appalling notions that all men were equal, with no respect for rank or birth.

The mountain man seemed disinterested, unless money was involved. "Hey, sir," he said, the word laced with mockery, "thought you should know, me and the other boys noticed awhile back but we wasn't sure 'til now."

"Noticed what?" Bracebridge asked.

"We're being followed."

"Blades?" asked Staunton, turning to the mage. He'd anticipated that other Blades might appear. Those damned gadflies had a way of showing up even in the most remote, godforsaken corners of the globe. The Heirs were prepared, though. Once Bracebridge perfected his spell, they would be even more prepared.

"Just one person," the guide said. "An Indian woman. Ain't nobody else but her."

Staunton felt a flare of irritation. He didn't have time for importunate Natives. "What the hell does she want? Money? Whiskey?"

The guide shrugged. "Don't know. She ain't coming forward to say. Want me to go after her? I could bring her back to camp, make her talk." He rocked back and forth on his heels, eager. The prospect of capture and torture seemed to thrill the mountain man.

"No, don't bother." Staunton waved his hand, dismissive. "She's just some red-skinned beggar whore. We have more important tasks that demand our attention."

"If you say so." Visibly let down, the guide trudged back to where he and his fellow mountain men were busy gnawing on plugs of tobacco and telling stories of killing bear. They all groaned in disappointment when word came back that the Indian woman was to be left alone.

"Maybe you should let him go and get the squaw," Bracebridge suggested. "I think he'd like the entertainment."

"He can amuse himself when we have what we've come for." Little interested in discussing hexes and spells with the mage, Staunton strode off. He couldn't leave the encampment, however, not without a guide, and those laggards weren't moving. So there was nothing to do but pace back and forth, knowing that he was punishingly close to fulfilling his every ambition.

Nathan followed Astrid's gaze as she glanced up to the darkening sky. The day was already drawing to a close. "We'll have to make camp soon," she murmured.

Camp meant bed, and bed did not mean sleep. Not to him. Not with her. Two days. It had been two days since they'd made love, and he'd felt every minute since then like needles of fire. He liked anticipation as much as any man, but there was anticipation and then there was torment.

It didn't help that she seemed to be thinking similar thoughts. Throughout the day, he'd feel her eyes on him. Need and desire in her gaze that she tried to disguise but couldn't. They hadn't touched once since their kiss. In fact, they had barely spoken since the ice field, and it was a strange silence, not quite comfortable, not entirely uneasy. Weighted.

He glanced around. The ground was rocky and sloped, a poor choice for camp. "Not here."

"The valley below should furnish a good place. Should be warmer, too. For me, anyway," she added with a small smile, "since you're equipped with your own furnace."

He was burning, all right. But like hell would he pull her to the ground and take her impatiently in the dirt. He'd done that once before. He wanted more. He would show her what they could be capable of.

The bottom of the valley furnished a welcome surprise. A lodge, of wooden poles and green moss, standing in a forest clearing. It was roughly the size of her single-room cabin, though taller. No smoke came from the opening in its roof. As Nathan and Astrid circled the lodge's perimeter, he scented the air.

"No one's been here for weeks," he said. "Abandoned?"

Astrid peered into the open doorway, one hand resting on the butt of her revolver. "The Stoney have these lodges scattered around, and I guess the Earth Spirits do as well. They are for travelers. No one lives in them permanently." She slipped inside, Nathan right behind her. Light filtered in through the hole at one end of the roof. Remains of a fire lay just beneath the hole, and a few bowls were stacked against the wall, near a large iron kettle. The ground was covered with soft hides.

She walked to the remnants of the fire and, slipping the straps of her pack off with a grateful groan, knelt down. "Anyone is welcome to use these lodges," Astrid explained.

"Not anyone!" cried a shrill voice in Nakota.

The fire blazed to life.

Nathan leapt to Astrid, trying to shield her, and she stumbled back, pistol drawn, right into Nathan's arms.

"Show yourself," Nathan growled.

"I am here!" The fire leapt and sparked, growing in size.

Both Nathan and Astrid peered closer at the fire. The flames shaped themselves into a rough approximation of a face—two scowling eyes and a sharp-toothed mouth.

"An elemental," Astrid breathed, straightening. She stood still, pressing her back to Nathan's front.

"The guardian of my people," cried the fire spirit. "You must leave this lodge at once, outsiders!"

Nathan didn't care for anyone, not even an elemental, telling him what he could and could not do. "And if we don't?" he challenged.

The fire roared bigger, and Nathan, shielding Astrid with his body, pulled her away so that she was wedged between him and the wall. He hissed as the flames singed his skin. Then the flames receded. "Stay and be roasted," cackled the fire spirit.

Astrid tried to edge around Nathan. "Perhaps we should go."

But he wouldn't be deterred. Sharing this lodge with Astrid, sleeping on hides, and enjoying the luxury of a real roof and some damned privacy was exactly what Nathan wanted. "'Your people?'" Nathan repeated to the elemental. He blocked Astrid's path. "The Earth Spirits."

"Do not despoil their name by speaking it!" The fire spirit flared with indignation.

"I can't despoil their name when I am one," Nathan answered.

"You?" The elemental looked skeptical, if flames *could* look skeptical. "I sense the coldness of the white men's world around you."

"Look deeper and watch." Nathan cast off his pack and removed his clothing. Astrid avidly watched him disrobe, and he vowed to make good on the hunger in her gaze. He let the change come over him, and it happened within the drawing of a breath. So much faster now. He could do it with ease as Astrid looked on, no more fear of vulnerability. Now a wolf, he circled the fire and nipped at its smoke before transforming back into a man.

The fire spirit actually appeared apologetic, burning a little redder. "Welcome, welcome, Brother Wolf! This roof is yours. My flame is yours. And," the elemental added, with a wink of one glowing eye, "your mate is welcome to my heat as well."

Nathan, securing his breechcloth, gazed at Astrid, who watched him with trepidation and desire. "Thank you, Guardian," he rumbled, "but tonight, she shares my heat."

Chapter 10

By Firelight

She still marveled that he'd gone after her. He might have done the same with anyone, not content to let another fight for him or his people. And he was determined. He would not have taken kindly to being left behind.

He'd gone after her, and not only for these reasons. It was *her* he pursued. And, damn them both, she wanted him to. During the day, her thoughts had been full of their quest, but now, finally taking further moments for herself, he was all she could think about, all she could feel. In her mind, her heart, her body.

Astrid watched Nathan as he entered the lodge, bearing the iron kettle full of water, drawn from a nearby creek. The heaviness of the large pot, combined with the weight of water, caused the muscles in his arms to stand in curved, potent relief as they strained against his shirt. She followed the fluid, strong grace of him as he moved. He maneuvered the kettle toward a metal stand placed over the fire and set it down.

"Not too hot," he warned the fire spirit. "We want warm water for bathing. Don't cook us."

"Yes, Brother Wolf!" the elemental chirped, happy to be of service.

Astrid nodded her thanks when he crouched nearby, forearms braced on his lean thighs. "That was something I always missed," she said, "when I was on a mission for the Blades. Baths." Using her knife, she cut away at the tough outer skin from thistle roots. She'd also gathered some glacier lilies, dandelions, and violets to supplement their dinner of cutthroat trout, and the flowers lay spread upon a blanket. An Arcadian meal.

He watched her work, smiling slightly, and as a soft drizzle began outside, the lodge filled with languorous domesticity. She felt both at peace and restless, a curious but not unpleasant combination.

"The grime never bothered me," she said, "when we were in the middle of it. A bit of dirt was nothing when facing man-eating Fijian bird demons, or Heirs' bombardment. But as soon as things slowed down a bit, there was nothing I wanted more than a good, hot bath."

"No tubs here," he said. "You've got two choices: a thorough but cold plunge in the creek, or a warm but partial rinse here."

She glanced out the doorway, where dusk turned the forest into purple shadows and icy rain pattered against the tree trunks and onto the woodland floor.

"A rinse," she said, fighting a shiver. "I've got a bit of soap in my pack. Not my favorite, Pears, but it will do." She stood and, with a small bit of coaxing, the elemental provided a second, smaller fire, over which she spitted and roasted the fish.

"I want to hear about it," he said, following. "Your missions for the Blades."

Settling down closer to the fire, Astrid pulled off her coat and set it aside. "You want to hear about that? Truly?"

He folded his legs beneath him, muscles in his thighs and calves catching the firelight. "I do. It's not just our own mission we're undertaking, but the Blades, too." There was nothing dissembling or counterfeit in his tone, his face. He was honestly interested.

She shrugged. "Nearly five years' worth of missions. I wouldn't know where to start."

"Anywhere. Your favorite."

A sudden smile touched her mouth. "Oh, that would have to be tracking the Zägh through the Eastern Anatolian mountains."

"The what?"

"Zägh. It's an enormous bird, but it has a human face, and it can speak. It knows the secrets of the universe—Michael and I had to be sure the Heirs couldn't capture the Zägh and force it to reveal its knowledge."

"Dangerous?"

"Very." And her heart spiked with excitement to remember.

"Tell me what it looked like."

"Wings as wide as this lodge," she said, opening her arms. "Talons the size of wagon wheels. It took a little piece of me here"—she touched her fingertips to her back—"but spoke beautifully, like a troubadour."

And so, for the next who knew how long, Astrid recounted for Nathan her many adventures as a Blade of the Rose. She thought perhaps he might grow bored or restive, but he asked numerous questions and seemed as rapt in the telling of the tales as she was relating them. They ate their meal of fish and flowers as she drew pictures in the air with her words and hands. So many places she had been, from the icy wastes of Russia to the arid plains of Abyssinia. All of them as wondrous as any storybook could promise, and more, because they were real, and she was real, as real as her need to explore and learn everything she could. And he understood.

Nathan laughed when she recounted her attempt to disguise herself as a beardless youth in Amideb, only to attract the attention of the city's most sought-after prostitute. He frowned, serious and intent, when she described the siege between her, Michael, and the Heirs on the rocky coast of Portugal, only to have the Source they guarded captured by a smoke demon summoned by the Heirs. Small victories and cutting defeats. And the homecomings, to the Blades' Southampton headquarters, where Blades would gather in their ramshackle parlor and trade stories and compare scars, boast and guffaw, sometimes mourn, drinking whiskey and tea and eating plates of Cook's celebrated cinnamon biscuits. Until someone was called away on another mission, and it began all over again.

"You're smiling," Nathan said, leaning back on his elbows, his legs stretched out to the side. Handsome legs, solidly muscled, the worthy subject of a master sculptor.

"Am I?" she asked, surprised.

"Been smiling almost the whole time we've been talking."

"No wonder my cheeks ache." She pressed her palms to the sides of her face as if to keep her smiles at bay.

He considered her, eyes warm and gleaming. "It's wonderful to see. Beautiful."

She ducked her head, suddenly shy in a way she had never been, not even as a girl in her Staffordshire village. Something about this man, direct and unafraid in his intentions and desires. His insight into her was both frightening and glorious. She hadn't wanted someone so close, fitting inside her as a hand slides into a glove, warming the cool leather. Not only one body within another, but another's self snug against her own. She did want, she did not want. And this . . . peculiar man . . . fit. Not with perfection, because that was impossible, but there was a certainty in him that she recognized. She had opened herself to him, yet not fully. There were parts of herself she still hoarded. He wanted everything of her and would give her everything of himself. She had but to unlock her innermost chambers. The key was in her hand. And she hesitated.

"I admit that I . . . miss it," she confessed as she looked down at her hands in her lap. "Being a Blade."

"But that doesn't go away, does it?" he said. "It's a part of you. Anyone can see that. Can hear it when you speak."

"I tried," she said, wry. "Tried to forget, to pretend I could just cast it off, like a dried, dead husk." She could not believe the words coming out of her mouth, things she had dared not admit to herself for years, yet here, in this warm forest lodge, with *this* man, she felt the bolted cabinet within her open on rusty hinges, releasing clouds of dust and memories and truths.

"Not dry and dead," he said. His voice was low and rough. "Alive. As you are. No other woman so full of life as you."

She raised her gaze up to his and the intense heat shining there. Smoky tendrils of long banked desire wove through her, turning her flesh sensitive, making her want. Want so badly her heart began to flutter in the aviary of her chest, in time to the throb that centered between her legs, sultry.

I don't know what I'm fighting.

"I think . . . ," she said, her breath scarce, "that I should like . . . that bath now."

He said nothing, but his nostrils flared as she rose up and drifted toward the large pot of water.

"I kept it warm for you," piped the fire spirit. "Not too hot, not too cold."

"Many thanks, kind spirit," Astrid murmured, while Nathan continued to stare at her with a hunger that nearly stole her ability to think and move. "You have been so helpful."

The elemental flared, pleased with itself and the service it had rendered. Its flames curved into a grin.

"Would it be possible," she continued, addressing the fire spirit, "to keep the fire burning but have your gaze averted?"

The flames pointed down in a frown of confusion. "Gaze averted?" the elemental repeated. "You mean, look away?"

"Yes," said Astrid, locking her eyes with Nathan's. She

knew precisely what she was asking, what she wanted. "Some privacy for Brother Wolf and me."

There was a minute pause as both the elemental and Nathan took in what she said. Nathan's eyes narrowed.

"Oh," yelped the fire spirit, turning red. "Yes, yes! I can do that. Let it be known that I am hospitable in everything!" With that, the face within the flames vanished, but not without sending Nathan another wink.

Which left Astrid and Nathan alone. They had a large pot of warm water, a roof, a soft hide floor, blankets, and the whole night. The Heirs were out there, she had no doubt, and tomorrow brought a thousand dangers, a thousand doubts, but tonight . . .

Tonight, the key gleamed in her hand.

"In my pack," she said, "are some cloths."

He retrieved them and stood in front of her within seconds. Already, his chest rose and fell with the speed of one who had been in full pursuit. Firelight carved him, the clean blade of his nose, the hollows of his cheeks, the sensual fullness of his mouth.

"Let me," he said. He tugged her shirt from her trousers and began undoing the buttons. As her skin was revealed, each long finger gently brushed against it, creating fever bursts.

She glanced down. He had already removed his moccasins. Beyond that, he wore only the hide shirt and breechcloth—which, she noticed, already pulled tight against the growing hardness of his erection. She knew he wanted her, but to see corporeal evidence made her head light and her pulse erratic.

"I'm not used to being tended. I always . . . took care of myself." Her skin prickled with sudden bashfulness, knowing that she spoke of more than removing clothing.

And he understood. He growled, "I will give you everything. Take off your boots."

She raised a brow at his commanding tone. A bath had been *her* idea, after all. Still, with the hunger and raw need in his voice and eyes, echoing what she felt turning her bones liquid, she was willing to concede. Just this once.

So she pulled off her boots and socks and threw them aside. Both barefoot, he became taller, and she had to tilt her head back farther to look up into his eyes. She did not feel overwhelmed, yet there was a subtle shift between them, the delineated borders between male and female that served to draw them closer together, polarized.

He resumed unbuttoning her shirt, a frown gathered between his dark brow as he focused on his task. The loosening fabric brushed against her nipples, already beaded into sensitivity. She bit her lower lip at the sensation. Then the shirt was open, revealing a slim column of skin that ran, uninterrupted, from her throat to below her navel. He dragged one fingertip down this expanse, a line of fire.

Nathan peeled the shirt off of her, delicate but forceful in his movement, and let it drift to the floor.

"Ah, God," he sighed, ragged.

She was bare now, from the waist up, and let him look his fill. And he did look. Not just at her breasts, but everywhere: arms, shoulders, the bows of her clavicle, her ribs forming arcs beneath her skin. She realized she was much thinner than fashion dictated, if fashions were much the same now as they had been four years ago. Life in the wilderness stripped away extraneous flesh. Pampered, soft women, of yielding, plush limbs could never endure. Only strength mattered here. So she was not ashamed as Nathan looked at her lean body, but proud that she had the mettle to survive.

What he saw, he liked. His rasped breathing and the straining length of his cock within the breechcloth told her so. And she was glad. She wanted his desire.

"Touch me," she said.

But he gave his head a small shake, almost as if waking. She scowled. What was he doing? Would he just strip her and stare, letting her burn? She felt exposed, undefended, and fought the urge to cover herself. Let him see her. She must. For him. For herself.

He saw her struggle, and admiration showed in his face at her willingness to keep herself open to him. He took up one of the cloths and dipped it into the kettle of water. Then, with deliberate, unhurried strokes, he drew the wet cloth over her bared skin. Everywhere he touched grew warm, and not merely from the water. Starting with her arms, then, rotating her, over her back, and then he returned to her front and ran the cloth along her throat. She watched him. His eyes were black, black and sharp as obsidian knives, and he drank in the sight of her with a voracity that made her tremble.

He dipped the cloth back into the water and then, at last, drew it over her breasts. Warm, damp fabric cupped her, rubbed deliciously against her nipples. She did not try to stop her soft moan. Yet he did not linger there. Instead, he moved the cloth over her ribs and in circles over the top of her belly. Astrid wanted to curse in frustration at the methodical pace, which only served to build her need higher.

Then he cupped her breasts with his hot, capable hands, his fingers coming up to play over her nipples. She stiffened, arched, and when he bent and took one nipple into his mouth, his tongue lapping at it, she hissed and threaded her fingers into his hair, pressing him closer. Each lick reverberated through her and concentrated between her legs, where she sweetly ached. She could come from this alone.

The exquisite torture ended. He straightened as she made a choked noise of protest. His eyes were heavy-lidded as though to bank the conflagration within them, his lips wet from his ministrations.

"Now me," he rumbled, handing her the cloth.

The fabric soft and damp in her hands, she realized he

would bare himself to her as she had done to him. A show of trust. That he could allow her access to all of him.

His shirt was made without buttons or fastenings of any kind, for ease of removal when shifting forms. She let her hands drift underneath the soft hide garment and hover just over his skin. He growled. But it was a tactic she could not adhere to for long. She had to touch him. Her palms flattened against his flesh, and she allowed them freedom to explore the masculine topography they discovered. Everything she felt was burning hot, satiny smooth, and solid as faith.

More growling came from him, and did not stop as he watched her hands on him. She pushed back the hide shirt, and he helped by practically tearing it off. Then there were no obstructions for her to look and touch as much as she pleased. And she pleased. How completely male he was. With one hand, she ran the wet cloth over him, and the other traced patterns of desire over his skin.

Experimentally, she scraped her teeth over his pectorals, nipped lightly at the ridges of his twitching abdomen.

He snarled, then snatched the cloth from her hand. "Not so quickly," he panted. "I want this to last." As he dipped the cloth into the kettle, he said, "Take off your trousers."

Her heart jumped as a surge of arousal filled her. "Aren't you supposed to tend to me?"

"*You* have to do it."

He would see her stripped entirely, in every way. Ensure they both savored each touch, each sight.

This was not the simple quenching of bodily desire. It was much more. She unfastened her trousers and pushed them, and her drawers, down past her hips, until she stepped out of them and cast them aside. Now she was entirely nude. She glanced up to see him watching her with an intensity that verged on frightening, if it wasn't so exciting.

Reverential, he knelt before her and ran the cloth over her hips, down her legs, and back up again, his touch devotional and, she suspected, somewhat proprietary. She pushed that thought from her mind, focusing instead on the sensations he created, the demand in his eyes.

"Such incredible legs," he murmured. "A huntress."

"And you are my prey."

"I'll let you catch me." He turned her around and ran the cloth over her buttocks, and the growl he made was loud and insistent.

A shocked laugh escaped her mouth as she turned back to face him. His growl wasn't poetry, but she didn't want flowered words or exotic metaphors. She wanted real desire. And she had it.

He rubbed the cloth over her belly. She began to shake as need built. The cloth dipped lower, over her mound, but only brushed it before going lower to the insides of her thighs. She could not tell if the warm trickling she felt there came from the cloth or her own devastating arousal, yet when she heard him draw in breath through his nose and curse his approval, as though scenting her, she had her answer. She widened her legs to give him further access.

Nathan rewetted the cloth and then finally worked it over her, between her cleft, through her folds. Against the fiery bud of her clit. She gasped and had to grip his tense, rippling shoulders to keep herself from collapsing.

"Oh, Lord," she whispered. "Yes."

"More," he rumbled. With one hand, he gripped her buttocks, and the other held her hip as he drew forward, bringing his mouth against her.

She . . . she screamed. There was no way to stop herself. Sound burst from her as pleasure decimated reserve. No hiding. His tongue dipped into her, discovered her, a living, wet creature that knew her most secret self. He teased, he adored, he consumed. She writhed as he held her fast in his hands, more and more noises of ecstasy being pulled from her like silken banners. Her fingers tangled in his hair.

She felt walls around her collapse. She wanted to flee, retreat, but his onslaught saw no cessation, no mercy. It was too much, this pleasure. It was not enough. Dimly, she thought, *How can I protect myself?* And the answer—she could not. He refused her withdrawal. Sensing her fear, he plunged onward. Sucking her clit into his mouth, stroking it with his tongue. And she arched into it, offering herself without regard for anything, including her heart.

The orgasm hit her so hard, it robbed her of sound. She could only bow backward like a supplicant as he held her upright. Awareness ebbed. All she knew was pleasure, the pleasure he gave her.

Her legs shook, yet she managed to remain standing. His breath feathered across her belly as he pressed kisses there, kisses that soothed as well as inflamed. She was torn between wanting to curl up into a protective ball and throwing her arms around him with murmured endearments. Who was she? What did she want? He kept chipping away at the barriers she'd flung up until she was left with the mystery of identity.

He started to draw her down to where he knelt, but she resisted. He wanted completion, the joining of their bodies. But if he devastated her, she would do the same to him.

Instead of joining him on the floor, she reached down and took back the cloth.

He looked up at her, surprised, disgruntled, and, yes, excited. Astrid saw that he liked the fact that she had enough strength to resist capitulation, that she could meet his force with her own. The angles of his face became even sharper. His breath came in quick, shallow bursts.

"On your feet," she commanded.

He didn't have to obey. The power of this man radiated out like the mountains. No one could make him do anything he did not want to do. Yet he chose to submit. To her. She could not fail to understand the significance of this.

Eyes locked with hers, he slowly rose. Waves of heat and masculine desire rolled off of him, and a subtle, spicy scent that brought to mind animals in the springtime, feverishly mating in celebration of the sun. She caught his scent and it played havoc with her senses. She thought herself satisfied after her climax, but fresh need slammed into her. A bond tightened, one that existed between her and Nathan alone.

Once he stood, it was time for her to act. She undid the breechcloth and it fell to the ground. Her attention was wholly riveted by the sight of him, naked, aroused, firelight sculpting him into the primal essence of man. When they had coupled before, on the banks of the rapids, she had been impatient and frenzied, hardly seeing anything but her own demands. Now she saw him completely.

His erect cock was . . . beautiful. Full and gently curved, stretching up toward his navel. It twitched with impatience under her gaze, which nearly made her smile, but she wanted him too much.

Astrid's eyes climbed back up to his and he stared back at her. What she saw made her tremble.

Everything. Everything was there, in his eyes. He held nothing back from her. Not his desire, not his fear, not his heart. He had given it to her, whether she felt prepared for the gift or not. He was completely unafraid in his vulnerability, and this made him even stronger.

He is much more courageous than I.

She knelt down and, after dousing the cloth in the water, began to slowly bathe him. There was no superfluity of flesh on him. He was all sinew and strength. His skin glowed like polished copper, glistening, as she rinsed him. She followed the lines of his tense thigh muscles, the hard curves of his calves, up the back of his legs to his firm buttocks.

She moved back to face him, still on her knees, and ran the damp cloth down the length of his penis. He hissed, but she did not stop, gripping the shaft and stroking it with the cloth, then moving lower to gently cup his sac.

A string of curses from him, and then he could not speak, because she dropped the cloth and, without hesitation, took his cock entirely into her mouth. Almost entirely. He was too large to fit completely, so she wrapped her hand around the base. God and goddess, the taste of him . . . Musky and male. Exquisite.

She ran her tongue along the shaft, then teased over the perfect round head, where she tasted a pearl of salt. She began to dip her head down, to take him in farther, but he pulled away.

Astrid gazed up at him through hazed eyes. Why had he stopped her?

"I want," he rasped. He quickly bent and took up the end of her braid. In an instant, he'd undone the plait and combed his fingers through her loose hair. It fell about her shoulders in golden waves, teasing the tops of her breasts, and he rumbled his approval. She became, suddenly, woman embodied. And also entirely herself, without the armor of her braid.

She took him back into her mouth, and lavished him with the gift of her tongue and hands. She was rewarded for her efforts with yet more hoarse swearing as he shook and tensed and gleamed with sweat.

Nathan cupped the back of her head, lightly but firmly guiding her. His hips moved as she sank down, then up, and down again. Again, she tasted it, the saline drop that proved he was close to release, and she sucked at it. She needed his climax, his surrender, as much as he did, even as renewed slick moisture gathered in her pussy. She could come simply from bringing him to orgasm. She would.

Then he pulled from her mouth and was kneeling before her, eyes afire, breath labored. "This. Now." His hands still cupping her head, he brought them together in a kiss.

She clung to him as they savaged each other's mouths. They were almost too hard with each other, scraping teeth and crushing lips, and yet it was a gorgeous savagery that they both needed. Their bodies pressed close, both slick with sweat, and at that full contact of skin to skin, they groaned into each other. His cock urged against the curve of her stomach, hot and thick. She cradled her hips into him. He found his way between her soaked folds, sliding between them. Never had she been so wet, so wanting. She had pried herself apart for him, and he had done the same. They could not hide from each other.

She gripped his shoulders, lifting her head to whisper, "Us, now." She pressed him down, and he went willingly onto his back, legs stretched out, arms open to receive her.

Astrid took a moment just to look at him. This man who had roared into her quiet life, who had pulled her from her solitude through force of will and strength of heart. Lying on his back did not lessen his potency. He commanded from wherever he had positioned himself, and now he beckoned to her, a demand but also a request. This was her choice.

She was afraid. She wanted to leap. She hesitated, knowing that what they were about to do meant much more than their earlier, frantic lovemaking. Going back into the fortress she had constructed around herself would be impossible after this. And that meant inviting more pain.

"Brave," he murmured. "You are brave, Astrid Anderson Bramfield."

"I am," she said. And she straddled him. Their gazes held as his hands gripped her hips and she braced her palms on his shoulders. Then she sank down onto him. They both moaned.

He filled her, filled her absolutely. Yet she could no more be still than hold back an avalanche. She had to move. She slid up and down, and each stroke caused more and more of herself to dissolve. It could not be possible for anything to feel this good. Yet, as he had proved many times, to him, there was no such thing as impossible. Because pleasure kept soaring higher and higher, as she rode him and he thrust up, and they were joined, deeply joined.

Astrid lost the power to hold herself upright. She draped herself over the hard length of him, and he wrapped his arms around her. With her head tucked into the curve of his neck, she gave herself over, freeing herself. Her release tore through her, violent, merciless, and wonderful. She threw her head back and cried out, tightening around him.

He gave her a few breaths, only a few, before rumbling, "Everything, Astrid. I'll give you everything."

He pulled out, a devastating loss, and she found herself positioned on all fours, while his hands stroked everywhere over her slick body and she writhed. He was behind her, one hand again gripping her hips, the other pressed against her belly. He paused, the sleek head of his penis positioned at her opening. She tried to push herself back, to impale herself on him, but he kept himself just out of reach.

"What do you want?" he demanded.

She growled her frustration.

"Tell me what you want," he said, voice hard with hunger. When she faltered, he would not show her pity. "This?" he rasped, stroking her with the head of his cock. "Is this what you want, Astrid? Tell me."

"Yes," she moaned.

"Tell me."

"I want you," she finally gasped. "I want you inside me. I want you to take me. Now."

"Now." Dark satisfaction. And he plunged into her. Again. Again. Hard, insistent thrusts that made her pant. The hand that splayed on her belly moved lower, so that his rough fingertips rubbed at her clit. His other hand drifted up from her hip to wrap in her hair. She felt her head tugged back, baring her throat.

Sounds came from him, animal sounds that thrilled her beyond reason. Against her back, she felt him cover her with his body, and then his teeth on her neck. Holding her as he marked her and made her his mate.

Impossibly, she came again. Moments later, she felt a sweet stab of pain as he bit her harder while emptying himself into her. Wracked with pleasure. His release went on and on. Then he was wrung out, panting, cradling her to him as he nuzzled her.

Slowly, they sank down to the ground together, so that they were cupped like shells. His hand pressed against her chest as if to feel the racing of her heart, the heart over which she no longer had control.

He rummaged through the packs until he found blankets and a canteen of water. Laying upon the hide floor, she drowsily watched him moving around the lodge, barely able to move except to turn her head slightly to follow him.

He cast shadows upon the wooden walls, recalling the beginnings of the world, when mankind was newly aware and walked upon the earth, creating, becoming legends. There was Nathan, gleaming skin, muscle, and bone, and there was his shadow, his dark shape that was an enchantment.

Nathan saw her watching him and smiled. What a smile he had, rare but brilliant. This man was himself enchantment, for she felt herself submerging under his thrall. Not a binding spell, but something that required an offering from the one being beguiled—a lock of hair, or a handful of trust.

Her eyes closed as he lay beside her. The sound of the canteen being set down, and then the rustle of woolen blankets draped over them both, their damp, worn bodies. He arranged their limbs so they twined together, and the energy of him beside her, around her, hummed beneath her skin.

They took sips from the canteen. The cold water was a blessing after the heat they had created. Then the canteen was put aside and he enfolded her in the tight satin of his arms.

"Tell me about your life in Victoria," she murmured.

"Not much to tell. Had little life outside my work."

"You said something about helping a Chinese laborer win a case against a white banker. Were all your cases like that?"

He sighed. "Not enough. Usually I handled property disputes, but I hunted down the cases nobody wanted. I'd go to the Indian settlements or Chinese camps and ask around, search out who'd been wronged and try to make it right. At first, I'd have to convince them that I could and would help—they were scared."

"Of what?"

"Retribution. Or that they might bring a grievance and wind up getting punished. It happened too often."

"You said 'at first,'" she noted. "Something changed."

She felt his smile on the back of her neck. "The Indians and Chinese started to seek me out after I won some cases. Mostly theft. Some slander—an Indian running a chowder shop lost his business when a white competitor scared off his customers, told them he cooked cats instead of fish. But I got the Indian restitution, and he reopened his shop. I said he didn't have to pay me back, but he insisted on bringing me free chowder every day."

"How was the soup?"

"Delicious. But the partners at the firm didn't like what I was doing. Too many dark people lingering around the office. I wouldn't stop, though. So I had my pro bono cases come at night, after the office closed down. Doubled my workload, but I didn't mind."

Incredible, the fighting spirit of this man. Who had made love to her as if she was more precious than sunlight.

She remembered the very last time a man had held her after lovemaking. Michael, the night before he died. In their tent, in the wilds of Abyssinia. He'd been unusually forceful that night, making love to her with a demand that bordered on prescient, as if he knew he would not get the chance again, and needed to brand the sensations and feelings into her and him.

His touch had faded from the memory of her skin. She tried to call it back, but too much time had passed. He was a warmth around her heart, but not a physical presence. The first time she had forgotten something about him—whether he had read *The Woman in White*—she collapsed into grief that lasted weeks. And then, then the process of losing him became . . . if not easier, then more familiar.

"Are there many Blades of the Rose who are husband and wife?" Nathan asked. As if he read her thoughts and knew she was thinking of Michael.

"Only a few," she answered softly. "Arabella and Douglas Westby. Cassandra and Sam Reed. The Chattons, but they're retired from the field now. One Italian couple. I never met them. Though men and women can be Blades, we aren't actively encouraged to marry one another. Makes things a little more . . . complicated."

"No man wants his woman in danger."

She rolled over, propping herself up on her elbow, and scowled at him. "And if the woman's a better shot than he is?"

His face had softened with repletion, the corners of his eyes turning up with a smile. "Then he makes sure she has enough bullets." He ran his fingers back and forth across her collarbone, pausing to circle the hollow of her throat.

Though she was sated, his touch still called forth sparks along her skin. "No Blade ever goes into the field alone. We always travel in groups of at least two. And *no one* wants to see their partner injured. Male or female."

"But it's worse for a man to have his woman hurt. It's his job to safeguard her."

Astrid raised a brow. "I thought that, rebel that you are, you'd have a bit more progressive attitude."

"Some things are carved into a man's blood and bones." His smile faded as his look grew more pensive. He raised his eyes to hers. "Like the need to protect his mate."

She did not answer. Instead, she turned onto her other side and tried to settle, his arm around her a comfort and a weight. Unease shifted through her. They had shared something profound, something of such complexity that she could not yet face it. He had given her all of himself, and she had done the same, but years of protecting the damaged beast of her heart could not be undone in a night, a week. How long would it take before she was ready to fully bestow everything? She feared she would need a lifetime.

Chapter 11

The White Lake

The Métis guide was frightened. He didn't want to show his fear, so he withdrew into impassivity, but Catullus could tell by the thin set of Jourdain's mouth, the whiteness of his knuckles as he held his reins.

"This is the Earth Spirits' territory," he said tightly. "They are whispered about amongst the Métis. A secretive people of strange power. They keep themselves hidden."

"And no one has ever explored their land before?" Catullus asked.

"None have dared."

"I'm no stranger to traveling through forbidden territory," Catullus said. "We will avoid populated settlements. What is the power of the Earth Spirits?"

Jourdain had been brought up a Christian, and he crossed himself now. "I cannot speak of it. Too dangerous."

Catullus wished he had more information, but wouldn't press the guide. Blades often rode into unknown situations, and he knew that he was as prepared as he could be for any eventuality.

As they rode through dense woods and across open meadows, Jourdain cast alert, anxious glances over his shoulder, worried that any moment could bring an attack from unfriendly Natives.

Catullus's fear had another origin.

"She won't be happy to see us," he said to Quinn, riding beside him.

"I never met Mrs. Bramfield," answered the Bostonian. "But you two are friends."

"It has been a long time since she answered any of my letters. She made it clear she wanted to be left alone."

"Doesn't matter if she's happy or angry," said Quinn, plainspoken as always. "There's no choice now."

Catullus sensed the presence of the Heirs. It followed them like a rotten miasma. Heirs had traveled this very trail not long ago, and he hoped like hell that he could reach Astrid before they did. He checked his Compass again, a now habitual gesture, and the needle pointed him onward. To Astrid.

"No," he said grimly. "There is no choice."

It rather alarmed Astrid how easily she awoke beside Nathan, their bodies entangled. She hadn't shared a bed with a man in years, and now here she was, feeling the solid weight of him all around her. He felt very different from Michael, who had been a big man with the large, golden-haired limbs and chest of his Saxon ancestors. Nathan was sleek, streamlined, and tight, with a dark nest of curls at his groin. And they fit well together. She did not feel trapped with his arms around her.

They were attuned to each other's needs and rhythms as they readied for the day. Bathing, dressing, and breakfasting quietly, yet the silences between them were not awkward. Only when he tried to gather her close for a kiss did she pull on the threads of tension, giving him her lips but unable to give him more. Words and vows tried to spring forth, yet she could not give them voice. She clutched her heart close, reflexive. As he drew back from the kiss, she saw in his gaze a flare of demand, then deliberate—but temporary—letting go. His eyes swore that he would not retreat.

After thanking the fire spirit for its hospitality—and receiving demands of a return visit from the elemental— they set off northward. The elemental knew from the conversations of the lodges' past guests that an ice field lay within half a day's steady trek. So it was with greater confidence that she and Nathan pushed onward toward their goal—the first totem.

They hiked as quickly as terrain and body would allow. Speed was everything. The Heirs could be just up ahead, or directly behind. The falcon was absent from the sky. No way to know where the Heirs were, and uncertainty urged Astrid and Nathan forward.

"There," Astrid puffed at midday. She pointed ahead to a mountainous ridge. "An ice field is just on the other side of those peaks. I can see the snow along the mountaintops."

"And I can smell the ice," he said, drawing in a deep breath. He drew straighter, vigilant and ready. "I feel it, too. That magic neither of us could sense before. It's here."

They shared a glance of growing excitement. Their goal was near. But they were just starting to ascend the peaks when Nathan halted, growling.

"The Heirs of Albion," he snarled. "They're close. Very close."

Astrid's hand immediately went to the butt of her revolver as her pulse spiked. Her rifle was loaded and standing by, too. A sound overhead brought her and Nathan to look up. "*Jävlar,*" she cursed. "Is that—"

"The same damned falcon," Nathan said, teeth clenched. "We'll stand and fight them."

"No—we can't. Our best chance is to get to the Source before they do." She pointed to a notch in the mountains surrounding the ice field. "We'll take that pass into the valley."

Before he could argue, she began scrambling up the rocky slopes as fast as she could, using a long walking stick she had fashioned en route. Haste made her stumble slightly, but she moved quickly and heard Nathan behind her. Icy, gritty snow clung to the mountainside, soaking through her gloves as she hauled herself up. The air thinned, became brittle. Her breath gusted in short, white clouds.

The peak grew steeper, and soon, she and Nathan took turns helping haul each other up the rocks. She glanced down the mountain and swore again, her blood chilling further. A group of seven riders approached from nearly the same route she and Nathan had taken. The thick fir trees clustered at the base of the slopes blocked her view. She fumbled for her spyglass.

"No time," Nathan said. "We're almost at the top."

Damn, but he was right. So she pushed herself on, the Heirs too close, but too far to know which of the bloody bastards pursued. Didn't really matter. She hated them all.

The pass was a cleft between two peaks, lined with snow. They had to pause here, to catch their wind. She looked around for boulders or something else to block the pass, but found only more and more icy snow climbing up the sides of the mountains framing the gap. No trees to be found above the timberline. Damn, again. Her mind whirled, trying to figure a solution.

"Astrid," Nathan said, placing a hand on her shoulder. "Look." He turned her around so that she faced into the valley.

She did look, and her breath caught in wonder. The valley, shaped like a bowl, glittered in the sunlight as a vast field of gleaming, pure white ice stretched across the bottom. Blue cracks spread throughout the ice, a network of crevasses running like rivers of air. Impossible to tell the depth of the fissures, whether they were shallow or deep, and how many of them lay beneath the surface of the ice. The valley was encircled with snow-covered mountain peaks. Astrid stared at them for a moment, squinting against the glare. The shape of the mountaintops, how each one had two sharp spires, and square rocky projections pointed into the valley, recalled something . . . .

"Wolves," she said aloud. "They look like the heads of wolves."

A low chuckle from Nathan. "By God, they do."

"The white lake where the pack hunts," Astrid murmured.

"I feel it, too," he said. "The magic of this place. It's as if someone lit a hundred lamps beneath the surface of my skin. And," he added with a grimace, "it's hard as hell to keep from changing into the wolf right now."

The totem's doing. "Can you hold off?" she asked with concern. "We need our packs, but I can't carry them across the ice on my own."

He gave a clipped nod, though she felt the tension radiating out from him, the barely restrained beast trying to break free.

"Let's get this totem," he gritted, "before the Heirs reach it, and before I lose control."

Descent into the valley had its own challenges. Too slow across the snow, and they sank. Too quick, they skidded and slid, knocking into rocks that thrust upward. The heavy pack on Astrid's back wanted to pull her into a tumbling fall, a sure recipe for breaking her neck. By the time they reached the ice field at the base of the snowy slope, her legs shook and sweat chilled her back as she clung to her walking stick. Nathan, too, looked winded.

"I hear them," he panted, bracing his arms on his bent legs. "They left their horses at the base of the mountains. Now they're just about to reach the pass."

Astrid cursed as she wiped a sleeve across her forehead. "If we could just block the pass, they couldn't breach the valley, not for a little while, at least. But there's nothing to use. The only thing in abundance is snow."

Overhead, as if to jeer at them, the falcon shrieked.

Both Astrid and Nathan stared at each other as a notion occurred to both of them simultaneously, eyes widening.

"Avalanche," they whispered.

* * *

God, she was perfect.

When this was over and the wolf totem was safely in his hands, Nathan would show courageous and cunning Astrid just how damned perfect for him she was. He wouldn't let her withhold anything of herself, either. She'd shown him clearly last night that she was as bound to him as he was to her. And damn, with the totem's force urging his beast on to a fever, it was all he could do to keep from claiming her here, on the white, shimmering ice.

But that was going to have to wait. Right now, they had an avalanche to start.

"Sound triggers avalanches," she said. "And the snow along the pass is in a lee. It's built up. All we need is enough noise to get it going."

They both glanced around, as if a cannon was going to conveniently appear. None did.

She slid off her pack and took up her rifle. "I could try and shoot into the snowbank. That might cause enough percussion to get it going. Otherwise, I can't think of anything that might work."

Nathan had a sudden inspiration. He also pulled off his pack, but then removed his shirt and started to tug off his moccasins. In response to her quizzical look, he explained, "There's something I can do, as a wolf." Shoes removed, he undid the breechcloth. Hell—he might not feel temperature as strongly as he used to, but being naked on an ice field was not kind to a man's most precious belongings. At least Astrid didn't seem to notice. "When I give the signal," he said, "fire."

"And the signal will be?"

"I'll . . . bark." He glowered at her when a smile tugged on her lips. "Not a word."

She mimed sealing her mouth, but that didn't stop her eyes from twinkling like sunlight upon the gray ocean.

One last warning glare, and Nathan finally unchained the beast. Too long confined, lured by the totemic spirit within the ice field, it burst from him, savage and joyous. Skin turned to fur, the softer flesh of hands and feet hardened into paws, teeth lengthened. It would have been painful, had it not felt so damned right. Magic was everywhere here, it flowed through him in glowing currents.

He glanced at Astrid. She smiled encouragingly at him, then aimed her rifle up toward the pass. Nathan heard the voices of the Heirs, sensed their bodies and greed moving up the other side of the mountains, poisonous. They wanted him. They would hurt Astrid. He wouldn't let that happen.

He gave a low bark. Astrid shot and the bullet slammed into the snow with a loud crack. At that same moment, Nathan gathered up all the magic he could contain within himself. Pushed it out as he threw back his head and howled. His wolf's howl—the sound of his soul. Wild and rebellious.

And angry. He'd never howled before, didn't know what he was capable of, but the sound he made was aggressive, coarse. Deafening. *Stay back. This is my land. My woman.*

At first, nothing happened. Stillness. Then a deep boom, as if a huge charge of dynamite exploded. Both Nathan and Astrid started from the sound.

"There," she gasped, pointing up, but Nathan already saw.

A white torrent plunged down the tops of the mountains, gathering in size and speed as it thundered into the pass. Sheets of snow plummeted in waves, throwing up clouds of ice, and shaking the ground. Even far at the bottom of the valley, Nathan felt it through his paws. He crouched in readiness.

The pass quickly filled with snow. More snow overflowed, but it mostly spilled down the other side of the mountain ridge before the avalanche slowed, then stopped. With any luck, the Heirs of Albion would be buried in white, cold graves. At the least, thcy couldn't force their way into the ice field for a long, long while. Not quite as satisfying, but he'd take it.

Astrid's own vicious, victorious smile revealed she felt the same way. "A hell of a howl," she said, grinning as she turned to Nathan. With a laugh, she added, "Your tail's wagging."

He made a *woof* of mock irritation. Then readied himself to change back into a man. They still had to locate the totem in the midst of all this ice.

"Wait," she said, sensing what he was about to do.

He cocked his head to one side, curious.

"Remember the legend?" she asked. "Once at the white lake, we were to lend our voices to song. Not sing, but howl. Wolves circle their prey when they hunt—just as the mountains here are in a circle. And when you howled a moment ago, the sound echoed from every peak. Save one. I'm not certain which, though. You should hear it better than I."

He gave another soft bark, understanding. Turning so that he faced into the valley, the mountains encircling the ice field around him, he howled again. Then waited, listening.

As she had thought, the sound echoed around the valley, bouncing off each of the wolf-headed mountains. Except one. It stood on the far side of the ice field, but the strange and complete absence of sound returning from this peak was immediately evident to Nathan. Once he had confirmation, he shifted back into his human form, though it was difficult to corral the beast in him.

"That one," he said, donning his clothes and nodding toward the mountain. "Not only did it not echo, the sound just moved straight past it. Almost as if it wasn't there."

"That is where the wolf pack is incomplete," Astrid deduced.

He saw what he had to do. "And I must complete it."

Easier in theory than practice to cross an ice field. The whole of the icy plain was riven with cracks and crevasses, faults that hid their depth beneath thin crusts of ice. A wrong step could send either Nathan or Astrid plummeting twenty or more feet into white nothingness. They tethered themselves with rope, and she shouldered her rifle in order to carry a short pickax to chop into the ice, should one of them start to fall. Only one set of grappettes in their gear, and Nathan insisted that Astrid wear them to keep her footing secure.

"What about you?" she asked.

"My footing's better without shoes." The ice on his bare feet felt cool but not bitter.

So she strapped the four-spiked grappettes onto the front of her boots, and, with the aid of her walking stick, they began to slowly, slowly cross the ice field toward the peak that did not echo.

The rope stretched between them as she would step, test the strength and depth of the ice with her walking stick, and then move on, Nathan behind her. His beast snarled at being led, yet the man knew it wasn't a leash but a source of strength. Only a damn fool would go bounding across the ice field without guidance or care, and he wasn't that.

"It's good there hasn't been any recent snowfall," she said over her shoulder. "Hides the crevasses. Very dangerous. Makes every step uncertain."

"I know something about uncertain steps," he said, dry. "Every day in Victoria was that for me, a constant danger."

Astrid threw a wry smile of understanding over her shoulder.

"This icy crossing," he said. "It's like life."

"How?"

"Two people, bound together," he said. "Doubt in each step should the world collapse underneath them. And if one falls . . ."

"The other would plunge down, too," she finished.

"Or be the means of their salvation."

She paused for a moment, giving him a charged look that

sent heat and awareness sparking through him, before turning back to their trek.

She was careful as she moved over the glacial field, but confident. Alert, yet unafraid. Becoming, with each foot forward, more the girl she had been before the death of her husband, as well as the wise woman she had developed into afterward. Maybe Nathan had helped shape her change. He wanted that. He wanted to imprint himself onto her as she had marked and changed him.

His reverie snapped as a patch of ice Astrid tested suddenly buckled. A chasm opened. Slabs of ice shattered, spreading out in a lace of fractures. The ice beneath her feet shuddered, then fell. She fell with it, too fast to use her ax for purchase, too fast to speak even a word. The tip of her braid disappearing into the ice was the last he saw of her.

Nathan threw himself back to stop her fall. He dug his heels into the scraping ice and skidded, scrabbling for a foothold. He grabbed the rope leading from his waist, felt the burn of it sliding through his palms. Then there was a hard tug as the length of rope played out and she dangled in free fall. He gritted his teeth against the pull, the combined weight of her and her heavy pack suspended in midair.

Holding tight to the rope, he turned over and dragged to the edge of the chasm, knees digging into the slippery, granular ice. He braced himself above the opening in the ice, arms shaking as he wedged against the frozen breach, and looked down. Astrid hung over a crevasse that seemed to stretch down into oblivion. Hot terror coursed through Nathan as the rope between them groaned, threatening to split.

"Drop the pack," he called.

She looked up, naked relief in her eyes, then frowned. "Our gear—"

"Your life," he shot back.

Seeing that there was no choice, she began to tug the straps off her shoulders. Her efforts ran up the rope, pulling on him with sharp jerks, and he tensed his entire body to brace them both. Sweat chilled his back. He clenched his teeth with effort until his jaw throbbed. Then, relief. The pack fell from her, careening down into the icy void. He didn't hear it land.

She still held her pickax and stuck it into her belt, her rifle over her shoulder.

"Climb," he yelled.

Lips tight, she did. Hand over hand, she drew herself up the rope, while Nathan supported her weight over the opening. She was a hell of a lot lighter without that son-of-a-bitch pack. When she was high enough, he leaned back and hauled up the rope, arms aflame. After several agonizing minutes, her hands appeared at the edge of the crevasse. He grabbed her slender, strong wrists and pulled until he groaned.

Then she was out, and he wrapped his arms around her with enough force to make her gasp. Dimly, he realized he was shaking. But not from effort.

Her arms were also around his shoulders, her fingers interlaced behind his neck, as they both half lay, half sat at the rim of the chasm, breath coming in frantic puffs, hearts knocking against each other. Finally, she raised her head, and he pulled back enough to look into her flushed, lovely face.

"Another typical afternoon for the Blades of the Rose," she murmured.

"Insanity." He brushed his lips over hers.

She returned the kiss. "No better way to live."

"Or die," he countered.

Her look was surprisingly thoughtful, considering she had just been dangling over frozen death minutes earlier. Thoughtful, but the darkness that once might have overtaken her did not appear, and that gladdened him. She murmured, "That's the price for an extraordinary life."

"And we are extraordinary."

"We are, without a doubt."

* * *

The walking stick was lost to the icy recesses of the chasm, so the rest of the journey across the ice field to the base of the mountain proceeded at a crawl. He wanted to run, knowing the Heirs of Albion were barred only temporarily from the valley.

"And they'll find a way in," Astrid said with grim certainty. "It is merely a matter of when."

But haste meant even more danger. A slow progression, then, much as Nathan, and his beast, hated it. The closer they got to the mountain without an echo, the more the animal in him lunged and clamored for release. He was already worn almost to breaking from the trek in, and recovering Astrid from her tumble into the ice. Forcing down his beast was yet another strain on his taxed will.

Almost at the base of the mountain, he halted. She turned when she felt the tightening of the rope.

"Here," he rasped. Energy ran through him, demanding, alive. His body was a lightning rod, every cell vibrating, the beast pushing hard against the boundaries of his flesh and spirit.

"Where?"

Hand trembling, he pointed. To an enormous crevasse ten yards ahead.

They carefully approached the slender, deep fissure and peered in. The opening was narrow, barely enough for a man to slide through, but they could see that, past the first feet through the thick ice, the crevasse opened wider. How much wider, neither could tell. Everything within looked blue and frigid.

"Down there, somewhere," he said.

She lowered onto her stomach and looked into the crevasse. "I think I see a floor of some kind. Made of ice. And something embedded in the ice."

Nathan removed his pack. "I'm going in."

She looked up at him, alarmed. "No, you aren't. I am."

"I don't want you down there." Fear and anger hardened his words. "Too dangerous."

Astrid surged to her feet, glowering, just as angry. "I appreciate the sentiment, but your chauvinism is unacceptable. Do not forget that *I* was a Blade for years, and, until a short while ago, you were merely an attorney. I have experience with Sources. You do not."

"I won't let you down there alone," he snarled.

"And I won't let you go by yourself, either."

They glared at each other, at an impasse. She would never consent to wait for him. A compromise.

"We go together," he finally gritted.

She didn't answer, but went to his pack and pulled out another length of rope, along with some loop-topped metal spikes. "At least two-timing Edwin was prepared," she muttered. She fastened one end of the rope in a strong knot through one loop. With the side of her ax, she hammered the spike into the ice several feet from the opening of the crevasse, then untied the rope from her waist and spliced it to the end of the other rope.

"I go down first," he said, stepping forward and taking the pickax and remaining spikes from her. He tucked them into the waistband of his breechcloth.

The scowl she sent him was ferocious, but she did spare him a dispute. As he neared the entrance to the chasm, gripping the rope, her anger was replaced by apprehension. Nathan realized how she more easily showed her emotions now—very different from the stoic hunter he'd met at the trading post—and it pulled fiercely on his heart. Just before he lowered himself into the crevasse, she took one of his hands and gave it a hard squeeze, her lips compressed whitely into a line.

He held her gaze with his own, an unspoken promise, and then lowered into the entrance of the rift.

The first few feet pressed in close, hard walls of ice, and he hammered in a spike, through which he threaded the rope.

He went down a little farther, and the opening widened. Gusts of glacial air spun around him, blue and mineral, and he found himself within an ice cavern some two dozen feet across. The walls shimmered and glowed without sunlight, sparkling as if made entirely of diamonds. As he climbed down the rope, Nathan thought he saw, within the swirling patterns in the ice, forms of wolves. Running, hunting, heads back in eternal howls. His throat tightened as his heart raced. Beautiful. This place was part of him, and it was beautiful.

The rope did not quite reach the icy floor. He jumped the few feet remaining, and, finding the floor solid and stable, called up to Astrid, "I'm down."

He waited just below as she climbed down, ready to catch her should she fall. Yet she was strong, and didn't lose her grip. Soon, they were in the ice cavern together, staring at the wolf shapes as their breath puffed.

"This is marvelous," she breathed. "But where is the totem?"

He felt the pull, at his feet, and looked down. His heart shot up, and plunged. "There."

She followed his gaze and murmured her own mixed blessing and curse.

Embedded several feet farther within the ice at their feet was the totem. A wolf tooth, the half length of his forearm, belonging to a wolf of mythic size. Nathan tried to imagine the beast to which it belonged. A being of legendary scope that walked the surface of the earth back when magic covered the globe, unhidden, omnipresent. Power emanated from the totem in unseen waves that shook Nathan to his core.

"Someone else had the same idea," Astrid whispered.

Curled close to the totem, also trapped within the ice, lay a human body. Caught in its moments of final agony as it stretched its hand toward its prize, thwarted.

Thick ice made it difficult to tell whom the unfortunate treasure-seeker had been. Astrid knelt and wiped at the ice with her glove. "This body could date to last week or a thousand years ago."

"Whoever, whenever he was, he failed."

"We won't," she said. Absolute confidence energized her voice as she stood.

He warmed himself on the flame of her strength, knowing it to be the equal of his own. "We have to break through the ice."

She stepped close, and in the shimmering icy light, her face became ethereal, like a star come down to earth. When she reached toward his breechcloth, excitement and confusion battled.

"Here?" he asked, raising a brow. Not that he had any objections. He'd have her whenever, wherever he could. Even an enchanted ice cavern. Still, the Heirs could arrive at any moment, and the wolf totem played hell with his self-control.

"I want another kind of cleaving." With a wicked smile, she pulled the pickax from the band of his breechcloth and held it in both hands.

A rueful chuckle. "Cat," he teased.

"This is a better claw," she said, hefting the pickax.

"Sharper, not better." He moved to take it from her, but she stepped back with a shake of her head.

"I'll chop, you stand ready, should anything crop up. We don't want what happened to our friend"—she nodded toward the body imprisoned in ice—"happening to us."

Even though he was physically stronger than her, he let her experience in dealing with Sources guide them. He took a few paces back, giving her room. She positioned herself over the totem.

Astrid adjusted her grip on the handle, raised the ax, then brought it down with a forceful chop into the ice. Shards of ice flew, splintering mirrors. The chiming sound echoed off glassy crevasse walls. Tiny chips of ice sparkled on her cheeks, her eyelashes. Again and again she lifted and swung the ax, hacking into the hard, frozen surface, each blow hard and sure. Nathan wondered if he was a deviant because he found the sight of her wielding a pickax to be potently arousing.

He felt it before she did. A rumbling under the ice. "Stop," he commanded.

No sooner were the words out of his mouth, than the ice over the totem erupted into spikes of ice. Nathan lunged forward and pulled her back, just as a spear shot up precisely where she had stood. Like an avenging spirit, the frozen body pitched upward, impaled on icy lances. Jagged pieces of ice stabbed through the corpse's eye sockets. Its clothes were ancient, hides covered in beading and quills, but the body shattered into pieces as it was thrown aloft, pierced.

Nathan sheltered Astrid with his body, but they both stared as the totem rose up, borne upon the spikes. Liberated from its icy vault, the wolf tooth was even larger, nearly the length of Nathan's forearm, and wickedly white and sharp. Someone had threaded a thin leather thong through its wider end.

The totem was free of the ice. At once, the ice stopped rising, leaving a circumference of frozen spikes, with the totem in the middle.

He and Astrid shared a wondering glance. Could it be so simple? The Source was being delivered right into their hands.

He started toward it. Her hand on his arm stopped him. "Look—the ice," she breathed.

Groaning, splintering, the ice shifted. The gleaming spikes gathered around the totem, arranging themselves into—

"A mouth, a wolf's mouth," he whispered.

Like a wide-open jaw, the tooth and the icy spears gaped. Then shifted again. The jaw slammed shut as a huge wolf grew from the cavern floor, entirely formed of ice. The totem became one of its massive teeth. The rest was made of ice, but yet it had the motion and movement of a living wolf. It turned crystal eyes to Nathan and Astrid, its paws gouging the ice at its feet. Then growled. He'd never heard a sound like it, a sound of magic and threat, reverberating in the crevasse.

Astrid pulled from Nathan's arms, her gun out, ax clutched in her other hand.

Spikes of angry fur rose along the giant wolf's back as it bared its teeth in a snarl. It crouched, ears upright, tail stretched out so that it scraped the icy walls. The unspoken language of hostility and dominance.

Nathan stepped forward. The damn beast would have to get through him to reach her, and that wouldn't happen. He became pure instinct, barely having time to throw off his shirt and breechcloth before his own wolf burst free with a ferocious snarl.

It didn't matter that the ice wolf dwarfed him. Bristling, Nathan faced the other wolf, his own sharp, ready teeth brandished. His growl thundered deep in his chest. Human thought vanished. Aggression, the need to protect Astrid and dominate this challenging wolf—all he knew and felt. He gave his beast complete freedom.

He and the ice wolf circled each other, their growls filling the cavern. The moment stretched, tensed.

With a snap of its immense jaws, the ice wolf feinted, aiming for Nathan's throat. Astrid, behind him, cocked her gun and brandished the ax, ready to take on the other wolf if necessary. But Nathan wouldn't yield, standing his ground. The other wolf's ploy revealed to be merely that, a ploy. The wolf pulled back and hunkered into a crouch, as if taunting Nathan to try the same gambit.

Nathan lunged. He launched himself at the ice wolf with a growl. Its gullet, vitals. He would tear them out if he had to. Ice or flesh. Didn't matter.

But Nathan's teeth met only air.

The ice wolf's crouch had shifted into a cower. Its tail lowered and ears flattened as its back curved into an arch. The wolf's head sunk down to the ground, muzzle pointed up at Nathan.

When Nathan advanced, still growling, the other wolf rolled onto its back, tucking up its paws and exposing its stomach. A plaintive whine threaded from its throat.

"It's submitting," Astrid whispered, but Nathan knew instinctively.

The ice wolf opened its jaws wide, not to bite, but to reveal the totem within its mouth. It waited like this, patient.

Nathan's beast would not relinquish its hold on him, too lashed to aggression and animal demand, so, denied words, he gave a soft bark. Astrid understood, and edged forward, until she stood in front of the submissive wolf. She started to reach toward its open maw, but cast a quick, questioning glance at Nathan. He ducked his head briefly in assent. The ice wolf wouldn't dare hurt her, the alpha's mate.

Astrid stretched her hand out and wrapped it around the totem. The moment she touched the enormous tooth, the ice wolf dissolved into cold vapor, swirling around her and Nathan. When the mists disappeared, she was left holding the totem, the thong dangling down as if waiting to be looped around someone's neck.

They were alone in the crevasse, with only the broken, frozen human body for company.

Without the threat of the ice wolf, the shift came over Nathan at once. He pulled himself up from the ground to stand on two feet, heart pounding, power surging through him. He felt immense, the size of planets, utterly without fear.

Astrid gazed down at the totem in her hands, her expression reflective. "This is the first," she breathed. She glanced up at him. "The first Source I have seen or touched in five years. And we recovered it, together." Her mouth curled into a smile, then, with a last, almost wistful look, she handed him the totem.

Gravity and strength in his hands, the history of generations of wolves, the nocturnal forests and joy of the hunt. Pups whelped, wolves challenged, mates taken, birth and death. Millennia racing like clouds over the moon. The new threat of man, the subjugation of wolves into dogs, servants. The wolf of the woods remained free as Nathan was free. But here, cupped between his human hands, was the means to preside over all Earth Spirit wolves. Their strength and ferocity and communion—his. If that was what he desired.

All wolf Earth Spirits his to dominate, so long as he held the totem. To be in command, no longer the outsider. A fierce temptation.

"Nathan?"

Astrid's voice, her hand on his arm, concern in her storm-colored eyes.

He forced himself to breathe calmly. "Keep this," he said, his hoarse voice more animal than human. He held the totem out to her. "It tantalizes me."

Astrid closed his fingers over the totem. "It belongs to you, and the Earth Spirits."

"I want to—it makes me—"

"I know," she said gently. "And that's why you must be the one to carry it."

He looked down at the totem, running his thumbs over the grooves in its smooth surface, the leather cord threading through his fingers. He drew in a breath, then straightened his shoulders and nodded.

"You held such power many times when you were a Blade," he said. "You held it just now, and didn't yield to its pull."

"I'm not immune," she answered. "But the feel of a Source's magical power in my hands is something I am familiar with. Familiar enough to let it go."

"And this," he held the totem up, and the crystalline light within the chasm limned it with silver radiance. "This is my challenge. My temptation." He gazed at the totem, the emblem and control of shape-changing wolves, saw its potential and his own. "I can face it. You've shown me things about myself—that I'm a better man than I had realized."

She stared at him for a long while, as if caught between

one breath and the next. Something shifted in her face, the further reveal of the woman beneath the cool warrior. Then she leaned close and kissed him. "The strength of you," she whispered against his lips. "You make me feel things. I thought myself incapable of feeling anything again. I did not want to. Yet you . . ."

"Anything," he said, low and sure. He kissed her hungrily. "For you, I'll do anything."

It did not seem strange to him that he should make such a vow here, in this white, enchanted place. Speaking his heart to Astrid within the frozen, glittering cup of the earth's magic, he was himself spellbound. And found no sweeter sorcery than what he tasted in her lips and saw in her eyes. They would face the next challenge, and all the challenges to follow, together.

Chapter 12

Alliances and Reunions

After Nathan dressed and everything was secured, they climbed out of the crevasse, bringing themselves up, blinking, into the sunlight like newborns. Their shadows cast blue monoliths upon the ice field as the sun moved across the sky.

Astrid watched Nathan wrap the totem in cloth before carefully packing it away. And if his fingers lingered on the Source for a brief moment, absorbing its power, she could not fault him. Such magic tempted many, even Blades. Especially Heirs.

As though reading her thoughts, he said, "The Heirs of Albion couldn't have taken the totem. The ice wolf would have protected it."

"Nothing is out of their grasp," she replied. She checked her rifle and pistol to ensure they were both loaded and ready. "One blast of Zhu Rong's Fist would have melted that wolf like so much slush."

Nathan stood, shouldering the pack. "Zhu Rong?"

"Chinese fire god. The Heirs have a cadre of mages whose only task is the conquering of dark magic spells."

"While the Blades of the Rose have only magic that is

theirs by right or gift." He shook his head, but smiled. "A bunch of madmen."

"Do not forget mad*women,*" she added, smiling back. Seeing him, standing straight and potent upon the frozen field, warmth flooded her. What a force he was, a force she could not long withstand.

"There's only one madwoman I won't forget." He stepped close, enveloping her with his heat, and kissed her. She felt yet another barrier around herself fall softly away.

The screech of a bird ripped them apart to glower at the sky. Circling high above them was the Heirs' falcon, reminding her and Nathan that they were hotly pursued.

"If only that damn thing flew lower," Astrid muttered, gripping the strap of her rifle.

"We'll have our hunt later." Nathan took her hand. "But we won't stay here to become prey."

The avalanche had sealed the most accessible route in or out of the ice field, so they had no choice but to make the arduous climb up the northernmost peak with no aid from trail or pass. Clinging to icy rocks, they scaled the mountain. The valley gathered cold winds to scour at their hands and faces, and even Nathan, warmed by the fires of magic within him, felt their bite. Alone, it would have been impossible. Working together, they pushed, pulled, cajoled, threatened, encouraged. When one slipped, the other was there to grab hold. When one could not muster enough energy to clamber over yet one more boulder, the other helped call forth untapped reserves of strength.

As they took a moment to catch their breath, clutching the side of the mountain, she felt the blood coursing through her exhausted body with a joyous wonderment. "This is what I missed for so long," she gasped. "Scraped hands, steep odds, steeper mountain." She glanced over at Nathan, who wore an expression of battered glee that matched her own. "Someone beside me for the ascent."

"The descent, too," he added.

They could not linger. In painful, slow increments, they took the mountain. No sooner did they reach the top, both her and Nathan panting and spent, then he whirled around to look back into the ice-filled basin. A growl sounded in his chest.

"The Heirs?" Astrid asked, leaning down so she braced her forearms on her thighs.

"They've breached the valley."

Straightening, she followed his gaze. She squinted and was only just able to make out several dark forms at the farther edge of the ice field. She reached for her spyglass, then cursed when she realized it was lost with her pack.

"They still have to cross the ice field," Nathan said. "Gives us time to move on."

Further words were not wasted. Without her pack, descent was easier, but she stayed close to Nathan as they wended down the mountain. Soon, snow gave way and trees appeared, the icy heights giving way to warmer Chinook winds blowing from the west. The warmth made her hands ache as they came back to life. By silent agreement, they pressed on, keeping conversation to a minimum.

Rocky spurs at the base of the mountain sloped into foothills, dotted with stands of aspen. White tree trunks, spotted with dark markings, rose around them as they pushed forward on legs shaking with weariness. The foothills rolled on ahead, and, as she and Nathan took another rise, she saw that a wide swath of verdant late-summer meadowland lay just beyond the hills. And past that, a range of austere mountains stretching up as if toward redemption. In the late afternoon light, golden and rich, the land became a wondrous, unforgiving heaven.

"I feel I've dreamt this place," Nathan murmured as they rested a moment. "Or seen it before."

"Perhaps in dreams, before you came here," suggested Astrid. "The buried part of yourself struggling to the surface."

"But I didn't dream that," he said, voice hardening as he

turned back. They both gazed toward the vale that ran along the base of the mountain ridge surrounding the ice field. From the green depths, something flashed. Then flashed again in a rhythmic pattern. Astrid's throat constricted as her heart attempted to leap out. She knew that pattern.

"More Heirs of Albion?" Nathan growled.

Her mouth oddly numb, she forced words out. "No. It's a signal. From other Blades of the Rose. They're here."

Her first instinct: Run. Hide. Take Nathan by the hand and flee with him, deep into the wilderness where they could not be found.

It was one thing to acknowledge that she was still a Blade, to take up their work again. Alone. Nathan fought at her side, and fought well, but of the two of them, only she was a Blade. Something altogether more weighty and momentous to join forces with other Blades on a mission. It made her return more concrete.

Four years. She had left them four years ago. And suddenly, time folded like paper so that those four years disappeared.

"How did they find us?" Nathan asked.

From her coat, Astrid pulled out her Compass and opened its lid. Its face stared back at her, the four cardinal points a small star in her hand. Each directional point was a different blade—pugio, rapier, scimitar, and kris—representing the many corners of the world and the many nations that composed the Blades of the Rose. "This. Blades can track each other with their Compasses. When I took it from my cabin, I never thought . . ." Ambivalence roiled within her. She both longed for the company of other Blades and feared it.

"Stay or go, Astrid."

Her gaze snapped up to him. He watched her, expression carefully neutral, but she could see within the gleaming blackness of his eyes that he knew precisely what she felt. The idea settled warmly low in her back, like a steadying hand.

"The choice is yours," he said.

The signal flashed again.

She gave her head a shake. He had shown her so much, not only revealing himself, but uncovering her, too. She drew a breath, taking strength from the resilience of her body. "What I fear, I must face," she said. "And," she added, wry, "it never hurts to have a little help managing the Heirs."

She turned the face of her Compass toward the light, creating her own responding signal. "I've answered," she said, lowering the Compass.

Nathan's mouth at the back of her neck sent heat through her, as his arms came around her waist. The lean potency of his body behind her. His sultry kiss, full of promise. She recalled vividly the night before, when he gripped her with his teeth as he plunged into her eager depths, and she shivered with need.

"You awe me, huntress," he murmured against her skin.

She drew in his praise, felt it nurture the blossom within her, the seedling of her heart. Yet she could not let herself grow too distracted. She signaled again to the waiting Blades, whoever they might be, and read their response. Wait there. They would join her soon.

"Who are you?" she signaled. Then lost her breath at the response.

Catullus. Catullus was coming.

Astrid slipped the Compass back into her coat with hands she fought to keep steady. She leaned back, using Nathan's strength to bolster her own—just this once. She had run and hidden, but now it was time to face her past.

"I'll be. She's answering." Quinn said this as if Astrid's response had been in doubt. In truth, it had been. Catullus half believed she would ignore his signal and slip away into the wilds, leaving her Compass behind and any means of tracking her.

No. She stayed. Her signal indicated she would wait for him and the rest of the party to catch up.

Catullus responded with the affirmative, his heart an ache in the confines of his chest. In a few hours, he would see her again, speak with her. And whomever she traveled with, since Jourdain had seen two sets of tracks—a man who walked beside Astrid. Questions elbowed against each other in Catullus's mind. He would soon have answers. He wondered whether he would want to hear them, after all this time.

"She's waiting," Catullus said to Quinn and the guide. He clicked to his horse to urge the animal forward, then pulled on the reins when he saw Jourdain was not moving.

The Métis didn't bother trying to hide his fear. A whitened hand on the pommel of his saddle, eyes wide. "I won't take you there," he said, voice strained.

Catullus and Quinn shared concerned glances. "Why not?" asked Quinn.

"I took you into the Earth Spirits' territory, and that's bad enough," Jourdain said. "But those foothills ahead, and the mountains, they're dangerous big medicine." He shook his head to dispel evil spirits. "If I took you there, I'd be sending you straight to hell, and me along for the ride."

"We can handle big medicine," Catullus said.

"Maybe so, but *I* sure can't." Jourdain walked his horse close to Catullus. "I know you're a smart feller, Graves. So I'm telling you now, best thing for you to do is turn back. Your friend's already lost."

"No," said Catullus. He fought down a tide of anger, knowing that the guide was only trying to be helpful, but Catullus could no more abandon Astrid than he could stop his mind from churning out new inventions. Both were necessary and unstoppable.

"Is there anything I can say to make you change your mind?" Jourdain pressed.

"No," Catullus said again. "I'm moving forward. Quinn?"

"Right behind you," the Bostonian answered without hesitation.

Jourdain's shoulders slumped. "That's too bad. I liked you folks." He brought his horse around so that he faced the direction from which they'd come. "I'll wait for you at the camp just beyond the big river. If you don't come back in a week, I'm moving on."

"I still have to pay you the rest of your fee," Catullus said.

But the guide held up a hand. "Keep it. It wouldn't be right, taking money from a dead man." Then he kicked his horse into a canter and rode off into the woods, not sparing a glance behind him in his haste to flee.

That left just Catullus and Quinn. And Astrid. The woman who had once been his dearest friend, now separated by a handful of miles and many years.

No need to bother with the ice field. Crossing it would take far too long, and, by then, the Bramfield woman would be far ahead. The Heirs struggled back up the pass and convened at the base of the mountains.

So close. They were so damned close, Staunton could taste the metallic flavor of success, gleaming like a knife against the tongue.

"Bracebridge," Staunton said, turning to the mage, "can Duchess slow them down?"

"Not yet," was Bracebridge's answer. "There's more work to be done there. But," he added with a growing grin, "I've got something else in mind to pin them down."

"Do it," Staunton commanded.

While the mage dismounted and rummaged through his saddlebags for the necessary materials, Staunton, the other Heirs, and the mountain men all impatiently waited. Each moment was precious time lost into the yawning maw of failure, which he would not abide. He'd worked too hard for this. Staunton refused any possibility other than success.

He heard something rustling in the scrub just a few yards from him. Something that sounded human.

He drew his gun. "Enough of this skulking," he shouted. He cocked the gun. "Out."

An Indian woman slipped out from behind the cover of the bushes. She seemed of indeterminate age, neither a girl nor a crone, with the tough bones of a hard life. No fear marked her posture or her face as she stared back at him, eyes dark and defiant. From her belt hung a well-used knife.

Everyone but preoccupied Bracebridge drew closer to see this wonder. Even the looks of pure, brutal lust from the mountain men did not dim the insolence of the woman's expression or stance.

"Put your gun away, white man," she sneered. Her English was remarkably clear. "Or do you fear one woman so much you must hide behind bullets?"

Muttering curses, Staunton holstered his gun. Like hell would he let some squaw shame him. "You have been following us. Why?"

"I seek a mutually beneficial arrangement." When one of the mountain men approached her on horseback, the chilling glance she sent him caused the guide to pull up short. Dispassionate anger clung to her like frost.

"What on earth could *you* have to offer *us*?" Richard Halling snorted.

"Quiet, fat swine," the woman said. "I will speak only with the chief of this war party."

Staunton almost laughed to see Halling turn purple with indignation, but was gratified that whoever this squaw was, she knew leadership when she saw it. And Staunton was the leader here.

The woman addressed him, though there was little deference in her tone. "You follow the path of the Earth Spirits' totems. So does your quarry. I know the legends. I can lead you to where they will go next, so you do not chase them like litter runts."

"We have means of slowing them down," Staunton said, nodding toward where Bracebridge labored over a spell.

"Would it not be better to have your prey come to you?" the woman countered. "Have the advantage over them?"

The idea appealed, hating having to chase the Blades, but Staunton was cautious. "How do you know where they are heading?"

"I was once a member of the Earth Spirits' tribe," the woman said, and her words grew bitter. "My brother, Winter Wolf, and I. We sought to keep the tribe's territory free of all outsiders, to protect the tribe from polluting strangers. Earth Spirits are the favored children of the Great Spirit. We should not have to endure the filth of ordinary folk. It is an insult!" Her copper cheeks grew dark with rage and hate gleamed in her eyes.

Everyone edged backward, even imperturbable marksman Milbourne, instinctively fearing this lone woman.

"Winter Wolf and I patrolled the boundaries of the Earth Spirits' lands," she continued, regaining some composure. "Other members of the tribe patrolled, but none had the courage as my brother and I. They simply chased the interlopers away. But we knew we had a duty to preserve our purity. Whatever unlucky fool stumbled into our path, Winter Wolf and I killed. We could not tolerate anything less than complete destruction of outsiders. And for that, for *that,*" she spit, "Winter Wolf and I were exiled."

Staunton could understand the squaw's need to preserve the integrity of her tribe, even if they were just a bunch of red-skinned heathens. Magical heathens, but still only savages. "But you were trying to protect your tribe," he said.

"Yes," the woman said, her teeth predatory as she snarled her frustration. "Yet the tribe did not see it that way. The chief felt we went too far, were," she jeered, "*cruel.* Iron Wolf cast us out. And the rest of the tribe agreed. They drove us from our lands, our home."

"Is your brother here?" asked Staunton. Having a wolf shape changer would be most useful, even if it wasn't Lesperance.

Raw sorrow marked the woman's face. "He is dead. Trappers murdered him when he had taken the form of a wolf. Now Iron Wolf and the other Earth Spirits owe me his life."

Too bad about the wolf changer. He would have been a good pawn. "Revenge, then," Staunton said. "You will guide us to gain retribution against those who wronged you."

"Justice, not revenge," the woman snapped.

Semantics, as far as Staunton was concerned. He eyed the woman, the severe set of her mouth, her hands curled with the need for vengeance. How trustworthy was she? He had no desire to wake up with a knife in his eye.

Perhaps Bracebridge could work up a spell to determine whether the squaw spoke the truth. Trouble with lies, though, was that many people were so strongly ensnared in their falsehoods, they believed their own fabrications.

Yet the idea of finally leading this chase, rather than lurching after Astrid Bramfield and her Native friend, held immense appeal. The Heirs of Albion were encouraged to exploit any advantage.

"She seems willing to help outsiders," Milbourne noted. "Even though she was banished for killing them."

A good point, and one Staunton wished he had thought of.

"Since my exile I have no people," the woman said. "No allegiances. Everyone is an outsider, as am I. My hand is raised only to extract retribution from those who were once my own."

"Very well," Staunton said, eager to retake command of the discussion. "You may guide us. But, be warned"—he jabbed a finger—"anything suspicious, and I'll set loose my men. They've been waiting patiently."

The mountain men grunted their approval, but quieted

when the woman shot them a gaze filled with unadulterated contempt.

"They may try," she said. Her hand rested on the hilt of her knife. "But I'd advise against it, if they value their stones."

The mountain men slid protective hands between their legs.

Staunton smiled. Even though she was an Indian, he rather liked this icy-hearted bitch. She possessed the precise attitudes valued in Heirs.

"Your name?" he demanded.

"Swift Cloud Woman," she answered.

He inclined his head. "You follow on foot, Swift Cloud Woman."

She nodded, as if expecting this.

"It's ready," Bracebridge called. "The spell is ready."

"Then get to it," Staunton yelled back without breaking his gaze from the woman. "It's time to take charge of this mission."

"You know which Blades are coming."

Astrid swallowed hard at Nathan's statement. He knew her far too well to miss her signs of unease, no matter how hard she tried to force them under a barrier of stone. As they waited together at the top of the hill, looking for signs of the Blades' progress, she made herself stand still rather than nervously whittle on fallen branches. Nathan crouched nearby, his forearms braced on his thighs, hands loose.

"One of them," she answered. "His name is Catullus Graves. English, like me. His family has long served with the Blades." A small smile crept over her mouth. "The Graveses are . . . extraordinary."

"Magic?"

"Intellectual magic. They are incredible inventors. The devices they create are beyond imagining. And Catullus may be the most brilliant of the whole clan. The things he can fashion, from seemingly ordinary objects." She realized she was smiling.

"And what is he to you?"

His question was deliberately casual, but she sensed the edge beneath it.

"A friend," she answered. "An old friend. Ten years now."

"A long time," he said, tight.

She saw in the hard angle of his jaw the unnamed, scarcely acknowledged fear. He never showed fear, not facing the prospect of death at the hands of the Earth Spirits, not against the huge ice wolf. Yet here, with her and the arrival of the Blades, was fear.

For the whole of Nathan's life, he had lived on the outside, not fully Native, not white. He belonged to no one and no place. Even the Earth Spirits had not truly been a home to him.

Yet *she* gave him a sense of belonging. He'd said so. His truest self emerged with her. A thought at once humbling and wonderful.

Now came Catullus, the embodiment of her past, of a world where she *did* belong. She might be lost to that world, that past. Lost to Nathan. The Blades were not his home, as they were to her. If she disappeared back into the Blades, what would become of Nathan? He might have no place, no home, granted once and then cruelly stolen away.

"You don't have to fight anyone for me," she said.

"Except you."

Oh, God. He leveled her with a few words and searing looks. She felt herself in a dizzying plunge, wanting the flight, worried about the landing. "I give as much as I am able," she said.

"I know," he answered.

Again, he demolished her. Such courage he had, to face uncertainty and the possibility of terrible hurt. She had not possessed the same, not for a long while. That was changing, however. In slow, tentative steps that might or might not be enough.

She began to speak, then stopped herself, frowning. She felt a change before seeing anything. Sticky cool moisture unspooled from the south, unlike anything she'd ever experienced here in the Northwest Territory—and she had been witness to many strange forms of weather.

"Look," he said, pointing toward the south. A damp, cold miasma began to creep over the land, thick and yellow.

"That fog is decidedly . . . not normal."

He inhaled. "Smells of . . . dirty river water and . . . coal smoke. No factories out here. Or coal-burning fires."

Astrid drew in a breath, and memory assailed her, followed shortly by a bolt of alarm. "It's a London fog."

Nathan scowled even as he started with amazement. "The Heirs' doing."

They watched as the low-lying fog rolled toward them, smothering everything in an impenetrable murk. Within a minute, she and Nathan found themselves enveloped in a sulfurous, clammy gloom. Trees scarcely a few yards away disappeared. Even Nathan, just beside her, grew hazy. The sun could not penetrate the fog, leaving Nathan and her trapped in a world of tawny vapor.

Astrid pulled her gun. "The Heirs will likely try to attack us."

"I can sniff them out," said Nathan. "No surprises. We take cover."

"We cannot. Catullus will be looking for us in this fog."

"You said earlier, if he's got a Compass, he can find you."

"I won't make it more difficult for him. He may have a Compass, but to him, this land is unknown. He hasn't got a wolf's senses to guide him. He could get badly hurt. I shan't allow that. And if you want to seek shelter, so be it, but I am staying."

They stared hard at each other, enshrouded in the mixture of smoke and mist, two forceful people coming up against the unyielding surfaces of their wills. Both of them, balanced atop the precarious ridge of tension. She refused to leave. He did not want to stay. Would he concede, as Michael might have done? Would he try to force her to submit?

Suddenly, this decision became so much greater than simply staying or going.

Eyes narrowed, he gave a curt nod, but began pulling off his clothing. "I'm not leaving you. But don't light a fire, and don't expect conversation." With that, he shifted into a wolf.

Another rampart within her gave way. Compromise. Astrid ran her fingers through the warm, soft fur at his neck. He rumbled under her touch.

She settled herself onto the damp ground, gun in hand, rifle across her lap, and prepared to wait for Catullus. But not alone. Nathan paced in alert circles around her, a sentry. Between the two of them, she felt they could face anything.

"What the hell?" Quinn's amazement penetrated the deep fog blanketing them.

"Son-of-a-bitch Heirs," Catullus muttered. "Brought some of the Thames with them."

The horses, unfamiliar with the sickly, unique properties of a proper London fog, whinnied and danced in fear. Both Catullus and Quinn held tight to the reins to keep the animals under command.

"Think they know we're here?"

"Hard to tell." Catullus removed his moisture-slicked spectacles and wiped them on a cambric handkerchief. "Even if they don't, we must get to Astrid as soon as possible."

"Don't know how we can do that without breaking our necks. We've got our Compasses, but they might lead us right into a gully—or worse."

Catullus's mind hummed with an idea. Of course, his mind *always* hummed with ideas, a family trait that caused most

Graves kin to sleep only a few hours at a stretch and ensured grumpy spouses. Catullus hadn't a spouse, much to his father's vexation, and seldom had a woman in his bed for longer than it took for both him and the woman to secure several hours of pleasure. He generally preferred to use the woman's bed for lovemaking, since it enabled him to return home and go straight back to his workshop. His lovers all knew this, and none tried the Sisyphean task of trying to make him stay. Still, he wished some woman, at some point, desired his presence enough to make the attempt. But that would then mean having to talk with them, connect with them in a way beyond the physical. And then . . . that's where his intellect failed him.

His brain could unlock any puzzle. Yet he could not solve the mystery of the hearts and minds of women.

He should consider himself lucky. He was unencumbered. Free to work as much or as long as he pleased. Free to go on missions without fretting about someone at home, worrying about him. If only he wasn't so damned lonely.

But that was inconsequential now. He and Quinn had to get to Astrid, and quickly.

Dismounting, Catullus held the reins of his jumpy horse and rifled through a bag on the packhorse. His fingers brushed an assortment of things—brass fixtures, tubing and wire, lengths of specially treated canvas. The usual organized jumble that composed his traveling equipage. One never knew what one might encounter when on a mission. At last, he found what he sought.

He pulled a length of what appeared to be ordinary chain from the bag. It resembled in thickness and material the kind of chain that might be used to counterbalance a large clock. A round lead weight was attached at one end of the chain.

Quinn eyed him with curiosity. "Going to chain up the fog?"

Catullus led his horse to Quinn and gave him the reins. "I can't do this too close to the animals. It will likely frighten them." He stepped away, putting distance between himself and the horses.

"Do what?"

Slowly at first, then with increasing speed, Catullus began to swing the chain in a circle in front of him. A low whistle sounded as the chain cleaved the air. The weight on the end of the chain kept its momentum.

"Something I have been working on," he explained to Quinn as he increased his speed. The fog around him swirled. "The metal in the links is a special alloy and shaped just right, like little funnels. Took me months to get the proper combination. It has the strength of regular iron, but it propels air with greater ability. Observe."

"Jezebel's drawers! Look at that!"

The haze through which Catullus spun the chain began to eddy, and then, gradually, the fog dissipated, forming a cylinder of clear air as wide as the chain's diameter.

"You're coring the fog like an apple," Quinn marveled.

"It's not absolute clarity," Catullus said, "but it should provide enough visibility to travel the mile between us and Astrid."

"Do I want to know why you had that in your bag?" Quinn asked drily.

"The chain creates wind," answered Catullus. "I thought we might need it, if we tried to sail on becalmed waters. I can lead us to clear a path, but you'll have to use your Compass to guide me."

"Can do. And we can trade places, when your arm gets tired." Quinn chuckled. "They said to me, 'Max, that Graves fellow, he's an odd one, but smart as a fresh dollar bill.' And they were right."

"Thank you, I think," Catullus murmured. As he carved a path through the dun-colored fog, he wryly mused that the assessment of his character was rather accurate. Yet, if that meant ensuring the safety of the Blades, including Astrid, then he was willing to live with the price of his intellect.

* * *

Sitting in the opaque fog with only a wolf for company, expecting an attack from ruthless exploiters, waiting for the friend she had spurned, Astrid understood in a sudden, silent crash that the quiet, insulated life she had tried to create for herself was entirely over. The thought did not trouble her. Something had always felt wrong about secreting herself away in her cabin. Years of deliberate numbness ensured she never examined this feeling overmuch. She could pretend to herself that being a solitary mountain woman was precisely the existence she wanted.

Nathan had changed all that.

He circled her now, never still, padding on silent wolf's paws as he patrolled. He might have been angry at her decision to stay, but he'd compromised, meeting her will with his own. In all her years, even as a Blade, she'd never met a man his equal.

"I know why you became an attorney," she said softly. She did not want to raise her voice, lest she alert any Heirs to her presence, but Nathan's hearing caught her words. She could tell by the swivel of his ears.

"To fight," she continued. "From the inside. Happiness and power were taken from you by the government, by people who weren't your own. And you do not want anyone to go through what you experienced, to be hurt as you have been hurt. The best way, the most devastating way, was to take the establishment apart from within the very system that most harmed you. Am I right?"

Nathan made a low sound of surprised agreement. He stopped his pacing, continuing to peer into the thick fog, though his ears were turned to her.

"It is like me, with the Blades," Astrid said. "Perhaps it was because I had no brothers or sisters that, as a child, I wanted for little. Whenever I saw anyone being denied, or subjugated, it . . . enraged me. I could not bear it. Why should one have everything, and the other, nothing? Had it been an option for women, I may well have gone into law. But," she sighed, "it was not an option. And what the Blades offered me was so much more gratifying."

Although he continued to keep his surveillance, Nathan backed up so that Astrid was able to place a hand on his back. He gave a rumble of approval. Beneath his fur, inside his form of a wolf, she felt him, the essence of who he was, a call that resounded within herself. So strong, these feelings. They engulfed her but, she was beginning to understand, they buoyed her as well.

"Push me," she said, "I push back. I have always been that way. My mother called me Little Star, but more as a jest. Nothing precious or twinkling about me. More like a nova," she snorted.

The sound Nathan made seemed to say, *I like you this way.*

"Thank you." She smiled. Here she was, conversing with a wolf. Surely some women would appreciate this arrangement—no opportunity for a man to speak back. But Astrid welcomed the time when Nathan assumed his human form. She needed his words, the sound of his voice.

"We are a pair, aren't we?" she murmured. "A couple of born scrappers. I should think we would tear each other apart."

He broke from his vigil and turned to her. Astrid's hand still hovered in the air from where it had rested on his back, and he pushed his warm muzzle into it, closing his eyes. One paw he placed upon her lap.

Her heart, freshly mended, did not fall to pieces. Yet it trembled. And became stronger.

Nathan suddenly pulled away with a growl. He faced out, staring into the fog with vision far sharper than her own. Astrid leapt to her feet, pistol in hand. Nathan started forward, then glanced back at her, as if deciding whether to attack whoever approached or to stay with her. He stayed, sinking into a ready crouch. Meanwhile, his growl grew louder, more menacing. Even Astrid's blood chilled at the sound.

"How many?" she whispered to Nathan, then cursed when she realized he couldn't answer her.

There was eerie, thick silence, all sound muffled by the dense fog. Then Astrid heard it. What seemed like slow, steady hoof falls, but the fog played havoc with sound so that she could not tell their number. And above the *clop-clip* of the horses, another sound, strange and fluting, like a creature of air and sky keening. Perhaps the Heirs had summoned some unknown beast. She had fought creatures before. She could again. And not alone.

Astrid glanced over at Nathan. His lips peeled back to reveal long, deadly teeth that demanded blood. The bristles on his back looked made of steel. She had witnessed him kill to protect her before. She might again, within moments. Astrid wanted to spare him the numb pain of becoming too accustomed to killing.

A column of wind pushed over her and she braced her feet. She cocked her gun. Aimed into the fog.

The yellow mist began to twist and churn, blown by this new wind. A circle of clearing air emerged, features such as tree trunks and grass materializing. She peered into this radius of visibility.

A figure strode forward. In its hands was some kind of rope or chain that it swung in circles, causing a breeze to drive away the fog. Behind this figure was another, this one mounted, and leading two horses. There were more than two men in the Heirs' party. Yet she could not allow herself a moment of solace. Not until she was certain.

"North is eternal," she called.

Nathan tensed at her words. He did not understand their significance.

Almost immediately came a response from the figure swinging the chain. "South is forever."

The man on horseback added in an eastern American accent, "West is endless."

Then the three of them spoke in unison. "East is infinite."

Astrid felt relief wash over her, at the same time that her heart seized with anxiety. "Easy," she said to Nathan. "These are friends. They are Blades."

Nathan rapidly changed into his human form, but the frown had not left his face. As he donned his clothing, Astrid stepped forward. The fog cleared even more, showing her details of the man with the chain, which he quickly stilled. Another amazing invention. She might have known.

Gleaming boots, even here in the middle of the wilderness. Perfectly fitted trousers tucked into the boots, and an equally perfect dark coat. If she had any doubt who emerged from the fog, those doubts were banished the moment she espied the black-and-silver embroidery on the waistcoat.

"Catullus," she said.

"Astrid," Catullus answered.

And suddenly, she and the man she regarded as her closest friend stood facing each other. Four years after they had last spoken. Because she had run away and spurned his every effort to contact her.

For some time, she and Catullus stared at each other. He was still, as always, sculpturally handsome, his eyes dark and clever behind his spectacles. Wariness, too, in his gaze, as if he was unsure whether she would bite him.

"The goatee is new," she said.

He touched it reflexively. "I started growing it shortly after you left."

"Ah," she said, feeling awkward. She glanced up at his close-cropped hair. "No gray hairs, either. I was not so lucky." She heard Nathan come up to stand beside her, but it was almost impossible to turn away from Catullus. Dimly, she was also aware of the man on horseback dismounting and approaching their group.

"Astrid," said Catullus, and the sound of his voice was so

familiar it nearly made her weep, "why in God's name are we talking about grooming habits?"

Her laugh was strained. "I think . . . it is because I am . . ." She searched for the right words. Profoundly sorry. Deeply embarrassed. Angry. Joyous. "Glad to see you."

"Are you?"

She blinked. "Of course I am."

"I did not know what sort of reception I would receive."

In truth, had he tried to see her less than a month ago, she might have chased him off with her rifle. But much had changed since then. *She* had changed.

"Folks," said the gangly, fair man standing beside Catullus, "you think we might have this touching reunion later? Seeing as how there's a gang of Heirs out there who'd just as soon roast us for supper."

"Agreed," Nathan said.

Astrid gave a guilty start. She had been too immersed in her own spectacle to have given Nathan proper consideration.

She quickly introduced Nathan to Catullus, who then performed the same service for the other Blade, a man called Max Quinn from Boston. Both Nathan and Catullus gave each other a thorough sizing-up, two prime males eyeing each other for possibility of threat. There was no mistaking Nathan's proprietary hand on her shoulder. Astrid was at once amused, irritated, and bashful, made more so by Catullus's raised, questioning brow. She wondered what Catullus might think of her, to have a man besides Michael in her bed, especially since it was her grief over her husband's death that had driven her to self-imposed exile.

"What the devil are you doing out here, Astrid?" Catullus demanded. "Quinn and I find your cabin in shambles, a body rotting away inside, Heirs on your tail, and we're apparently trespassing on some powerful tribe's territory."

"I've been trying to figure out what's going on for a week now," Quinn added, "and I can't understand it at all."

Astrid drew a deep breath, then, as concisely as possible,

related everything that had transpired since the moment she arrived at the trading post. Nathan filled in details in his precise, direct fashion. By silent agreement, she and Nathan did not discuss their growing attachment, and especially not the times they had made love. That would be akin to discussing sexual techniques with one's older brother.

As they related all that had happened, Catullus nodded and absorbed information, while Quinn made soft, colorful curses of amazement. Occasionally, Catullus asked questions, but mostly he was silent and attentive.

When at last Astrid reached the end of her narrative, exactly to the moment when Catullus and Quinn arrived, she took another breath. "And that is why Nathan and I are making such haste. We have to get to the remaining totems before the Heirs do. They will want the Sources to control the shape changers, and we cannot allow that to happen."

Catullus and Quinn shared a look, and that made Astrid very, very nervous. She clenched her hands into fists as Nathan's hand tightened at her shoulder, offering support.

"The Heirs aren't here for the totems or the shapeshifters," Catullus said.

"Perhaps they came on a scouting mission for Sources," Astrid answered. "But when they encountered Nathan, they found what they were looking for. They kidnapped him."

"I allow," said Catullus, "that when presented with an opportunity to acquire more Sources, the Heirs took that opportunity. But, Astrid, that isn't what brought them out to Canada in the first place."

"What *did* bring them here, then?" Nathan demanded.

Catullus stared at Astrid, and the chill seeping into her had nothing to do with the lingering fog. "You, Astrid. They came for you."

Chapter 13

The Solitary Hunter

Rain began to fall, clearing away the fog. It was a chilly, steady rain that ran down the back of the neck and turned the ground to mud. None of this registered with Astrid. She could only stand and gape at Catullus, burning cold.

"No," was all she could say.

Catullus's expression shifted from wariness to something akin to pity. "Yes," he answered. "They left England with the express intention of abducting you, and taking you with them back to their headquarters in London. Our inside source confirmed it."

"What do they want with her?" Nathan demanded. His voice was steel and stone, a weapon.

Catullus sent Astrid another sympathetic look. What he said next made her heart stutter to a stop. "They have the Primal Source."

Not once in her entire life had Astrid fainted, not even when Michael had had to take a bullet out of her shoulder without a drop of whiskey to sedate her. Yet she wasn't aware until she felt Nathan's steadying hands on her that she'd even begun to list. The world grew nebulous around the edges as she struggled to comprehend what Catullus just said. If it was true, that the Heirs did possess the Primal Source, nothing could be worse. For everyone.

"Steady, love," Nathan breathed, supporting her.

She shook her head and tugged herself away, needing her own strength, but her legs would not cooperate, and he wrapped strong arms around her to keep her upright.

"Astrid spoke about this Primal Source," Nathan said to Catullus. "Can you tell me more?"

"It is the first Source," Catullus explained, "the one from which all other Sources originate. There is no Source more powerful, and to harness its power for oneself is to be in command of the world's magic."

"I don't see what that's got to do with Astrid," said Nathan.

"Africa," Astrid muttered. She managed to rouse herself enough to stand on her own. "Michael and I were studying the Primal Source in Africa, learning its history, its abilities. Not to exploit, but for the sake of knowledge. If Blades knew more about the origins of magic, we could protect it better. And while Michael and I studied the Primal Source, Heirs tried to take it. There was a fight. The Source was safe, it disappeared back into nature, but Michael . . ." She knew how this story ended, with her covered in Michael's blood and a solitary boat trip back to England.

"Mrs. Bramfield knows more about the Primal Source than anyone," Quinn said. "That's why the Heirs need her now. They want to use her knowledge to exploit the Primal Source even further."

"Further?" Astrid repeated with a sick dread.

Catullus nodded briefly. "Not long ago, the Heirs' dark mages activated the Primal Source. And that means," he added, addressing Nathan, "that they can now use its power. But they want Astrid's expertise to capitalize on it."

"With the Primal Source under their command," Astrid said, "there is nothing standing in their way of utter dominion. Their dream of England's imperial supremacy will come true. If they know how to feed the Primal Source their wishes, they will have everything they want." She felt the urge to scream, to tear the earth apart with her bare hands. Activated the Primal Source. Nothing, not a damned thing in the entire world, could be worse.

"This makes sense," Catullus said, thoughtful. He seemed so calm in the face of complete disaster, but, then, he'd had a good deal longer to accustom himself to the idea than she. "It must have been when the Primal Source was triggered, that's when Sources everywhere became charged with even greater power. And Astrid's earlier, long exposure to the Primal Source had already imbued her with some of its strength. After the Primal Source was activated, it must have also increased its strength within Astrid. In the case of Lesperance"—he nodded toward Nathan—"Astrid and the totems' response to the awakening of the Primal Source enabled your latent abilities to emerge."

An awful thought struck Astrid, and she turned to Nathan, furious with herself. "I did this to you," she gritted. "Your change into a wolf, your kidnapping. And the Heirs' being led to the totems. It was all my doing."

"Enough," he said, jaw tight. He gripped her shoulders, facing her, direct and unwavering. "None of that's true. The Heirs alone are responsible, not you. And I'm not sorry at all about being able to change. It's made my life a hell of a lot more worthwhile. *You* make my life worthwhile."

She swallowed hard, taking him in, as rain pattered around them. Nothing back. He held nothing back, and she kept giving him meager handfuls. He deserved better than that. She would set things to rights.

But not now. Now the world was verging on complete subjugation. After giving Nathan a look that stated clearly that they were far from finished in that discussion, she turned to Catullus. "I thought the Heirs were after the totems, but they are not. If so, we oughtn't lead those sons of bitches to them." Thank the gods she was with other Blades, and Nathan, who were long familiar with her unladylike language. No one blinked or looked askance at her words.

"You know Heirs," Catullus said grimly. "Once they know of a Source, they must claim it for themselves. Especially now that each Source is more powerful than ever, thanks to the Primal Source."

"We have to get the remaining totems before they do," Quinn said. He glanced up. "Looks like the rain's finally stopping. Sure miss my old saloon back home, but," he added with a grin, "if I didn't like dragging my gangly behind through the mud, I wouldn't have become a Blade."

The plainspoken American helped lighten the group's mood as everyone muttered their agreements. It took a special breed of fool to become a Blade of the Rose, a combination of courage, determination, and masochism.

"You must know where the next totem is," said Catullus.

Astrid and Nathan glanced at each other. In truth, they had been so busy avoiding the Heirs and then waiting for Catullus and Quinn, they hadn't discussed the whereabouts of the totem.

"The Earth Spirits' medicine man told us a legend," Astrid said. "From that, we piece together our direction. We have only just acquired the first totem. As for the next . . ."

"*Travel the path of the solitary hunter,*" Nathan recited, "*to the gray forest.*"

Everyone pondered this. "They never give much, those legends," said Quinn. "Like the ancients are trying to drive us out of our minds. Crazy bastards."

Catullus made a wry laugh, and it reminded Astrid of the many nights she, Michael, and Catullus used to sit by the fire at headquarters, talking about missions until they grew hoarse and their sides ached from laughter. No denying it now, there was a decided strain between her and Catullus, a strain that she had engendered.

For now, they focused on what needed to be done. "Which path?" Catullus asked. "Which hunter?"

"Bears hunt alone," Astrid noted.

"As do hawks," said Nathan.

But they already knew the totem they sought belonged to either the bear changers or hawk changers. Which left them exactly where they had been earlier.

In frustration, and to quiet the chaos of her heart, Astrid turned away to gaze at the broad meadow stretching just beyond the foothills where she and the others stood. She had found a measure of stability out here in the wilderness, and sought that stability now. Twilight was coming soon, and the sinking sun caught the dispersing rainclouds in bands of fiery pink and gold. The rain washed away the dank London fog, leaving the air tonic and clear as it hovered over the meadow. The broad field was not perfectly flat, rather dipping here and there. She would not have noticed these small hollows, but rainwater had collected within them, forming gleaming shapes scattered across the surface of the meadow.

She peered closer. "Those pools," she murmured.

Everyone turned to see what had captured her attention.

"They look like tracks," Nathan observed.

It was true. The pools were not scattered randomly across the meadow. They stretched in groups in a rough line over the grassy expanse. Each group was composed of a larger, ovoid pond with five small ovals at the top.

"Human footprints," Catullus ventured.

"No." Astrid recognized the shapes of the tracks. "Bear. They look very similar to human prints." She pointed to a series of other pools, smaller than half the ponds. "Those are the front feet. Bear tracks."

"Damn big bear," said Quinn. Which was an understatement. The trail was one of a bear of enormous scale.

"A legendary bear," Nathan amended.

"And look," Catullus said, directing their attention further. "The trail leads to those mountains beyond the meadow." Sure enough, the giant tracks did precisely that, heading toward soaring gray peaks capped with glittering snow.

Astrid said in wonder, "The gray forest."

The four of them, three Blades of two countries and one shape-changing Native, stood in silence as they saw the task that lay ahead of them. Difficult enough to scale the bear totem's mountains, but the Heirs were somewhere out there as well, ready to kill, ready to capture Astrid. She'd no doubt that, if she did manage to wind up a prisoner of the Heirs, she would be tortured. For that was the only way she would divulge anything about the Primal Source.

She also had to contend with the towering monument of her abandonment of Catullus, her rejection of his friendship, which cast its own bleak shadow. And the fact that every day, every moment she spent with Nathan, he'd become as necessary to her as blood. Her heart rebelled at the notion at the same time as it rejoiced.

Such a byzantine maze she found herself within. To consider all of it at once was to court paralysis. She had to keep moving.

"We know our path," she said, breaking the silence. "Now we must pursue it."

First, a campsite had to be found. Even with Nathan's sight to guide them, traversing the wilderness in darkness had its dangers. And everyone sagged with fatigue. The day had been long, tumultuous. Every day afterward would be the same.

As Quinn and Catullus readied their weary horses, Nathan drew Astrid aside. He softly ran his long hands down her hair, over her face, tracing warmth and emotion that almost made her sigh. Today alone, she had seen him scale mountains, face down a mythical beast, challenge and defend her, and now he touched her tenderly—not reverentially, not as though she was made of sugar, for he knew she had more resilience than that—but the gentleness of his hands upon her filled her heart to bursting.

"I'm with you through this," he said. "Every step, I'm beside you."

"We have help now on the mission." She flicked her eyes toward Catullus and Quinn.

"More than the mission," he said, linking their hands together, "and the totems, and the Primal Source. You aren't alone. We fight together." The dark heat and promise of his eyes soothed and inflamed.

She rose up onto her toes and pressed a kiss to his mouth, soft and ardent. Their mission had changed, yet his strength had not. It grew, as did her own, because of his support. "Knowing that is enough," she whispered against his lips. "And I'm sorry we are to lose our privacy, for many reasons. Not the least of which," she added with a small, wicked smile, "is that I want you. Quite fiercely. Nothing like seeing a man intimidate a giant ice wolf to ignite the passions."

He nipped at her bottom lip and growled. "I'll terrorize whole packs to be alone with you." They drew closer, body to body, and it was a wonderful torment.

Hearing Catullus and Max finish with their horses, Astrid drew reluctantly away. She missed the heat and solid strength of Nathan immediately, but turned to face the other Blades, standing and holding the reins of the animals. Catullus's expression remained carefully neutral.

"I spotted a dry site in the meadow," she said. "It's high enough to keep us out of the damp, but not so high that we'll catch the wind."

"Glad somebody knows what to do out here," Quinn replied. "Our guide hightailed it."

Astrid started. "Your guide *abandoned* you?"

"He tried to have us turn around." Catullus's voice was also deliberately toneless.

"But what if you didn't find me?"

"Have I ever turned back or abandoned a colleague?" Catullus answered.

"No," she said after a long pause. "You may have new whiskers, but you are still Catullus Graves, tireless and obstinate."

Hard to know whether it was the lowering sun glinting off his spectacles or a flare of old, shared humor that she saw in Catullus's eyes. She hoped it was the latter. Having glimpsed what she and her erstwhile friend once shared, she found herself with a powerful yearning. Nathan's presence showed her what she had so ruthlessly denied.

Wordlessly, the four travelers made their way through the foothills to the site Astrid had identified. While waxed canvas tarps were laid down atop gathered tree branches, Astrid built a fire pit and set up a line on which everyone could dry their soggy clothing. One at a time, they slipped away to change into dry clothes. The moment of utter disrobing in the frigid air stole Astrid's breath, but she hastily pulled on fresh garments, grateful that at least some of her belongings had been spared a tumble into an icy crevasse.

Everyone gathered close to the fire, warming their hands and watching their rain-drenched clothes steam. It had not escaped Catullus's notice that Astrid and Nathan would share a pallet that night, but he said nothing. A tight silence spread like a sail, buffeted by winds of tension. Several times, Quinn attempted conversation, but his efforts were met with awkward, monosyllabic answers.

"Say, Lesperance," he said, rising to his feet, "I bet we'll need more kindling. I'll need your wolf eyes to help me find some. There's a pal."

A more naked attempt to put Astrid and Catullus alone together could not have been fashioned. Nathan sent Astrid a hard, questioning look. If she wanted shelter, he would provide it.

She gave a miniscule nod. This was something that she must do. He understood and rose sinuously to standing. After a narrowed glance at Catullus—promising retribution should anything happen—he strode from the camp with

Quinn loping beside him, one fair and gangly, the other dark and sleek.

Another weighted silence pressed down. Astrid resisted the impulse to fidget, as she'd done when about to receive a scolding from her parents—usually with good reason. She had been rather a handful as a child, so willful and apt to get into scrapes of both the metaphoric and literal kind. But Catullus wasn't her parent. He was her equal.

"How is working with Quinn?" she asked, because she needed some way in.

The firm line of Catullus's mouth bent in one of his restrained smiles. "He's a good man. Eager, but able."

"I remember hearing about him. He and Tony Morris were in the Yucatan, keeping the Heirs away from some feathered serpents."

"Tony's dead. The Heirs killed him almost a year ago."

Astrid's heart seized. Tony Morris had been the most genial man she'd ever known, always making a fuss whenever she and Michael were at headquarters, and running out in the dark of night to get the kind of boiled sweets Michael craved when on a mission.

She croaked, "Anyone . . . anyone else?"

Catullus listed names, grief hardening his voice. "Pritchard. The German cabal, facing him in the South Pacific. Sarah Halpin came back from St. Petersburg with a limp. She's been retired from fieldwork."

"Oh, God." Astrid scrubbed her face with her hands as if to pull away a mask of anguish. So many names, faces, people she had known and fought beside, to have them lost or wounded. It was the price of being a Blade, a high price that had cost Michael his life and Astrid her heart. But Michael and Tony and Jim Pritchard knew the risk, as every Blade did, including herself, and they all took it willingly.

"But there are good tidings, too," Catullus continued, his words growing lighter. "Thalia Burgess is married now, and she and her husband, Gabriel Huntley, are both Blades."

Astrid remembered dark-haired, emerald-eyed Thalia, tall and dynamic, and imagined that any man she might have selected for herself would be just as tall, just as forceful.

"She always wanted to become a Blade," Astrid murmured.

"She earned it, too. I was with her and her husband in Mongolia—an assault on a Buddhist temple in the Gobi. They both fought well, and a Source was saved."

Surely a larger story lay behind those simple words, one she longed to hear, but another time. Her desire for news must have shown in her face, because Catullus said, "And here's a sign of Armageddon: Bennett Day is also married."

Astrid could not have been more astonished if Catullus suddenly ripped off his perfectly tailored coat and sprouted a pair of butterfly wings. Her mouth truly did hang open.

"Was he smoking opium at the time?"

Catullus chuckled. "He was entirely and ashamedly sober. And loves his wife as he does everything: immodestly and joyously."

"I cannot imagine the paragon that ensnared him," Astrid breathed. She was quite convinced that the word "rake" would forever have to be retired and struck from the vocabulary, since no man could ever embody the term more perfectly than Bennett.

"His bride is London Edgeworth."

Fortunately, Astrid had not been taking a drink from the canteen, or surely water would have gushed out of her nose. "Joseph Edgeworth's daughter? The man who is one of the most powerful Heirs? *That* London Edgeworth?"

"The same. And Edgeworth is dead. His son has assumed his role. London is now a Blade. I was at her initiation in Southampton."

Yet more stories. Her head spun with them. She wanted tea. And whiskey. "I feel as if lifetimes have passed me by."

"That was your choice."

Ah, the preliminaries were over. Anger edged Catullus's

voice, though he kept himself as restrained as always. She did notice, however, that his hands were busy, methodically stripping away the damp bark from a stick.

"It was," she said evenly. "And, at the time, it was what I needed." She thought about Nathan, about the family he never had, never having a place or people of his own, and his wrath that she should have all of these things, yet deliberately abandon them. "It was also," she continued, "bloody selfish."

His surprised eyes met hers, but he kept mute.

"He was everything to me," Astrid said simply. "No one, not even you, can know what it's like to have the person you love more than anyone else die in your arms. And I had to bury him, too. Alone. So, until you have experienced that, I daresay you cannot judge my actions." There was no heat in her words, only simple statement of fact. That old pain no longer haunted her, and she knew that Nathan's presence allowed this.

Catullus bowed his head before looking up again. "You are right. We were all of us hurting after Michael's death, and I remember . . . ," he said, growing slightly fond, "I remember such times the three of us had." He smiled at some memory, doubtless one of the moonless nights where she and Michael had helped test some of Catullus's more daredevil inventions. Shingles were likely still missing off of headquarters' roof. "I had hoped that you and I might find a way to negotiate grief together, support each other through it, but you just . . ." He spread his articulate hands, encompassing her absence.

"I did not think of anyone but myself," Astrid acknowledged. A renewed pain to think of hurting Catullus, that he might need help, too. Her dear friend became much more real in that moment, as brittle as any human, with his own needs. She reached over and took one of his hands with her own. Those inventor's fingers, more precise than the finest instruments. They both contemplated the sight, her roughened hand grasping his after years apart.

"We have all learned the secrets of magic," she murmured. "Yet there is no way to undo time. The only incantation I can say is that," she paused, allowing herself to feel the gravity of her words, "I am sorry."

Catullus stared at her.

She let air into her suddenly tight chest. "I know that does not make everything right, but I hope in time you and I should be friends again. For I have missed you, Catullus. Very much."

He was silent for so long, Astrid felt a chill creep into her. She began to pull back, but his hand stopped her.

"You damned woman," he grumbled. "Don't you know?"

"Know what?"

"I will always be your friend. Always."

Oh, damn it. Her throat and eyes burned. "Always?"

His grin, dazzlingly white, transformed the scholar into an imp. "If I can forgive you for nearly burning my workshop down that one time, I can forgive you a little lapse in correspondence." And, bless him, he respected her enough to leave it at that.

Their hands came apart, but now with the ease of old friends.

"And you," Catullus said. He looked her over, from her boots to her heavy coat. "You have evolved into a mountain woman. I hope you haven't taken up chewing tobacco."

She chuckled. "This place has a tough glory. It's a hard and beautiful land, and there's something of the wild Viking in me that responds to that."

"And Lesperance?"

Her face heated. Just to hear Nathan's name spoken sent her pulse quickening. She both did and did not want to speak of him. To distract herself, she picked up a twig at her feet and began toying with it. "We have grown . . . close. He saved my life. In many ways."

"He loves you."

The twig snapped. She lost the ability to draw breath as her heart shied like a startled horse. "He hasn't said so."

Catullus made a wry face. "Men and words. A contentious relationship."

"Not with him. He says what he means." Stupidly, Astrid thought, *We must be near the ocean.* Because she heard a loud roaring, a whoosh and crash, yet Catullus did not seem to hear it. And then she realized, *No, it is within me. It is my blood.*

"But *those* words are the hardest to speak."

She tried to align herself with ordinary life, which meant talking. "Have you ever said them?"

"Not yet."

"Have you wanted to?"

Catullus looked away, taking himself from the light of the fire, and now that the sun was almost completely down, she could barely see his face, obscured as it was in shadow. "No."

"Don't worry, Lesperance," Quinn said with easy camaraderie. "She'll be fine."

Nathan and Quinn drifted in arcs just past the boundary of the firelight. The pretense of collecting kindling had been abandoned almost at once, which left Nathan enough time to pace and brood. There was history there, between Astrid and Graves, a history in which Nathan played no part. He couldn't lay claim to her past, had no wish to, but not too long ago, she'd been so mired in her history she couldn't move forward. Graves might spirit her back, the changeling returned and the woman restored to her rightful place. Leaving Nathan without her, bereft, howling in pain and fury. His life without her held nothing but chill emptiness.

The realization slammed into him like a fist. This was the danger, he saw, of giving someone your heart. If they left, you had nothing within but a chasm. He'd been on his own his whole life. Yet that was nothing, nothing compared to how alone he'd be without Astrid.

He couldn't answer Quinn, but continued to pace. Night sounds of insects and rousing animals drifted up from the meadow and nearby. If he wanted, he could attune his hearing to the low murmur of conversation around the fire. Yet he had to give Astrid her privacy, much as he burned to know what she and Graves said to each other after years apart.

Many minutes stretched.

"He's not a rival," Quinn added.

Nathan stopped in his pacing, frowning. He glanced at Quinn, who was busy weaving long pine needles into something.

"He talked about her a little," Quinn continued. "Not a lot, because I learned that Graves, he's a reserved kind of fellow. But he doesn't think of her like a lover."

"I trust her," Nathan said at once.

"But do you trust Graves?" asked Quinn, wry.

"Not yet."

Quinn chuckled. "Don't trust me, either, I bet."

"No."

Quinn didn't take this as an insult. He shrugged affably. "Makes sense. You just met me and Graves, and I bet you don't have a lot of reason to trust people. Especially ones you don't know." He held up the needles, which, Nathan could tell now, had been fashioned into a doll. "What do you think? I was going to give it to my niece."

"She'll like it." Though Nathan had no experience with children. Still, he could imagine a small girl might like a doll made from needles found in the Northwest Territory. They would still carry the sharp, clean smell of the wilderness.

Quinn contemplated the toy he'd fashioned and smiled. He tucked it into his pocket.

"Tell me about being a Blade."

Nathan's demand didn't seem to surprise Quinn. "We're all a bunch of harebrained fools," he said affectionately. "Running all over the damned place and putting our lives in danger as regularly as some folks drink coffee. Our numbers are small, and our enemies just keep getting bigger and stronger. And we just keep trying to fight them, even though we can't ever truly stay ahead."

"Then why do it if you can't win?"

Now Quinn looked puzzled, as though Nathan's question was patently obvious. "Whether we defeat the Heirs," Quinn said, "or any of the others, that doesn't matter. It's the fact that someone has to stand up and do what's right, regardless of the outcome. It's the fight."

Nathan nodded, understanding this. He'd done the same his whole life. It would be strange, though, to continue his own rebellion with someone beside him. To have comrades in arms, sharing his struggle. Dusting him off when he fell. He'd taken so much upon himself, he never thought to have anyone help. There were many advantages. Still, he would be accountable to others. To ask their opinion. To act, but consider someone besides himself.

The sound of soft laughter drew his attention. Graves and Astrid, chuckling. Then their voices again, low and familiar. Nathan wouldn't allow himself to hear the specific words. But he could tell the tension between the friends was gone.

"We can go back," he said to Quinn.

After they both gathered armfuls of kindling to help everyone maintain the pretense, he and the tall Blade returned to the camp. Nathan's gaze immediately went to Astrid. The fire shaped her in clean planes of gold as she smiled up at him. Something in his chest broke free into flight to see the unfettered soul gleaming in her eyes. A burden had been lifted from her, and though he wanted to shoulder all her burdens, he couldn't resent their lack.

He sat beside her, taking her hand, absorbing what he'd learned about his feelings for her. She threaded her fingers with his, pressing their palms together and, in full view of Graves and Quinn, kissed him. Deeply. He barely kept himself from groaning at her taste, her openness. And when she and Nathan did reluctantly pull apart, he saw more than relief from old weight in her eyes. As she gazed at him, those storm silver depths shone with such tenderness that he forgot the rudiments of breathing. Everything coalesced into a single moment of heart and breath.

I love her.

She knows. And she isn't afraid.

A meal was shared, talk exchanged about the next day's trek up the mountains, and Nathan began to appreciate Graves's dry humor, his incisive mind. Quinn, too, was a good-humored sort whose cheerfulness, even in the face of damp ground and future entanglements with the Heirs, couldn't be dimmed.

But, honestly, Nathan cared for only one thing, one person. He burned with need for the woman beside him. Not simply her body, but all of her. There was a pleasure of sitting with her by the fire, sharing conversation, knowing they were bound together in a way that couldn't be undone. His body wanted hers, but his heart wanted her heart more. And had it, if her kiss and sweet gaze spoke true.

Tomorrow would be another long, perilous day. Soon after they finished their meal, everyone crawled off to their respective pallets to sleep. When Astrid stretched out beside him, fitting her body to his and sighing as she relaxed into slumber, his noble impulses to chastely savor their connection disappeared like birds flushed from the briers. He gritted his teeth until his jaw ached. His beast clamored for her, needing to mark her as his. He couldn't give in, not now. Yet it was a small price, to suffer this want, knowing that she gave herself the strength to accept his love.

He debated between changing into a wolf and staying human. As Nathan and the Blades started their ascent of the mountains, he decided it was best to have the ability to speak.

The horses had been released, since the animals could never scale a mountain. Which meant everyone shouldered their gear and weapons. All the Blades had revolvers and rifles.

Nathan pulled himself over a tumble of rocks forming the scree slope at the base of the peaks. Graves was just behind him. At their rear was Quinn. Astrid took the lead—far more familiar with mountaineering than any of them.

"Use the foot and handholds that I do," she called back to them. "We don't know what's stable and what's likely to fall."

The men all grunted their acknowledgment as they sweated their way up the angled slope. Cold sunlight beat down on them. "Day's just getting started," Graves muttered, "and I'm already quite bored by these rocks."

Nathan didn't speak, but he wasn't relishing the idea of climbing any more than Graves. Still, ever since they'd approached the base of the mountains, he'd been feeling an odd buzzing throughout, a sharp awareness that grew with each tug upward.

Must be the wolf totem. That was the only reason he could determine. It called to him more strongly than any other, since the wolf was his other form. And he kept the totem close, for safety.

They were still within the timber line, and fir clustered in groups like gossips, rustling. The trees could hide Heirs. Nathan drew on his heightened senses to search for signs of Heirs. Yet something within these mountains created disorder—he tried to grasp scent, sound, and came away with so many discordant impressions, he was almost as lost as if he'd been an ordinary human. Strange that he should grow, in such a short amount of time, comfortable with his new senses so that he missed them when they were gone.

He tuned himself to Astrid, her lithe form moving over the surface of the mountain like a creature of nature. Sun caught in her braid, a gilded rope swinging across her back, and the flex and stretch of her muscles underneath the fabric of her trousers entranced. Occasionally, he was awarded with a view of her utterly gorgeous, pert buttocks. She guided him in the sureness of her body, the intent of her hands and feet. Sometime during the night, he'd been able to drift to sleep and was glad, not just for the rest he so badly needed, but because waking with her limbs woven with his was a heady, drowsy pleasure. Yet it had taken many moments of deep and controlled breathing before he could stand to face the day—he'd awakened hard as iron and aching with desire.

That desire was banked now, but the fire of it would never burn out.

Everyone convened at an outcropping, surveying the route they'd come and where they needed to go. He felt himself tugged forward, but without focus.

"Where do we go from here?" Graves asked, wiping his forehead with a crisp handkerchief. Nathan wondered how the man managed to look so spotless and elegant, even after a night sleeping in a damp meadow and a morning climbing boulders.

From the outcropping, they had several choices. Four mountains stretched above them. "The totem could be on any of those," Quinn noted. "And I'm not much relishing the idea of clambering up four different mountains to play Find-the-Source."

"There must be something to lead us," Nathan said, glancing around. "My damn senses aren't telling me anything."

Astrid also looked about. Gray slopes stretched out around them, interspersed with groupings of evergreens. Tall rocky spires rose up, like spines, and twisted along the sides of the mountains. Astrid squinted against the glare bouncing back from the stone, peering up at the spires. Nathan followed her look, trying to see what she saw.

She took a step closer to one of the spires, then pointed up. "Those are bear territorial markings," she said.

Quinn and Graves also looked to where she pointed. "Those scratches at the top of that rock?" asked Graves.

"The diagonal claw marks are the same as a bear makes

when marking territory," said Astrid. "And a few feet lower, the gouges in the stone are consistent with the tooth marks bears also leave."

"Not in stone," Nathan felt compelled to note.

"And not twenty feet up," Quinn protested.

"No," acknowledged Astrid. "Bears use trees to mark their territory. They stand up on their hind legs to make the marks—a show of force for anyone who thinks about intruding."

"Trumpeting their size," Nathan determined.

Astrid nodded. "And strength. But none are strong enough to bite and claw through stone. And even the biggest bear couldn't reach as high as those markings."

"Unless," Graves ventured, "this is no ordinary bear we are dealing with. One *did* leave enormous prints in the meadow."

"The ice wolf guarding the totem was gigantic," said Astrid. "Though," she added with a blinding smile in Nathan's direction, "Nathan faced it down."

"Nicely done!" Quinn knocked his fist into Nathan's shoulder, grinning, and even Graves looked impressed. But none of that mattered, compared to the admiration in Astrid's eyes and the unfettered freedom with which she allowed herself to show it.

"It would make sense," said Nathan. "If we're dealing with magic, the scale of everything becomes bigger, mythical."

"Do the markings continue?" asked Graves.

Astrid approached the rocky pillar that had been marked, and peered beyond it. "Yes, there." She pointed to another stone steeple, this one several yards away and farther up the side of the mountain. "I see the markings again."

"That's our path," said Nathan. "The path of the solitary hunter."

"Shall we follow it, then?" Graves asked.

Nathan nodded, feeling odd that consensus had to be reached before moving forward. He was still acclimating himself to working with others. With Astrid, they acted so smoothly in concert, hardly any discussion was necessary, and what disputes they did have were soon resolved. Now Nathan had two more opinions to consider.

But there was no conflict here. Everyone agreed that following the trail of markings in the stone was the best way to find the totem. It frustrated him that his senses and attunement to Earth Spirits' magic could have grown so anarchic that he couldn't provide more help. Yet Astrid proved again the depth of skills that made her a mountain woman and Blade.

He drew up beside her. "You're a wonder," he said, pulling her close for a kiss, which was enthusiastically returned.

"Glad *I* didn't find those tracks," drawled Quinn, passing them.

Nathan couldn't stop himself from smiling. "Your moustache would scratch."

"But that's precisely what the ladies like," Quinn answered, stroking proudly the facial hair in question. "A little rough with the sweet."

Graves and Astrid rolled their eyes. Soon, everyone was scrambling up the mountainside, following the markings, the terrain too uneven to permit anything but the most important conversation. Despite the fact that the going was slow and tough, Nathan felt an unfamiliar swell of lightness inside. Hell, was he actually *happy*?

He might very well be. The woman he loved was with him. He pushed himself toward an important goal. And, regardless of how Quinn or especially Graves felt about him, a kinship of purpose already began to weave around them. He'd never felt anything like this in Victoria, not even with the youngest attorneys at the firm. There, he was the outsider, the rebel. Here, he was a man, part of a team.

"Ahead," he panted, gesturing forward. "The dark spot in the side of the mountain. A cave."

"A bear den," agreed Astrid. "The totem must be there."

Breathless, everyone assented, and renewed energy flowed

through them. The totem was close. As they neared, Nathan's body began to thrum with awareness. He was drawn closer to the mouth of the cave as if impelled by invisible hands. He and Astrid and the other Blades were about to achieve what the ancients believed to be impossible. His heart nearly charged from his chest.

The first bullet slammed into the ground at his feet.

Chapter 14

A Battle of Bones

"Fall back!"

Quinn, Astrid, and Nathan had already made for cover behind a stand of fir trees as Graves shouted his command. The barren, rocky ground leading up to the cave held no shelter. Bullets whined all around, shattering stone and tracing lines of deadly heat.

Nathan and the Blades threw themselves behind the cover of the trees as pieces of bark splintered. Everyone took seconds to secure their firearms. Astrid pressed her revolver into Nathan's hand as she took up her rifle.

"Wolf or no," she said, low and urgent, "you're just as vulnerable to bullets as the rest of us."

He didn't protest. He'd handled plenty of guns, though he'd never fired at a human being before.

Another bullet gouged into the tree behind which he and Astrid crouched, coming damned close to her head. No, he'd have no concerns about shooting a person.

"Damn it," a man's voice roared. "Don't shoot the woman! We want her alive!"

Astrid cocked her head to one side, as if trying to identify a sound. Then she, Nathan, and the other Blades began to return fire.

The Heirs had taken up a position behind a large cluster of rocks on one side of the cave's mouth. Nathan couldn't see their faces, since they kept themselves hidden, only the barest glimpse of their eyes and hands and the flash of their gun muzzles as they shot at the Blades.

"No way to get into the cave," Nathan said over the barrage. "Not without being either exposed to gunfire or taking out the whole nest."

"They want me alive," Astrid said. She peered around the tree and fired a round. "I could head out, provide cover."

"No," said Graves and Nathan in unison.

She scowled at them. "Don't be foolish," she snapped. "Not if I can give us an advantage."

"I'll think of something," Graves barked. "Something that doesn't involve using you like a shield."

All discussion stopped as another heated volley of gunfire careened between the Heirs and the Blades. Nathan swore and ducked as he fired back, wanting more than anything to let his beast out. The savage need to protect his mate roared through him. He wanted blood. Blood in his mouth as he ripped apart the men who threatened her. Yet Astrid had been right. Even an angry, big wolf was susceptible to bullets.

"How the hell did the Heirs know about this place so they could get a jump on us?" Quinn snarled.

"Because of her," Astrid muttered. She nodded toward a smaller rock, set a little ways apart from where the Heirs screened themselves. A Native woman crouched there, and, even at that distance, her eyes glittered with avarice and anger, like a long-buried curse. She carried no gun, but watched the gunplay eagerly.

"Who is that?" asked Graves.

Nathan had never met her, but he knew at once. "Swift Cloud Woman. An exile from the Earth Spirits' tribe. Must have a grudge."

An explosion of heat. Nathan and the Blades reared back as their covering trees burst into flame. Not a single spark or gradually growing fire, but an eruption of flames that engulfed the trees at once. A tiny hell on the side of a mountain.

A dark-bearded man with the Heirs grinned as he chanted, his hands moving and drawing patterns in the air.

"Bracebridge," Graves said through gritted teeth. "A mage, and a bloody powerful one. Forcing us out."

The trees gave no shelter, only a means of burning. There was no choice but to make a run for the cave.

"I'm laying down cover," Astrid yelled, and before anyone could stop her, darted out and began firing as fast as she could at the Heirs. Shells from her rifle flew in a blur as she fired, cocked, and fired again with incredible speed.

Nathan swore violently and ran after her. He dimly heard Graves and Quinn behind him, bolting for the cave's entrance and shooting at the Heirs.

Whomever had called the order to keep Astrid alive, his words proved true. No one fired at her, though everyone else was fair game, and, as she stood her ground to provide cover for her comrades, none of the Heirs or their henchmen aimed for her.

One of the Heirs stood up slightly, pointing his gun at Nathan. Nathan and Astrid shot back, but then her eyes widened as she caught sight of the man. For the barest moment, her finger hesitated on the trigger of her rifle. Color drained from her face. She looked as though she'd be sick at any moment, and then rage replaced her sickness.

She started toward the man, fury contorting her features. Hell, it looked like she wanted to gut the man with her bare hands.

Nathan grabbed Astrid's arm and hauled her toward the entrance of the cave. Incredibly, she fought him, trying to break free.

"Let me go," she snarled. "He's mine. I'll take him."

Nathan held her fast as he sprinted to the cave. "Inside. *Now.*"

As he pulled her to what he hoped was safety, Quinn darted ahead to secure their position, while Graves kept up the rear. Nathan had to admit, for a scientific genius, Graves was mighty handy with a six-shooter. A heavyset Heir yelped in pain as one of Graves's bullets sliced into the man's shooting hand.

Even though Astrid continued to twist and struggle in Nathan's grasp, he managed to get them closer to the cave. Then there was a clattering, and Nathan pulled Astrid down as large rocks were flung at them. He threw them both onto the ground, catching sight of the mage commanding the rocks through outstretched hands.

"Graves, down!" Nathan shouted. Too late.

One of the rocks crashed into Graves, knocking him in the head and sending him crumpling to the earth. Blood seeped, scarlet and wet, from a gash on Graves's head. Astrid shouted his name as she struggled up. Graves didn't move. Bullets whined and chipped the earth around him.

A lanky shape dashed out from the cave. Quinn. He'd thrown off his pack and was heading toward Graves. "Get to safety," he shouted at Nathan. "I'll grab Graves."

With a clipped nod, Nathan leapt to his feet, Astrid's wrist firmly in his grip. At least she didn't fight him as they sprinted for the cave.

Once inside, Nathan and Astrid spun around to offer up more coverage for Quinn. The Bostonian had Graves slung over his shoulder and ran as fast as he could, given that he had a tall, unconscious man draped over him like a rag.

Quinn had almost made it to the cave's entrance when he cried out, staggering. A crimson circle appeared on his thigh, and he sank to one knee. Graves slid from Quinn's shoulder.

"Take him," Quinn panted to Nathan.

Both Nathan and Astrid leapt forward to grab Graves's arms and drag him into the cave. As they did this, more shots rang, and Quinn gave another hoarse cry. He glanced down at his chest, where a stain of red blossomed and grew.

He caught Nathan's gaze as they both saw the wound. Somewhere between a smile and a grimace, Quinn said, "Well, damn it." Then he pitched forward and lay still.

Seeing that Astrid had Graves secured, Nathan darted to Quinn. He turned the man over and blood coated his hands. Sightless eyes, now empty of humor, looked back at him.

Quinn was dead.

Rage. Everything, everywhere. He'd never known a fury so strong, so potent, pouring through him.

Nathan saw Quinn's lifeless body, the blood pooling around him, and a mindless, rioting rage took over. His beast broke free. He never felt the change, the gradual shift into animal form. One moment, he was a man, crouched beside a body, and the next . . . Scraps of leather littered the ground around him. They'd been torn apart in his transformation.

He bellowed his wrath at the Heirs. Nathan didn't recognize the sound. It was unlike any noise he'd ever made before, even as a wolf. He stalked toward the side of the cave closest to the Heirs. And the Heirs stared back, their weapons hanging in stunned hands, as they gaped. Up. At him.

"Oh, my God," Astrid breathed behind him.

"The One Who Is Three," yelped Swift Cloud Woman.

Nathan couldn't hear. All he knew was fury. He rushed the Heirs with ready teeth and enormous claws. The men scattered like leaves as he swiped at them. Dimly, the vestiges of his humanity marveled at his giant, heavily furred claws. These were not a wolf's paws. His height was not a wolf's height. And the sounds he made were not a wolf's challenging growl. Deep and guttural, he roared.

The Heirs and their mercenaries ran. They would not run from a wolf, even one who attacked. They would run from a bear. One of the Heirs, a heavier one, face white and terrified, lagged. Nathan lashed out and tore through the man's coat with long, straight claws, ripping all the way down to the skin. The blood he saw welling wasn't nearly enough.

I am a bear. I give death.

He could chase. He could kill them all. Wanted to. Wanted their blood for Quinn's. He charged in pursuit.

"Nathan!"

Astrid's voice, commanding and urgent, stopped him. His massive body lurched around and he saw her staring at him, her face ashen. Graves knelt at her feet, struggling to regain sense. Graves saw Quinn's body and started. Shock and anger crept over his face, reigniting Nathan's rage. He started to turn to continue his pursuit of Quinn's murderers.

"Nathan," Astrid said, her words tight. "We have to move on. Catullus is hurt and we must get the totem." Then, somber and sorrowful, she added, "Please."

His hesitation dissolved with that one word. Nathan ambled toward her, familiarizing himself with his new, immense body. He had none of the speed of his wolf, his hearing and eyesight dimmer, but a thousand times more power. When he reached Astrid, she held out a hand to him, knowing full well that, deep as he was within his new beast's form, he could take her hand off with no effort. But she used it, the scent of her flesh, to bring him back.

He drew in the smell of her, warm woman, *his* woman. And felt himself coalesce back into a man.

Naked, he crouched on all fours and saw the much smaller shapes of his human hands upon the rocks. When he stood, the world was lower.

"Take some clothes from Catullus's pack," Astrid said. She pressed a length of muslin against Graves's head, stanching the bleeding. Her hands, so slightly as to almost be invisible, trembled.

Numb with anger and shock, Nathan did so, pulling on a

pair of trousers and a shirt. His moccasins were entirely lost, and there weren't more boots. He refused to take Quinn's.

"We have to bury him," he rasped.

Astrid's silver eyes reflected pain and resolve. "No time. The Heirs will regroup in moments."

"Quinn—"

"Is dead." Her voice was as hoarse as his own, but firm. "There's nothing to be done now." She held Nathan's gaze, and he saw old and new heartbreak with strength beneath. "I had to do the same with Michael. I came back afterward to bury him. We will do the same. But later. Now we owe it to Quinn to complete the mission."

Though his neck felt like snapping from tension, he nodded. But he went to Quinn and carefully closed the dead man's eyes, then hefted the body and set it a little farther within the cave so that it was not so fully exposed. Nathan hesitated, then reached into Quinn's jacket pocket and took out both his Compass and the little doll Quinn had made the night before. Someone would know how to reach Quinn's family. His niece would have her toy.

He turned, slipping the doll into one trouser pocket, the Compass in another, to see Astrid watching him. Her eyes did not glisten with tears, but sadness glimmered there.

Graves tried to stand, holding the bloodstained cloth to his head, but he could not gain his balance. He stumbled, groaning. Astrid immediately supported him, draping his arm over her shoulders. Graves was a tall man, and his size caused both him and Astrid to stagger. Without a word, Nathan took Graves's other arm and put it around his shoulders so that he took most of the Blade's weight.

"Hell," growled Graves, his voice slurred. "Quinn."

"Gone, Catullus," Astrid said gently.

"God damn him," Graves swore, then pressed his lips tight until they paled. Even in his addled and weakened state, fury blazed in his dark eyes, behind his cracked spectacles. "Didn't have to—"

"He did." Astrid's tone was even. "He was a Blade. We see to our own."

Rage for the Heirs and for himself, for failing to save Quinn or kill the Heirs, ate at Nathan like acid. His words came out in a snarl. "Either we stay and talk and bury Quinn, or we go into this cave and get that son-of-a-bitch bear totem."

"Which is your totem, too, it seems," Astrid said. "Did you know?"

"I knew there was a beast in me," Nathan answered. "Wasn't just wolf. Too big to be contained by only one animal. But I had no idea that I could . . ." It seemed impossible but also exactly right.

"Have you ever seen or heard of someone changing into more than one animal?" Astrid asked Graves, and the wounded man shook his head slightly.

"Answers inside," Nathan said, grim. "Maybe."

The three of them carefully turned to face where the cave pushed on into the mountain. It yawned, a black chasm, and damp, musky air swirled out. No telling how deep the cave went, or where the totem might be. The darkness whispered to Nathan, calling to him. He knew now what pulled him—the bear, also beneath his human's skin.

"We'll need lanterns," said Astrid.

Graves shook his head, and the motion made him bite back a groan. "Heirs will be following. No light."

"I can lead," Nathan said. "Either as wolf or bear." Incredible that he could be both.

But Astrid disagreed. "I can't hold Catullus by myself. We still have to carry our gear. Even Catullus."

"Can walk," Graves insisted. "Don't need help."

"Like hell," Astrid fired back.

"No light," Nathan rumbled. "No animal to guide us. How in God's name are we supposed to find our way through that?" He tipped his head toward the beckoning cave.

"In the packs." Graves struggled to speak through a haze of pain and disorientation. "A small, green canvas bag."

Astrid released Graves, who sagged onto Nathan, and darted to the packs. After rummaging for a moment, she produced the small green bag, then opened it.

Two objects lay inside. One was a pair of goggles, fashioned of leather, brass, and dark glass. The other resembled a music box, complete with a slightly oversized crank and a small metal megaphone inset into the box.

"Employs sound," Graves muttered. "To reflect off objects. See in darkness—like a bat. Astrid. You must use. Guide us." He turned filmed eyes to Nathan. "Going to hurt. Your ears."

"Doesn't matter," Nathan answered, impressed as hell by Graves's device even though he did not quite understand it.

After everyone shouldered their packs, divesting Quinn's of anything essential, they all stared somberly at Quinn's body. No one spoke, a tacit agreement to let their silence serve as the best eulogy.

"We'll come back for you," Nathan said, breaking the silence.

"Amen," said Graves and Astrid.

Then the three of them—Graves, Astrid, Nathan—turned their backs to the sun and moved into the darkness.

Astrid slid on the goggles. "I cannot see anything," she said. "The glass is dark."

"Will become clear," Catullus mumbled. "Turn the crank on the box. Megaphone facing out."

She did so, and it emitted a whirring sound.

"Faster," Catullus urged.

Obeying, she turned the crank more rapidly, and the pitch of the whirring rose. "I still cannot see."

"Turn until you can't hear the sound."

Astrid's hand spun on the handle. Sure enough, the

whirring rose higher and higher until the sound disappeared altogether. Disappeared, but only to her and Catullus.

Nathan hissed in pain. She stopped immediately.

"Keep going," Nathan gritted. "If it gets us through the caves."

"Your hearing—"

"*Go,*" Nathan growled. He moved, and she heard him heft Catullus higher on his shoulder.

She had no choice but to continue. As she turned the crank, the whirring started up again, increased its pitch, and then vanished. Nathan sucked in his breath—it decimated her to cause him pain, yet she had to go on. Nothing happened at first, and then dim shapes emerged from the darkness, somehow shaped in grainy reddish relief within the dark lenses of the goggles. The walls of the cave, stalactites and stalagmites, the twisting stone passages that wended deeper into the mountain.

"I can see," Astrid exclaimed. "How?"

"Material in the lenses," Catullus said. His words slid and slurred, but he could not quite contain the pride in his voice. "Gets excited by the sound waves bouncing off surfaces. Creates . . . vision."

She never lost her wonderment at Catullus's intellect. She had not years ago, and it was true today. "The Blades are damned lucky to have you on our side."

"I know."

Astrid smiled faintly at this. Yet there was no luxury of time. Soon, the Heirs would return. And the faster she, Catullus, and Nathan found the totem, the sooner she could stop torturing Nathan's sensitive hearing.

So, carefully, as quickly as they could, given Catullus's injury and the dimness of the images produced by the sound and vision device, they pushed into the cave. Ghost images appeared in the dark of the lenses, the close walls pressing down, coiling passageways that were sometimes narrow, sometimes vaulted. Once, as an experiment, she lifted up the goggles. They were moving through utter darkness.

"I can stop for a moment," she said to Nathan. "If you need some time."

"No." His pained growl caught her straight in the middle of her chest.

Even if he insisted on continuing the torment, Astrid had to give herself a respite from hurting him. "A bear," she whispered. "You truly didn't know."

"No," he said again, but the word encompassed everything—surprise but a strange inevitability.

"Neither Iron Wolf nor He Watches Stars said anything about an Earth Spirit changing into more than one animal." She kept her voice a soft murmur. "You are special."

She felt but could not see his rueful smile. "Never doubt that." Then the smile left his voice. "We move forward. I feel the Heirs returning."

Astrid nodded, then realized he likely couldn't see her. So she slipped on the goggles and continued. They all moved forward in cautious steps, avoiding sudden gaping holes that appeared along the floor of the cave. If they were traveling blind, one of these pits would surely have claimed one or all of them. To Nathan, the cave was filled with terrible sound, but to Astrid and Catullus, there was only the shuffling of their feet, the rasp of their breathing, and the moan of long-trapped wind, like a phantom haunting the stone.

Quinn was back there. Alive that morning. Jesting and eager. Now only a husk of cooling flesh, the essence of what made him, *him*, fleeing into memory. Like Michael.

"You didn't tell me." Her words to Catullus were a whisper, in deference to Nathan and to protect their location. But a hard whisper, the edge of it cutting. "Staunton. He's here, with the Heirs." Merely saying the name of the man who had murdered her husband filled her with sickness, like swallowing poison.

"What. Would you have done. Had you known?"

She couldn't answer, but renewed anger surged through her. At the Heirs. At Catullus. At life and fate and everything that could not be controlled. "You should have told me," she muttered. "I deserve to know."

"Thought you might. Want revenge."

She did. She wanted to make Staunton suffer. The idea of his agony pleased her, an urge that shocked her. She had been wild, sometimes reckless and headstrong, but never sought another's pain, never enjoyed hurting someone.

That urge pushed her when she heard distant voices behind them. The Heirs. Nathan, too, stiffened and growled. She felt the warm mist of his change begin to engulf him and stopped cranking the sound device.

"My beast wants vengeance." His words were deep, hardly human.

She wanted nothing more than to join him. Leave Catullus alone in the dark, taking her rifle and pistol. Find the Heirs. Make them pay with their lives. Cold, merciless death. She couldn't survive, though. There were too many Heirs. Even if she killed Staunton, her own life would be lost.

Then, she heard herself say, "No, we move forward."

Nathan's growl swelled. "The Heirs—"

"Will face judgment. Someday."

"Not soon enough," Nathan snarled.

Catullus said, "To be a Blade. Means putting aside thoughts. Like revenge. For the greater. Good." He added, his voice wearying, "I want it, too. Vengeance. But there is more. Than what any of us. Want."

Astrid and Nathan were silent. There were exchanges that had to be made. The freedom of being a Blade came at a price. The price of ethics. If those beliefs were abandoned, unchecked by a larger sense of purpose and duty, then what stopped any of them from becoming an Heir? Ruthless, manipulative. Selfish.

She stiffened when she felt a hand brush her own, then relaxed. Nathan. He threaded their fingers together and squeezed, a sign of communion, solidarity. His touch grounded her, as she did the same for him. In his touch, she felt resolve. They would move onward, together.

Then he inhaled sharply. "They're getting closer."

No need for clarification as to who "they" were. She, Nathan, and Catullus wove through the caves, damp stone walls surrounding them. Muffled through layers of rock came the sounds of footfalls, hard voices.

Forward, then. She resumed turning the handle on the device, illuminating the world dimly through the goggles. They walked on until the tunnel suddenly opened up, and both Nathan and Astrid froze.

"What?" asked Catullus.

"We have to make a choice," she answered.

They stood at a crossroads. Seven tunnels branched off from the chamber, each twisting into separate paths. "I don't know which passage to take."

"Bear markings?"

"Only rocks and more rocks, but none of them scored with claw or bite marks. Hell." A false turn, and they could be lost within the cave, or trapped. She stopped turning the device, plunging herself into darkness, as she considered their choices.

She heard Nathan move. "Can you walk on your own?" he demanded, turning to Catullus.

Catullus, moving away from Nathan, took a step forward, and then another. "Holding steady."

"Good. Astrid, put the seeing device away."

"Done."

Clothing rustled. And then the warm mist of Nathan's changing.

She heard the rustle of his fur, the shift of his paws upon the stone. Reaching out, her fingers brushed his shoulder and she realized with a start that he had taken the form of a wolf.

"The bear is too new," she murmured, and he pressed the

warmth of his muzzle into her hand in agreement. Then he was gone.

She and Catullus waited in darkness, hearing Nathan pad from one tunnel to the other as he drew in their scent and power. Finally, he made a soft bark. He padded back to where she stood with Catullus, then stepped underneath her hand.

"You will lead us now," she said.

Nathan *woofed* in agreement.

"Take my hand, Catullus."

"If I touch you," Catullus noted drily, "he'll bite me."

"No biting, Nathan," she warned.

He rumbled a response, saying without words, *Very well. But you ask a lot.*

Then, with Nathan in the lead, Astrid's hand upon his back, and Catullus's hand clasped in hers, they formed a strange, small chain and delved farther into the mountain's secrets.

A silent journey in darkness. Yet not entirely silent. The voices of the Heirs and their mercenaries grew louder, though they could not be seen.

"Which one, damn it!" Staunton shouted. "Woman?"

"This I do not know," said Swift Cloud Woman, voice brittle and bitter.

Staunton cursed. "Bracebridge?"

"Can't say. Perhaps that one—"

"You," said another English voice. "Go investigate."

"Why me?" asked someone with a Canadian accent.

"Do it."

Grumbling and swearing, the mountain man stomped off to obey.

Whichever tunnel the mercenary had chosen ran alongside the one through which Astrid, Nathan, and Catullus ventured. They could hear the man's rough voice shouting through the stone close beside them.

"Ain't nothing here but—" Then a shout, and the sound of rocks tumbling.

"What the devil's going on down there?" Staunton yelled.

"Slipped . . . gonna fall! Somebody come quick!"

But no urgent footfalls came from the Heirs.

"Hey! You bastards!" the mountain man bellowed. "I can't hold—" Another shout that turned into a scream, before it faded away.

Astrid's stomach twisted. She gripped Nathan's fur harder, and he moved on, away from the Heirs' betrayal of their own. And if Nathan had not been able to sense the right passage, they, too, might have plummeted to a black, empty death.

Thank God, she did not fear close spaces, or the dark, for both pressed in on every side. Yet she still felt their oppression, as much as she felt the oncoming threat of the Heirs. They may have lost one of their mercenaries, but that did not diminish their menace.

Nathan stopped abruptly, but the momentum from Astrid and Catullus sent them all pitching forward into nothingness. A vertiginous drop, and she flung her hands out, trying to scrabble for purchase. She imagined herself falling as the mountain man had fallen, to become a broken body at the bottom of a chasm.

She landed, abruptly, with a clatter. Astrid scrambled on her hands and knees, feeling hard, brittle shapes all around. Sightless, she picked up one of the objects. Slightly porous, some long, some short, knobbed on the ends. Bones. Her heart tried to push its way out of her chest.

"Nathan," she rasped.

"Here." He took her outstretched hands and pressed his face against them. His breath warmed her chilled fingers. They were alive. In a pile of bones. Nathan asked, "All right?"

"Yes, but—where's Catullus?"

"Shield your eyes," said Catullus, somewhere out in the darkness.

"All right," she said, doing so. A sudden flare of light appeared between her fingers. Slowly, she peeled her hands from her face. Even though she had covered her eyes, it took several moments before her vision cleared. When it did, she saw that Catullus held a brass cylinder aloft—another of his newer devices—unearthly green light glowing from within it and turning the scene into something from the underworld. They knelt in a large cavern, its roof soaring up into blackness. At the opposite end of the cavern was the entrance to another tunnel. Animal bones covered the floor, piled high like mounds of calcified driftwood.

She gazed over at Nathan, his face a pale jade mask as he took in the sight. He rose to standing, shoulders back, eyes sharp. Only when Astrid noticed Catullus modestly glancing away did she realize that Nathan was unclothed. She had grown so used to Nathan naked—she actually rather preferred it. The pale green light turned his lean body into a gleaming idol, ready for worship.

The thought made her smile, even in this macabre place.

"What . . . ah . . . what sort of bones are these?" Catullus asked, showing a deep preoccupation in examining the bones in question. For all his work with the Blades, Catullus was still very much an Englishman. At least he sounded as though he'd regained his rather decorous wits after his blow to the head.

"Bear," said Astrid and Nathan in chorus.

She glanced at him, eyebrows raised. Likely he'd never seen bear bones prior to this. Yet he would know them instinctually. They were in him, in some form.

"One of these is the totem," she said, rising to her feet. She wobbled. The bones lay so thick, the actual floor was buried beneath. "Now we have to determine which."

Catullus cleared his throat. "Perhaps, Lesperance, you can scent out the proper one. Like a hound."

"This whole place is full of scent," Nathan grunted. "Bear *and* human."

For a few moments, they all waded through tense silence and the rattling piles of bones, trying to find one that stood out in some way.

"There," said Catullus, breaking the silence. He pointed at a large, long claw that rested atop one of the piles of bones. It appeared nearly three times the size of an ordinary claw. A hole had been bored into it, and a leather thong threaded through, just as it had with the wolf totem. "Rather easy," he murmured, mistrustful. "Sources never come so readily."

Astrid stood closest to the totem, so she cautiously started to move toward it, but Nathan's voice stopped her.

"Stop. This totem might not want someone who isn't an Earth Spirit to claim it. I'll go." He advanced toward the totem.

Nathan reached out to take it. The pile of bones upon which the totem rested began to shake and clatter. Men's harsh voices drifted into the cavern, dim at first, but growing steadily louder. The Heirs. Heading straight for them.

Nathan regained his footing even as the bones shook harder. Suddenly, they exploded upward with a hard rattle. The bones moved deliberately, shifting against each other, moving into place. Upward, they gathered, a construction from the ground up.

They assembled themselves. Into an enormous bear's skeleton—the massive, vacant-eyed skull with enormous, lethal teeth, the barrel-sized rib cage, empty of organs and life, the stark claws bereft of flesh but gleaming and deadly. The skeleton reared up, towering fifteen feet high, its skull nearly scraping the top of the cavern. With a hollow, unearthly roar that came from no lungs and no flesh, it struck out with a claw that held the totem. Astrid felt the roar deep within the marrow of her own bones.

She shouldered her rifle. She would use it on the skeleton or the Heirs. Or both.

As she did this, Nathan hunched over. Before his hands hit the ground, he changed. Within the mist, his body swelled, grew burly and tough, and suddenly, he transformed. Before, it had happened so quickly, she hadn't time to truly take in the metamorphosis. And now she saw Nathan reform into a bear—massive and powerful. His body was broad and brawny with muscle, covered with dark, thick fur tipped with silver. He opened his black, square muzzle to bellow his challenge, revealing teeth the size of daggers and more deadly. One swipe from Nathan's claws could kill a man.

Yet the skeleton was far greater in size. And undead. Whereas Nathan was very much alive. Nathan bellowed again at the bear skeleton, standing up on his hind legs, a terrible and wonderful sight.

"Will they fight?" Catullus called above the din.

"He had only to challenge the ice wolf," she called back. "A show of dominance."

"Let's pray it's the same here," muttered Catullus.

No sooner had Catullus spoken, than the skeleton charged.

The sound was something between a clash of marble and a steam train. Both bears roared at each other. Nathan met the beast head-on and, each clutching the other, they grappled. Astrid and Catullus fell back as the two furious creatures battled, a collision of tooth and claw. But the skeleton had no flesh, giving it an advantage. Astrid hissed as its claws raked Nathan's side, staining his fur with thick blood.

Her rifle would be useless, and the chance of hitting Nathan too great. So she slung her rifle onto her shoulder and dove for her pack. When she brandished her ax, Catullus called out, "Astrid, no!"

She shook her head at him and darted toward the brawling creatures. She edged around the perimeter of the cavern, positioning herself behind the skeleton. When it lunged for Nathan, she launched herself forward.

Swinging the blade high, she brought it down on the skeleton's back leg bones, hacking, but not breaking through, the tibia and fibula. Splinters of bone flew up as the beast roared. Unbalanced, it swung around and charged toward her. She ducked, rolled away, but felt the burn of claws across her shoulder.

The opening gave Nathan the opportunity to pounce on the skeletal beast, gripping the bones of its throat with his teeth. The two bears crashed to the ground, sending other bones spinning into the air. Nathan and the beast rolled and tumbled. With desperate, furious claws, the skeleton gouged at Nathan, tearing his flesh, trying to dislodge him. But Nathan took the pain and used it to push himself harder.

"Lesperance," Catullus shouted. "Hurry! They're nearly here!"

Above the sounds of the battling creatures, Astrid heard the Heirs shouting, their pounding footfalls. She glanced toward the opening from which she, Nathan, and Catullus had come. Firelight from torches and lanterns began to paint the walls as the Heirs neared.

A savage snarl, and with a deafening crunch, Nathan crushed the bones of the skeleton's neck. The beast shuddered, then went still. Another clatter, and the bones that composed its form lost cohesion, collapsing onto the other bones like so much lifeless matter. The totem gleamed, ready to be seized.

Astrid was at Nathan's side before he finished transforming back into a human. When he did, she cursed, seeing his lean body viciously cut and bleeding. She held him up as he sagged on unsteady legs, his hair and skin damp with sweat.

"The totem," he rasped.

"Here," she said, grasping it and handing it to him. She helped him tie the strip of leather around his neck, so the claw hung between his pectorals. Parallel gashes from the skeleton's claws cut across the smooth muscle. It would take all of his healing ability to recover and, if he did, he would be forever marked.

"You?" he breathed. He reached up to gently touch the

tears in her coat, the slashes limned in her blood. Fury darkened his features.

"Nothing at all," she said quickly. There was no time to spend on fretting over her minor injuries. "Can you walk?" She smoothed her fingertips over his face, tracing the beloved, hard planes, and careful to avoid the scrapes.

He nodded, but exhaustedly.

"Good," Catullus said, his voice clipped. He hurried toward them, brandishing his own rifle. At that moment, the Heirs, led by Staunton, appeared at the entrance of the cavern. "Because we'll need to run."

Chapter 15

Gaining Perspective

Cover was absent. Nowhere in the cavern offered shelter from the Heirs, as they gathered at the cave's entrance with guns at the ready. Even though Astrid had known she would see Staunton again, she still shook with rage to glimpse his face, alive and eager for power, while Michael's face existed only in memory. Keeping herself from launching across the cavern to wrap her hands around his throat took every fiber of her self-control.

Nathan. Catullus. The totems. She used them all to ground herself when fury threatened to devour her.

"Stop making this tiresome, Mrs. Bramfield," Staunton called. His voice echoed off stone walls, hollow and ringing. "Or you prefer us to kill Graves and your red-skinned companion like we did your gangly friend."

A hot, jagged stab of guilt pierced her. Quinn died because the Heirs wanted *her.* She'd be destroyed if anything happened to Nathan or Catullus. Would it be better if she surrendered herself?

Nathan, bleary as he was, holding on to her shoulder to stay upright, caught her eye. "They're trying to tunnel into your mind," he growled. "Fight back."

"Yes," she said. Nathan showed her the way back from darkness. Heirs picked their enemies apart ruthlessly, even from the inside. She wouldn't allow them to control her.

She, Nathan, and Catullus had to keep moving. Astrid took advantage of the fact that the Heirs wanted her alive. As she and Nathan struggled toward the cave's exit, she fired her pistol at the Heirs. Her aim was wild, distracted as she was, and the shot went wide, but it kept the bastards back. They all ducked as the bullet ricocheted, then lodged into stone.

With the Heirs positioned at the cave's entrance, Astrid clambered up to the cavern's exit, and, with Catullus's shove from behind, pulled Nathan up beside her. A rifle being cocked across the cave drew her attention. She cursed to see John Milbourne, the Heirs' master marksman, take up position. Even if Astrid draped herself like a rug over Catullus and Nathan, Milbourne could pick them off easily, all without so much as scratching Astrid.

"I've something to hold them off," Catullus muttered. He took up his own short-barreled shotgun and fired at the entrance to the cavern. Something wet exploded across the rocks lining the entrance.

The Heirs and their mercenaries ducked, then looked up with puzzlement. Nothing had happened, not even a corrosive liquid burning their skin.

Both Astrid and Nathan glanced at Catullus. "Don't think that worked," Nathan rumbled.

Milbourne took up his position again, readying to shoot.

"Patience," said Catullus, pulling his revolver. "Cover your eyes."

At least Astrid and Nathan knew not to argue. They both complied, though Astrid couldn't resist peeking through her fingers.

Catullus fired his revolver at the now wet cavern entrance, creating a flare of sparks with the strike of the bullet. The sparks landed on the wet patches of rock. Suddenly, the rocks surrounding the cave's entrance burst into flame. Astrid did shield her eyes then, and heard the Heirs and their mercenaries shouting in panic and anger.

Opening her eyes again, she saw the entrance to the cave now curtained in blue and white chemical flames. Behind the curtain stood the Heirs, cringing away from the blaze, unable to pass through it. They could only watch as Astrid, Nathan, and Catullus hurried away through the exit and down a tunnel. Nathan had regained enough strength to move on his own, though Astrid stayed close. Catullus lit the way with one of the brass illuminating devices, turning their retreat into a glowing green underworld.

"How?" she asked Catullus. The sounds of fire and chaos dimmed behind as she and her companions ran deeper into the mountain.

"The shotgun shell held viscous chemicals that adhered to the rocks," Catullus answered, panting. The light from the illuminating device, combined with fighting the injury to his head, leeched color from his face and made him ashen. "Sparks from the pistol ignited the chemicals. Burns for a long while." He sent a wry glance toward Nathan, though it skittered away at the sight of Nathan's undress. "Not as sensational as turning into a wolf or bear, but it worked."

Nathan's smile was brief but honest. "Next time, *you* can have a magical bear skeleton tear at your chest."

"Must I? Hate to ruin this beautiful waistcoat. It's Italian."

Astrid felt her lips twitch. They were all of them giddy with heightened nerves and present danger. Not for a moment did any of them forget Quinn, or the reasons that propelled them onward through the cave.

"Gentlemen, if I may interrupt your stirring discourse," she said as she sprinted, "where the hell are we going?"

Everyone stopped their run to contemplate this. Nathan took advantage of the brief pause to throw on clothing—mostly for Catullus's comfort. Certainly not for his own, because Nathan couldn't suppress his winces as the fabric contacted his wounds. Astrid promised herself she would see to Nathan's injuries as soon as time allowed. A shift of her rifle strap across her shoulder sent flaming pain through her, reminding her of her own wound. Yet she had suffered much worse in her time, and so gave it no more thought.

"There must be another way out of this mountain," Catullus murmured.

"There is." Nathan's voice held authority, the natural confidence so much a part of him. "I can scent it—fresh air ahead of us. Just keep going."

Neither Catullus nor Astrid felt any impulse to question or contradict. Nathan *knew* and that was that.

So, in silent agreement, the three of them moved on. Nathan in the lead, followed by Astrid and, lastly, Catullus, who remained alert for the sounds of pursuit, pistol drawn. At some point, Catullus must have retrieved a spare pair of spectacles to replace the ones that had broken, for the green light turned the glass into a subterranean creature's glowing gaze.

Cold air pierced the tears in Astrid's clothing. Her feet slipped on the stone floor. Looking down, she saw the rocks were slick with ice. The whole of the tunnel gleamed as frost grew thicker, the air growing colder until their breath came in puffs. Dark stone gave way to glossy white, becoming aquatic as ancient ice glistened in the green light.

The tunnel steepened. Even sure-footed Nathan slipped on the sudden decline. The ground quickly dropped and, despite all their efforts, everyone stumbled, fell, then found themselves shooting downward in a mad slide. There wasn't even time to shout in surprise. One moment, Astrid balanced on precarious feet, Nathan ahead, Catullus behind. And the next—she careened down an icy chute.

"Bugger!" Catullus shouted, sliding behind her.

They slid in a tumble of flailing limbs through the ice-slick tunnel, knocking against each other, fighting to get upright. But it was a losing battle. Faster and faster they slid, rocks and ice passing in a blur. Cold wind pushed at their faces.

The tunnel twisted and curved, sending everyone skidding up the walls as they banked.

When a large boulder appeared ahead, right in the middle of the chute, everybody twisted to keep from slamming into it, but that didn't stop Astrid from bumping her leg hard against the rock, nor Catullus from almost snapping his neck. Only Nathan could direct his slide, moving feet first as he plummeted down.

"Link up," Nathan called back. "We can control our slide better."

Fighting to reach out to each other, they finally caught hold. Catullus wrapped his legs around Astrid's middle, and she did the same with Nathan.

"We lean together to turn," Nathan yelled. "Hard left, *now.*"

As one, Astrid, Nathan, and Catullus leaned, and narrowly avoided colliding with another boulder.

"Now right," Nathan shouted.

They slid past a yawning gap on the left side of the tunnel that would have sent them hurtling into dark oblivion.

A sudden memory of sledding with her father, the wild ride down snow-covered hills as her mother stood at the bottom, peering between her gloved fingers. Mother lived in fear of those sledding sessions, but Astrid and her father took to the hills anyway. No self-respecting Swede could keep their child from playing in the snow. Here she was, an adult, roaring down an icy chute as part of a human toboggan.

The wind tugged a smile from her as she, Nathan, and Catullus hurtled through the tunnel, gaining speed. Oh, her bottom was going to be quite sore once the chill wore off. Yet she couldn't mind it now.

A blinding blue-white light lay dead ahead.

"Daylight!" Astrid cried.

And, like a cork popping from a bottle, they burst out into the day. For weightless moments, they soared as they lost hold of each other. Their toboggan broke into three parts: Catullus, Astrid, and Nathan. From so long inside the mountain, Astrid couldn't see, but was engulfed in white radiance, dazzling her, while clean, open air surrounded her.

Then, landing. She flew into snow and rolled. Astrid pulled her arms close, holding her rifle, knowing she could only wait out the tumble or risk breaking a limb. Over and over she rolled through powdery snow. Faintly, over the crystal crunching of snow filling her ears, Astrid heard Nathan and Catullus in their own tumbles. All she could do was hope they didn't start an avalanche or smash into any rocks or trees.

Her roll halted. She heard Nathan and Catullus slide to their own stops nearby. The world continued to spin, so she turned onto her back and stared up at the spotless blue sky, willing the sun to stop its dizzying twirl.

Finally, she sat up. The earth tilted, then righted itself. Astrid saw that she, Nathan, and Catullus were halfway down the mountain. She realized that they had passed through the mountain, the cavern entrance all the way on the other side of the huge peak. Surely it had to have been miles they'd traveled through solid rock. Hills and forest lapped against the base of the mountain, more unknown territory.

"Everyone all right?" Astrid asked.

"Limbs still attached," said Nathan.

Catullus muttered, "Stop the carousel, Mother."

Nathan regained his feet before Catullus did. Glittering with snow that clung to his hair, his eyelashes, his clothing, Nathan stood on legs that wobbled only slightly and went straight to her. She took hold of his outstretched hands and felt herself soar up, into his arms. Despite the snow, he radiated warmth, and she felt herself wonderfully surrounded.

"Shall we go again?" he asked, eyes aglow.

"Yes, please," Astrid answered at the same time Catullus groaned, "God, no."

* * *

Level heads and seriousness overtook them. As each gained their feet, the shimmer of shared excitement faded to be replaced by the cooler gleam of gravity and purpose. Max Quinn lay dead at the mouth of the cave, having surrendered his life to ensure the Blades' success. They could not tarry, should the Heirs follow. And they would follow. It was never in doubt. The only question was how long it would take the Heirs to catch up.

The bear totem still hung from Nathan's neck, and the wolf totem was secured within a rucksack. Possessing two totems, two powerful Sources, was enough to draw the enemy. And, no one forgot, Astrid was the Heirs' target.

What remained of the gear was loaded up onto backs. No one—not Catullus with his bruised head, Astrid with her torn shoulder, or Nathan, rife with bite and claw wounds—was spared from bearing the weight. Personal discomfort mattered not at all, and nobody complained.

In a line, they descended the mountain. Astrid glanced at the obvious trail they left in the snow. Three sets of footprints across a pristine white expanse.

"No more stratagem," she murmured. "We've a race, now."

"They know where to find us," said Catullus. "And the Sources. That Native woman guides the Heirs."

"She can take them to the last totem." Nathan rubbed his hand on the clean lines of his jaw, where claw marks from the skeletal bear already began to heal.

"They are too opportunistic to waste a chance to get another Source," Astrid agreed. She stepped gingerly over where the snow ended and the bare earth began. A good, hot fire to dry her clothes was a distant and lovely dream. And a cup of tea. Oh, now *that* was a beckoning paradise. "Especially now that they have the Primal Source."

"Which is why they abducted you, Lesperance," Catullus said. "They want all Source magic and magical beings under their control. No prospect squandered."

"And I won't give up a chance to rip those bastards' throats out," growled Nathan.

That was a plan Astrid could support.

Down, farther, they went, putting behind them the snow-capped mountain, until they were well within the welcoming shelter of an evergreen forest. The treetops held the gold of the sun as it journeyed toward the horizon. Soon, camp would have to be made. All of them swayed on their feet with exhaustion and hunger. No matter what losses they had faced this day, their bodies had the temerity to continue to function and make demands. Astrid knew this from experience.

At a small creek, the packs were lowered and injuries tended. A fresh bandage was wrapped around Catullus's head, which made him cantankerous. "I look like a damned drumstick," he muttered.

After Astrid had cleaned the healing cuts covering Nathan, he saw to her shoulder. She sucked in a breath as she peeled off her coat and shirt, while Catullus suddenly became enrapt with adjusting and cleaning his spectacles. For a man whom she knew had experience around unclothed women, her old friend was circumspect in her partially clad presence.

Nathan, meanwhile, focused only on her. He frowned over the slashes along her skin, dabbing carefully with a dampened cloth. When she hissed at the touch, he rumbled, "An ax. You attack a giant magical bear skeleton with a god-damn ax."

She was turned away and couldn't see his face, but heard the commingled anger and admiration in his voice at her risk. "Bullets are too unpredictable," she said. "I could not risk hitting you."

"And got yourself in striking distance," he added darkly.

"I had to." And the words were thick in her throat, yet she found a way to say them. "For you."

A bare, brief moment of terror. She'd said it aloud, making it real for both of them. And, even though she did not doubt him, still the flutter of fear to launch herself like a bird in hopes of flight.

Instead of answering, his fingertips grazed over her bare back, careful around her wound. Her braid was tenderly lifted aside, and his lips swept along the sensitive nape of her neck where, she knew, small puffs of escaped blond hair brushed his mouth. Not a kiss, precisely, for she felt his indrawn breath. Taking in her scent where it was concentrated. And then, she shivered as he very, very lightly bit her neck—a reminder that she was his, in the most primal way.

They could not tarry, much as she reveled in Nathan's touch, its meaning. Poor Catullus would polish his spectacles into granules of sand. And, always, the threat of pursuit.

So Nathan wrapped scraps of clean cloth around Astrid's shoulder, and she donned her shirt and coat.

"What is the legend for the hawk totem?" asked Catullus, gratefully turning around when given the all-clear.

"*From the sky you will see the way of the green river,*" Nathan recited, rising to his feet.

"How do we get up into the sky?" asked Astrid. As she stood, she gave Nathan a speculative look and he raised his brow in response.

"Me?" he said.

"We know you can change into a wolf *and* a bear," she answered. "Would it not make sense that you have the ability to become a hawk as well?" A remarkable thing to ask, yet everything was possible. Even a man who could fly.

Nathan's pensive expression did not alter. "At this point, I can't rule it out."

"Can you try now?" asked Catullus. "The way you did with the bear and the wolf?"

Nathan closed his eyes, then, after a moment, opened them, his face shadowed. "I don't know how. The wolf and bear came out when I was angry, when someone was hurt or threatened."

"Perhaps you can make yourself angry," Catullus suggested.

He did not say aloud, but everyone thought, that Nathan might attempt to remember Quinn.

Nathan tried again, closing his eyes, an expression of intense concentration turning his face into sharpened planes. Then he shook his head, frustrated. "No—it won't come. Damn it."

Astrid placed a hand on his chest, and beneath her palm felt the steady throb of his heart, the firmness of his flesh that marked him as real and living and hers. *Hers*. "No anger now," she soothed. "When the time is right."

He was only somewhat mollified. "Still need to get up into the sky."

Astrid glanced up with a small smile at the tall fir trees surrounding them. "I know a way."

"I should go, too," Graves said, scowling.

Astrid disagreed. "You took a bad hit to your head. The last thing you should do is climb a tree."

"And stand around like a nursemaid whilst you and Lesperance play."

Nathan clapped his hand on Graves's shoulder. "Keep an eye on the prams. And no gossiping with the other nannies."

More grumbling from Graves and, in truth, Nathan couldn't blame the man. If given the chance to scale a five-story tree or remain on the ground, Nathan would choose the climb. A hell of a lot more interesting.

"Astrid's right," Nathan added. "You fall and smash open that valuable brain of yours, all that's left is your stunning beauty."

"I *feel* fine," Graves muttered, but he knew they were correct, and so, took up a watchful stance with his shotgun cradled in his arm.

Two trees stood within six feet of each other, so Nathan and Astrid took up positions in front of each. A test found the trunk to be just wider than his circled arms. Glancing up revealed that the tree narrowed as it stretched up toward the sky, but it seemed sturdy enough to hold his weight. Astrid, a good deal more slight than he, would be well supported. As he looked up, late sunlight caught in the high branches and needles, an amber-and-green mosaic.

He turned his gaze to Astrid, who had kicked off her jacket, boots, and socks, and had her arms wrapped around her own tree.

"Have you ever climbed a tree before?" she asked.

"What boy hasn't?" He had, truthfully, been whipped soundly for climbing up the imported English elm tree and onto the chapel roof beside it. Didn't matter how many times he was beaten for it, Nathan still climbed. He liked the view and solitude, the world grown small and him above it. "But that tree had branches."

"This one does, too." She looked up. "But they are higher up." Nearly twenty feet higher.

Her arms still encircling the trunk, she gripped the rough bark, pulling herself close, then jumped. She planted her bare feet on the trunk, half a yard off the ground. She slid her arms upward, then, with her feet, pushed herself up until she was two yards above the forest floor. She smiled down at him, part woodland elf, yet entirely real woman. "Now you. Use your legs, not your arms, for strength."

He drew in a breath, arms loose but ready, then jumped. His first attempt wasn't quite as successful as hers, his feet scrabbling on the trunk as he fought for purchase, then lost his grip to find himself standing exactly as he was before.

Graves snorted but, when Nathan glared at him, smiled beatifically.

Nothing like a little disbelief to push Nathan further. His second attempt went much better. Nathan leapt, gripping the tree, then used the strength of his legs to push him higher. Within a moment, he was level with Astrid.

"Excellent," she beamed. "Keep going. It gets easier when

we reach branches." Which were still nearly twenty feet above.

The world narrowed to the feel of bark against his feet and hands. He methodically climbed, glancing down every now and again to see the forest floor—and a watchful Graves—growing more and more distant. Heights did not trouble him, but he did start in surprise when he looked over to the nearby tree and could find no sign of Astrid.

"Up here," she called.

He followed the direction of her voice. And cursed, smiling.

She sat on a branch, some six feet above him, looking comfortable and relaxed. For a bare moment, fear gripped him. Fir needles blanketed the ground, but they wouldn't give enough cushion if she fell. And they were only going higher.

"Boys are not the only ones who climb trees," she said, reading him instantly.

Doubt fled. He trusted her strength and skill. In seconds, he had pulled himself up onto a branch and sat, as she did. They were deep into the canopy, surrounded by tree branches and afternoon birdsong. A few curious sparrows turned jet bead eyes toward them, unused to company so high up. One inquisitive female hopped onto Nathan's hand, her feet like living twigs, before taking flight.

"They're drawn to your magic," Astrid noted.

"I thought birds didn't react well to it."

"Depends on the bird. And the magic."

"Still a ways to go," he said, glancing upward. They needed to clear the treetops, and the sun sank lower. Dusk would come soon.

They clambered from branch to branch, and he felt the old boyish thrill to climb, to use an old tree to lift himself up. Was it the beast in him, or something else? Simply the pleasure a man took in conquering heights and making the world shrink, birthing himself into a giant.

Now and again, he glanced over to Astrid and saw the

same joy in her face, the need for motion and ascent. He allowed himself a moment of purely masculine admiration, to see her lithe, slim body move like a supple dream, all strength and sensual potential. And more than that, he was drawn in by the energy of her, the living soul that gave itself the might to withhold nothing. Now freed from the cage of her own making, Astrid soared. He burned to soar with her. He swore he would, and face all the demons of hell to do so.

Higher, higher they climbed, sometimes battling the branches that grew thickly the farther they went. The ground disappeared, obscured by boughs and shaking green needles. A few squirrels watched and chattered before bounding away. Precarious, the higher he and Astrid went, as the trunk narrowed. A slight swaying of the trees. Then the canopy thinned. Nathan and Astrid emerged into open air.

Low sunlight briefly dazzled before they could truly see. And then—

"Oh, marvelous," Astrid breathed.

Over fifty feet above the ground, the land flowed out around them. White-and-gray mountains carpeted lushly with forest. No sign of the Heirs on the mountains, nothing to foul the panorama. The shining blue backs of rivers, weaving in serpentine arcs. The sky, impossibly big and open, as though the lid of a box had been removed to reveal eternity above. A cool wind, fragrant with the multitude of life all around, swirled and pulsed and quickened the world.

The most arresting sight: Astrid, glowing, truly free. Her silver eyes shone, daylight stars, and he read in them not only the pleasure in a rare, exalted view, but that they could share it.

Up here, with the view of gods, everything fell away, everything cleared into precise focus. He knew himself—she had given him the means.

"I love you," he said.

A flicker of fear and then she became brilliant, another sun. Then, strangely, chuckled. "We need to work on your timing. I cannot touch or kiss you now." She glanced ruefully at the distance between them.

Her response wasn't quite what he had in mind—her own declaration of love would've been nice—but she was always herself, never someone else's idea of who she should be, and, damn it, if that didn't make him happy, then he was a miserable bastard who deserved precisely nothing. So he took her words and her bright joy and felt himself become a hundred times more than he'd ever been before.

"Let's find that green river," he growled. "Then we can climb down and I can say it again."

"A good plan," she said, smiling.

They both gazed out, searching for any sign of a green river. "All the rivers look blue," he said.

"Perhaps in certain light," she offered. "Or moss growing along the riverbanks makes them appear green."

"But the legend says, *From the sky you will see the way of the green river.* Why *from the sky?*" He continued to scan the landscape around them, drawing upon his every sense, human and beast, to reveal the land's secrets.

"The white lake was not truly a lake," Astrid said. "And the gray forest was not truly a forest, but a mountain range. So the green river must not be an actual river."

Nathan's attention snagged. He narrowed his eyes, and then a small smile of triumph curved his mouth. "Look there."

Astrid followed his point, and then she smiled as well. "The green river."

A trail of trees, taller by dozens of feet from those around them, cut through the terrain. It began close by and then wound in curving bends to the east. From the ground, the path of trees could not have been seen, but from far above the ground, the route revealed itself in the height of the trees.

"The trees are older than the rest of the forest," Astrid said, voice soft with wonder. "The ancients must have planted them long ago to serve as a pathway to the hawk totem."

"If it's a path," Nathan said, "it has to lead somewhere."

They both followed the course of the trees with their eyes. The green path twisted through forests, even cutting across a river, on for miles. Until it ended. At sheer granite cliffs.

Astrid said, "It leads there." Even from a great height and distance, both she and Nathan could tell the cliffs were fully perpendicular and extraordinarily tall. Scaling such cliffs would take more than experience and rope. It would take a miracle. Or magic.

As he and Astrid made their way back down, Nathan realized with a start that he already had his miracle. He glanced at Astrid, taking her in, her grace and resolve. A diamond, hard and beautiful, within the demanding seclusion of the wilderness. Yet diamonds were cold and cutting, and she was warmth itself, capable of profound tenderness.

And, as for magic, she had shown him there was much more of it in the world than he'd ever believed.

To follow a path of trees toward a sheer cliff seemed perfectly ordinary, or so Graves acted when told of their next objective. He just said, "Very good," shouldered his shotgun and pack, and started off in the right direction.

Being a Blade, it seemed, meant doing things that normal people would scoff at. But, out of everything Nathan had seen and done since meeting Astrid, following a trail of trees seemed downright routine.

But dusk already began to descend, especially down in the forest, where shadows lengthened long before the sun disappeared. And everyone began to stagger like drunkards, the day's turmoil wearing. Even the pleasure of climbing into the sky—and Nathan opening his heart—had its price.

Astrid found them a suitable campsite—he wondered how he'd ever get used to seeing her indoors, since she was as much a part of the wilderness as it was of her, but he didn't really give a damn, so long as he was with her, in a cabin or castle—and the three of them settled around the fire. Astrid and Nathan on one side, Graves on the other. A melancholy silence reigned as they ate a meal of roast fish and gathered berries. The absence around the fire was palpable.

"Quinn mentioned a niece," Nathan said.

Graves nodded, feeding the fire. "A married sister in Boston. His only family."

No one asked whether Quinn had a wife or sweetheart. Such connections seemed to be luxuries for Blades.

"There's never enough funds for a proper pension," Astrid sighed. "As it is, even the headquarters in Southampton is falling apart."

"Last winter, the library flooded," said Graves. "We had to put all the books in Bennett's room."

"What were his thoughts on the matter?" asked Astrid.

"He was never in his own bed enough to care." He turned to Nathan. "Quinn's sister will be notified. That is usually my job, writing those letters. If there are any personal possessions, I send those, too."

Nathan swore gently. What a hell of a job, writing to someone's family to deliver news of disaster. Made him respect Graves, more than he already did.

"Except with Michael," Graves added.

"I wrote those letters," said Astrid, staring into the fire. "He had a brother and an uncle. The brother wrote me back and said I was a worthless whore who led Michael to his death." She broke a twig and tossed it into the flames, her face a distant shore.

Anger surged through Nathan. "Where does he live, this brother? I'll find him and break his ribs, one at a time. Slowly."

Her smile was bittersweet as she placed a hand on his cheek. "A lovely sentiment, though the image is a bit grisly."

Even Graves looked furious and shocked. "You never told me about that."

She dropped her hand and moved her shoulders up and down, a negligent shrug. "At the time, I was too buried in grief to care what Clancy Bramfield said. One raindrop in the midst of a hurricane."

Graves and Nathan looked at each other over the fire in a silent agreement to locate Michael's brother and give him a thorough thrashing. Nothing quite engendered friendship between men than the prospect of beating the tar out of another man.

Nathan hated that he couldn't go back in time and undo all the hurts she had suffered. He hated that he couldn't protect her from any and all pain. He would take every pain for her, if he could. But none of this was really possible. She had been hurt, and all of it, the good and the bad, the sweet and the sorrowful, made her into who she was now. The woman he loved.

Who was, even now, in danger.

Hell, he couldn't wait until he could face those son-of-a-bitch Heirs and kill each and every one of them for even *thinking* about hurting Astrid.

He placed his hand on the back of her neck, just to touch her. The feel of her skin calmed and stirred him. She shifted beneath him, settling into his touch with a barely audible sigh.

"I dreamt about returning to Southampton," she said, as calmly as if she hadn't mentioned the fact that her brother-in-law once called her a worthless whore. "A few months ago. Strange—I seldom remember my dreams, but this one was quite vivid." She frowned at the memory. "I heard a woman's voice, a voice I almost recognized. She kept saying, over and over, 'Come back. The hour of the Blades is now. Come back.'"

Graves gazed at her levelly. "That was not a dream."

Her head whipped up as Nathan demanded, "What?"

"What you thought was just a dream," Graves explained, "was a beacon."

"How?" asked Astrid.

"You remember Athena Galanos?"

"The Blade from Greece," Astrid recalled. "She came from a line of witches who once held much power."

"Athena's magic has grown considerably. She is now one of the most powerful witches in recent history." Graves's look was direct and serious. "When the Heirs woke the Primal Source, it was time to gather the Blades to combat this new threat."

"Call in reinforcements," said Nathan.

"Precisely," Graves said. "We need all the help we can muster. So Athena sent out the plea, using her magic, summoning every Blade to England. What you thought was a dream, Astrid, was a call to arms."

Astrid frowned, absorbing this. She was being pulled back home, back to her old life and old world. She was a Blade—she, Nathan, and Graves all knew this.

But Nathan wasn't a Blade. He had one home, and that home was her.

She had to leave, had responsibilities and a code. A sense of honor. But he might lose her to that which he loved about her.

"How many Blades are there?" asked Nathan.

"Haven't done a formal count," said Graves, "but no matter what our numbers are, they will always be far fewer than the Heirs. Yet we must call on all of them. No matter where they are—even the most hidden corners of the world."

"The threat is so great?"

Graves held Nathan's gaze with his own and there was no embellishment there, only cold truth. Truth that froze Nathan to his marrow. "Everything," said Graves. "*Everything* is at stake."

Chapter 16

Vows

Night progressed and life continued in exchanges of words and sips from the canteen.

"The first Blade of the Rose was a woman?" asked Nathan.

"Frances of Strathmore," answered Catullus. "A master weaver. She made a pilgrimage to the Holy Land and discovered crusading knights trying to enslave a *djinn*. Frances and Jack Dutton, a blacksmith and fellow pilgrim, stopped them. But centuries passed before the Blades as we know them truly came to be."

Astrid, her mind clouded with swarms of thoughts, listened only partly as Nathan and Catullus talked of the history of the Blades of the Rose—the beginnings of the organization, its broadening purpose, the struggle to best an enemy that never stopped growing or striving. Nathan, in his incisive way, cut to the heart of the matter with direct questions, and she heard, in Catullus's straightforward answers, the tentative beginnings of friendship between the two men. Both of them, Catullus and Nathan, urged onward by a continual striving. Catullus impelled by his capacious brain to create new inventions. Nathan driven to right wrongs, fight for those who could not.

Time slipped away. She felt it as surely as if holding water in her cupped hands. No matter how tightly she kept the seal of her fingers, the drops kept running out and she felt soon she would have nothing but wet hands and emptiness.

She watched Nathan's face in the glow of the fire. His broad forehead, the dark slashes of his brows. The nose that would, on any other face, seem too large, too striking, yet on him fit perfectly. Lips belonging to a warrior angel, that spoke without compromise and kissed her without mercy.

Not so long ago, she had not known him. Yet it felt as if there had always been a part of her set aside only for him. Strange, that. Strange and terrible and wonderful. She had been so certain it was Michael and Michael alone who held her heart and that, with his death, he'd taken her heart with him to the cold land of loss and forgetting. Yet enough of her heart remained alive to grow and blossom in the tropical heat of Nathan's love.

"And when there are no more Heirs of Albion?" Nathan asked.

Catullus said, with no hesitation, "That may never happen, but there are always more enemies, more who want to claim magic for themselves, no matter how many lives are lost."

Michael. Tony Morris. Max Quinn. The roster of the dead. It would grow, unavoidably. A life could be extinguished in the span it took to douse a candle. Her own, or any number of people she cared about. Yet to hide away, protecting against pain, meant missing the beauty of this world, transitory as it was. Hardly a life, less than half. And protect herself against what, truly? Happiness, pleasure. Love.

Astrid rose to her feet, drawing the attention of Nathan and Catullus. Both men stood—the habit of polite society, even out here.

She wanted words. She could not find them, for they seemed too small to contain everything she felt. So, instead of speaking, she gave Nathan a look far more eloquent than she could say, and then slipped into the darkness just beyond the circumference of the fire.

Nathan might have said something to Catullus. Catullus might have answered. She hadn't ears to hear. She let the forest take her, enfold her in its night sounds and cloak of shadows. The crunch and scent of pine needles under her boots. Nocturnal birds measuring their territory in hoots. Her own pulse and breath as she felt herself at the very edge of safety.

Behind her, coming closer, gaining speed and nearly silent, Nathan padded. He'd taken the wilderness into him, now.

He came beside her within seconds. Yet he did not try to take hold of her or press her with questions. They fell into step naturally, side by side, delving farther into the forest. Silence both fraught and comfortable stretched between them like bands of light. They could not go too far, however. No one forgot the threat out there, somewhere, that none of them should be apart from the others for long.

At the base of an ancient pine, she stopped. Here, thick roots pushed into the earth, spreading in wizened profusion. The width of the trunk and roots testified to the age of the tree.

"This pine," she said, laying her hand upon its gnarled trunk, "was alive when Julius Caesar met his death in the Senate."

Nathan set his hand beside hers, and the sight of his long fingers close to hers but not touching sent a wave of tenderness and lush desire through her.

"It stood when horses first came to this continent." His voice was a rumble deeper than the darkness.

"And when London burned, and Bach composed his Brandenburg concertos." She turned and leaned against the trunk, facing him. "Destruction and creation."

His eyes gleamed in the shadows as he braced himself over her, then drew closer, so that only a few inches separated them. Their breath threaded together as she let herself absorb the heat of his lean body. Muscle and bone, the strength and hunger of this man, barely restrained. One word, one look. That's all it would take to open the floodgates. Holding himself back took every measure of control he possessed, and yet he did, for her, instinctively knowing what she needed at that moment.

"I have to go back to England," she said, low and urgent. "A battle is brewing there, the battle that determines everything. If we can secure the totems, I must return with Catullus to help the Blades."

"I know." His words were a rough caress, his eyes a starless promise.

She pressed her lips together, aware of his own mouth so close, aware of the swift beat of her heart. A dizzying combination of fear and excitement to speak further, yet she must. "There is no means of knowing how the battle will fare, if the Blades will succeed. Or even if I will survive."

"You will," he said, a harder edge in his voice.

She smiled gently, a little sadly. She knew well the tenuousness of life. "You can't know that."

"I know it." His jaw tightened with conviction, and the heat and determination in his eyes stopped her breath.

"If I *do* survive," she said, pressing on doggedly lest she lose her nerve, "I will come back. To you. If you will wait for me. Because"—she felt just as she had moments before plunging over the waterfall, just as terrified and exhilarated, the distillation of what it meant to be alive—"I love you."

She kept her hands plastered against her sides, needing to touch him but holding herself in check, for she would let nothing but her words speak for her. Words she had not believed she would ever utter again.

She waited for his answer. He had said, not a few hours before, that he loved her, but she couldn't be certain of anything until she heard him say so again.

He drew even closer, their bodies separated by less than an

inch, his mouth hovering over hers. His breath came as quickly as her own, his chest rising and falling as if heating the very earth. "I know that you'll survive the upcoming battle," he said, "because I'll be fighting right beside you, and I'll lay down my own life to protect yours."

"I . . . oh," she said. It took her some moments to understand. "You . . . will come with me?"

"Your fight is my fight," he said. Stark and direct, his words filled her with unsparing joy. "Your cause is mine. And more than that." He brushed her lips with his. "More than that. Your heart is my heart. I love you, Astrid. My place is with you. Always with you."

He kissed her, a deep, purposeful kiss that demanded everything and gave everything. She sank into his kiss, the sultry slick heat of his mouth, the shared hunger. Yet neither touched, except for their mouths, as though they both needed only a tap forward into free fall.

She felt compelled to pull her lips from his, long enough to gasp, "And your tribe? The Earth Spirits?"

"Their totems will be safe," he rasped. "And that's all. I left them to be with you, not just for this fight, but forever. Understand this," he growled. "You and I? The Earth Spirits called us mates, and that's what we are. Mated. Each for the other, and not a damned thing—not the Blades, the Heirs, or any magic—will separate us. Not ever."

She had thought herself exposed entirely. But she had one last, final layer. Gently, she removed her ring, pulling off the golden band. Ah, bittersweet. For a moment, she held it in her palm, feeling its shape press against her tender flesh, the unity of its circle, before putting it into her trouser pocket.

She held Nathan's gaze as she did this, an act as deliberate and daring as carefully stepping off a bridge. She felt a little dizzy, quite sad, and also—joyous. Done. It was done. And both she and Nathan understood precisely what it meant. For her and for him.

She did let herself touch him then, because she could no

longer stop herself. Her arms came up and encircled him, feeling the breadth of his shoulders, his narrow hips, his sleek body that inflamed not only for its beauty but because it was him, the physical manifestation of *him*. "My lover," she murmured, taking back his mouth. "My love."

Groaning, hc plunged back into the kiss, wrapping her in his own taut arms. Their bodies pressed against each other, and at the contact, hips cradling hips and the immediate awareness of their shared arousal, they both gasped.

For a moment, they allowed themselves the exquisite torture of being still, feeling the sensual potential of their bodies. Between her legs, his cock was a welcome, insistent presence, full and striving toward her innermost recesses. She loved the feel of it, of him, his animal lust and human desire, and, when she could no longer bear being still, arched up into him so that his thickness rubbed precisely where she wanted him most. A bestial growl sounded deep in his throat as she pushed and moved against him.

It was not enough.

Their mouths met and held in long, molten kisses. She wanted to touch him everywhere, yet could not, because she clung to him as one might cling to shelter in a storm. But he *was* the storm, and she wrapped her legs around him, throwing herself into the tempest. She wasn't afraid anymore.

"Nathan," she gasped. "Now. Please . . . now."

He looked down at her, his face tight with need, eyes burning. "You know," he rumbled. "You know what this means."

"I do," she said. Her gaze held his, and they saw in each other everything—loss and joy and fear and strength. And love. Love, above all. Terrifying and marvelous.

They wasted no further time. Nathan stepped back just long enough to strip and Astrid, impatient, tugged off her boots, her socks, her trousers. She unbuttoned her shirt, but before she could pull it off, he had her again, wrapped in his arms. His bare chest pressed to hers, both already damp with sweat, and they abandoned themselves to a kiss.

Astrid twined her legs around him as he lifted her up. The swollen head and shaft of his cock slid between her folds, and she nearly felt embarrassment at her wetness. She wanted him so badly.

As he wanted her. His cock surged, solid and demanding, at the intimate contact. She moaned. Their gazes caught and locked again as he lifted her up higher and then brought her down, slowly, so slowly, filling her. Every inch of him sliding into her, breath by breath, flesh within flesh. He branded himself upon her with his deliberate heat and thickness. His retreat was just as slow, just as deliberate, and she felt his absence in her body like grief.

Astrid canted her hips to take him inside her once more. Another immersion into complete ecstasy, one that made her eyes flutter. But she would not allow herself to close her eyes. She kept them open, holding Nathan's gaze, as he moved in and out of her with purposeful strokes, teasing, testing, taking them both to a place where bodies fused and hearts merged. They would not allow themselves to hide. *This is who we are,* their gazes said. *Together.* They sealed their bond through touch and sensation, as intimate as if they had opened their hearts like books to be read and studied.

Pleasure built, a conflagration atop an inferno. She gripped him with her arms and with her inner muscles. She would hold him however she could.

"I want," she panted. "All of you. Now."

"This," he growled, punctuating the word with a hard thrust of his hips.

She cried out at the sharp pleasure. "Yes."

He braced her against the trunk of the pine and drove into her again. "This."

Exquisitely speared by him, she did not feel the bark at her back, only the thick slide of him within her. "More. Yes." She was frantic now, driven only by need, as she impaled herself on him. Then she lost the ability to speak, only made formless sounds of desire and demand. Nothing had ever felt this good—continents could be formed upon the mass of her ecstasy. It overwhelmed everything.

His thrusts grew faster, harder, as he abandoned himself to the pleasure she eagerly offered. His breath came in harsh rasps. The whole of his body gleamed with sweat, and he held her as he delved as deeply as he could into the welcoming heat of her, urging them both toward coalescence and release.

She bucked, crying out, with the force of her climax. White fire consumed her. She became nothing but ashes and pleasure. And then she did something that seemed entirely right.

She bit him. On the neck.

Hers. She marked him as hers.

At the touch of her teeth against his skin, Nathan jolted, then his body completely stiffened and a fierce, rough groan tore from him. It sounded like murder or resurrection. Or a mix of both. Her name was a benediction on his lips as he flowed into her, molten, like the core of a planet.

He trailed kisses of satiation over her face, her throat while she made formless sounds of contentment. And gradually, reluctantly, they loosened, her legs sliding down his, so that she stood upon the ground. Even then, they did not take their arms from each other, but leaned together against the tree, foreheads touching, and breathed in the forest at night, as though the world had only just been created.

By the light of the fire, Catullus examined his Compass. No one had made alterations to the design, not since Portia Graves's time, and it seemed about due for some improvements, incorporating innovation and new technology. Lately, he'd been thinking about adding a means of measuring distance and possibly height. Such options could prove useful for Blades in the field.

He looked up briefly when the breeze carried the sound

of a soft moan. Astrid. Out there in the darkness with Lesperance.

Catullus was forty-one years old. He knew precisely what Astrid and Lesperance were doing.

Bending back to his work, Catullus took a small screwdriver from a slim case and began to carefully remove the front plate of the Compass. He knew what he'd find within the Compass, having disassembled his own hundreds of times. Whenever he found himself in the field, away from his workshop, and needing a distraction for his busy mind, he invariably dismantled his Compass to search for ways of refinement.

Yet the mechanism and magnets could not hold his attention tonight. He didn't want to think about Astrid and Lesperance making love, but, for all the attention his brain received from the world, he was still a man, with a man's needs.

Penelope Welham. The last woman he'd taken to bed. That was . . . six weeks ago? Eight? A prosperous mercer's widow in Southampton, Penny had a long-standing arrangement with Catullus. When he was in town and found time away from his workshop, he made semiregular visits to her bed. Neither Penny nor Catullus expected fidelity from the other. In truth, they expected nothing more than a few hours of sex. Conversation was kept to a minimum. Neither inquired about the other's life. They were convenient for each other, and that was all.

Catullus forced himself to concentrate on the Compass. Such a simple device, yet he knew it could be made better with only a few small adjustments.

He was happy for Astrid, truly. He could not resent her moving forward. And that she had found love not once, but twice, astounded him. Catullus had spoken truthfully when he told her he'd never once been in love. He felt like an alchemist, hearing tales and seeing with his own eyes the transformation of lead into gold, yet unable to make the metamorphosis himself.

When it came to sexual experience, Catullus had his fair share. But beyond the physical act of making love, he was nearly as green as a youth half his age. He found that, when out of bed, he and his lovers barely understood each other. The women were fascinated by either his skin color or his intellect, finding him to be an intriguing enigma but not truly a man. Conversations were awkward, stilted, and he never truly knew what to say. The women were largely blank. His mind drifted back to his work. At least there, he found something that stimulated more than his body.

A growl unfurled from the darkness. Somewhere between a man and an animal. But entirely carnal, utterly erotic.

Catullus gritted his teeth together at the sound. He couldn't fault Lesperance and Astrid for making love this night. Quinn's death hit them all hard, and it was natural to affirm life, and love, through the joining of bodies. Yet still, bloody irritating to be reminded that, while Astrid and Lesperance had discovered love with each other, Catullus was deeply, profoundly alone.

Usually, he could combat those feelings being out in the field. Not this time.

He came from a venerable line of intellectuals, all blessed—or cursed—with extraordinary minds that perpetually churned out ideas and inventions as readily as most people ate. And almost everyone in his family, with the notable exception of odd Aunt Sabrina, had managed to find spouses or long-term romantic partners. Some of the marriages were more successful than others, yet, for the most part, domestic felicity had been attained by generations of Graveses. The very fact that he was alive attested to this.

Why was he different? Were his standards simply too high? Should he try to make himself more accessible to the average woman?

He didn't *want* the average woman. He wanted a woman with whom he could be fully himself, in all his peculiarity, and who engaged him on every level. He knew it would be nigh impossible to find a woman whose brain worked as his did, constantly at work on dozens of inventions simultaneously, his mind picking apart the world and searching eternally for the whys and wherefores. That would be excruciating, for both of them. Yet there had to be a woman out there, *somewhere,* who wasn't silly and wasn't dull or strident or insubstantial or pedantic or . . . ordinary.

Such women did exist. They were Blades of the Rose. But he had learned early the important principle that female Blades were for friendship and the shared goal of protecting Sources. Not lovers.

Oddly, the flame-haired Miss Murphy from the trading post popped into Catullus's mind like an errant spark. She had a luscious figure, it was true, but he'd seen something in her bright blue eyes that attested to a depth and energy he'd seldom found outside of the Blades. He remembered how she took in the dilapidated saloon, missing nothing, alert to everything around her. Including—nay, especially—him. Intriguing.

He would never see Miss Murphy again, and, even if he did, it would not matter. He reminded himself of this as he closed up the Compass. He, Astrid, and Lesperance were on a desperate bid to protect the Earth Spirits' totems and Astrid herself. Already their search had cost one Blade his life. And, should they succeed, the Heirs still held the Primal Source and would be unleashing it upon an unsuspecting world—soon. Very soon. Nations and the lives of millions hung in the balance. There wasn't time or room for Catullus to brood and feel sorry for himself. The sorrows of his heart held no place here.

Yet, as he waited by the fire for Astrid and Lesperance to return from their nocturnal tryst, Catullus wondered only half in jest if he might be able to replace his heart with one made of clockworks. A mechanical heart could never feel lonely.

* * *

Swift Cloud Woman stood with her arms crossed, watching from her place in the forest encampment with sardonic detachment as the men who called themselves Heirs swore and spat and blamed each other for their defeat in the caverns.

Back in the caves, their medicine man had extinguished the flames that barred them from the totem's cave, only to find their prey—and Swift Cloud Woman's prize—gone.

Rather than chase their quarry like clumsy idiots, the Heirs and Swift Cloud Woman had retreated, back through the caverns, and then out, past the body of the slain man. He had died well, she thought, a courageous warrior defending his brothers. That hadn't stopped her from rifling through his pockets, searching for anything of value. Nothing there except a bone-handled folding knife and a few wilted wildflowers. She took the knife.

They had staggered back down the mountain, everyone in foul temper, until one of the guides found a good place for the night's encampment. No sooner had the tents been pitched than the men all began arguing, carrying on or else sulking.

"They were right there!" the fat white man whined and readjusted the bandage over the slight bullet graze on his hand. "Already had the totem!"

"You shoot worse than a blind drunkard," the tall one called Milbourne snapped.

"But *you're* the marksman," sneered the fat man. "And you didn't even hit the Indian. And *you,*" he yelled, rounding on the bearded medicine man. "Bloody lot of good your spells did us, Bracebridge. Light a few trees on fire and then nothing! Just a sodding flint, you are."

"Careful, Halling," seethed the medicine man. "Or I'll make your balls swell like rotten melons and explode."

"Muzzle it, all of you," the leader spat.

"Why?" the fat one sulked. "You need silence so you can devise yet another brilliant plan?"

Meanwhile, the remaining two mountain men passed a jug of wretched liquor back and forth, as disinterested in the death of their fellow guide as they were in the argument.

Men were fools—white men especially. Never taking responsibility for their actions. Never thinking beyond a handful of moments in the future. They stumbled forward, fists flailing, cocks out, and then bawled like elk when they didn't get what they want.

Winter Wolf had been different, though. A noble warrior. And wise. Wise enough to know that the territory of the Earth Spirits had to be kept pure from defilement. Her brother understood that, of the two siblings, she possessed the sharper mind. Without her guidance, he acted recklessly, so she planned their attacks against trespassers, their routes for patrol. She hadn't the ability to take an animal's shape, so Winter Wolf became her weapon. And he was proud to do it.

Fresh outrage surged anew to think of her brother's death. He had been foolish, hunting alone while she was busy plying miners with cheap whiskey heavily laced with water hemlock. She had intended to take their valuables when the convulsions began. But she had felt something was wrong, and left the white men to froth and seize. Winter Wolf was not at their little camp, and did not return for many days. Only when she ventured to a nearby trading post did she see him—or what was left of him. His wolf pelt hung off the back of a trapper's packhorse. Where his body lay, she never knew, but she knew precisely where to find the body of the trapper who killed her brother. Behind a saloon, where she had lured him with lusty promises and then slit his throat. Yet it did not bring Winter Wolf back.

Foolish boy. Swift Cloud Woman dragged her fist across her leaking eyes, furious. With herself, for leaving her reckless brother alone. With Winter Wolf, for being so rash as to get himself killed. With the white man, who befouled her lands with their greed. But most of all, with the Earth Spirits.

She would have retribution. She would make the Earth Spirits suffer. In the best possible way. They thought themselves so proud and free, valuing their independence most of all. But they would bend to her. Each and every one. Even, and this was best, the One Who Is Three. The most powerful Earth Spirit, hers to control.

Such wonderful plans she had. A hard smile twisted her mouth. With the totems in her possession, Swift Cloud Woman would command the wolves to eviscerate their own parents, the bears to tear the limbs from their own children, the hawks to peel at the flesh of their spouses. And One Who Is Three would drink the blood of his white lover.

Oh, Winter Wolf, you will see from the Hunting Grounds, and you will laugh, as we laughed at the pleadings of unclean intruders, begging for their lives.

She would see this all come to pass. Hate was such a wonderful fuel, burning cold and clean.

"Silence, everyone!" She strode into the middle of the encampment and felt a thrill of triumph when every one of the men was rendered speechless. She regarded all of them, each in turn, and they gaped at her like mice beneath a hawk's shadow.

"Stupid white men," she said, derisive. "Perhaps your medicine man can conjure up some testicles for each of you."

They continued to stare at her, stunned, until the fat one recovered enough to trundle forward. "I'll thrash you, redskinned bitch," he blustered, finger pointing through the bandage on his hand.

His howl split the air, followed by an arc of red that spattered in the dirt. The fat man cradled his hand and gawked at the tip of his finger, now lying in the dust. "You cunt!"

Swift Cloud Woman sheathed her knife coolly. "Threaten me again, and I will flay you. Slowly. Beginning with your big pink belly and ending with your big pink rump."

The medicine man and the tall man chuckled as their fat

companion sniveled, retreating. The leader, Staunton, however, narrowed his eyes as he gazed at her.

"I'd appreciate it," he said, silkily, "if you don't wound any of my men. They're no good to me injured."

"Make sure they give me no cause," she answered.

He tipped his head in acknowledgment, then held out a hand. "Now that the floor is yours, please enlighten us."

She ignored the thread of sarcasm in his voice. "Tell me—what is it you all seek? Why have you come so far from home?"

"We come for the glory of England," Staunton answered at once. "We seek whatever means we can to help our nation."

"The triumph of Britain," threw in the medicine man.

"All the world will belong to the Crown," added the tall man.

"*Most* of it," amended Staunton quickly, seeing her flare with alarm at this idea.

The fat man only whimpered.

She shook her head. "No, this is what you claim, but it is not truly what you desire. Each of you claims to work for a greater power, yet in each of your hearts, all you covet is power for yourselves and none for your fellow warriors. Like a child hoarding berries, stuffing them into his face until his belly aches. Then one of you is sick and the rest have nothing. As you have nothing now."

The medicine man and the tall man both snorted in derision, but the leader raised a brow at her. He was truly listening to what she said. It seemed he was well suited to his role.

"If this is true, what would you suggest to remedy the situation?" he asked, only slightly ironic.

"Remember that all that matters is the tribe," she counseled. "Do not try to be the lone warrior with the most coups, for that does not bring victory, only boasts. You are all part of the same tomahawk, working as one to cut down your enemy, and you"—she pointed at Staunton—"are the tomahawk's blade."

The leader made an ironic grimace. "I'd ask you to refrain

from saying the word 'blade.' However," he continued, "I see your reasoning. Perhaps we can work somewhat more . . . co-operatively."

"Yes, a plan for the next battle. Each of you to play a part that leads to one thing—conquest."

"What would you know of tribes?" challenged the tall man. "Yours exiled you."

Hot humiliation and anger darkened her cheeks. "Everything that my brother and I did was for the tribe. Yet they were too weak, too soft. They were not willing to be strong and merciless. And for being what they should have been, my brother and I were cast out. For that," she clipped, "I vow to see them punished."

"Sounds selfish," noted the medicine man.

"No," she said proudly, drawing herself up. "It is righteous."

"Exactly," agreed Staunton. "As righteous as what we do in service to our country."

Native woman and white man shared a look of mutual understanding. They alone truly grasped what it meant to dedicate oneself to the greater good. Strange that she would find that insight with a white man, her enemy. Yet it did not change her plans for the future.

"So, now that we've reached a true agreement," Staunton continued, clapping his hands together, "it's time to plot our strategy. *All* of us."

"Agreed," Swift Cloud Woman said, allowing herself to smile. She could hardly wait for what was to come next.

Despite yesterday's bitter loss, despite the omnipresent threat of the Heirs, the group traveled this morning with a definite sense of lightness and purpose. Two of the three totems were in their possession and safe. For now. The third, final totem was within a day's journey. Yes, the Heirs still wanted her, but she would not allow herself to dwell in fear of them.

"I think," she said softly, "we just might succeed in this mad venture."

Nathan, sharing in her enthusiasm, flashed her a grin that set the tinder of her desire alight.

"Careful, Astrid," warned Catullus, brusque. "Victory is never certain."

Well, *there* was someone who wasn't quite as optimistic or in good spirits as she and Nathan. Catullus had been silent, verging on sullen, ever since waking. She had a good idea why.

No one, not even scholarly Catullus Graves, would be particularly chipper after sitting alone and listening to people make passionate love in the forest. She had tried to take him aside earlier that morning and, if not apologize, at least thank him for his forbearance. He hadn't given her a chance to speak. Instead, he loaded up his pack and marched off into the woods. She and Nathan had scrambled after him before Catullus stomped away entirely.

"I do know that," she answered now. "Complacency leads to disaster. One of the Blades' tenets."

Nathan nodded, understanding. "Take nothing for granted."

Which she most definitely did not. As she and her companions threaded through the trees, following the path of the green river, Astrid could not keep her gaze from Nathan or stop her pulse from surging anew with each glance. Long-limbed and supple in purposeful movement, his body was known to her as intimately as her own. More, she knew the man who inhabited his sleek body, and when he caught her shamelessly admiring him, the heat flaring in his eyes nearly made her stumble. Or spin into the air like a loosened feather on a breeze.

Yet Catullus, surly as he was, spoke the truth. She was too seasoned a campaigner to fall into one of the most basic traps. So she kept herself alert to her surroundings, falling into old patterns of caution and readiness.

Silently, they pushed on through the dense, old forest, the

path of trees older and more wise than any mere human could ever hope to be. She listened to the sounds they made, their branches and the millions of fine green needles moving against each other, whispering ancient secrets.

As they passed a particularly weathered, aged tree, Nathan inhaled sharply, snaring her attention. His eyes were bright, sharp, as though they could see beyond the veil of time.

"I feel it," he said. His hand came up to hover over his chest. "Here. Growing stronger. A . . . rising, drawing me on. Up." He looked up, searching through the branches for something only he could see or sense.

Her own heart leapt with excitement. They were getting close. And another evolution in Nathan had already begun. "The totem is calling you."

Without speaking, he moved ahead, intent, and Astrid sensed it, too, the currents of power that flowed through the forest, the sky. She shared a glance of anticipation with Catullus, before Catullus remembered he was cross and walked on, his expression shuttered.

Afternoon, and the green river abruptly stopped.

They all stared up at the object blocking their path.

Nathan scowled, as if he could burn the thing down with the heat of his gaze.

"That is . . . rather tall," Astrid said.

"Like a cannon is a rather big gun," Catullus murmured.

A cliff, nearly a quarter of a mile high, towered over the three travelers. The cliff stretched toward the heavens, rocky face completely sheer, impassive, and flat. Nothing interrupted its indifferent surface—except a lone pine that grew halfway up the barren expanse. The tree pointed at an angle from the sheer face, toward the sky, isolated and proud.

And entirely inaccessible.

Chapter 17

Flight, Fight

"Not unexpected," Catullus murmured, looking up, as they all were. "But still, a surprise. I did not quite believe *anything*—aside from a titan—could be this tall."

"It's there," Nathan said, voice tight. "The totem. Held by the tree."

Astrid paced forward and placed her hand upon the stone. "There is nothing to hold on to. No way to climb. Unless," she said, turning to Catullus, "you've one of your ingenious devices in your pack."

"Alas, nothing that might work here." He looked almost sheepish at his oversight.

"Perhaps we could go around and try from the top," she suggested. "Lower ourselves down."

But Catullus shook his head. "We don't have enough rope." He gazed at the movement of the tree on the cliff. "And the wind would dash anyone to pieces against the rocks."

"And it would take too long to find a way around." Astrid swore, knowing the totem was so close but impossible to reach. She and Catullus stared up at the solitary tree, which seemed to taunt them from its height.

"There's another way."

Both Astrid and Catullus turned at Nathan's voice. He, too, was looking up, hands on his hips, expression focused, mouth a taut line.

"How?" asked Catullus.

Nathan's gaze snapped to his companions. "Fly."

Astrid's eyes widened. They had discussed the possibility that Nathan could change into a hawk, but he'd been unable to make the shift. "Can you now?"

He began pulling off his clothing. "Don't know," he growled. "But there's no choice. The totem's up there and we have to get it." He threw the last of his garments to the ground, readying himself, and then shut his eyes in concentration. Ragged inhalations sawed from him as he forced himself to focus inwardly, drawing upon the fury he had felt when first transforming into his other animal forms.

Astrid and Catullus held their collective breaths, waiting.

Nothing happened. Then, the mist of his change began to gather. Astrid clenched her fists in readiness.

The mists obscured Nathan, then dispersed. Leaving him crouched and snarling as his wolf.

The growl he made was pure frustration.

"It's all right," Astrid said, calm. "Try again."

His golden canine eyes closed, and the mists collected around him. This time, when they dissolved, Nathan hunkered in the enormous form of his bear.

He growled again, a sound so enraged that Astrid almost believed he would charge her and Catullus. Yet he retained the man within, and changed back into his human shape. He made use of this form by swearing long and viciously. Even Catullus, who had heard some of the coarsest language imaginable, started.

She went to Nathan, seeing the anger overtaking him. Anger for himself, because he refused to let her or Catullus or anyone down, but was met with the iron of his own resistance. His scowl was for himself alone.

"Nathan," she said softly. She placed her hands upon his

face, gently forcing him to meet her gaze. The fury blazing in his dark eyes left her breathless, that he could turn such anger upon himself. "Stop."

"I won't fail you," he snarled.

"You will not," she said, grave. "Nothing you do is a failure."

Catullus, bless him, had moved away to give them some privacy.

Finally, Nathan dropped his gaze and said, so low his words were a rumble, "I don't know what to do."

Her chest constricted. She could not imagine what it cost him to admit his fallibility, this proud man who was a born fighter. Yet he revealed the gap in his armor—to her, and only her.

She took one hand and laid it against his chest, feeling the hard throb of his heart within the enclosure of his ribs. He was hot satin beneath her palm.

"Here," she murmured. "The answer is here. It took anger to release the wolf and the bear, but I think you need to find something else within you to free the hawk."

"I don't know what that is," he grumbled.

She pondered. "What is a hawk? What does it mean to fly?"

At first, more frustration crossed his face. Then he subdued himself and listened, quieting. "Freedom," he said, after a moment. "The open sky. Lightness." The storm clouds in his expression began to dissolve, giving way to stillness, and the beauty of him allowing himself peace was a sight beyond magnificent.

"Yes." She kept her words soft but intent. "Find that in yourself. Whatever gives you that freedom."

His breathing slowed, the fast pounding of his heart eased, and a slow, wondering smile illuminated him as he looked at her. He stepped nearer, then leaned close and kissed her with an aching sweetness.

"You," he whispered against her lips. "*You* free me."

The bright pennant of happiness unfurled within her. And

then Nathan disappeared, enveloped in the mists of his transformation.

She felt the beat of wings, the lofting upward, and stepped back with a smile.

A handsome hawk hovered just above her—its wings a lustrous mosaic of russet and brown, tipped with black, its breast spotted tawny and umber, and the vivid red of its tail. She held out her arm, and the hawk alit, regarding her with its nobly shaped head and clear golden eyes. It held her carefully in its talons, though she knew the sharp claws could tear with no effort. The solid weight of the hawk surprised her a little, yet it was marvelous that such a relatively small body held all of Nathan.

"I knew you could," she said softly. She stroked the front of its chest with the back of her fingers, finding him as soft as a lullaby.

The hawk ducked its head, then gave a short cry. She could have sworn he smiled at her.

"That's Lesperance?" Catullus asked, coming nearer.

The hawk flapped its wings in response before settling itself.

Catullus chuckled, shaking his head. "Think of all the money you will save on train fare." Then, more seriously, he added, "Nicely done, Lesperance."

Nathan made a small chirp of acknowledgment, then ruffled his wings as a signal. She understood. Stepping away from Catullus, she gave her outstretched arm a slight push. A brief grip from his talons, the force of his body urging upward, and then—

He flew. Nathan soared upward. His wings beat powerfully, lifting him higher. First, in expanding curves, learning what it meant to fly. And then he grew confident, forceful, taming the invisible territory of the air and making it his. He let out a cry, wild and limitless. She had never seen or heard anything as beautiful.

Her eyes heated, blurred.

You, he had said. *You free me.*

Ah, if only she could be up there with him, enjoying the liberty of flying. But she wouldn't begrudge him his own flight. She watched him as he grew smaller, wheeling upward, her own feet firmly upon the ground. Love, she began to understand, also meant letting go.

A dream. This had to be a dream. Countless times, he'd dreamt of exactly this: soaring, released from the earth, the whole of the world beneath him in a patchwork of green and gray, all around him infinite air, wind and cloud and sun. Boundaries dissolved, he was completely free.

He hadn't the fledgling's fear. The sky was his. He knew instinctively how to use his wings, when to push against tides of air, when to glide. Drunk with possibility, he wheeled and dove, making the earth small and large and small again. He laughed, and the sound was a hawk's cry.

Astrid should see this. She should feel it. To share the sky with her was exactly right. But impossible. He was the rarest of the Earth Spirits, able to take the shape of not one but three animals. And she was only human.

He saw her beneath him, watching him, the precision of his sight allowing him to see the golden strands of her hair loosening from her braid and trailing across her cheek. She seemed so tiny, so vulnerable, and the world so gigantic. He had killed for her. Would do it again without a second's hesitation. But her smallness was an illusion. No one stronger than Astrid, not in the whole of the earth.

In this new form, he could fight beside and above her, wherever the battle took them. And he would. First, he had to get the totem.

Within his hawk's form, he felt the totem's power as surely as he felt the sun upon his back. It called out to him with the strength of a hawk's cry.

Nathan turned to the single, defiant pine, growing proudly

from the side of the cliff. He saw the totem at once, carefully nestled in the branches. The talon of an enormous hawk, nearly the size of an entire ordinary bird, a leather thong attached to it as with the others. God, would he have to battle a giant hawk, as he had the wolf and the bear? Didn't matter. He'd face whatever he must to get thc totem and keep it out of the Heirs' hands.

He brought himself close to the tree, then perched upon the branch holding the totem. Using his own talons, he edged closer, cautious. At any moment, some supernatural hawk could come screeching to life, and he had to be wary. He glanced down, seeing Astrid and Graves far below, watching attentively.

Astrid gave him a slight nod and smile, encouraging.

He moved forward, then stretched out a grasping foot toward the totem. When he touched the totem, surges of soaring power flooded him, the sensation of flying hundreds of thousands of miles above the earth, the hunt and the kill, rising and falling through the air. Literally in his grasp was the might to command every hawk Earth Spirit, to tame their will and make their wings his own.

Another temptation, one he would fight just as he had fought and mastered the temptations offered by the wolf and bear totems.

He waited, grasping the enormous talon with his own, but no colossal hawk appeared. It might truly be this simple—if turning into a hawk and flying up the side of a towcring, sheer cliff could be called simple.

The totem's size made it too unwieldy to hold in one of his talons. So he gripped it with both and prepared to take flight, bringing it to earth and ensuring its safety.

A familiar falcon's scream tore the air, and suddenly, it was upon him.

The falcon dove at him, screaming. Razor-sharp beak, slashing talons. It hacked at him everywhere—his face, his chest. A swarm of knifelike wounds, swathing him with burning pain. Wings slapped the air, a blur, as Nathan fought against the attack, balancing precariously on the branch.

He remembered this falcon—its shrill alert at the trading post had caused the Heirs to abduct him, and later, it had circled overhead, tracking and reporting their progress to the Heirs. Now, in his own avian form, he knew the falcon's thoughts, its pleasure in bloodshed, carefully cultivated by its masters. He saw in its mind its hunting without purpose, without the need to feed, but only for the amusement of killing. A specially bred monster. It wanted him dead, wanted the prize he clutched in his talons.

It launched itself at him, a frenzy of bites and tearing. In Nathan's talons was the totem. He had only his beak and wings to counterattack. Changing into his other forms wasn't possible. The branches of the tree were too slender to support anything other than a bird's weight. He had only the shape of his hawk with which to defend himself.

And so he did. He lunged and struck, aiming for the falcon's talons—the worst of its weapons. A satisfying scream of outrage when he hit home, tasting blood. Angry and surprised that its prey had the gall to fight back, the falcon charged, only to be forced back by Nathan's assault.

The falcon didn't give him much room as it flapped backward, but it was all he needed to take to the air. Better to fly than be cornered within the branches.

With a beat of his wings, he shot into the sky, the falcon in close pursuit.

"*Jävlar,*" Astrid hissed. She stared down the sight of her rifle, following Nathan and the Heirs' falcon as the two birds of prey wheeled in the air. The damn falcon had come from nowhere. Astrid had been careful to watch the skies and saw nothing. Yet here it was, attacking a hindered Nathan. She had to help.

Whatever distance Nathan was able to put between himself and the falcon never lasted long enough for Astrid to take a decent shot. Even if there was enough room between the two birds, not even an experienced riflewoman like Astrid could hit such a small moving target.

"Can you take a shot?" she asked Catullus, whose shotgun was also trained on the aerial battle.

"Too far up," growled Catullus. "And they're spinning like trick kites up there."

Astrid cursed again, burning with rage. Short of growing her own pair of wings, there was nothing she could do to help Nathan. Only watch as he fought for his life.

The falcon clung to him, a mass of feathers, beak, and talons, all ripping, scratching, thirsty for his blood. Without his own talons, he was at a loss to retaliate, to take the initiative. And that infuriated him. He could only dodge and defend as he clung to the oversize totem.

The totem threw his balance. Holding it hampered his maneuverability. The falcon, unencumbered, was a hell of a lot more agile, and that cost him.

He could lead it down. If he got close enough to the ground, he could shift either into human form or even wolf or bear. That gave him more options. And Astrid and Graves could protect the totem as he fought.

He banked and readied for descent. But the falcon saw what he meant to do, and its attack grew fiercer. It slashed at his wings, his talons. Scorching trails of cuts crisscrossed him, and he struggled to clasp the totem.

A better purchase was needed. He moved slightly to readjust his hold—the opening the falcon needed. Its knifelike beak stabbed at his talons. Reflexively, his grip opened.

The totem fell.

Damn it to hell. He and the falcon plunged down, racing to catch it. But his injuries—including those from the day before, not fully healed—slowed him no matter how hard he pushed himself. He and the falcon sped downward, the ground growing closer, the falcon edging ahead.

It grabbed the totem. And continued its dive. Nathan urged himself nearer. Talons free now, he tore at the falcon, felt the satisfying rip of feather and flesh.

Then it surged onward. Shook itself. And suddenly a wave of energy pulsed from it, pushing him back.

Engulfed in bright light, the falcon shrank, then expanded. Nathan dove forward and was thrashed back by the beat of enormous wings. He spun away. Stunned, he hovered for a moment, trying to gain his balance. Then mentally swore at what he saw.

The falcon was no longer an ordinary animal. Now it was a creature of legend, grown to the size of a carriage, wings broad as sails. Clutched in one of its massive talons, the totem looked no bigger than an infant's rattle. That alone sent a bolt of cold fury through Nathan. But true rage, blinding in its intensity, slammed into him when he saw that the falcon headed straight down. Right toward Astrid.

Words sputtered and died in Astrid's mouth. It could not be. Yet it was. Before her eyes, the Heirs' falcon abruptly grew. To monstrous size.

"Good Christ," Catullus swore. Aptly put. But it seemed that the will of heaven had nothing to do with what they faced now.

She'd battled giant creatures before, but never witnessed an ordinary animal transform into an enormous beast.

"Bracebridge's work, surely," Astrid mused, grim. And now it clasped the totem in one massive talon.

Nathan looked so small beside the falcon, and when the huge bird's wings knocked him away like a gnat, anger and fear gelled within her.

She raised up her rifle. She had a bigger target now. "Get closer, you parakeet," she snarled. "I'll blast you to pulp."

"I believe the parakeet heard that," Catullus said, voice flinty. "It's headed straight for us."

The falcon indeed sped down. Racing directly toward where she and Catullus stood. And the closer it got, the more Astrid realized how bloody *big* that bird was. Its beak could slice her in two. She suddenly felt like a defenseless rabbit in a field, seeing the huge shadow over her.

Like hell would she flee. She braced herself and took aim. In the corner of her eye, she saw Catullus do the same. They both inhaled, steadying themselves. Then fired.

The falcon swerved, avoiding Catullus's shot. But Astrid's bullet clipped the tip of one wing. It squawked as giant feathers scattered, large as fronds.

"I think we made it cross," muttered Astrid.

They reloaded, fired again, yet the creature dodged the bullets.

"Astrid," Catullus warned. "It's heading for *you.*"

She glanced up. And saw he was right. The falcon was diving straight toward her. Wings outstretched, eyes glittering with avarice, talons glinting like swords. A vision from the depths of hell.

She fumbled to reload with fingers that felt far too stiff.

Catullus bellowed, "No time—run!"

There wasn't a choice. The shadow overhead grew. The falcon was almost on her.

Astrid ran, heading for the cover of the trees. She heard Catullus shouting behind her, the blast of his shotgun, and Nathan's hawk screams of rage.

Almost to the trees. The pines grew too close together for the falcon to follow. She sprinted, nearly at the boundary of the protecting woods. Then felt herself wrenched backward. Hot pain shot through her shoulders and back. Her arms were pinned at her sides.

She lifted up, the ground disappearing beneath her feet.

Her rifle fell and became a tiny toy as it hit the ground below her. The falcon gave a triumphant shriek, piercing and loud.

The damned winged beast had her.

Thought fled. He flew forward, propelled by rage and horror. *No.* Astrid struggled, writhing and twisting, to free herself or at least reach the knife in her boot or her pistol.

But the falcon held her tight and nothing she did could set her loose. Didn't stop her from trying, though. He would have admired her spirit but was too choked with fury to do anything but reach her.

Nathan pursued. He no longer felt the pain of his wounds. There was only forward. Yet it didn't matter how hard he pushed himself, the falcon's wings were bigger, its speed faster.

He would reach her. *Had* to.

Another surge of strength rolled through him and he managed to draw close enough so that he flew beside her. His vision clouded when he saw the blood on her back where the falcon's talons clutched her.

He shot forward, intending to slash at the huge talons, then pulled back. A glance down revealed they were hundreds of feet in the air. If the bird dropped Astrid from this height, she'd never survive the fall. *Goddamn it.*

Astrid saw him, and alarm flared in her eyes. She snarled her frustration at her capture, hair whipping around her face.

"In my pockets," she shouted above the wind and deafening flap of the falcon's wings. "I put the totems there when you shifted into a hawk. Take them."

He didn't care about the damned totems. He wanted her.

At his hesitation, she growled, "Do it. Quickly."

Nathan flew closer, then plucked from her pockets the wolf and bear totems. He clutched them in his talons. And continued to fly alongside, keeping pace with the falcon. The giant bird paid him no heed as it soared over the forest. It had its prize, and Nathan was less valuable. But Nathan would fight the beast for Astrid.

"You have to change form," Astrid yelled.

Like hell, his gaze told her. The falcon had to land at some point, and when it did, he'd be there, ready. His best chance to follow was in hawk form.

She saw his refusal and clenched her teeth in frustration. "With the totem, they can control you as a hawk," she shouted. "Be anything. Wolf. Bear. Man. But not a hawk."

With a foul mental oath, Nathan realized she was right. With the hawk totem in the possession of the Heirs' familiar, he would have no free will in his hawk form. The Heirs could make him do anything. Including hurt Astrid.

It infuriated him that he couldn't speak. So he let his eyes say what he could not, holding Astrid's gaze. *I'm coming for you. I will not stop until you're safe.*

"I know," she said, quieting, her silver eyes warm. She held his gaze and tried to memorize him, as though—and this he couldn't allow—saying good-bye. "I love you."

He hated his animal forms. They took words from him, the multitude of things he had to tell her. That she was the breath in his lungs and the gleam of his soul. That he loved her beyond reason, beyond self. And would do so until the fabric of the world dissolved.

He *would* say these things. He refused to believe this was the last they would see of each other.

But he couldn't even *touch* her, damn it.

"Go now," she mouthed.

Heart torn into shreds, Nathan wheeled away. A rending within as the distance between him and Astrid grew.

He felt the hawk totem reaching out to him, snaking tendrils of control, trying to rob him of his will. Just before he became engulfed in its demands, he landed and shifted into his wolf form, already running. In his mouth, he held the leather thongs attached to wolf and bear totems. Dimly, he saw his body covered with cuts, oozing bright blood and staining his fur, but the wounds belonged to someone else.

He could still see her, above him, and he hurtled in pursuit. Eyes to the sky, he watched with helpless fury as the falcon and Astrid shrank with distance, no matter how fast he ran.

Sensing him, the falcon turned its head and let out a piercing shriek. The sound reverberated, a noise so shrill and high it stabbed through his sensitive wolf's hearing. He felt himself stumble, then realized it wasn't him that shuddered, but the ground beneath him.

The shriek did not stop, and, as it continued, fissures spread through the earth under Nathan. It quaked and rumbled, then split apart into gaping crags. Trees, dirt, and rocks tumbled down. Roaring, a fissure cracked open beneath his feet and began to widen.

He leapt, trying to keep on solid ground. But the fracture widened and he found himself tumbling down in a hail of debris. He scrabbled for a hold, shifting in mid-fall into a man. Yet every rock or outcropping he grabbed crumbled beneath his hands. He fell, the earth swallowing him, the last of the falcon's shriek ringing in his ears.

Astrid—

A hard slam as he hit bottom, then darkness.

The falcon's scream nearly cleft her head in two, but she tried to shake off its effects. She couldn't break free of the falcon. Fighting now would only use up her strength. She had to wait. It would land sooner or later, and when it did, she would be ready.

The earth below her sped past, a panorama of trees, valleys, mountains. Sky all around, vast as eternity.

A god's view. Beautiful, or it would have been, if she wasn't being abducted. As it was, anger and fear turned the sight rancid. Not minutes before, she had wished to be in the sky, to share with Nathan the wonder of flight. Now she hadn't that wish, but a travesty of it.

At least Nathan had heeded her directive, changing out of his hawk form. He would be safe from the totem's sway.

Would she see him again? She squeezed her eyes shut, allowing herself the barest moment of weakness. This capture might almost be easier to bear if she had nothing and no one. But he'd come crashing into her life, bringing energy and motion and love, and now to lose all this, to lose him was a deeper wound than she could bear.

No, she thought fiercely. Whatever awaited her when the falcon landed—and she had a good idea it wasn't going to be pleasant—she would fight and stand, until there wasn't breath or blood left in her.

As the falcon flew, Astrid kept a careful eye on her surroundings, noting direction. If she did manage to get free, she'd have to find a way back to Nathan. She didn't know this part of the Territory, but she was an able mountain woman.

The falcon banked, heading toward a forest clearing that held an encampment. Astrid tensed. People gathered there, pointing, their faces turned up to the sky. Waiting for her.

He was a boy again. He stood in Mr. Engleby's study, and the headmaster was angry. Once more, he'd been caught trying to run away, and, once more, Mr. Engleby railed at him, calling him an ungrateful heathen brat. Didn't Nathan know that most Indian children had to live in misery and godlessness? Nathan should be thankful to be the recipient of such generous condescension, to be brought up in the proper English way. If Nathan was truly lucky, he might one day become a carpenter or blacksmith or even, God willing, a teacher.

As Nathan listened to this blistering lecture, aware that it would be followed by a beating from Mr. Engleby's cane, he felt he had to leave. He had to leave *now.* Time was running out. Didn't Mr. Engleby know? Every second Nathan spent in his office meant that it was getting away, that she would be gone. He had to reach her.

"Now, this will never do, Lesperance!" snapped the headmaster. "I did not give you permission to turn into a wolf!"

Nathan glanced down and saw not his boy's feet, but the paws of a wolf, standing upon the faded Turkish carpet. *Yes,* he thought. *It will help me run. To catch her.*

"Such insolence," hissed Mr. Engleby. "I will show you who is master here, Lesperance!"

Then Nathan felt the sting of the cane. Again and again, but it was more of an insistent pelting than the usual bite that left red welts. Mr. Engleby kept hitting him, kept saying, "Lesperance! Wake up! Lesperance!"

He had to leave. Had to go. And he wouldn't stand another second of the headmaster's punishment.

He growled, swatting away the annoying sting.

The sensation abruptly stopped. "Thank God," someone said above him. "You're alive."

He was no longer in Mr. Engleby's study. Rocks and sticks poked into his back, and a coating of dust filmed his mouth. Everything felt stiff and sore. He cracked open his eyes from beneath lids that felt mortared shut, and winced at the crescent of light above him. Someone's head peered over the edge, but the person had two reflective circles instead of eyes.

"Lesperance!" the man called. "Can you hear me? Are you injured?"

Nathan struggled to sit up, every part of him protesting the movement. His head spun for a moment before the ground beneath him righted. Looking around, he found himself at the bottom of a deep ravine, surrounded by fallen tree trunks and rocks. He struggled for several seconds to remember just where the hell he was, still drifting between dream and waking. He fumbled beside him and felt the barest relief when his hand closed over both the wolf and bear totems. At least something was safe.

"I lost the falcon," the man shouted down. "There was no way to keep up."

Damn it. Astrid.

Nathan surged to his feet, ignoring dizziness and blinding pain. His body was a network of bruises and cuts in different stages of healing, some more fresh than others. Something wet trickled down his side and, when he touched it, his hand came away red. He wiped it on his thigh, leaving a smear of blood.

"Easy," Graves called. "You took a bad fall. Actually—you look like hell."

Nathan glanced around, assessing the situation. The chasm was thirty feet deep, fifteen feet wide. The walls rose up steeply. The lower part of the walls was composed of huge, smooth slabs of granite, while farther up, smaller rocks jutted out. If he could trust taking his hawk form, flying out would be simple, but the hawk totem belonged to the Heirs, and so flight wasn't a choice.

Astrid. Every second he was here, the farther away she got. The Heirs might have her already.

He almost sank to his knees, slammed with rage and panic.

"Can you climb out?" Graves asked.

Shoving aside his fear for Astrid, Nathan strode to the wall and made a few jumps, trying to reach the part of the wall that had more hand- and footholds. But they were too high up, and every time he landed, excruciating pain shot through him.

"Can't," he growled. "Any rope?"

Graves cursed. "In Astrid's pack, back at the cliff."

Nathan hadn't any idea how far he'd run or how long he'd been unconscious. All he knew was that to have Graves go back for Astrid's pack and then return would take too long. There had to be another way out. He scanned the bottom of the chasm again, searching for something he could use, and his gaze alit on the jumble of tree trunks scattered like jackstraws. He realized with a start that he'd been damn lucky not to have been crushed underneath any of them as they fell with him into the ravine. But now they offered a solution.

"Got an idea," he called up to Graves.

He allowed the shift to come over him and, in an instant, looked down with dark satisfaction at his bear's giant claws. With his mouth, he picked up the thongs laced to each totem. Then felt the brute strength of his ursine form as he moved toward the piles of fallen trees.

He put his paws against one of the trunks on top and shoved. The pine rolled as easily as a twig rather than a trunk with a two-foot diameter. In his human shape, he'd never have enough muscle to move it on his own. But as a bear, incredible strength was his for the using. He pushed the log, sliding it along the ground until it came up against the wall of the chasm. Another shove, and the trunk tipped upward, braced between the ground and the wall. It wasn't easy, though. He had a bear's strength but not a human's dexterity. A frustrating process of trial and error until he got the log just where he needed it.

"Good man," Graves called down in approval. "Or, uh, good bear!"

Nathan shot him a glance before throwing himself back into his task. After testing the sturdiness of the propped trunk, he dug his claws into it and began to climb. The tree protested under his weight, threatening to splinter. Nathan growled. He would have only one chance at this. None of the other trees at the bottom of the ravine would support him.

"Try your wolf," Graves suggested. "It's lighter."

A good suggestion, and one Nathan immediately took. He felt his body grow smaller, sleeker. Ah. Better, though fractures still spread throughout the tree. Balancing, he climbed up the wedged log until he was within a few feet of the chasm wall.

Nathan leapt, using the powerful muscles of his back legs, aiming for the closest handhold with his claws. At the same time, the tree beneath him groaned, splintering. It gave a loud crack before splitting in two and tumbling to the ground.

"Careful, Lesperance!" Graves shouted.

Nathan pushed himself upward, forcing the shift faster than he ever had before. And scrabbled on the handhold with human hands. He had just enough grip to hang in midair, his feet dangling fifteen feet above the ground. Agony burned his arms as they bore his full weight. He clenched his teeth around the totems' thongs, the claw and tooth swaying and knocking into his chest.

"Climb ten feet more," Graves urged. "I've got a branch up here just long enough to reach you."

Drawing in a fiery breath, Nathan pushed himself upward, hunting for handholds. Blood trickling from his fingers and palms made his grip slippery. He searched, and found, narrow wedges in the rock wall, and hefted himself up. Dug his toes into the rock and used the force of his shaking legs to propel him higher. Each ascending inch was a torment, his body demanding surrender, but he ignored all of it. Only Astrid mattered.

Then, lifetimes later, Nathan saw a stout branch lowered by Graves. "Take it," the man urged.

Nathan wrapped his arms around the branch. Using his feet, he helped push himself up as Graves pulled. A minute later, Nathan found himself sprawled at the lip of the ravine, gasping. He raised his head to see Graves, gleaming with sweat, lying on his back.

"You're damned heavier than you look," Graves panted.

"Thank . . . you . . . ," Nathan rasped. He cast a glance over at the branch that had been used to haul him up. "Very . . . soph . . . sophisticated design."

Graves offered a wry smile. "Yes, the best my famed brain could come up with under duress. The most primitive lever."

Nathan pushed himself up onto hands and knees before

staggering upright. He took a step before his legs shuddered under him.

Graves was supporting him within a second. "Slowly now, Lesperance. You're banged up worse than a regimental drum."

"Astrid—" Nathan rumbled, hating the shaking in his limbs.

"Doesn't need you killing yourself," Graves said sharply. "I want her back, too, but you're of no use if you push yourself too hard. Sit."

There was little choice as Graves lowered Nathan to the ground, then handed him a canteen. Nathan took several sips of water and felt slightly better. He noticed that Graves had both Astrid's rifle and his own shotgun, as well as the pistol at his waist.

"Why didn't you stay with them as a hawk?" Graves asked.

"It's got the damned totem." Any reminder that he'd had to let Astrid go sliced him open. "The Heirs could make me their puppet. Almost did."

Graves cursed, understanding the truth.

"I'll get her back." Nathan's voice held enough edge to cause sparks.

"She still has her Compass." Graves took his own Compass from his pocket and showed it to Nathan. Sure enough, the needle pointed in the direction where the falcon headed. "We can track her with this."

The other man's slightly trembling hands revealed his own barely contained anger.

Nathan shook his head. "I don't need the Compass to find her."

"How—?"

"Here," he gritted. He placed his fist in the center of his chest, where a sharp, cutting pain screamed, obliterating everything but the need to reach Astrid. "I feel her. We're . . ." He tried to think of a word that contained everything he felt for her, which was everything, and the living connection that stretched between them like a shared sense. But words were lost in his fury and fear.

He could only say, "We're bonded." He sent a defiant glare to Graves, as if challenging him to contest this.

Graves, wisely, didn't argue. He saw at once that Nathan spoke in dead earnest. He gave a clipped nod and put the Compass in his pocket.

"Take these." Nathan handed the totems to a shocked Graves. "If anything happens to me, keep them safe."

"They belong to your people," Graves protested.

Time was slipping away. Darkness would fall soon, making their task that much more difficult. "I trust you. And," he added with a grim smile, "I don't have pockets." He rose to his feet, glad to have regained some of his strength.

Graves also stood. "We'll find her, Lesperance." He held out a hand.

Nathan clasped the offered hand, sealing the vow. "I know." Because there was no alternative. And he knew that if there was one man he could count on as an ally, at least where Astrid was concerned, it was Graves. He released his grip on the other man's hand. "I'll see you there—when it's time to annihilate those bastards."

Graves nodded. "That you will."

Nathan broke into a run, releasing his beast simultaneously. His body shifted, re-formed into his wolf, running first on two feet and then four. Fur and fang, deadly intent and instinct.

Yes, this was exactly right. He had the speed and the will to kill. And he would. Blood would be spilled that night. Until Astrid was safe, he would cut down anyone in his path. Without her, he had nothing, only rage and sorrow.

He paused, just long enough to throw back his head and howl, pouring everything into the sound.

It echoed throughout the wilderness, his howl, through the forest, the mountains, over rivers and fields of ice.

Enraged and heartbroken and louder than an army of cannons. Nothing hidden. The best part of him was gone. He mourned. He threatened.

Everywhere, all around, the forest stilled, arrested in motion by the wolf's howl. It held the wilderness in its frozen, furious grip. Everything shivered.

Let the Heirs know he was coming, he thought, savage. Let them know that death awaited them.

He bound on swift legs into the forest, not sparing a backward glance for Graves. The other man would catch up. As the earth sped beneath Nathan, he vowed that he would get Astrid back, and kill as many Heirs in the process as he could. If his own life was lost to ensure this goal, it was a price he was willing to pay.

Chapter 18

The Assault

Her husband's murderer. Years had passed, but his face was a recurring nightmare. An incongruity. The face of a killer should be twisted and ugly. Yet Albert Staunton was a rather pleasant-looking man, of medium height, well formed and possessing regular, even features. A model of British manhood, hale and gently bred. Someone's perfect son.

She fought gagging on her disgust and wrath.

As the falcon neared for its landing, Staunton ambled forward with a welcoming smile, an amiable host. Still a dozen feet off the ground, the falcon opened its talons, releasing Astrid. She landed in a ready crouch, reaching for her pistol.

"Please, Mrs. Bramfield," Staunton said, grinning affably. His mild voice brought back a flood of bitter memories. Rage swept through her, leveling everything in its path. "Let's not make this troublesome."

"Let's," she answered. She pulled her gun and cocked it with one motion.

Then found herself utterly frozen, gripped by an invisible fist.

Darkest fury misted her sight. Trapped, utterly trapped, and entirely helpless.

Bracebridge walked forward, his hands making patterns in the air, chanting softly. His spell held her immobile. As he neared, he passed the now earthbound falcon. The mage gave his familiar a fond pat, and the bird stuck out one talon, the totem within it offered up like a kill. Bracebridge took the totem, cooing his gratitude, as if the falcon was merely a pet and not a monstrous beast. The two grizzled mountain men nearby eyed the falcon warily.

"Good girl," Bracebridge murmured. "Did you work the Earthsplitter Spell? Did you? Such a good girl."

Earthsplitter Spell? Astrid did not like the sound of that at all. Was Nathan all right? The scream of the falcon still rung in her ears, and she had seen the earth begin to shake, cleaving apart. Nathan might have fallen, or been crushed by tumbling rocks. He could be hurt, or worse. She wanted to scream her frustration, but forced herself to silence.

Instead, she took in the layout of the camp, the people within it, to learn as much as she could. The encampment stood in the middle of a clearing, with thick evergreens encircling the perimeter. Beyond lay the forest, and possibly freedom, if she could reach it. But she need not run. She could use her environment to her advantage. Five tents were scattered in the clearing. Packs and gear lay strewn about. At the center of the camp, a fire burned—openly, displaying the Heirs' arrogance. They did not care who was aware of their presence.

Of the Heirs themselves, all four were accounted for—Staunton, Bracebridge, Richard Halling, and John Milbourne. Faces she knew all too well. The mountain men left little impression beyond their fur-covered coats, matted beards, and greedy eyes.

The Native woman, Swift Cloud Woman, stood off to the side, watching everything vigilantly. Only Astrid noticed the woman staring at the totem greedily.

"Halling, take her weapon," Staunton said.

While Astrid remained bound by the spell, a heavyset Heir

she recognized as Richard Halling approached tentatively. A bloody bandage was wrapped around his hand. He cast a glance at Staunton, uncertain.

"Take it. Follow the plan." Staunton's pleasant demeanor chipped a little with his snapped command. "She can't hurt you."

Halling edged closer and reached for Astrid's pistol, as one might reach into a basket containing a serpent. She hissed at him, and he jumped back. Petty of her, but she'd take what victories she could.

Seeing that she truly could not move, Halling sauntered forward. He plucked the pistol from her hand, smirking.

At least she still had her knife, if she should get free of this spell.

"Check her boot," said John Milbourne.

Astrid bit back a curse. Halling took the opportunity to slide his doughy hands down her hips and legs. Acrid bile burned her throat at his touch.

"Just another reason why women shouldn't be in the field," Staunton said with a pretense of dismay. "Someone might take advantage of them."

Knowing chuckles from the other Heirs, including Staunton. Halling found her knife, then, after slithering his hands up the insides of her legs, stepped back with a triumphant grin.

"Declawed the cat," he crowed. "She can't hurt us now."

Astrid found that the binding spell still allowed her to speak. So she said, "Your father bought your way onto this expedition, didn't he? No other reason why you would be here. Unless," she added thoughtfully, "the Heirs had a halfwit quota they needed to fill."

Halling turned red, then moved to strike her.

"Careful, Richard," Staunton warned. "Remember the plan. We don't want to hurt Mrs. Bramfield. Not unless we must."

With a mulish sulk, Halling stomped off, but not before giving Staunton her pistol and knife. Staunton tucked the gun into his belt and tossed the knife into the fire. He strode to Astrid, his eyes almost pitying.

The closer he got, the more Astrid shook within the confines of her invisible prison. Each step revealed his humanity, the fact that he was no more than another person of flesh and breath. No longer the colossal embodiment of evil, but only a man. A man who killed without compunction. Somehow, this revelation made everything worse, because Staunton was simply human, with will and vulnerability, who made the choice to commit murder for his ambitions.

"I think you know what we want," he said.

"You know I won't tell you anything," she replied.

He placed his hands on his hips. "Your answer is not unexpected."

"Then you understand," she said, "that as soon as I can, I will kill you."

"Death is part of our work, Mrs. Bramfield," he replied mildly. "Your husband knew that."

"It was *your* bullet that killed him. And since he is dead, and I am not, I will see you punished for that."

He was unmoved by her vow. "Whether there will be more death is entirely up to you."

She narrowed her eyes, but said nothing. God—if only she could break this bloody spell. Her pistol, so close. Even without a weapon, just to be able to move and wrap her hands around Staunton's neck, crush his windpipe. Killing Staunton could not bring Michael or Max Quinn back, but it might provide a small measure of justice. Or satisfy her need for vengeance.

At her silence, Staunton continued. "I offer you generous terms. Tell us what you know about the Primal Source—"

A harsh sound approximating a laugh scraped from Astrid's throat.

He shot her an annoyed glance. "Tell us everything you know, and in exchange, we shall grant you freedom. You've grown close with your Indian comrade. Danger can do that to people. He wouldn't object to warming your bed, too. Just think of it," he added, cajoling. "You and the shape changer, safe in your little wilderness cabin. Perhaps coming to love each other. No more Heirs. No more Blades. Only peace."

"And a litter of half-breed babies," threw in Halling with a snicker.

"Shut it," snapped Staunton over his shoulder, then turned back to Astrid, gentling his expression. "Doesn't that sound lovely, Mrs. Bramfield? A quiet, safe life. Never again having to confront the prospect of the man you love dying in your arms. Could you face that again? Seeing your Indian paramour gasping his final breaths, and you, powerless to help him?"

She swallowed thickly around fiery pain, desperate to block out the images his words conjured. But she could envision it plainly: Nathan, lying as Michael had, bathed in blood, his eyes going glassy, his sleek body cooling as she cradled him.

"And if you refuse," added Bracebridge, "you will most assuredly see that come to pass."

Staunton asked, "So, what is it to be? Give us what we need and save your future lover's life, or refuse and watch him die."

Everyone waited, watching her. Even Swift Cloud Woman stared at her, awaiting her answer.

Astrid felt each beat of her heart, even as her body was paralyzed. She had not noticed when in the falcon's clutches, but now she sensed it. An invisible yet gleaming, luminous band around her heart. It spun out from her like a web, fine but strong. Stretching out, reaching. Connecting her. To Nathan. Somewhere out there, in the forest, far away but getting closer. And even with the distance between them, he was there, in her. The bond had been forged over the past weeks, and made everlasting the night before, when she revealed her love and they cemented their bond through the joining of their bodies.

Once, she might have been afraid of severing that bond, might have even consented to obliterate her every principle in order to preserve it. Now her bond with Nathan gave her the strength to do what she must. She knew he would understand her choice.

"There's a third option," she said.

"Yes?"

"I tell the lot of you to go bugger yourselves."

Staunton heaved a sigh like a disappointed parent. "You *are* going to be tiresome." He turned to the assembled Heirs and their mercenaries with a snap of his fingers. "Pack up. We formulated a plan, and we shall adhere to it. We have the woman, so we're moving out."

"But it's almost dark," complained one of the mercenaries. "We can't travel at night."

"No time for niceties," Staunton barked. "We leave tonight." As everyone hurried to do his bidding, he swiveled back to Astrid. "I may have neglected to mention something rather important."

"Your parents sold you to a carnival for the price of gin. You're really a French tightrope dancer."

A corner of Staunton's mouth turned up. "Ah, droll humor. The last refuge of the desperate."

"Just ask your wife."

He shook his head. "Alas, I am not married. Women tend to make life exceedingly aggravating. As you are graciously proving now. But what I failed to mention to you before is that, if you did not consent to disclose what you know about the Primal Source, we will be forced to take you with us."

Icy fear clutched the back of Astrid's neck, yet she said, "To the circus?"

"To England. Yes, my dear Mrs. Bramfield," he said in response to her unguarded look of shock, "my fellow Heirs and I are most eager to have you enjoy our famous hospitality. You see," he continued with a warm smile, "at our headquarters in London, we have a lovely, quiet room in the basement. Equipped with sound-deadening panels and the very latest in persuasive devices. And all waiting just for you."

Miles unraveled beneath him as darkness fell. He crossed forest and river, vaulting over rocks, skirting mountains. Animals scurried out of his path, alarmed by the sight of a large, dark wolf tearing through the wilderness, a beast possessed. His paws took scrapes and cuts as he sped across sharp stones and unstable earth.

It meant nothing. He felt only the pull on his heart, the searing pain of Astrid's loss. No. She was not lost. He could find her. *Would* find her.

Nathan raced on, drawn forward by the bright path of energy she left in her wake.

Confined within her invisible prison, watching the Heirs and their mercenaries pack up their camp, she was losing her battle against panic. To be taken back to England, away from Nathan, kept like a rat in the basement, tortured—

No. Thousands of miles stood between her and that basement. Somehow, some way, she would find a way free. They could not keep her captive in this spell forever. She would seize any opportunity en route to escape.

The Native woman, seeing the Heirs distracted by their preparations, edged around the camp's fire and sidled close to Astrid.

"The totems," she hissed at Astrid, eyes bright and avaricious. "Where are the other totems?"

"You truly believe I will tell you where they are?" Astrid answered.

A hard, cunning expression settled over Swift Cloud Woman's face. "You are white, but not a fool."

"But *you* are a fool," said Astrid, "if you think you will be able to wrest any of the totems from the Heirs."

No answer from Swift Cloud Woman but a flash of fury in her dark gaze. Though frozen in place, Astrid almost recoiled from the violence and hatred in the Native woman's eyes, a hatred directed toward everything and everyone. Astrid realized that, out of all the people within the Heirs encampment, perhaps Swift Cloud Woman was the most dangerous.

"The One Who Is Three," she sneered.

With an internal jolt, Astrid remembered the Native woman saying this before, back at the cave entrance. When Nathan made his first transformation into the bear. The first sign that he was not an ordinary Earth Spirit.

"I heard his howl. The sound of a beast pining for its lost mate." Swift Cloud Woman pushed the words out like a taunt. "He is coming for you."

A thrill of joy and terror burst inside Astrid, but she said nothing.

"Only once every seven generations sees the birth of the One Who Is Three. A warrior of legend. He comes now," Swift Cloud Woman said, then voiced what Astrid was afraid to think. "It will not be enough. These men will kill him, and you will watch."

Astrid felt these words as surely as a stab to her heart. "I will not tell you where the other totems are."

At this, Swift Cloud Woman's mouth arched into a tight smile. "Despite yourself, white woman, you are wise."

"Such sagacity wasn't easily gained."

The Native woman shared a look with Astrid. Shining in her eyes, like a tiny, flickering flame, were the last vestiges of Swift Cloud Woman's humanity—that still loved and mourned. But hatred damped this flame, nearly extinguishing it. Soon, the flame would be gone forever.

My God, she's not that different from me. Or how I once was.

But no one had brought Swift Cloud Woman back from her darkness, and she dwelled there, forever.

"What?" the Native woman demanded, seeing the expression change on Astrid's face.

"There is no hope for you," Astrid said quietly. "All the vengeance in the world will not bring back the dead."

Swift Cloud Woman shied back from Astrid and, with a snarl, stormed away, leaving Astrid alone to twist upon the spikes of fear and hope. She desperately longed to see Nathan, but she knew that the Native woman spoke the truth. Even with Catullus providing assistance, the likelihood that the Heirs would slaughter both men was too great. If it meant never seeing Nathan again in order to save his life, Astrid would readily consent.

But such a choice would decimate her.

He'd never faced a more difficult decision. All he wanted—*needed*—to do was race into the encampment and start tearing out throats, slicing men to tatters. Everything within him demanded he do just that.

Yet, as Nathan crouched in wolf form just beyond the boundaries of the Heirs' campsite, watching them, he knew that to do that, to unleash his animal impulses without thought or plan, would not only kill him, but endanger Astrid.

He stifled the growl that wanted to rumble from his throat. A growl of both relief and rage. Relief that she was unharmed. Rage to find her captive. She was there. Standing not thirty feet from where Nathan hid, her back to him. Something kept her immobile, though. He saw it in the rigidness of her posture, her unnatural stillness. He had a strong suspicion the magic-wielding Heir was responsible for that.

Again, he forced down the need to just slam into the Heirs' encampment and start spilling blood. A direct assault wouldn't work, not with men so dangerous and Nathan on his own. His mind spun with plans, strategies. If he went for the mage first, Nathan could free Astrid, then, with her armed, they could both take down the Heirs. But, even though he knew the Heirs wouldn't risk killing Astrid, they had no issue with killing him. Even in bear form, he was just a creature of mere flesh. One well-aimed bullet would see him dead, and Astrid still captive.

How, then, to do this? On his own, there seemed no possible way. He was unarmed, save for his teeth and claws. The Heirs had a hell of a lot more magic at their disposal. One man—or wolf, or bear—against six, plus the Native woman and the enormous falcon. Nathan could not do everything himself.

He needed help. He needed Graves.

A surprising, humbling moment. Nathan had spent the whole of his life acting on his own, guided by only his judgment and impulses. Even when he had left the Earth Spirits to follow Astrid, he'd answered to his heart alone.

Yet he saw now, there was a value in being part of a collective. Knowing that someone else would be there, watching his back, tending to the tasks he could not do alone. It wasn't weakness, but wisdom.

But how long would Nathan have to wait? The Heirs were packing up their camp, which meant they were moving out, and soon. If Graves didn't show up quickly, Nathan would have no choice but to act, and hope like hell he had enough fury in him to see Astrid safe.

"Something's troubling Duchess."

Staunton glanced over to Bracebridge, who was patting and soothing the giant falcon. The bird—seemed ridiculous to call it that when it was the size of an outbuilding—shifted from foot to foot, ruffling its feathers and making chirrups of unease.

"Magic is close," Bracebridge said.

"You've got a Source literally hanging from your neck," noted Staunton.

"Perhaps," the mage allowed, hand hovering over the hawk talon. "All the same, I should make preparations, in case we do have visitors. And you?"

Even though he knew it was there, Staunton touched the pouch that hung from his belt. "I am ready for callers as well."

"Should be a lovely gathering," Bracebridge grinned, already anticipating being able to use his newest spell. What the mage had planned made Staunton's gut clench in revulsion, but Bracebridge was always eager to advance his magic use. Better that he should try the spell than Staunton.

With a nod, he left Bracebridge. As he strode to finish breaking down his tent, he was pleased to see a growing look of unease on Astrid Bramfield's face. Good. Her mettle always annoyed him, the fact that she inherently believed herself as good or strong as any man. A poor example of British womanhood—not the docile, ornamental female who dedicated her life to pleasing and serving men, to creating a warm and welcoming haven in the home. Of course, Staunton had little experience with that himself, with no wife of his own and a mother dead in childbed, but in principle it needed to be upheld. An empire was built upon the stability of its foundation, and women were the foundation of everything.

Movement in the corner of his eye snared his attention. The Native woman was pacing like a metronome, back and forth, glancing between Astrid Bramfield and Bracebridge. Or, more specifically, the totem around the mage's neck. Swift Cloud Woman looked ready to pounce at the slightest provocation. He wasn't sure what to do about her. Now that the Heirs had Astrid Bramfield and one of the totems, they had no more use for the Indian female.

He'd have to get rid of her somehow. Either pay her off, or something a bit more drastic. A shame, really. She had more intelligence and understood him better than most of Staunton's men. Which made her dangerous.

Staunton surreptitiously checked his pistol, ensuring it was loaded, then again touched the pouch at his waist. Whatever happened, he would be sure to be ready. His goal of mastering the Primal Source was too close, and he would be damned before anyone got in his way.

A faint rustling nearby. Nathan tensed, then let out his breath.

"I smelled you coming," he whispered after shifting into his human form.

Graves, crouched low, face shining with perspiration, grimaced as he neared. "At this point, none of us are particularly crisp. Even me." He glanced down ruefully at his once-pristine waistcoat, now grimy and torn, and the scuffed toes of his formerly gleaming boots. Thank God it was dark, or else the man might have been so dismayed by his appearance he'd be inconsolable.

"You made good time," Nathan said in an undertone.

A handkerchief, somewhat less than snowy, appeared from Graves's pocket, and he used it to clean his spectacles and mop his brow. "Thank God I take exercise every day, else I'd be whimpering in a ditch somewhere." The square of cambric returned to his coat. "I half expected to arrive and find you already paws-deep in Heirs and bullets."

Nathan softly snorted. "Came damned close."

"Glad you didn't," answered Graves. "You might have the makings of a Blade, after all. If that's what you want," he added.

"I can't think that far ahead," Nathan rumbled. "Only now matters." The wait for Graves had destroyed what patience he had, so now he was a bundle of lit fuses, ready to detonate. His only consolation was that his wounds had more time to heal. He jerked his head toward the encampment. "They're pulling out, which doesn't give us a lot of time."

Graves, peering through the undergrowth, surveyed the scene, lit by firelight. "Four Heirs. Two guides. The sodding big falcon. And that Native woman—she looks like a viper." He studied Astrid and cursed. "Bracebridge has our girl in a binding spell."

"How do we break it?"

"Either he breaks the spell on his own, or we need one of his teeth."

Nathan's smile was feral. "That won't be a problem." He and Graves turned to observe the camp. Nathan spoke low and quickly. "I've made a survey of the area. We've dense forest all around us—should provide some good cover—but it hinders maneuverability. Two paths lead out; they'll be taking the southern one. There's nothing in the camp we can use for protection. Even the tents are being taken down. All the men are armed with at least one pistol and plenty of ammunition."

"Very good, counselor," murmured Graves with admiration.

It surprised Nathan that he actually enjoyed Graves's approval. "And you're the tactician. So, what kind of plan can you formulate?"

After they quickly came to an agreement on their tactics, Graves smiled darkly. "Much as I love science, there's nothing quite so inspiring as an old-fashioned fight." He silently loaded his shotgun and closed the breach.

"Tonight, you'll have plenty of inspiration."

She couldn't abide helplessness, yet there was nothing she could do while Bracebridge's spell held her tight. Only watch as the camp was broken down. The tents were collapsed, the pack animals loaded.

Staunton paced toward her. "I believe it's time for us to leave, Mrs. Bramfield. Rather a shame your Indian and

Graves didn't show. I was hoping to tie up those loose ends, but," he said regretfully, "we can't have everything we want."

"I know," she answered. "Otherwise I would have gutted you long ago."

He opened his mouth for a retort, but the words never came.

Instead, Astrid's heart leapt into her throat as a familiar wolf sprinted out of the darkness, her rifle gripped in his jaws.

The camp burst into a frenzy of excitement as men whipped out their guns. A volley of shots from all around, but the wolf ran straight through the encampment, between the men, so that none could take aim without risking shooting their comrades. Nathan cast her one quick glance, weighted with everything, before disappearing into the darkness on the other side of the camp.

All the guns turned to the direction in which he'd vanished, opening fire. A storm of bullets chopped into the brush. Astrid's stomach seized in terror as she seethed at her imprisonment. If only she could grab someone's gun—help balance the odds.

Then, the sharp crack of returning gunfire from the darkness. The Heirs, their mercenaries, and Swift Cloud Woman all scattered, looking for cover, before shooting back. But the muzzle flash of Nathan's rifle kept revealing his location, so that no sooner did he get off a shot than the Heirs traded fire. Even if Nathan kept changing position, sooner or later, the Heirs would find him and cut him down. He couldn't possibly hold them off on his own—and she was no help to him.

A shotgun blast boomed from the other side of the camp—opposite where Nathan sniped. Yet there wasn't time to wonder where the blast came from. The encampment suddenly filled with blinding light. A flare. And Astrid had a very good idea who was responsible.

She smiled as the camp shattered into chaos.

* * *

Nathan allowed himself one vicious smile as Graves's flare turned the encampment into brightly lit anarchy. Knowing the flare was coming allowed Nathan to shield his eyes, and as soon as the light flashed, he seized his chance.

He shot into the camp and managed to frighten the already terrified horses. The animals bolted into the forest, taking the Heirs' gear with them. At the same time, Graves, stationed opposite him, fired his shotgun, clipping the arm of an Heir. The falcon shrieked.

One of the mountain men spat and swore. "I'm gonna get that son of a bitch," he snarled and charged into the woods, heading straight for Nathan. The mercenary's pistols blazed. Hot trails of bullets whizzed inches from Nathan.

Enough with the damn weapons. Nathan dropped his rifle and felt the surge of massive strength through his body as he shifted. The mountain man had just enough time to lurch to a halt before screaming. But by then, it was too late.

Catullus, creeping closer, heard the scream, followed by the bear's bone-chilling growl. Everyone in the camp froze in terror as the scream turned into a wet gurgle. Even Catullus shuddered at the sound.

The other mercenary panicked. With a yelp, he bolted into the forest—right toward Catullus. Just enough time for Catullus to flip the shotgun and swing it like a club. The butt of the shotgun collided with the grizzled man's head. He sprawled, insensible, in the scrub, hardly uttering a groan. Catullus surveyed the mercenary at his feet dispassionately after taking his pistol. If the mountain man ever did regain consciousness, he'd be rewarded with a blistering headache.

Four Heirs left, including the goal, the mage. Catullus slung his shotgun over his shoulder and drew his pistols. His plan with Lesperance seemed to be succeeding. Which meant it was time to create a diversion.

* * *

Astrid couldn't duck as pistol shots rang out from the forest, but she trusted Catullus's aim—for that's who it had to be. A spark of elation flared within her. They were both here. Catullus and Nathan. And despite the frenzy of bullets and shouts around her, she couldn't have been more glad to hear the sounds of gunfire. If only she could join in rather than stand around like a useless statue! This was beyond infuriating.

In the confusion of gunfire, no one saw Nathan in human form spring from the darkness. He launched himself at Bracebridge. The two men grappled together, rolling in the dirt. From Nathan, a hail of punches and blows, direct and fierce, eyes glittering. Astrid gaped at the sight. She'd seen him fight in his animal forms, but never before as a man. He spared nothing for the mage, but Bracebridge fought back, as adept with his fists as he was with magic. The mage plowed his knuckles into a barely healed wound in Nathan's side, and Astrid sucked in a breath to see Nathan wince in pain.

Blood darkened the dirt around them as they brawled. Whenever one of the Heirs tried to throw themselves into the fray, shots from Catullus forced them back. But when there was a snap, and the hawk totem suddenly skidded in the dust, both Richard Halling and Swift Cloud Woman threw themselves at it.

Heir and Native scuffled, each struggling for the totem. Hate for the other twisted their faces. Halling didn't care if his opponent was female—he threw punches as if she were a stevedore, not a woman. And for her part, Swift Cloud Woman fought back just as viciously, digging her fingers into the soft, unprotected parts of Halling's body. The man howled when she jammed a knee between his legs, but he retaliated with an elbow to her throat.

"You'll pay for that, too," panted Halling.

"Not if you die first," rasped Swift Cloud Woman.

Astrid dragged her gaze from the struggling pair back to Nathan and Bracebridge. Nathan's punches aimed for the mage's face, his mouth, until Bracebridge bellowed in pain and spat out a blood-covered tooth. The moment the tiny white tooth hit the ground, Nathan dove for it, abandoning Bracebridge.

As the mage cradled his injured mouth, Nathan, kneeling, held the tooth. Bracebridge's eyes widened. Nathan whispered something into his cupped hands.

"Goddamn it!" The mage's curse was more a spray of saliva and blood than words.

Suddenly, Astrid stumbled forward. Free. She was free.

She ran to Nathan, but there wasn't even time to throw her arms around him. His eyes burned her, searing with intensity.

"I am well," she answered in response to his unspoken demand. "You—"

"I'm here. Always."

They shared a kiss, brief and fierce. But now was not the time. Now she was free, and she would fight. With Nathan beside her.

Staunton whirled and, seeing her liberated from her prison, bellowed his rage. And Bracebridge, wiping his bloody mouth on his sleeve, rose up with a snarl.

Astrid and Nathan exchanged a glance, wry and affectionate. Time to do battle. So, with a final squeeze of assurance, they sprang apart, ready to face whatever came next.

Just to touch her again filled Nathan with a rush of power. Not even holding the totems had given him such a surge. But to feel her, whole, alive, and primed for combat, was as potent and bright as a strike of lightning.

He saw her grab a knife from the dirt and face Staunton. The two stared at each other across the expanse of the camp—two old enemies preparing for their final clash. Much as Nathan wanted to help Astrid, this was her fight. Staunton belonged to her alone, but like hell would Nathan let the Heir hurt her. If it meant saving Astrid's life, Nathan would kill Staunton himself. Better to face her anger at depriving her of her revenge, to keep her alive.

Nathan had his own battle to fight. He turned and faced Bracebridge. "Your damn magic tried to kill me," he growled at the mage. "And take her. But all that's going to end tonight."

"Oh, I definitely agree," smirked Bracebridge. "I've been waiting for this, red man." He raised his hands, curling them into claws, and muttered something in a language Nathan couldn't recognize.

He didn't know what Bracebridge was chanting, but he absolutely did not want him to finish saying it. Nathan sprang toward the mage. And was knocked back by a roiling wave of heat and animal stench.

The mage grinned at him. Then his grin faded, replaced by a grimace of pain as he bent over, convulsing. Something pulsed beneath the surface of his skin, as if his muscles pulled and swelled, reshaping themselves. Bracebridge screamed. He lurched upright, jerked up by an unseen hand, and a loud cracking filled the encampment as his bones split and grew. His clothing tore apart, unable to contain his growing body. Thick, black fur sprouted over his skin, covering everything, even his face. His scream turned into a snarl as his mouth and nose lengthened, his teeth elongating into wicked daggers, and his ears grew pointed. The nails of his hands and feet blackened, thickened into claws.

And then the transformation was over. Nathan stared at the enormous, unholy combination of man and wolf, neither one nor the other but something awful in between.

"Now, little dog," the mage growled, his words more animal than man, "let's see who is alpha wolf and who is dead."

With a snarl, Nathan's wolf surged out of him, and the two animals threw themselves into the fight. Only one of them would see the morning.

* * *

The sight riveted her. There were legends, of course, as old as time. Some internal scholar flipped through her mental archives, remembering the names. Loup Garou. Upir. Anjing Ajak. Werewolf.

Reading and hearing of such a beast compared not at all to seeing one. The visceral horror at seeing this profane transformation. A creature born of dark magic. Created from a man's body for one purpose—death.

Nathan's death.

"I do not want to kill you."

Her attention torn from the awful vision, Astrid's mouth formed a taut line as she stared at Staunton. "Your decency is commendable."

The Heir scoffed. "Words such as 'decency' are meaningless when forging global empires."

"Then there should be no empires."

His laugh grated. "The naïveté of you Blades never ceases to charm me."

Smiling coldly, Astrid brandished the knife in her hand. "I am a most charming woman." She motioned Staunton forward. "Let me show you."

He saw now. There was no way to take her, not alive. Whatever she knew about the Primal Source would die with her. A momentary slump of his shoulders, frustrated at the loss of her knowledge, before he straightened them.

Polite as a courtier, he said, "As you wish." Then he drew his pistol and pointed it at her heart.

Chapter 19

A Most Unusual Battle

The mage—or what the mage had become—lunged for him. At the same time, Nathan sprang toward the beast, aiming for his vitals. But the change had sharpened the mage's skills, and he knocked Nathan aside with a sweep of his arm, scoring Nathan with his claws.

Nathan rolled and recovered swiftly, then launched himself, teeth first, at the werewolf. He felt the gratifying sensation of tearing flesh, ripping away at the fur-covered skin across the beast's forearm. It howled, something between a man's shout and a wolf's yelp.

Maddened by shedding blood, the werewolf pounced, catching Nathan under his front legs. They fell, spinning together, in a fever of bites and slashes.

A movement distracted Nathan. He turned just enough to see Staunton with his gun aimed directly at Astrid, and her armed only with a knife. *No.*

Nathan thrashed to loosen himself from the werewolf's grasp, but the damn creature held him in a vise. He had to break free. Had to reach her.

The air suddenly filled with piercing hawk cries.

Everyone, the werewolf, Staunton, even the Heir and Native

woman grappling with each other, stopped in mid-motion and stared up at the sky. The falcon let out an alarmed screech.

And then they descended. Two dozen hawks, maybe more, diving and shrieking, beating their wings. A flurry of talons and beaks. All directed toward the Heirs. The men waved their arms and swatted at the attacking hawks, but the birds' assault was relentless.

Astrid, thank God, seized the distraction. She leapt forward and kicked the pistol out of Staunton's hand. The gun flew into the air and was caught in a hawk's talons. Nathan could have sworn the bird winked at him as it wheeled away.

Nathan felt something choking him, a burning in his throat. He struggled for a moment, thinking the mage was cutting off his breathing, then realized with a start it was something else. Emotion. Hot, unruly emotion.

They'd come. The Earth Spirits had come to his aid. They must have heard his howl of desolation and known he needed help. So they had left the safety of their village and come to give their support. And, of course, the hawks arrived first, the fastest of the Earth Spirits.

He had dismissed them, this tribe where he thought he didn't belong, but they hadn't given up on him so quickly. And now, here they were, fighting with him for the life of his mate.

Renewed energy pulsed through his body. He let it overtake him, felt his wolf give way to his bear, and felt viciously triumphant when he threw the werewolf back. The beast snarled up at him, but with a new fear as Nathan reared up on his hind legs, bellowing.

Oh, he was going to enjoy this.

But before he could attack, a barrage of talons and wickedly sharp beaks came at him from all sides. He grunted in surprise. The Earth Spirit hawks were bombarding him. And Astrid. But why? Moments earlier, the hawks had been his allies. Now he dodged their assault, growling with each scratch and bite.

"No!" Astrid shouted. She tried to evade the hawks as they swarmed her. "We're *friends*! Stop!"

Nathan didn't understand what could have caused the hawks' treachery. Until he saw the Native woman lying in the dirt, cradling her bleeding head, while the heavy Heir crouched nearby. Clutching the hawk totem.

The Earth Spirits were under his command.

Catullus had mulled allowing Halling and Swift Cloud Woman to kill themselves in the struggle for the totem, sparing him the effort. He did not particularly enjoy killing, and if someone else could do the work for him, he had no qualms reaping the benefits.

And when the hawks had thrown themselves into the battle, providing even more distraction so Catullus might return fire with Milbourne, so much the better. But then Halling snuck in a hard jab at the Native woman's temple, sending her toppling, and grabbed the totem. The Heir trumpeted his victory as he clutched the totem, and then the birds were his to control. Halling wasted no time in implementing his new weapon. The hawks launched themselves at Lesperance and Astrid while Halling and the other Heirs guffawed.

Nothing for either Astrid or Lesperance to do but bat the attacking birds back. Even Lesperance in his giant, brutal bear form couldn't really defend himself. Impossible to hurt one of the hawks while they were under the command of the Heirs.

Time to abandon the cover of the forest. Catullus charged.

Halling, caught up in his victory, didn't see Catullus until it was too late. Catullus tackled the Heir, then attempted to pin him down. Damn, but the man was heavy. And surprisingly agile. Catullus's punches landed in soft belly, and Halling squirmed like a fish as he tried to throw Catullus off. They both struggled for the totem, Halling holding it away from Catullus's reaching hands.

Then a feminine snarl, and someone latched onto his back. A rabid jackal. No—the Native woman. She wrapped one arm around Catullus's neck and squeezed. At the same time, Halling flopped beneath Catullus, trying to wriggle free. The corners of Catullus's vision began to darken.

Catullus hauled himself back and up, gripping the Native woman's arm, but Swift Cloud Woman wouldn't relinquish her choke, despite the more than a foot height difference between them. She snarled in his ear, "You and all intruders will be destroyed. I will see my land made pure."

With no breath of his own to waste, he didn't bother responding. Instead, Catullus dragged his shoulders up and ducked his chin, giving him a tiny measure of release. He stepped back, hooking his leg around the woman's. Then he pivoted, gripping her arm, and threw her to the ground.

She slammed into the dirt with a gasp. Catullus, fingering his abused throat, winced to contemplate what his mother might think of him hurting a woman. He hated having to do it. But Swift Cloud Woman recovered almost immediately and launched toward him. As he dodged her assault, he grimly reflected that his mother might forgive him in these extenuating circumstances.

The hawks dove at him, as they continued to attack Lesperance and Astrid. Catullus, ducking to avoid their assault, strode to where Halling was staggering to his feet.

"It's mine!" shrieked the Heir. Red stained his cheeks, like an overtired boy having a tantrum.

"Impolite to hoard your toys, Richard." Then Catullus plowed his fist into Halling's chin. This, at least, wasn't protected by fat, and as the Heir's head snapped back, Catullus seized the totem from Halling's weakening grasp.

The moment Catullus had the totem, he broke its hold over the hawks. The birds immediately stopped their bombardment, leaving Astrid and Lesperance free to face their enemies. But not before both sent Catullus looks of thanks.

Swift Cloud Woman sat up, a look of terror and hate

crossing her face as she gazed into the forest. Then Catullus understood why.

He didn't think he had ever been happier to see so many wolves.

Staunton spat out a clot of swearing as twenty wolves leapt into the encampment. They snarled, baring acres of gleaming teeth. The Heirs cringed. One of the wolves Astrid recognized as Iron Wolf, even bigger and more menacing than the others. At least, she thought with a bubble of giddy relief, the wolves were on her side.

"Don't worry, Staunton," Astrid said. "They won't kill you. That's *my* job."

"I wouldn't plan your victory celebration just yet," Staunton retorted. He reached for a pouch at his waist. "Be sure to set some extra places at the table." Then he flung the contents of the pouch onto the ground in a hail of numerous small, white objects.

One landed at Astrid's feet. It was a rune—a little bone tile with an ancient symbol chiseled into its surface. She had only a moment to wonder what Staunton planned on doing with the fortune-telling stones when they all sank into the dirt as if being drawn under by unholy gravity. The ground shook.

Astrid staggered back as something began to rise up out of the earth, where each of the runes had disappeared. At first, she thought they were worms—pallid, thick worms that writhed in the dirt. But then the worms grew, and she saw something was attached at the base of each worm, a larger, fleshy object connecting the worms together. Then she sucked in a horrified breath. Those weren't worms. They were fingers. Attached to hands. Which were connected to moldering arms. That were anchored to shoulders, and torsos. What looked to be scraggly weeds poking out of the earth pushed up in mounds, and then she realized the weeds were hair. Hair that patchily covered heads rising up from the dirt. Bits of skull showed between thatches of braided hair. The smell of decomposed flesh choked the air.

The creatures shoved and groaned their way out of the crumbling soil. Their skin held on to their bodies in rotted clumps, revealing gleaming bone beneath. Most of them were missing parts of their faces, their noses eaten away, cheeks either sunken or gone, eyes nothing but staring orbs in lidless sockets. All of the monsters wore crumbling leather armor and clutched rusty, heavy swords. A few held shields embossed with Celtic knotwork.

The creatures' awful moans settled like sickly vapor in the clearing. With shambling, shuffling steps, they started toward the wolves.

Astrid stared, horrified, at Staunton, who grinned wildly.

"The undead?" she rasped. It was disgusting, a violation, and the Heir couldn't have been more pleased.

"A good hostess should always be prepared for unexpected guests, Mrs. Bramfield. Quite sorry we don't have Quinn's body, or even your husband's. Otherwise we could have resurrected them both and had them join the festivities."

His taunt chopped into her. She had once wished so desperately for Michael to be brought back from the dead. Oh, she would see Staunton suffer. But first, she was going to have to do something about the zombie in her path.

In Nathan's animal form, the reek of the undead warriors struck like a blow. But their smell wasn't the worst of their arsenal. Though the creatures moved slowly, they were relentless. As wolves darted and snapped, the zombies pressed forward, swinging their huge, heavy swords. A yelp of pain announced that one of the undead had struck its target.

Nathan couldn't count the number of undead summoned—close to four dozen, at least—but they outnumbered the wolves. Worse, nothing seemed to stop the warriors. No sooner would a wolf rip out a creature's innards than it would rise again. Short of tearing the zombies into tiny pieces, there seemed no way to defeat them.

A host of guttural growls rolled from the darkness. When a group of fifteen bears appeared at the edge of the campsite, Nathan rumbled his own greeting. Among their number was Yellow Bear Woman, who had once captured him and Astrid and had been prepared to kill them for trespassing. Now she let out a quick growl of surprise to see him in bear form. But she and the other bears wasted no more time. They lumbered into the fight, and here at last the undead warriors found their match.

The wolves pushed zombies right into the path of the oncoming bears. With deafening roars and tearing claws, the bears shredded the creatures, even knocking one or two warriors' heads clean off. Yet the warriors fought back, hacking and slashing with their hefty swords. The encampment became a loud, frenzied battleground—wolf, bear, hawk, undead, and human.

More humans. Yelling war cries, human Earth Spirits ran into the encampment, brandishing war clubs and battle-axes. Men and women, and all fighting expertly, facing off against zombies without a break in stride. Including, Nathan saw with a start, wizened little He Watches Stars, who wielded a formidable ax and darted, quick as a lizard, into the storm of animal and undead bodies.

But there was more here than animal and human. In the middle of the camp stood a werewolf. Distracted for a moment by an assault of wolves and humans, Bracebridge whirled back to Nathan. On powerful legs, the mage hurled himself at Nathan, and they grappled, a mass of claw and tooth.

"A fine rug you'll make," snarled Bracebridge.

Nathan responded by tearing deep gouges in the werewolf's back.

A bird's shriek sliced the air. Not a hawk. Falcon. The Heirs' huge familiar had taken to the air, chasing hawks. It snapped at the smaller birds. Nathan watched grimly as one hawk screamed and fell, blood and feathers accompanying its descent. He shoved Bracebridge away and, shifting to wolf, leapt to intercept its fall.

Nathan just managed to catch the hawk on his back before carefully easing it down to a sheltered spot, where it made soft sounds of distress. A promise in his eyes that he would see to the hawk's wounds, but something first had to be done about the falcon.

With a vault, Nathan sprang into the air, changing into his hawk. He pushed his wings, forcing himself up, dodging bullets shot by the Heirs' marksman and the swords of the undead. As he rose higher, he cast a quick glance down. Below him, the battle was a churning throng of animal, human, and other. Astrid feinted and slashed at two advancing zombies. Graves sprinted toward the marksman, sidestepping attacks. Both Blades fought with precise skill, veteran warriors.

He neared the falcon, then joined the skirmish. The falcon stabbed with its massive beak and screamed its thirst for blood. Several hawks whirled away, carried off by injuries, thinning the numbers of Earth Spirits.

Nathan darted forward until he was just underneath the falcon. He flew beneath it, weaving from side to side to avoid its talons. He dipped a wing and rolled onto his back. He'd never flown upside down, and felt the challenge of staying on course. He heaved himself up and dug his talons into the falcon's chest, then shifted into his bear.

The falcon screeched as his weight pulled them down from the sky. They spun toward the earth, the falcon frantically tearing at him with its talons and stabbing with its beak. But Nathan's huge jaws and claws held more power. With a growl, he plunged his teeth into the bird's neck, his claws into its chest, and tore.

Blood and viscera rained down onto the battle.

They landed together, Nathan with a grunt, the falcon

without a sound. Nathan hefted himself up, shoving the bird's limp carcass to the dirt.

Above, the hawks cried out their tributes. Then circled down to rejoin the fight.

Bracebridge saw the lifeless body of his pet and howled in rage. The mage lunged for him. This time, when the werewolf and Nathan clashed, Nathan knew there would be no more distractions. One of them would die. And soon.

Catullus had no experience fighting the undead, but he was quickly learning the process was both arduous and disgusting. The damned creatures didn't know when to stop, no matter how many limbs he hacked off with a borrowed battle-ax. Which left the ground littered with decaying arms and legs and other . . . things. Things he really had no wish to examine closer.

He stepped in something, dodging a swinging sword, and slipped, going down on one knee. An unidentified substance dampened and stained the knee of his formerly immaculate Saville Row trousers.

"If I make it out of this maelstrom," he muttered, "I'm burning all these clothes."

Thank God he had allies. The encampment was filled with what had to be the most unusual battle ever recorded. Everywhere was a surging mass of fur, flesh, and feathers. Wolves, bears, hawks, and humans attacked the zombie warriors, while some grappled with the remaining Heirs.

Catullus turned at the sound of a man's scream. Not one of the Earth Spirits, but Halling. Judging by the pistol in his hand, the Heir had tried to shoot at an advancing wolf. But the wolf gripped Halling's hand in its mouth, drawing blood. His shooting hand incapacitated, there was nothing the Heir could do but weakly hold up an arm to defend himself when a bear lunged at him. Halling's next scream was cut abruptly short. He fell onto his back, and Catullus could only see flailing limbs as wolf and bear savaged their prey. One final twitch of Halling. And then he was dead.

But there was still the matter of Milbourne. The Heir coolly fired into the melee, wounding and felling Earth Spirits as calmly as if shooting tin cans rather than living beings. Catullus went for his own pistol.

And suddenly found himself thrown to the ground.

Swift Cloud Woman straddled him, her face twisted with rage, a jagged knife in her hand. She pinned his arms with her knees and held the knife to Catullus's throat. The edge of the blade bit into his flesh, and he felt a warm trickle down his neck.

"Give them to me," she hissed. "Give me the totems. Or I will cut your throat, black-skinned interloper."

"Have . . . we . . . met?" Catullus rasped.

Teeth bared, she pressed the knife against him with one hand, while the other scrabbled over him, searching for the totems. Including fumbling over a very private part of his anatomy.

"Awfully . . . forward," he said, hoarse.

He rocked one arm free and pushed it between her arm and his neck. He knocked her arm aside, taking the knife from his throat. She kept her hold on the hilt but was sufficiently unbalanced for him to rear up and throw her backward.

Swift Cloud Woman stumbled back, cursing in her native language, then spun when she collided with a large, dark wolf. Both wolf and woman snarled at each other.

"Iron Wolf," she jeered. She beckoned with her knife. "Now Winter Wolf's spirit will sleep, glutted on your blood."

The wolf growled, then crouched, readying to spring.

Catullus had a fairly decent idea who might win that encounter, and as he turned away to focus on Milbourne, he heard the woman's outraged screams. Looking back, he saw she lay unmoving in the dirt, the front of her buckskin dress black with blood. The wolf stood over her, its mouth stained red.

That Catullus did not kill Swift Cloud Woman might assuage his mother's conscience, but it wouldn't wipe his memory clean of seeing the Native woman's torn, still body.

Milbourne fired in rapid succession, sending Earth Spirits scattering for cover.

Spotting an opening in the battle, Catullus sprinted for the darkness of the forest. The sounds of struggle masked his movements as he pushed, quietly and quickly, through the brush. He edged around until he was situated behind Milbourne. Some might call Catullus's positioning dishonorable, but honor had little place when fighting for the lives of his friends and the safety of magic. Then he raised his own pistol and pulled the trigger.

The chamber clicked, empty. And so the next, and the next. Swearing silently, Catullus patted down his clothes, but found not a single damned bullet. He snorted at the irony. Famed inventor Catullus Absalom Graves, of the renowned Graves family, caught without enough ammunition.

He holstered his gun but moved forward. Time to take care of this without the advancement of gunpowder.

Milbourne didn't know Catullus was behind him until Catullus's hand chopped down on Milbourne's arm. The Heir's hand spasmed, causing him to drop his gun.

When Catullus spun Milbourne around, the Heir's sangfroid vanished. Face dark with anger, he threw himself at Catullus.

The name he called Catullus wasn't an unfamiliar one, but that didn't make the oath any less ugly. "Colored men have no place in England," Milbourne sneered. "It's only for the worthy whites."

"This from a man whose ancestors farmed and ate shit," replied Catullus.

Milbourne snarled, then attacked with a swift series of blows that made Catullus realize the Heir wasn't only an expert marksman, but a trained pugilist as well.

But so was Catullus. Thrice a week, at "Potato" McLaren's

boxing salon—more of an abandoned warehouse than a salon, but no one faulted Potato for his ambition.

The craggy Irishman's lessons were deeply ingrained, as well they should be, after Catullus had frequented the salon for over a decade. So Catullus launched into a series of jabs and hooks at Milbourne that would have made his trainer proud.

Catullus took a hard jab to the chest, temporarily winding him, but he shoved past the pain. When Milbourne came at him again, Catullus caught him in a lock, threw him down to the ground, and jabbed a paralyzing elbow into his solar plexus. The look of shock on the Heir's face was almost worth painting in miniature and wearing as a locket.

"That's not . . . gentlemanly," wheezed Milbourne. He sprawled, stunned, in the dirt.

"The benefits of training with a former merchant marine." Catullus took a length of thin, tough cord from his coat and, in seconds, had Milbourne trussed like a calf. He crouched down to the feebly struggling Heir and gave his face a friendly pat. "I think the local population will truly enjoy treating you to their hospitality."

Milbourne glanced over to where the Earth Spirits were busy reducing their undead enemy to pulp. Panic flared in Milbourne's eyes, and he tried to twist free. Catullus sighed.

"This should help," he said, and promptly knocked Milbourne unconscious.

Astrid spun away from the undead lurching toward her. They just kept coming. When one reached up to strike with its sword, she slashed, using her knife. The creature's rotted flesh split beneath her blade until her knife rested against bone. Swallowing her revulsion, she trapped its arm between her own in a lock, then twisted. With a wet crunch, the zombie's forearm broke off.

She snatched the creature's hand before it hit the ground,

then pried its fingers open and grabbed the sword's grip. She let the forearm and hand fall to the dirt. And swung out with the sword.

It was a heavy weapon, but its weight gave it power. Using both hands, she chopped her way through the zombies that cluttered her path to Staunton, scattering limbs and, in one case, a head.

Staunton watched, smirking, as undead warriors swarmed her. But his smirk faded as she hacked down zombies—little caring that she was spattered with bits of flesh and slivers of bone. And when nothing stood between her and the man who had killed Michael, fear turned Staunton's face chalky. No doubt she looked like a Valkyrie, her battle-crazed eyes, wild hair, and torn and bloody clothes.

They faced each other. The battle raging around them receded. Staunton clutched a knife while Astrid held a sword.

"Mine's bigger," she panted, smiling brutally.

"You are the most troublesome bitch," Staunton clipped. He ripped a sword from the hand of a nearby zombie, then waved it in front of him. "It was a pleasure to kill Bramfield, and it will be a pleasure to kill you. And then Graves and your Indian."

"Please try," she offered.

He lunged. She blocked his swing with her sword, and they pushed against each other, struggling for dominance. They fell apart, then slammed together again in a torrent of blows and parries. He looked stunned that a woman could wield a broadsword as well as she could. She didn't tell him about the mock Viking battles she used to have with her father. When she saw her father again, she'd be sure to thank him.

If she saw him again.

Staunton thrust, then pivoted, bringing his sword around too quickly for her to block. She bit back a yelp when the blade caught her across the left arm. Blood ran from the gash and turned her hand sticky.

Seeing her wound, Staunton smiled. "I used to think there was no challenge in killing women."

"How delightful that I changed your opinion."

She unleashed a volley of strikes, with Staunton deflecting and striking his own thrusts. Both she and Staunton held their weapons in two-handed grips, putting everything they had into each blow. He had the advantage, being bigger and a hell of a lot less injured. She gritted her teeth against the pain shooting down her arm, and the older wounds left by the falcon on her shoulders and back.

Astrid's gaze strayed to Nathan, needing to see him to help push her forward. The sight chilled her—him, in bear form, locked in a furious struggle against the werewolf. Like her, Nathan had been fighting, and fighting hard, for too long. He'd run untold miles in pursuit of her. While the mage was, if not rested, then certainly less tired. As she watched, the werewolf struck at Nathan with jagged claws, and Nathan growled in pain.

No. Please, no.

She didn't know whether they could prevail, whether she, Nathan, Catullus, and the Earth Spirits could hope to overcome the odds. And that thread of doubt sapped her.

Staunton, seeing her weaken slightly, pushed his advantage. His assault tripled, a fast blur of strikes, and she only able to defend herself, never take the lead.

Winning this fight would take more than strength, more than just raw rage and a desire to hurt. At this pace—exhausted, injured, thwarted—she would be joining Michael much sooner than she ever wanted. And leaving Nathan.

Another blow from Staunton rattled against her sword, sending jolts through her body, and Astrid sank onto one knee. Her head bent, hair curtaining her face, as her shoulders drooped. She let fall her sword arm, as if too heavy for her to support its weight, though she did not relinquish her hold.

Staunton looked down at her, his mouth curling into a

vindictive smile. Astrid peered up at him as the breath grated in and out of her lungs.

"The best part about killing Bramfield," he said, also panting, "was you. Watching you. As he died in your arms. To see his life drain away, and you couldn't stop it."

She stared at him.

He raised his arm up for the killing blow.

And Astrid sprang forward, thrusting her sword up, into his chest.

She pushed the blade so deep, only a few inches separated her from Staunton.

She looked into his shocked eyes. "Perhaps I'll feel the same way watching you," she said. Then she stepped back, leaving the sword lodged in place.

Staunton gazed at the sword in his chest, the hilt angled down where Astrid's hands had left it. Astrid studied him, the play of emotion across his face as he realized that death had finally come for him and could not be averted.

As he turned ashen and stumbled to his knees, she said, "I was wrong. I don't feel anything at all."

He gaped at her, dismayed.

Then he pitched forward and was still.

Astrid waited. But Staunton did not move. Did not draw breath. With the toe of her boot, she turned him over. He stared up with sightless eyes, now a thing, no longer a man. She looked down at him, waiting for a sense of peace, of justice served. But she did not feel exultant. She did not feel relieved or renewed. All she felt was tired. So damned tired.

Animal sounds unlike any other drew her attention. She looked up and, across the seething battle, again saw Nathan in bear form, grappling on the ground with the werewolf. A pitched battle, animal against beast. They each savaged the other. Nathan was wounded, but he fought on, courageous.

That was when her heart soared. Not with the death of her enemy, but with the life of her beloved.

Picking up the sword that had dropped from Staunton's hand, Astrid ran to join Nathan.

The hell of it was, Nathan couldn't go to Astrid. He fought against the werewolf, trading bites, claws, all the while intensely aware of her battle with Staunton. Peripheral in Nathan's vision but not his heart. When he saw her fall to one knee, Staunton poised with upraised sword above her, rage and terror unlike anything he'd ever experienced roared through him. He had to help.

But then Bracebridge, with his unnatural strength, caught Nathan about the waist and sent them both tumbling to the ground. Bracebridge gripped his throat with his teeth. Nathan lost sight of Astrid as he struggled for his own life.

As he rolled and grappled, she stayed in his mind. He had to drive onward, to protect her. If he failed in that—

"Nathan!"

Her voice. He glanced up and saw her close by, bloodied but alive. His glance flicked to Staunton's body, sword sticking from it like Excalibur, then back to Astrid. She'd done it. Triumphed, and with her own strength.

The smile she gave him, exhausted but encouraging, gave him what he needed.

Growling, he lunged up, and the werewolf staggered back. Nathan advanced, slashing. He raked his claws over Bracebridge's head. The Heir yowled in pain as Nathan's claw caught him across his scalp. Nathan pressed his onslaught, and the werewolf shuffled backward, directly toward the fire burning in the middle of the encampment. What had been a small campfire now blazed, fed by several burning undead who now piled in a heap of ashes and bone. Thick, black smoke billowed up in a dark column, darker than the night sky overhead.

Seeing himself backed up against the fire, Bracebridge

desperately surged forward. Nathan drove the werewolf back again with a snap of his teeth.

Bracebridge shuddered, then shrank. He shriveled into his human form, all pink flesh and red wounds. The crouching Heir looked down at his hands, no longer topped with claws, and groaned.

"No!" he cried. "My spell." He glared up at Nathan. "Filthy savage. You cost me my magic."

Nathan changed, casting off the cumbersome weight of his bear form, back into a man. "Then we finish this as equals." He advanced, and Bracebridge scuttled back, until the fire stopped him.

"Careful, Nathan!" Astrid shouted. "The fire—"

Within the fire, a black shape materialized. Not smoke or burning timber. A figure.

It emerged from the fire. At first, the flames hid the form so that it appeared only a tall, dark shape. Then, as it stepped out from the blaze, it became a man. In English clothing. With a face scarred, misshapen. He'd been burned, Nathan realized. Terrible burns that had healed but left the man disfigured, a web of thick, angry flesh. One eye had fused shut, his mouth permanently twisted. None of that was as awful as the hate glinting in his gaze.

Bracebridge, cowering at the scarred man's feet, looked up, eyes terrified. "Edgeworth! How did you—?"

"I've learned the fire now." The man surveyed the encampment, the bodies of Heirs scattered like heaps of refuse. He glared at Nathan and Astrid in turn, and when he saw Graves advancing, the man's sneer deepened. "You and your Hottentot family have been a thorn in the side of the Heirs for too long, Graves."

Graves did not blink. "We've been Blades for nearly two hundred years, Edgeworth. How long has your family been Heirs?"

His remark hit home, because the man winced as if slapped. So he turned back to Astrid. "This does not matter," he spat at her. "The Primal Source is ours and we will command it without your knowledge, stupid whore."

Nathan growled, stepping forward. Whoever this Edgeworth was, he'd pay for his insult to her.

Before Nathan could reach him, Edgeworth grabbed Bracebridge by the arm and hauled the mage backward, toward the fire.

"No! No!" shouted Bracebridge. "I'll be burned!"

"Not if you travel with me." Edgeworth retreated, and flames licked at him and the mage without harm.

"Edgeworth! Here—help me!" Milbourne, bound and powerless, cried out.

Yet Edgeworth seemed little interested in aiding him. "Bracebridge has some of his magic left," he said, scornful. "All you have is failure." Then he and the mage sank back into the flames. The blaze engulfed them, and with a hiss, they disappeared into the fire, leaving Milbourne behind.

The captive Heir cursed. Then the battle lines moved over him. Undead warriors trampled him in retreat from advancing bears and wolves, uncaring that their errant swords slashed at the man on the ground. Heavy bears lumbered over Milbourne, crushing him. The sounds of his shattering bones and skull were lost underneath the clash.

This didn't matter to Nathan. Neither did the sounds of battle, growing quieter now as the Earth Spirits destroyed the last of the undead. And Nathan didn't care about the bodies of Staunton, Halling, Milbourne, the mercenaries, or Swift Cloud Woman. Even the totems, which Graves held out to Iron Wolf, were of no importance. He cared about one thing, one *person,* only.

Bloody, battered, he turned to Astrid, opening his arms.

She ran to him, and they held each other as if allowing even an inch to separate them meant the destruction of the world. As he embraced her, as she him, the length of her shaking body pressed against his own, he couldn't feel his wounds or exhaustion. Instead, with her hands on him and her warm breath in his ear as she whispered, again and again, "Love you, love you," and he saying exactly the same thing, he felt the perfect rightness of their hearts locking together. Being made, finally, whole.

Chapter 20

The Battle Ends, the War Begins

Bittersweet, the end of battle. Sweet, because Nathan walked beside her through the encampment, his fingers laced with hers, his presence warm and strong—though tired and wounded—and she felt herself so replete with love for him, it eclipsed nearly everything.

But not all. Here was bitterness. As she, Nathan, Catullus, and Iron Wolf surveyed and tended the injured Earth Spirits, they found He Watches Stars in a small heap, stained with blood, face drawn and ashen, his breath rattling. Near him lay his heavy war ax, streaked with a surprising amount of gore.

As dawn began to lighten the sky, Astrid knelt beside him, cradling him in her arms, as the others gathered close. He Watches Stars' slightness surprised her, as if most of his soul, and weight, had already fled. Astrid shared a worried look with Nathan at the shallowness of the old man's breathing.

"Warrior *and* medicine man," Astrid murmured, brushing his damp gray hair from his forehead. "You are a man of many arts."

He Watches Stars gave her a small, tight smile. "This world is made up of more than spirit. It always pays to know how to wield an ax." He winced as pain moved through him.

"Be at rest, Grandfather," said Nathan, placing a hand on the old man's shoulder. "We will tend your honorable wounds."

"Morning Hawk Woman," Iron Wolf called over his shoulder. A young woman hurried forward. "He Watches Stars has need of your healing skills."

"No," rasped the medicine man. "I saw this night, long ago. The night I was to join the stars and sky. But I am glad." He turned ancient eyes to Nathan. "For I have seen and fought beside the One Who Is Three." He took Nathan's hand in his own, shaking. "Your journey does not end here." His other hand wrapped around Astrid's, and it was both fragile and strong. "And you will not be alone." The medicine man gazed at Astrid. She felt herself pulled into the dark, powerful currents within his fathomless eyes. "No longer Hunter Shadow Woman. Bright Star Woman. And her mate. Together . . . a force . . . unstoppable."

Then, under many watchful, stricken eyes, He Watches Stars stilled. She felt it, when the spirit left behind the shell of his body, for he grew lighter, and what she held in her arms was as substantial as a fallen leaf.

Astrid carefully lowered him to the ground, closing his eyes. Her throat ached. She wearied of death, because it never seemed to end and was, ultimately, inescapable. At some point, everyone must pass through the shadowy veil into . . . she did not know.

Nathan's broad, warm hand against her cheek brought her back to the realm of life. His gaze held hers. There, she saw his own sorrow at the medicine man's passing, but also the promise and fulfillment of joy. Once, she would have run from such promise. Now she ran toward it, toward him.

One consolation—He Watches Stars was the only casualty of the Earth Spirits. There were many wounded, but, to a one, each member of the tribe gloried in their injuries, proof of a battle well fought.

Nathan gave her another caress before moving toward Iron Wolf, hand extended.

"I haven't words to truly thank you," Nathan said, gruff. "Not as you and the tribe deserve, for coming to my aid."

The chief stared down at the offered hand before taking it. "You are our brother. We heard the sorrow in your howl, and we came. The tribe sees to its people."

Nathan, solemn-eyed, clasped the chief's hand and seemed to grow even taller. Astrid's heart brimmed.

Though she hated to disrupt the moment of connection between Nathan and his tribe, she had to ask, "What is to become of the totems?"

Iron Wolf released his grasp of Nathan's hand. "He Watches Stars told me what must be done, should the totems be restored to us." He glanced up at the lightening sky. "Now is the time. Come."

Everyone moved through the forest, to stand upon the banks of a nearby river. It flowed, wide, quick, and clean, before branching into three directions.

Iron Wolf gripped the totems by their leather cords, holding them over the rushing water. "Great Spirit," he intoned, "and the spirits of these sacred mountains and rivers, your children entrust their medicine to you. Take these totems, these vessels of power, and hide them from those that would corrupt their strength through greed and foolishness. This, your children humbly ask you."

The chief cast the totems into the river. The assembled people watched silently as the totems disappeared into the roiling white water. A gasp sounded from the crowd as the hawk totem was flung up into the air by the churning foam. But the totem did not fall back into the water. Instead, it rose up into the air, as if carried by an invisible hawk, disappearing into the clouds.

All eyes turned to the two remaining totems. The wolf totem sped down one path of the river, the bear down another. Soon, they had both vanished into nature.

Iron Wolf nodded. "The Great Spirit is wise, and now none shall have knowledge of the totems."

Quietly, the crowd returned to the encampment, everyone quiet and awed by what had transpired, even Astrid, Nathan, and Catullus.

"There will be many scars and many stories," said Iron Wolf. "Such tales will last for generations." He glanced at the burning mounds of the undead, now very much dead, and at three Earth Spirits, who strode forward to heft the falcon's carcass onto the growing bonfire. No one touched the bodies of Swift Cloud Woman, Staunton, Milbourne, and Halling, leaving them to scavengers.

Fitting, thought Astrid. The Heirs were nothing but carrion.

But not all of them.

Nathan followed her gaze, and a crease appeared between his dark brows. "Bracebridge escaped," he growled.

"To England," she answered.

Catullus said, "The man in the fire, Jonas Edgeworth. He is the leader of the Heirs now."

"That scarred madman?" asked Astrid.

Grim, Catullus nodded. "He's been warped by rage and magic. Which makes the fact that he has the Primal Source all the more terrifying."

"So we must leave for England," Nathan said at once. "Right away."

At his words, Astrid felt as if the sun rose not overhead but within her, radiant with love. He held true to his vow, that he would go where she went, that her battles were his.

Iron Wolf could not understand their conversation, since they spoke in English, so Nathan turned to the chief. "I must leave the tribe."

"But you are the One Who Is Three," Iron Wolf objected.

"What does that mean?" asked Astrid.

"The One Who Is Three is a bringer of peace in times of trouble. And now that the white man draws closer and closer to our territory, as the Earth Spirits hear of the harm done to other Native people, we have more need of the One Who Is Three than ever." Iron Wolf frowned, deeply troubled.

Nathan turned to Astrid. "When the fight against the Heirs is over, will you come back with me?" He held her hands in his own, his gaze black and penetrating, full of strength and steel, yet also, beneath, revealing a core of need. She knew it cost him to expose this need, and felt humbled and joyous to be the one he trusted.

"Of course," she answered immediately.

He actually let out a breath, as if nervous about her answer, then smiled so brilliantly she felt herself borne aloft.

But Catullus's rueful chuckle brought her back down to earth. "You are both awfully confident of our triumph against the Heirs. There is a war to be fought," he said. "And we will be on the front lines of that war. Nothing, especially victory, is certain."

Nathan tugged Astrid closer, then wrapped her in his lean, capable arms. His lips pressed against the top of her head. She breathed him in, the scents of blood and dirt and sweat. He was solid and real, a man who had fought through the ramparts she'd built around her heart, to bring her back to life.

"True," she said. "But there's no excitement in certainty, and if there is anything that rebels love, it's risk." She gazed up at Nathan. "And I am more than willing to take that risk."

"We'll tear the world down," Nathan rumbled. The animal shone within his eyes, wild and fierce, and the man, as well, just as ferocious.

As they came together in a heated kiss, she understood. Love had not tamed him. Nor her. They were both creatures that could never surrender. She saw in him the mirror of her soul, and knew that together they would set the world ablaze.

The sun broke over the tops of the trees, and morning began.

Epilogue

Hunting a Story

She really should leave.

Gemma Murphy looked around the muddy yard surrounding the trading post, hands planted on her hips. She paid no attention to the rain that dampened her hair, since she had grown used to an almost incessant drizzle for the past week. It was one of many signs that winter was fast approaching. Soon, the Northwest Territory would be blanketed with snow, making travel nearly impossible and extremely dangerous.

Though it might make for an interesting coda to the piece she had been writing, she hadn't much desire to freeze to death on her way back to Chicago. It was not as though she lacked material for her story.

Two months had seen her penning a series of articles she planned on titling "One Woman's Journey into the Heart of the Wild." She'd watched countless fur trade transactions, lived for a spell with a trapper and his Native wife, even stayed with a local Stoney Indian tribe. In truth, she could write a whole book about her adventures here in the Canadian Rockies, but she wasn't a novelist, she was a journalist. And, by God, she would prove it to those narrow-minded lummoxes at the *Tribune*.

Gemma strode through the yard, nodding her greetings to the men lingering there. She felt their eyes on her, but she was well used to the sensation. At the paper, she was one of two female writers, and out in the Northwest Territory, women were in short supply. However, the men out here in the wilderness were a good sight more respectful than the sniggering jackasses who called themselves reporters. Each time she walked through the paper's doors and into the nest of cramped desks, everyone stared at her as if she was some stranger who had wandered in off the streets. A stranger with a full bosom.

Instead of slogging through mud, she envisioned herself marching into her editor's office with a sheaf of paper under her arm. She would triumphantly slam the articles on Ludlow Hallam's desk. His pipe would drop from his mouth, scattering tobacco on the floor.

"There," she would say as everyone gathered outside, gaping. "I am never writing another piece of tripe about gardening or spring fashions or household tips *ever again.*"

What a wonderful moment that would be. She absolutely could not wait until it happened.

So why was she lingering at the trading post, when she really should be going home? Something was keeping her there, and she found herself delaying her departure, mystified by herself.

Suddenly, she had her answer.

Three people on horseback approached the trading post. At first, they were too far away for Gemma to make out anything about them. But then they were in the yard, and something thrilled through her.

He was back.

A variety of people visited the trading post. Trappers. Miners. Naturalists. Mounties. Natives. Missionaries. Of every color and stripe. Gemma made note of every one.

Yet none of them had left such a lingering impression as he did.

Instinctively, Gemma slid behind an outbuilding and watched as the three riders dismounted. One was the capable, serious mountain woman. Another was the Native attorney, now dressed in buckskins. They both surveyed the yard, alert and aware. Their movements were perfectly attuned to the other, as though connected by, and communicating through, an unseen bond. Even vigilant, they were continuously aware of each other. It was a union so profound, Gemma's breath caught to see it.

But they did not hold her attention for long. *He* did. Granted, his clothing was not nearly as dazzling as before—he looked, in fact, grimy and threadbare. But his spectacular wardrobe had not drawn her as had his eyes. In all her life, Gemma had never seen eyes like his. Not so much the dark color, but the powerful intelligence gleaming there. The precision of mind and immeasurable insight. Truly, someone extraordinary must reside behind those eyes. Someone she desperately wanted to know.

The fact that he had a gorgeously sculpted face and body was also something of an incentive. His tall, muscular body had held her riveted, the width of his shoulders and absolute assurance in his walk, his movements.

Strange indeed. Men usually did not affect her so strongly. She'd always prided herself on her cool head, interviewing even the most handsome light-opera tenor without blushing or flirting. Something about this man, though, pierced her professionalism, reaching beneath her journalist's armor to find the woman beneath.

Gemma continued to watch him as he and his companions led their horses across the yard, straight toward where she was hiding. She could not stop watching him. And when he and his friends stopped, just around the corner from where she stood, Gemma flattened herself against the wall to listen in on their conversation.

Yes, she was eavesdropping. Rude—perhaps. But one

didn't become a respected journalist by following the rules of polite society.

"Will it take long to reach England?" asked the Native man.

"Perhaps a month," was the answer. "We'll take a stagecoach to St. Louis, then a train to New York, and from there, a steamer to Southampton."

Gemma's heart knocked against the inside of her chest to hear *him* speak. That voice! Rich and low, and with the most delicious British accent. Women melted at such voices and, as much as she prided herself on being different from the average woman, in this she was no exception. Beyond its mere sound, though, was the intellect thrumming beneath. Profound. What secrets and insights might he harbor? Gemma needed to know.

"I hope that isn't too long," said the woman.

Why? For what?

"You think the Heirs might still make use of the Primal Source?" *he* asked.

"It's entirely possible," answered the woman. "They might not know precisely what they have, but the Primal Source is too powerful to be still for long, especially in the hands of those who would exploit it. We need to reach England."

"And soon," finished the Native man, as if speaking the same sentence.

"If we are too late," the woman continued, her words perfectly transitioning from the man's, "the consequences will be disastrous."

Every journalistic bone in Gemma's body hummed to life. She had no idea what these people were talking about—Heirs, Primal Sources, disastrous consequences—but it sounded not only fascinating, but dangerous. Precisely the sort of thing she loved to write about. If her instincts were right, and they always were, then whatever this trio was involved in was a thousand times more extraordinary than a few articles about life in the Northwest Territory.

"I'm going to check in with Sergeant Williamson," said

the Native man. "Tell him to forward Prescott's belongings on to the office in Victoria. Along with my letter of resignation." He made a soft noise of amusement. "Something so small as that task brought me here. To you." There was no doubt from the warmth and devotion in his voice that he was addressing the woman.

"I'm glad it did," the woman answered, with just as much tenderness. She added, her voice more businesslike, "And I'll let the sergeant know that Edwin Mayne attacked me in my cabin but was killed by my feral dog."

"Feral dog?" repeated the Native man, almost as if insulted.

"Vicious wolf," amended the woman fondly.

"Better," said the man, also affectionate.

How odd.

"I can stay with the horses," *he* said, and Gemma heard the footsteps of the Native man and the mountain woman heading toward the Mounties' office.

Gemma debated whether to slink away or pretend to just arrive, when she heard *him* say, "Please, do come out. I hate to think of you lurking like a footpad."

Oh, dear. Gemma never had anyone catch her before. Well, nothing to do but brazen it out. She tilted up her chin and rounded the corner, careful to keep her expression cool and assured.

Of course, seeing him up close, talking with him—his height, that voice, those eyes—had the unwonted effect of making her blush. Since she was a redhead, that meant her freckles turned crimson. Delightful.

"Unless you *are* a footpad," he said, wry. But then he stared at her face, at her freckles, actually, and seemed to lose the thread of the conversation. They stared at each other for several long moments, Gemma deeply aware of him, and he seemingly in thrall by her. A few feet separated them, but even that felt strangely intimate, the air hot and alive.

They both blinked, collecting themselves. "I'm *not* a

footpad," she answered. "I was merely taking a . . ." What was that English word? "A constitutional through the post."

"How much did you hear?" he asked, and while his tone was sharp, his eyes lingered on her lips.

Come to think of it, he had a beautiful mouth. Sensuous and full. It probably felt wonderful pressed against one's skin. Dear God, *what* was she thinking?

"Oh, nothing," she replied. "Something about a dog."

That seemed to placate him, though only slightly.

She stuck out her hand, knowing that, back home, a white woman shaking the hand of a Negro man was forbidden. But she was in the wilderness now, and normal rules could go rot. "I'm Gemma Murphy."

He eyed her ungloved hand for a moment before extending his own. His hands were large, but agile, and as he clasped her hand with his, she felt a sudden current, as though a coil of light unwound inside her. His own breathing came a little quicker, his eyes widening slightly behind his spectacles.

She longed to delve deep into those eyes, learn what mysteries they held. This was a most intriguing man, and he drew her in not only for the intelligence illuminating his face, but the stories he held. What a life this man must lead! The journalist in her was unbearably captivated, as much as the woman.

"Catullus Graves," he murmured, slightly dazed.

"You were the talk of the trading post, Mr. Graves," she said, "not that long ago."

"Why is that?"

"Your guide, Jourdain, came back and said you and your companion insisted on going into some dangerous territory. He thought you might be dead." The news had unexpectedly saddened her, more than she would have anticipated about someone who was, in truth, a complete stranger.

A shadow fell across Catullus Graves's face. "I am not. But my friend is. We had to bury him in the mountains."

"I'm sorry," she said, sincere.

"Thank you. But he died doing what he loved, so there is some comfort in that."

"And if you died doing what you loved," Gemma asked, "what that might be?"

He thought about it. "I would be in my workshop. Having just invented inexhaustible and clean fuel."

"Are you an inventor, Mr. Graves? What sort of inventions do you create? Do you have any with you now?"

"You ask an exceptional amount of questions, Miss Murphy." But his tone wasn't shocked or reprimanding. Almost . . . admiring.

"A terrible habit that I cultivate tirelessly," she answered.

He seemed a little startled by her response. But then he smiled at her.

She thought she might actually lose consciousness. Good gracious, did this Catullus Graves have a beautiful smile. Warmly, slowly unfurling. And even a bit shy.

"Catullus?"

Both Gemma and Graves turned at the sound of the mountain woman's voice. She and the Native man were striding toward them, wearing matching, wary expressions, completely in tune with each other.

Graves dropped Gemma's hand, surprising her. She hadn't realized they were still holding on to each other. "Ah," he said, sounding a bit flustered. "Astrid, Nathan, this is Miss Gemma Murphy. She's something of a habitué of the trading post."

"But not for long," Gemma added. "I'll be leaving soon."

"Going home?" asked the woman, with more than a touch of suspicion.

Gemma didn't like to outright lie, so she said, "Mm," which was neither a confirmation nor a denial.

"Everything's settled with Sergeant Williamson," said the Native man to Graves. "He said we can get a stagecoach at Fort Macleod."

"Excellent," said Graves. He turned to Gemma. "I have to go. I'm sorry."

They were both taken aback at the sincerity in his voice.

"Maybe we'll meet again," she said.

"Unfortunately," he replied, "I doubt that."

"Is it?"

"Is it what?"

"Unfortunate?"

He gazed at her, holding her with the sumptuous deep brown of his eyes. She felt herself under a minute inspection, as though he was reaching inside her and carefully, thoughtfully sorting and categorizing her into discrete elements. Like one of his inventions, perhaps. But she was more than a machine.

"Yes," he said slowly. "It is unfortunate."

"Catullus," said the mountain woman.

Again, Gemma and Graves glanced over and saw the woman and Native man mounted on their horses and waiting.

"Good-bye, Miss Murphy," said Graves. He hovered for a moment, as though trying to decide whether to shake her hand, kiss her, or just walk away. Finally, he settled on shaking her hand, though they were both a little awkward in their movements. And then he let go. With motion far more graceful than when he shook her hand, he strode away and mounted his horse.

A final glance at her, the faintest hint of puzzlement in his expression, and then he and his companions wheeled their horses around and rode away.

Gemma waited just long enough for Graves to disappear before breaking into a run. She needed a horse, a guide, and a gun. She was hunting a story, and something told her the one she now chased would be spectacular.

Don't miss the rest of the
Blades of the Rose series,
coming this fall!

In September, we met a WARRIOR in Mongolia . . .

To most people, the realm of magic is the stuff of nursery rhymes and dusty libraries. But for Capt. Gabriel Huntley, it's become quite real and quite dangerous . . .

IN HOT PURSUIT

The vicious attack Capt. Gabriel Huntley witnesses in a dark alley sparks a chain of events that will take him to the ends of the Earth and beyond—where what is real and what is imagined become terribly confused. And frankly, Huntley couldn't be more pleased. Intrigue, danger, and a beautiful woman in distress—just what he needs.

IN HOTTER WATER

Raised thousands of miles from England, Thalia Burgess is no typical Victorian lady A good thing, because a proper lady would have no hope of recovering the priceless magical artifact Thalia is after. Huntley's assistance might come in handy, though she has to keep him in the dark. But this distractingly handsome soldier isn't easy to deceive . . .

Her father called out, "Enter." The door began to swing open.

Thalia tucked the hand holding the revolver behind her back. She stood behind her father's chair and braced herself, wondering what kind of man would step across the threshold and if she would have to use a gun on another human being for the first time in her life.

The man ducked to make it through the door, then immediately removed his hat, uncovering a head of close-cropped, wheat-colored hair. He was not precisely handsome, but he possessed an air of command and confidence that shifted everything to his favor. His face was lean and rugged, his features bold and cleanly defined; there was nothing of the drawing room about him, nothing refined or elegant. He was clean-shaven, allowing the hard planes of his face to show clearly. He was not an aristocrat and looked as though he had fought for everything he ever had in his life, rather than expecting it to be given to him. Even in the filtered light inside the *ger*, Thalia could see the gleaming gold of his eyes, their sharp intelligence that missed nothing as they scanned the inside of the tent and finally fell on her and her father.

"Franklin Burgess?" he asked.

"Yes, sir," her father answered, guarded. "My daughter, Thalia."

She remembered enough to sketch a curtsy as she felt the heat of the stranger's gaze on her. An uncharacteristic flush rose in her cheeks.

"And you are . . . ?" her father prompted.

"Captain Gabriel Huntley," came the reply, and now it made sense that the man who had such sure bearing would be an officer. "Of the Thirty-third Regiment." Thalia was not certain she could relax just yet, since it was not unheard of for the Heirs to find members in the ranks of the military. She quickly took stock of the width of the captain's shoulders, how even standing still he seemed to radiate energy and the capacity for lethal movement. Captain Huntley would be a fine addition to the Heirs.

There was something magnetic about him, though, something that charged the very air inside the *ger,* and she felt herself acutely aware of him. His sculpted face, the brawn of his body, the way he carried his gear, all of it, felt overwhelmingly masculine. How ironic, how dreadful, it would be, if the only man to have attracted her attention in years turned out to be her enemy. Sergei, her old suitor, had wound up being her enemy, but in a very different way.

"You are out of uniform, Captain Huntley," her father pointed out.

For the first time since his entrance, the captain's steady concentration broke as he glanced down at his dusty civilian traveling clothes. "I'm here in an unofficial capacity." He had a gravelly voice with a hint of an accent Thalia could not place. It was different from the cultured tones of her father's friends, rougher, but with a low music that danced up the curves of her back.

"And what capacity is that?" she asked. Thalia realized too late that a proper Englishwoman would not speak so boldly, nor ask a question out of turn, but, hell, if Captain Huntley *was* an Heir, niceties did not really matter.

His eyes flew back to her, and she met his look levelly, even as a low tremor pulsed inside her. God, there it was again, that strange *something* that he provoked in her, now made a hundred times stronger when their gazes connected. She watched him assess her, refusing to back down from the unconcealed measuring. She wondered if he felt that peculiar awareness too, if their held look made his stomach flutter. Thalia doubted it. She was no beauty—too tall, her features too strong, and there was the added handicap of this dreadful dress. Besides, he didn't quite seem like the kind of man who fluttered anything.

Yet . . . maybe she was wrong. Even though he was on the other side of the *ger,* Thalia could feel him looking at her, taking her in, with an intensity that bordered on unnerving. And intriguing.

Regardless of her scanty knowledge of society, Thalia *did* know that gentlemen did not look at ladies in such a fashion. Strange. Officers usually came from the ranks of the upper classes. He should know better. But then, so should she.

"As a messenger," he answered, still holding Thalia's gaze, "from Anthony Morris."

That name got her attention, as well as her father's.

"What about Morris?" he demanded. "If he has a message for me, he should be here, himself."

The captain broke away from looking intently at Thalia as he regarded her father. He suddenly appeared a bit tired, and also sad.

"Mr. Morris is dead, sir."

Thalia gasped, and her father cried out in shock and horror. Tony Morris was one of her father's closest friends. Thalia put her hand on her father's shoulder and gave him a supportive squeeze as he removed his glasses and covered his eyes. Tony was like a younger brother to her father, and Thalia considered him family. To know that he was dead—her hands shook. It couldn't be true, could it? He was so bright and good and . . . God, her throat burned from unshed tears for her friend. She swallowed hard and glanced up from her grief. Such scenes were to be conducted in private, away from the eyes of strangers.

The captain ducked his head respectfully as he studied his hands, which were gripped tightly on his hat. Through the fog of her sorrow, Thalia understood that the captain had done this before. Given bad news to the friends and families of those that had died. What a dreadful responsibility, one she wouldn't wish on anyone.

She tried to speak, but her words caught on shards of loss. She gulped and tried again. "How did it happen?"

The captain cleared his throat and looked at Franklin. He seemed to be deliberately avoiding looking at her. "This might not be suitable for . . . young ladies."

Even in her grief, Thalia had to suppress a snort. Clearly, this man knew nothing of her. Fortunately, her father, voice rough with emotion about Tony Morris's death, said, "Please speak candidly in front of Thalia. She has a remarkably strong constitution."

Captain Huntley's gaze flicked back at her for a brief moment, then stayed fixed on her father. She saw with amazement that this strapping military man was uncomfortable, and, stranger still, it was *her* that was making him uncomfortable. Perhaps it was because of the nature of his news, unsuitable as it was for young ladies. Or perhaps it was because he'd felt something between them, as well, something instant and potent. She did not want to consider it, not when she was reeling from the pain of Tony Morris's death.

After clearing his throat again, the captain said, "He was killed, sir. In Southampton."

"So close!" Franklin exclaimed. "On our very doorstep."

"I don't know 'bout doorsteps, sir, but he was attacked in an alley by a group of men." Captain Huntley paused as Thalia's father cursed. "They'd badly outnumbered him, but he fought bravely until the end."

"How do you know all this?" Thalia asked. If Tony's death

had been reported in the papers, surely someone other than the captain would be standing in their *ger* right now, Bennett Day or Catullus Graves. How Thalia longed to see one of their numbers, to share her family's grief with them instead of this man who disquieted her with his very presence.

Captain Huntley again let his eyes rest on her briefly. She fought down her immediate physical response, trying to focus on what he was saying. "I was there, miss, when it happened. Passing by when I heard the sounds of Morris's being attacked, and joined in to help him." He grimaced. "But there were too many, and when my back was turned, he was stabbed by one of them—a blond man who talked like a nob, I mean, a gentleman."

"Henry Lamb?" Franklin asked, looking up at Thalia. She shrugged. Her father turned his attention back to the captain and his voice grew sharp, "You say you were merely 'passing by,' and heard the scuffle and just 'joined in to help.' Sounds damned suspicious to me." Thalia had to agree with her father. What sort of man passed by a fight and came to the aid of the victim, throwing himself into the fray for the sake of a stranger? Hardly anyone.

Captain Huntley tightened his jaw, angry. "Suspicious or not, sir, that's what happened. Morris even saved my life just before the end. So when he gave me the message to deliver to you, in person, I couldn't say no."

"You came all the way from Southampton to Urga to fulfill a dying man's request, a man you had never met before," Thalia repeated, disbelief plain in her voice.

The captain did not even bother answering her. "It couldn't be written down, Morris said," he continued, addressing her father and infuriating Thalia in the process. She didn't care for being ignored. "I've had it in my head for nearly three months, and it makes no sense to me, so I'll pass it on to you. Perhaps you can understand it, sir, because, as much as I've tried, I can't."

"Please," her father said, holding his hand out and gesturing for Captain Huntley to proceed.

"The message is this: 'The sons are ascendant. Seek the woman who feeds the tortoise.'"

He glanced at both Thalia and her father to see their reactions, and could not contain his surprise when her father cursed again and Thalia gripped a nearby table for support. She felt dizzy. It was beginning. "You know what that means?" the captain asked.

Franklin nodded as his hands curled and uncurled into fists, while Thalia caught her lower lip between her teeth and gnawed pensively on it.

She knew it was bound to happen, but they had never known when. That time was now at hand.

In October, let SCOUNDREL whisk you away
to the shores of Greece . . .

The Blades of the Rose are sworn to protect the sources of magic in the world. But the work is dangerous— and they can't always protect their own . . .

READY FOR ACTION

London Harcourt's father is bent on subjugating the world's magic to British rule. But since London is a mere female, he hasn't bothered to tell her so. He's said only that he's leading a voyage to the Greek isles. No matter, after a smothering marriage and three years of straitlaced widowhood, London jumps at the opportunity— unfortunately, right into the arms of Bennett Day.

RISKING IT ALL

Bennett is a ladies' man, when he's not dodging lethal attacks to protect the powers of the ancients from men like London's father. Sometimes, he's a ladies' man even when he is dodging them. But the minute he sees London he knows she will require his full attention. The woman is lovely, brilliant, and the only known speaker of a dialect of ancient Greek that holds the key to calling down the wrath of the gods. Bennett will be risking his life again—but around London, what really worries him is the danger to his heart . . .

"Save those slurs for your grandmother," said a deep, masculine voice to the vendor. He spoke Greek with an English accent.

London turned to the voice. And nearly lost her own.

She knew she was still, in many ways, a sheltered woman. Her society in England was limited to a select few families and assorted hangers-on, her father's business associates, their retainers and servants. At events and parties, she often saw the same people again and again. And yet, she knew with absolute clarity, that men who looked like the one standing beside her were a rare and altogether miraculous phenomenon.

There were taller men, to be sure, but it was difficult to consider this a flaw when presented with this man's lean muscularity. He wonderfully filled out the shoulders of his English coat, not bulky, but definitively capable. She understood at once that his arms, his long legs, held a leashed strength that even his negligent pose could not disguise. He called to mind the boxers that her brother, Jonas, had admired in his youth. The stranger was bareheaded, which was odd in this heat, but it allowed her to see that his hair was dark with just the faintest curl, ever so slightly mussed, as if he'd recently come from bed. She suddenly imagined herself tangling her fingers in his hair, pulling him closer.

And if that thought didn't make her blush all the harder, then his face was the coup de grâce. What wicked promises must he have made, and made good on, with such a face. A sharp, clean jaw, a mouth of impossible sensuality. A naughty, thoroughly masculine smile tugged at the corners of that mouth. Crystalline eyes full of intelligent humor, the color intensely blue. Even the small bump on the bridge of his nose—had it been broken?—merely added to the overall impression of profound male beauty. He was clean-shaven, too, so that there could be no mistaking how outrageously handsome this stranger was.

She may as well get on the boat back to England immediately. Surely nothing she could ever see in Greece could eclipse the marvel of this man.

"Who are you?" the vendor shouted in Greek to the newcomer. "You defend this woman and her lies?"

"I don't care what she said," the Englishman answered calmly, also in Greek. "Keep insulting her and I'll jam my fist into your throat." The vendor goggled at him, but wisely kept silent. Whoever this man was, he certainly looked capable of throwing a good punch.

Yet gently, he put a hand on London's waist and began to guide her away. Stunned by the strange turn of events, she let him steer her from the booth.

"All right?" he asked her in English. A concerned, warm smile gilded his features. "That apoplectic huckster didn't hurt you, did he?"

London shook her head, still somewhat dazed by what had just happened, but more so by the attractiveness of the man walking at her side. She felt the warmth of his hand at her back and knew it was improper, but she couldn't move away or even regret the impertinence. "His insults weren't very creative."

He chuckled at this and the sound curled like fragrant

smoke low in her belly. "I'll go back and show him how it's done."

"Oh, no," she answered at once. "I think you educated him enough for one day."

Even as he smiled at her, he sent hard warning glances at whomever stared at her. "So what had his fez in a pinch?"

She held up and unfolded her hand, which still held the shard of pottery. "We were disputing this, but, gracious, I forgot I still had it. Maybe I should give it back."

He plucked the piece of pottery from her hand. As he did this, the tips of his fingers brushed her bare palm. A hot current sparked to life where he touched. She could not prevent the shiver of awareness that ran through her body. She met his gaze, and sank into their cool aquatic depths as he stared back. This felt stronger than attraction. Something that resounded through the innermost recesses of herself, in deep, liquid notes, like a melody or song one might sing to bring the world into being. And it seemed he felt it, too, in the slight breath he drew in, the straightening of his posture. Breaking away from his gaze, London snatched her glove from Sally, who trailed behind them with a look of severe disapproval. London tugged on the glove.

He cleared his throat, then gave her back the pottery. "Keep it. Consider it his tribute."

She put it into her reticule, though it felt strange to take something she did not pay for.

"Thank you for coming to my aid," she said as they continued to walk. "I admit that getting into arguments with vendors in Monastiraki wasn't at the top of my list of Greek adventures."

"The best part about adventures is that you can't plan them."

She laughed. "Spoken like a true adventurer."

"Done my share," he grinned. "Ambushing bandits by the Khaznah temple in the cliffs of Petra. Climbing volcanoes in the steam-shrouded interior of Iceland."

"Sounds wonderful," admitted London with a candor that

surprised herself. She felt, oddly, that she could trust this English stranger with her most prized secrets. "Even what happened back there at that booth was marvelous, in its way. I don't *want* to get into a fight, but it's such a delight to finally be out here, in the world, truly experiencing things."

"Including hot, dusty, crowded Athens."

"*Especially* hot, dusty, crowded Athens."

"My, my," he murmured, looking down at her with approval. "A swashbuckling lady. Such a rare treasure."

Wryly, she asked, "Treasure, or aberration?"

He stopped walking and gazed at her with an intensity that caught in her chest. "Treasure. Most definitely."

Again, he left her stunned. She was nearly certain that any man would find a woman's desire for experience and adventure to be at best ridiculous, at worst, offensive. Yet here was this stranger who not only didn't dismiss her feelings, but actually approved and, yes, admired them. What a city of wonders was this Athens! Although, London suspected, it was not the city so much as the man standing in front of her that proved wondrous.

"So tell me, fellow adventurer," she said, finding her voice, "from whence do you come? What exotic port of call?" She smiled. "Dover? Plymouth? Southampton?"

A glint of wariness cooled his eyes. "I don't see why it matters."

Strange, the abrupt change in him. "I thought that's what one did when meeting a fellow countryman abroad," she said. "Find out where they come from. If you know the same people." When he continued to look at her guardedly, she demonstrated, "'Oh, you're from Manchester? Do you know Jane?'"

The chill in his blue eyes thawed, and he smiled. "Of course, Jane! Makes the worst meat pies. Dresses like a Anglican bishop."

"So you *do* know her!"

They shared a laugh, two English strangers in the chaos of an Athenian market, and London felt within her a swell of happiness rising like a spring tide. As if in silent agreement, they continued to stroll together in a companionable silence. With a long-limbed, loose stride, he walked beside her. He hooked his thumbs into the pockets of his simple, well-cut waistcoat, the picture of a healthy young man completely comfortable with himself. And why shouldn't he be? No man had been so favored by Nature's hand. She realized that he hadn't told her where he was from, but she wouldn't press the issue, enjoying the glamour of the unknown.

His presence beside her was tangible, a continuous pulse of uncivilized living energy, as though being escorted by a large and untamed mountain cat that vacillated between eating her and dragging her off to its lair.

And in December, STRANGER brings the adventure
back to London . . .

He protects the world's magic—with his science.
But even the best scientists can fall prey
to the right chemistry . . .

LOOKING FOR TROUBLE

Gemma Murphy has a nose for a story—even if the boys in Chicago's newsrooms would rather focus on her chest. So when she runs into a handsome man of mystery discussing how to save the world from fancy-pants Brit conspirators, she's sensing a scoop. Especially when he mentions there's magic involved. Of course, getting him on the record would be easier if he hadn't caught her eavesdropping.

LIGHTING HIS FUSE

Catullus Graves knows what it's like to be shut out: his ancestors were slaves. And he's a genius inventor with appropriately eccentric habits, so even people who love him find him a little odd. But after meeting a certain redheaded scribbler, he's thinking of other types of science. Inconvenient, given that he needs to focus on preventing the end of the world as we know it. But with Gemma's insatiable curiosity sparking Catullus's inventive impulses, they might set off something explosive anyway . . .

Now was her chance to do some investigating. Surely she'd find something of note in his cabin. A fast glance up and down the passageway ensured she was entirely alone.

Gemma opened the cabin door.

And found herself staring at a drawn gun.

Damn. He was in. Working silently at a table by the light of one small lamp. At her entrance, he was out of his chair and drawing a revolver in one smooth motion.

She drew her Derringer.

They stared at each other.

In the small cabin, Catullus Graves's head nearly brushed the ceiling as he faced her. Her reporter's eye quickly took in the details of his appearance. Even though he was the only black passenger on the ship, more than just his skin color made him stand out. His scholar's face, carved by an artist's hand, drew one's gaze. Arresting in both its elegant beauty and keen perception. A neatly trimmed goatee framed his sensuous mouth. The long, lean lines of his body—the breadth of his shoulders, the length of his legs—revealed a man comfortable with action as well as thought. Though, until now, Gemma had not been aware *how* comfortable. Until she saw the revolver held easily, familiarly in his large hand. A revolver trained on her. She'd have to do something about that.

"Mr. Graves," she murmured, shutting the door behind her.

Behind his spectacles, Catullus Graves's dark eyes widened. "Miss Murphy?"

Despite the fact that she was in danger of being shot, it wasn't until Graves spoke to Gemma that her heart began to pound. And she was absurdly glad he did remember her, for she certainly hadn't forgotten him. They'd met but briefly. Spoke together only once. Yet the impression of him remained, and not merely because she had an excellent memory.

"I thought you were out," she said. As if that excused her behavior.

"Wanted to get a barometric reading." Catullus Graves frowned. "How did you get in?"

"I opened the door," she answered. Which was only a part of the truth. She wasn't certain he would believe her if she told him everything.

"That's not possible. I put an unbreakable lock on it. Nothing can open it without a special key that *I* made." He sounded genuinely baffled, convinced of the security of his invention. Gemma glanced around the cabin. Covering all available surfaces, including the table where he had been working moments earlier, were small brass tools of every sort and several mechanical objects in different states of assembly. Graves was an inventor, she realized. She knew her way around a workshop, but the complex devices Graves worked on left her mystified.

She also realized—the same time he did—that they were alone in his cabin. His small, *intimate* cabin. She tried, without much success, not to look at the bed, just as she tried and failed not to picture him stripping out of his clothes before getting into that bed for the night. She barely knew this man! Why in the name of the saints did her mind lead her exactly where she did not want it to go?

The awareness of intimacy came over them both like an exotic perfume. He glanced down and saw that he was in his shirtsleeves, and made a cough of startled chagrin. He reached for his coat draped over the back of a chair. One hand still training his gun on her, he used the other to don his coat.

"Strange to see such modesty on the other end of a Webley," Gemma said.

"I don't believe this situation is covered in many etiquette manuals," he answered. "What are you doing here?"

One hand gripping her Derringer, Gemma reached into her pocket with the other. "Easy," she said, when he tensed. "I'm just getting this." She produced a small notebook, which she flipped open with a practiced one-handed gesture.

"Pardon—I'll have a look at that," Graves said. Polite, but wary. He stepped forward, one broad-palmed hand out.

A warring impulse flared within Gemma. She wanted to press herself back against the door, as if some part of herself needed protecting from him. Not from the gun in his other hand, but *him,* his tall, lean presence that fairly radiated with intelligence and energy. Keep impartial, she reminded herself. That was her job. Report the facts. Don't let emotion, especially *female* emotion, cloud her judgment.

And yet that damned traitorous female part of her responded at once to Catullus Graves's nearness. Wanted to be closer, drawn in by the warmth of his eyes and body. An immaculately dressed body. As he crossed the cabin with only a few strides, Gemma undertook a quick perusal. Despite being pulled on hastily, his dark green coat perfectly fit the breadth of his shoulders. She knew that beneath the coat was a pristine white shirt. His tweed trousers outlined the length of his legs, tucked into gleaming brown boots. His burgundy silk cravat showed off the clean lines of his jaw. And his waistcoat. Good gravy. It was a minor work of art, superbly fitted, the color of claret, and worked all over with golden embroidery that, upon closer inspection, revealed itself to be an intricate lattice of vines and flowers. Golden silk-covered buttons ran down its front, and a gold watch chain hung between a pocket and one of the buttons. Hanging from the chain, a tiny fob in the shape of a knife glinted in the lamplight.

On any other man, such a waistcoat would be dandyish.

Ridiculous, even. But not on Catullus Graves. On him, the garment was a masterpiece, and perfectly masculine, highlighting his natural grace and the shape of his well-formed torso. She knew about fashion, having been forced to write more articles than she wanted on the subject. And this man not only defined style, he surpassed it.

But she was through with writing about fashion. That was precisely why she was on this steamship in the middle of the Atlantic Ocean.

With this in mind, Gemma tore her gaze from this vision to find him watching her. A look of faint perplexity crossed his face. Almost bashfulness at her interest.

She let him take the notebook from her, and their fingertips accidentally brushed.

He almost dropped the notebook, and she felt heat shoot into her cheeks. She had the bright ginger hair and pale, freckled skin of her Irish father, which meant that, even in low lamplight, when Gemma blushed, only a blind imbecile could miss it.

Catullus Graves was not a blind imbecile. His reaction to her blush was to flush, himself, a deeper mahogany staining his coffee-colored face.

A knock on the door behind her had Gemma edging quickly away, breaking the spell. She backed up until she pressed against a bulkhead.

"Catullus?" asked a female voice on the other side of the door. The woman from earlier.

Graves and Gemma held each other's gaze, weapons still drawn and trained on each other.

"Yes," he answered.

"Is everything all right?" the woman outside pressed. "Can we come in?"

Continuing to hold Gemma's stare, Graves reached over and opened the door.

Immediately, the fair-haired woman and her male companion entered.

"Thought it was nothing," the man said, grim. "But I know

I've caught that scent before, and—" He stopped, tensing. He swung around to face Gemma, who was plastered against the bulkhead with her little pistol drawn.

Both he and the woman had their own revolvers out before one could blink.

And now Gemma had not one but *three* guns aimed at her.